Beyond the

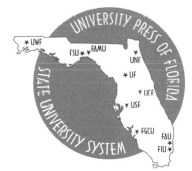

Florida A&M University, Tallahassee
Florida Atlantic University, Boca Raton
Florida Gulf Coast University, Ft. Myers
Florida International University, Miami
Florida State University, Tallahassee
University of Central Florida, Orlando
University of Florida, Gainesville
University of North Florida, Jacksonville
University of South Florida, Tampa
University of West Florida, Pensacola

A NEW AGE IN LATIN AMERICAN WOMEN'S FICTION

University Press of Florida

GAINESVILLE · TALLAHASSEE · TAMPA · BOCA RATON

PENSACOLA · ORLANDO · MIAMI · JACKSONVILLE · FT. MYERS

Beyond the Border

edited by Nora Erro-Peralta and Caridad Silva

05 04 03 02 01 00 6 5 4 3 2 1

ISBN 0-8130-1785-8
Library of Congress Cataloging-in-Publication Data are available.

Revised edition (first University Press of Florida edition) 2000.
First English-language edition, copyright 1991 Nora Erro-Peralta and Caridad Silva-
     Nuñez, published by Cleis Press, P.O. Box 8933, Pittsburgh, Pa. 15221. *Beyond the
     Border: A New Age in Latin American Women's Fiction* was first published in Spanish as
     Puerta abierta: La nueva escritora latinoamericana, copyright 1986 Nora Erro-Peralta and
     Caridad Silva-Nuñez, published by Joaquin Mortiz, Mexico City, Mexico.

Permission to reprint the following previously published material is gratefully
acknowledged: "The Immigrant" by Armonía Somers appeared in *Diana's Second
Almanac*, edited by T. Ahern, published by Diana's Bymonthly Press, Providence, R.I.,
1980. Reprinted with permission of T. Ahern. "Up among the Eagles" by Luisa
Valenzuela appeared in *Open Door*, published by North Point Press, San Francisco,
Calif., 1988. Copyright 1976, renewed 1978, 1998, Luisa Valenzuela. "Mercedes-
Benz 220SL" by Rosario Ferré also appeared in *The Youngest Doll*, published by
University of Nebraska Press, Lincoln, Neb., 1991. "The Judge's Wife" by Isabel
Allende orginally appeared in *Granta Magazine*.

The University Press of Florida is the scholarly publishing agency for the State
University System of Florida, comprising Florida A&M University, Florida Atlantic
University, Florida Gulf Coast University, Florida International University, Florida
State University, University of Central Florida, University of Florida, University of
North Florida, University of South Florida, and University of West Florida.

University Press of Florida
15 Northwest 15th Street
Gainesville, FL 32611–2079
http://www.upf.com

Contents

Foreword

The bookcases in Nora Erro-Peralta's office are filled with books of short stories, novels, plays, poetry, literary criticism, and photographs of writers: Isabel Allende, Nélida Piñon, Rosario Ferré, Laura Esquivel, Octavio Paz, Alicia Partnoy, Lucia Fox, Sabina Berman, Mario Vargas Llosa, Carlos Martínez Moreno, and on and on; a reflection of the artists' literature and of Nora's passion for sharing it with others. She has continually promoted Latin American literature, especially its women writers, for the last two decades, sharing her research, organizing conferences and public lectures, taking her students to book fairs and inviting some of the most recognized writers and critics to speak at Florida Atlantic University.

Cari and Nora, the editors of this collection and of the first edition, met at the University of Toronto while studying for their doctoral degrees in literature. They joined forces in an attempt to convince generation after generation of readers that the Castilian language has produced literary masterpieces of universal stature and appeal, calling particular attention to works written by women.

Both Cari and Nora belong to two countries: Cari, to Cuba and Canada; Nora, to Uruguay and the United States. This fact has made them adept at traveling back and forth between two cultures, between two languages, and has allowed them to navigate through the literary expression of each like fish through water, discovering a treasure of works that had been assailed by storms and buried for some time.

When it was published in 1986, their first anthology of short stories, Puerta abierta: La nueva escritora latinoamericana, was like a bullfighter's red flag waving in the face of the Latin American literary community, alerting it to the achievements of women writers from this continent. The anthology was an important undertaking because it showcased a group of writers who for the most part were virtually unknown, much less studied—even in their own countries.

Beyond the Border: A New Age in Latin American Women's Fiction translates this publication and makes it accessible to the English reader. The historical introduction and brief analysis of each story highlight the characteristics of each author and initiate the reader into an original, uncharted literary experience that reveals the extraordinary sphere of women's creativity and concerns.

Through the decades of changing attitudes and ideals, women writers labored and struggled, demanding to be included in the realm of the literary world. But except in Isabel Allende's case, women who wrote became discouraged and soon stop believing in themselves due to a lack of encouragement. Some of them went so far as to end their lives. For example, the Argentine writers Alejandra Pizarnik and Alfonsina Storni both committed suicide (Storni walked into the ocean, and her body was returned to shore by the waves); Antonieta Rivas Mercado, a Mexican writer and patron of the arts, put a gun to her temple and shot herself on the main altar of Notre Dame Cathedral (the gun belonged to her lover, José Vasconcelos, one of the major forces in the creation of the Mexican national identity, emphasizing its indigenous roots); Julia de Burgos, a Puerto Rican feminist, died all alone on a street in New York. Nellie Campobello, the only Mexican novelist to write about her country's revolution, opted for a dance career, which was surely more gratifying than literature; nevertheless, it was she who delivered Villa's personal archive to Martín Luis Guzmán, who used it to write his book *Memoirs of Pancho Villa*.

Over the last two decades a new generation of Latin American women have broken the moral and social ties that bound their predecessors, and not only do they have a lot to say, but they now have a forum where they can express themselves. Angeles Mastretta became a best-selling author with her novel *Tear my Heart Out*, Laura Esquivel achieved overnight success with *Like Water for Chocolate*, while Rosario Ferré and Luisa Valenzuela attracted critical attention for the way they play with language. In an attempt to overcome social and racial prejudices these women rewrote and revised history, bringing forth a feminine perspective. They strung their words together like the beads of a sumptuous necklace, presenting a unique gift to their readers.

This new era of literature written by women is represented in this book of short stories, which also includes a critical analysis and biographical and bibliographic information on each of the selections. The writers come from several Latin American countries: Argentina, Brazil, Chile, Costa Rica, Cuba, the Dominican Republic, Mexico, Peru, Puerto Rico, Uruguay, and Venezuela. The fifteen stories, like snapshots arranged in a collage, provide views of incest, abuse, solidarity, subversion, relationships, sexuality, traditions, violence, fate, power, freedom, victimization, life and death, eroticism, child abuse, and aging. Indeed, the editors of *Beyond the Border: A New Age in Latin American Women's Fiction* have played with these texts like photo essayists, using frame after frame of individual, social, and historical photographs, in color and in black and white, to reveal the development of contemporary Latin American women's literary history.

Elena Poniatowska

Acknowledgments

Our special thanks go to Deanna Heikkinen; this work would not have been possible without her assistance.

Translators

Bertie Acker
Claire B. Ashman
Nick Castor
Nora Erro-Peralta
Marguerite Feitlowitz
Rosario Ferré
Lucía Fox
Eloah F. Giacomelli
Anne Hohenstein
Ian Martin
Giovanni Pontiero
Margaret Sayers Peden
Brenda Segall
Caridad Silva
Cynthia Steele
Lisa Wyant

A Critical Introduction

When the first edition of *Beyond the Border* appeared in 1991, it became indisputable that a vast, rich body of fiction written by Latin American women was in existence; yet female authors were facing a traditional obstacle: the network that guarantees artists a place in literary history was still reluctant to acknowledge works by women. After we had looked at well-known anthologies in Spanish published up to 1990, many of which were used as reference works or textbooks at the university level, we came to the conclusion that they ignored fiction written by women.[1] Most of women's fiction was published in limited national editions that were poorly distributed. Frequently, anthologies and histories of Latin American literature repeated names of a few female authors as examples of rare classic phenomena, and they were always associated with the same story. A typical example was María Luisa Bombal and her story "The Tree." Nevertheless, some researchers, mostly women, were beginning to reverse this trend.[2]

When we compared the number of available English translations of Latin American male writers, especially those associated with the period known as the Boom,[3] with the limited availability of works by major Latin American women writers, it became evident to us that there was a need to publish and promote the latter.[4] The first edition of *Beyond the Border* intended to transcend cultural and linguistics frontiers that limited human exchange between Latin America and the United States.

Now, at the beginning of the year 2000, the situation has changed considerably: women writers are finally receiving significant recognition. In recent years, even readers with minimal knowledge of Latin America have suddenly become interested in Latin American women writers as a result of the myriad of anthologies, critical works, and translations produced throughout the 1980s and especially in the 1990s.[5] Today, some Latin American narrative works appear on best-seller lists. Writers such as Isabel Allende, Gioconda Belli, Rosario Castellanos, Laura Esquivel, Rosario Ferré, Griselda Gambaro, Elena Garro, Clarice Lispector, Angeles Mastretta, Cristina Peri Rossi, Nélida Piñon, Elena Poniatowska, Armonía Somers, Marta Traba, Luisa Valenzuela, and others enjoy international recognition.

However, many Latin American female authors of high caliber are still relatively unknown. It is clear that we need to look at the lost history of women writers throughout the continent to appreciate its valuable role in the development of Latin American culture. It would be inaccurate to assume that even within today's more positive context, women writers are allotted equal space with men in anthologies and in volumes of literary history.[6] The position of Latin American women writers is complicated by several factors: (1) until recently, Latin American literature in general was excluded from Western and even world literary canons;[7] (2) female as well as male authors were marginalized within the Latin American literary canon due to their nationality; writers from Argentina, Chile, Mexico, and Cuba were at the top of the hierarchy; (3) Brazilian literature was excluded from the Latin American literary canon primarily because Spanish was the language of privilege. This complex set of circumstances is changing thanks to a variety of efforts by scholars and publishers.[8]

It is important to remember that literature by women has flourished at certain moments in history and has then vanished when efforts to sustain it have declined.[9] We believe that there is an ongoing need to maintain the progress that has been achieved and to keep studying and disseminating the works of Latin American women. It is in that spirit that we prepared this second edition of *Beyond the Border: A New Age in Latin American Women's Fiction*. Our first task was to read the reviews of the first edition of the book and to monitor responses from colleagues, students, and readers in general in order to preserve what has been useful, to correct shortcomings, and to update the material.

The first edition of *Beyond the Border* received positive reviews for its mix of authors, which reflects a diversity of nationalities, ages, statuses, and artistic themes and styles. For this new edition, we kept the original selection of short stories and added one by Nélida Piñon, in an effort to give Brazilian women writers a fairer representation. Fourteen translators, including two of the authors and both editors, give the volume variety and artistic integrity. We updated and revised the bibliographies of primary, secondary, and general sources to better serve the needs of the English-speaking reader. We also added a list of Latin American short-story anthologies in English and a bibliography of Latin American women writers' works in English by authors who are not included in this anthology. We amended our brief historic overview of women writers in Latin America from the sixteenth century to the present and updated the biographical information on each author. This information has proven to be useful for readers in general and for background discussions in the classroom. For similar reasons, we retained, and made some revisions to, the critical comments for each story; they serve as guidelines for the reading experience. We hope that this edition will be of interest to the general reader, to students and specialists in the areas of literary studies, women's studies, gender studies, cultural studies, and the social sciences.

Brief Historical Background

During the period of colonization and up to the twentieth century, writing by women was produced by individuals who were isolated from one another. The first and most prominent Latin American woman writer was Sor Juana Inés de la Cruz (Juana Ramírez de Asbaje, 1651–95). Her life and work reflect the unfortunate situation of women at the time, when Latin American society offered women two choices, indeed two forms of prison: marriage or the convent. Faced with such limited options, Sor Juana, an intelligent woman from a well-to-do family, chose the convent as the only means to fulfill her hunger for knowledge. Nevertheless, she still was not free to continue her studies, for church authorities soon demanded that she abandon her intellectual activities as researcher and writer. Although she defended her right to intellectual freedom, eventually she gave up her studies and died at an early age, the victim of an epidemic, but also of society.[10] She left behind an accomplished body of literature: poetry, drama, and essays. Most of her work denounced the unfair rules imposed by men upon women, and, in so doing, she became the first Latin American feminist. Her best-known work, *Respuesta a Sor Filotea de la Cruz* (1691; *Answer to Sor Filotea de la Cruz*, 1994), a clever essay on women's rights addressed to Sor Filotea de la Cruz, the pseudonym used by the bishop of Puebla, is considered a masterpiece by critics.[11] Her literary works were recognized as the best of the period and earned her the name "The Tenth Muse" of the New World.

Two centuries later Gertrudis Gómez de Avellaneda (1814–73), a Spanish-Cuban, voiced her defense of the Indians and blacks.[12] Born in Cuba, she lived in Spain from the age of twenty-four until her death. She wrote poems, plays, and novels, among which was a famous antislavery novel, Sab (1841, 1993), in which she pointed out similarities between the lives of slaves and women, both victims of society. Although her writing was praised for its excellence, she was severely criticized and censured by society for her defiance of social convention.

Following this tradition of literary brilliance combined with personal rebellion against patriarchy, a Peruvian, Clorinda Matto de Turner (1852–1909), initiated the novela indigenista (indigenist novel) with her work Aves sin nido (1889; BirdsWithout a Nest, 1996). Her work gained national recognition and led writers into a new form of narrative, yet she herself was excommunicated and exiled by religious and political authorities for her anticlerical, liberal stand.[13] The other significant Peruvian woman of the nineteenth century, and a friend of Matto de Turner, was Mercedes Cabello de Carbonara, who wrote Blanca sol (White sun, 1888), a notable novel denouncing colonialism. Both women participated actively in a tertulia, a regular meeting of intellectuals—in the Spanish tradition—at which ideas were discussed over a wide range of subjects.

Two other women, both Argentine, shared the literary stage during this period: Juana Manuela Gorriti (1819–92) and Juana Paula Manso (1819–75). Gorriti made a pioneering contribution to indigenous literature with her two novels, El tesoro de los Incas (The treasure of the Incas, n.d.) and El pozo deYocci (The well ofYocci, 1869), and gave us a vivid historical portrait of her times in the serial story La hija del Mashorquero (The daughter of the Mashorquero, 1865). Manso collaborated with Argentine president Domingo Faustino Sarmiento in the field of education, where she dared to break with traditional structures in teaching methodology. Her political novel, Los misterios de la Plata (The mysteries of the River Plate, 1846), published during the dictatorship of Juan Manuel Rosas, captured the feeling of the time with an artistic mastery equaled only by José Mármol's Amalia (1851), a classic of the romantic movement. Both Gorriti and Manso faced reprisals and ferocious criticism for their ideas on liberation and educational reform.

The first half of the twentieth century brought important women writers to the narrative scene.[14] Although they were not recognized as genuine innovators by standard histories of Latin American literature, and were praised only condescendingly by male critics of their time, these writers broke new ground in the areas of fictional theme, language, and literary techniques and pointed Latin American fiction in a new direction. With their personal achievements, many of them also challenged society's assumptions about women. Such was the case of the Argentine Victoria Ocampo (1890–1979), who wrote not only her *Testimonios* (Testimonies, 1935–77) but also ten volumes of essays on a variety of subjects and an *Autobiografía* (Autobiography, 1979), which was published posthumously. In these works she spoke candidly and openly about herself in the first person, criticizing the restrictions that society imposed on women, even on wealthy, beautiful women, such as herself. Her life and work reflected an enduring commitment to self-development and to literature. As a young woman she wrote to her friend Delfina Bunge in 1908: "Can you see me burying myself with domestic cares? Because, needless to say, someone will have to take charge of the house. Can you see me leading that colorless life? That would be a true suicide of the intellect, of the 'self.' Never, never in my life will I be able to resign myself to abdicating my personality. And I understand that one must make this sacrifice for love. But not me, I can't."[15]

Earlier, in 1907, she had written to her friend: "I have made up my mind to have only one great lover: Art!"[16]

Ocampo was also a translator, a critic, the founder of the prestigious literary review *Sur* (South, 1931), and of the publishing house of the same name which promoted the works of many writers, among them *La última niebla* (1935; *House of Mist*, 1995) by Chilean María Luisa Bombal. Ocampo's travels, her encounters with famous artists from numerous countries, and her analytical insight into the human psyche constitute a fascinating source of aesthetic pleasure for the reader of her *Testimonios* and *Autobiografía*. In 1977 Victoria Ocampo became the first woman elected to the Argentine Academy of Letters. She dedicated this honor to all women whose efforts had never been recognized throughout history. Ocampo's life is a profound testimony to the fact that society's canons can be changed through personal achievements.

Teresa de la Parra, born in Venezuela in 1890 to a wealthy family, had a short life marked by illness. Parra wrote two novels: *Ifigenia, diario de una señorita que escribió porque se fastidiaba* (1924; *Iphigenia: The Diary of Young Lady Who Wrote Because She Was Bored*, 1994) and *Memorias de Mamá Blanca* (1929; *Mamá Blanca's Souvenirs*, 1993). *Ifigenia*, a feminist novel, translated into French by the poet Francis de Miomandre, achieved immediate recognition and success in Paris but was severely criticized in Venezuela as an evil influence on women readers. The novel's protagonist, María Eugenia Alonso, writes to a friend in Europe and later keeps a diary about her decision to marry a man she does not love because of social and economic pressures; the diary details the changes she subsequently observes in her personality. Her writing becomes a search for self-knowledge, during which she eventually accepts her weaknesses and inability to rebel. The whole process of self-inquiry is presented to the reader through a first-person narrator. However, Parra manages to avoid the intimate confessional tone usually associated with female writers by using different points of view and by maintaining a lucid narrative distance from her material. Her real purpose is to expose Latin American society's mistreatment of women. Yet her protagonist's inner journey represents a skillful exploration of analytical psychology by means of literature. This novel was widely read and, in spite of bitter criticism by her own society, gained her fame abroad.

La ultima niebla by María Luisa Bombal (1910–80) was another work of fiction that, when it appeared in 1935, was considered avant-garde because it dared to present the repressed sexual desires of an unhappily married woman who fantasizes an affair with a stranger. The nameless protagonist is unable to realize meaning in her life, becoming alienated from a husband who pays her no attention and a society that does not acknowledge her needs. She lives in a mental fog which prevents her from articulating her needs and integrating them into her life. Bombal's extensive use of poetic devices allows her to present the woman's sensuality in a frank but metaphoric manner, which brought the novel the success of seven editions and publication in eight languages. Bombal's novel was one of the first in Latin American literature to discuss the issue of women's sexuality; her efforts bore fruit during the second half of the twentieth century, when this issue was treated by many women writers with great success.[17]

An important literary figure in the early part of the century, the Cuban Lydia Cabrera (1900–1991) achieved prominence after the publication in Paris of her *Contes negres de Cuba* (Black tales, 1936). These short stories drew upon African popular culture in Cuba and the tradition of Latin American *criollista* literature. Her *Cuentos negros* was an attempt to preserve the Afro-Cuban legends for history and to capture their world through innovative language. Cabrera also wrote numerous fables and collections of short stories.

Cabrera's work represents one of the early successful female forays into the short story, a genre that reached its peak later in the century with the fiction of the well-known Argentine writer Jorge Luis Borges (1899–1986), whose work brought Latin American literature international acclaim. The publication of *Antología de la literatura fantástica* (Anthology of fantastic literature, 1940), edited by Jorge Luis Borges, Bioy Casares, and Silvina Ocampo, inaugurated a period of increased creativity, renewal, and intellectual achievement in Latin American literature, especially fiction, which has not yet diminished.

The 1950s and 1960s were marked by high productivity by authors and publishers. For the first time in the history of Latin American fiction, many authors were—and still are—translated, and their works successfully marketed abroad, reaching best-seller status in New York, Paris, Madrid, Barcelona, and other major cultural centers. With writers such as Carlos Fuentes, Julio Cortázar, Mario Vargas Llosa, Jorge Luis Borges, Guillermo Cabrera Infante, Gabriel García Márquez (Nobel Prize, 1982), Manuel Puig, and many others, the short story again became a popular literary form.[18]

However, the international success of Latin American fiction—known in literary circles as the Boom—really meant the success of primarily male writers. Women were largely ignored by Hispanic critics, historians, and anthologists. In response to this situation, and as early as 1950, the Mexican writer Rosario Castellanos (1925–74) began to call attention to works written by women, particularly in her essays: *Sobre cultura femenina* (On feminine culture, 1950), *Juicios sumarios* (Summary arguments, 1966), *Mujer que sabe latín* (Woman who knows Latin, 1973), and *Uso de palabra* (The use of language, 1974). She published many articles and short stories, which strongly protested the discrimination of women in Latin American societies and demanded change. Following in her footsteps, the Mexican writer Elena Poniatowska denounced the difficulties that women writers faced. The academics Rose Minc and Beth Miller compiled many studies of feminist literature. Lucía Fox-Lockert (Lucía Fox publishes literary criticism under the name Fox-Lockert), Gabriela Mora, Celia Correas de Zapata, Juana Alcira Arancibia, and Lygia Johnson broke new ground in research on Latin American women writers.

The journals *Letras Femeninas, Fem,* and *Hispamérica* became effective forums in which to publish—and promote—the work of women writers. The United Nations declared 1975 the International Women's Year, setting in motion a number of conferences devoted to the study of the works of women writers, among them Latin American women writers. The first Interamerican Congress of Women Writers took place at Carnegie-Mellon University, in Pittsburgh, Pennsylvania, in 1975; the second such congress, at the San Jose State University, California, in 1976; the third, at the University of Ottawa, Canada, in 1978; and the fourth, at the Universidad Nacional Autónoma de México in Mexico City in 1981. As a result of these meetings, women's studies programs were established in American, Canadian and Latin American universities. The efforts of North American female academics helped to overcome the traditional isolation of Latin American women intellectuals.

It is important to mention the names of a few women whose dynamism and generosity have made possible a dialogue between North and South America: Juana Alcira Arancibia, Celia Correas de Zapata, Margo Glanz, Martha Martínez, Beth Miller, Yvette Miller, Victoria Pueyrredón, Elba Torres de Peralta, Victoria Urbano, Rima Vallbona, and Alaide Foppa (who, it is rumored, was kidnaped and killed in Guatemala in 1980). These women continue the tradition of their intellectual sisters who, since the beginning of the century, have been working on their own to promote the arts in general and the works of women in particular. Victoria Ocampo, of the Plate region, was a pioneer in this field and the founder of the Argentine Women's Union. In the Caribbean, the collective work of a group of women led by Elena Mederos resulted in a major cultural contribution through the Liceum of Havana, Cuba. In Puerto Rico, Nilita Vientós Gastón founded and published *Asomante,* later *Sin Nombre,* a literary journal that has served as a distinguished cultural forum for Spanish American intellectuals.

By the 1960s, there was a noticeable increase in the number and quality of short stories written by women, due to a variety of circumstances (whose study falls beyond the scope of this book), such as: the economic prosperity of the 1960s; the support given by UNESCO to Latin American cultural activities; the establishment of more—and more accessible—

publishers, which in turn produced a significant increase in the number of readers; the international feminist movement; and the greater involvement of women in the workforce.

Over the last three decades, Latin American women writers produced a considerable body of literature, particularly fiction. Many writers have shown tremendous creative ability in experimenting with new forms of narrative that go beyond the boundaries of traditional genres. Such is the case of Luisa Valenzuela, El gato eficaz (Cat-o-nine-deaths, 1972); Rosario Ferré, Papeles de Pandora (1976; The Youngest Doll, 1980); and Elena Poniatowska, Hasta no verte Jesús mío (Until I see you again Jesus, 1969). Others have successfully cultivated several literary genres: Elena Garro, Marta Lynch, Julieta Campos, Hilda Perera, Griselda Gambaro, Beatriz Guido, Lucía Fox, Aída Cartagena Portalatín, among others.

The growing production of Latin American women authors from the 1960s to the 1990s, together with the arrival of modernist and postmodernist theories, has challenged and often dismantled the practice of marginalizing cultures, literature, and the artistic contribution of women. It is fair to say that by the turn of the twenty-first century many female authors are aware of their identity as Latin American artists but are also well versed in feminist theory. In innovative ways they explore issues of gender construction and ideology as applied to sexual relations in cultural and social practices, particularly in patriarchal capitalism. They are seeking to understand and explain female identity, vis-a-vis the act of writing, sexuality, and the use of power. Also apparent are some intellectual tendencies such as deconstruction, semiotics, psychoanalytical models of sexuality and subjectivity, which can be traced back to the writings of Jacques Lacan, Jacques Derrida, and Marxist theories of ideology.[19]

Given the great number of publications by women, their individuality, and their diverse approaches to creative narrative, it would be difficult to categorize them in groups according to subject matter, literary movements, social theories, and so on. It is beyond the length and scope of this introduction to offer a comprehensive account of all contemporary Latin American women who are publishing today. Instead, we offer a general view since the turn of the twentieth century by highlighting several noticeable literary developments and women writers associated with them.

A characteristic that can be traced as a constant through five centuries of Latin American writing by women has been the defense of marginalized people in society. In the last two decades, the engagement of women writers in Latin America with social issues has coincided in general terms with postmodernist practices of subversion, formal experimentation, and the questioning of authority. Yet this social commitment has taken unique paths of literary development which sometimes differ from modernism and postmodernism. One interesting development has been the so-called *literatura de testimonio* (testimonial literature).[20] In line with modernist and postmodernist practices, testimonial literature blurs the boundaries of literary genres and displaces an official voice of authority; this type of narrative cannot be labeled as fiction, short story, or even journalism. It is a form of narrative that documents community or non-official accounts of social events through the eyes of witnesses. However, in spite of its points of contact with postmodernist techniques, testimonial literature differs from postmodernist ideology by its belief in justice and truth. Some well-known testimonial works are: Elena Poniatowska's *La noche de Tlatelolco* (1971; *Massacre in Mexico,* 1975); Claribel Alegría's *No me agarran viva: La mujer salvadoreña en lucha* (1983; *They Won't Take Me Alive: Salvadoran Women in Struggle for National Liberation,* 1987); and the volume edited by Elizabeth Burgos-Debray based on interviews with a Guatemalan woman, *Me llamo Rigoberta Menchú y así me nació la conciencia* (1983; *I Rigoberta Menchú, An Indian Woman from Guatemala,* 1984).

Another noticeable trend has been the questioning of Western documented history as a valid objective voice of global experience. Some writers also question the validity of national recorded history and the role of history vis-a-vis the role of literature. Many authors deal with the interaction of history, literature, gender, and society. Some authors who have explored these topics are Angélica Gorodischer, Elvira Orphée, Reina Roffé, Ana Lydia Vega, Martha Mercader, Mabel Pagano, and María Isabel Clucellas.

A new development in women's literature occurred in 1983, when Susana Torres Molina published a collection of stories, *Dueña y señora* (Lady and Proprietress), in Buenos Aires which caused a tremendous shock in literary and social circles and legitimized the subject of lesbian literature. Lesbian themes had been introduced before by writers such as Armonía Somers, Isabel Edwards, and Cristina Peri Rossi, but they appeared sporadically, and not in an explicit manner. Writers who demonstrate an interest in lesbian themes are Sylvia Molloy, Marcia Denser, Rosamaría Roffiel, and Alejandra Pizarnik.

An exciting development of the last three decades that became firmly established in the 1990s is the inclusion of previously ignored groups of women writers in literary histories and anthologies. Brazilian authors have often been excluded for reasons of culture and language. Today the works of authors such as Lygia Fagundes Telles, Nélida Piñon, and Clarice Lispector appear regularly in Spanish and English. Writers from Central America, Bolivia, and Ecuador were often omitted but are now being published in Latin America and abroad. These include Carmen Naranjo, Gioconda Belli, Claribel Alegría, Giancarla de Quiroga, Gaby Vallejo Canedo, Eugenia Viteri, and Alicia Yánez Cossío. The work of Latinas, Chicanas, and women born in the United States who do not classify themselves as Latinas, and who write in Spanish or English, or both, have garnered international readership.[21]

At the beginning of the twenty-first century, we can be proud of the solid contribution made by many women in the areas of research, teaching, critical studies, translation, and publication. In addition, the continuing production of women writers from Latin America, along with the increasing interest in their works demonstrated by scholars, students, and the general public, indicates a consistent broadening of international horizon which will offer readers the opportunity to explore alternative views of human experience.

Critical Comments

The critical readings of dozens of contemporary Latin American short stories made us realize that it is impossible to classify them into literary schools or movements in the traditional sense, due to their individuality and their vast diversity of themes and techniques. However, we noticed that—taking into account themes, narrative structures, and linguistic codes—we could detect three areas of concern and general commonality. These areas do not refer to chronological periods of literary evolution in the traditional sense. On the contrary, they coexist chronologically, and authors move through them according to their own personal artistic development. Each area enriches the technical, thematic, and linguistic complexities of the one that follows and at the same time nourishes it. Some of the stories can be identified as belonging to one of these areas; others exhibit a comprehensive sum of all three of them. We use the image of these areas as an organizing principle to anchor critical comments, which may be useful guidelines for the reading of each story.

The first area of literary preoccupation highlights certain predominant themes: the unhappy marriage, women's passivity, sexual repression, unfulfilled love, loneliness, mother's duties, lack of self-expression, dependency, and evasion. There is a need to articulate women's issues from an emotional point of view. The authors use traditional literary techniques, first-person narration, and the female protagonist. The narrative tone is frequently confessional and dramatic.[22]

The second area of creative engagement is characterized by open and militant language and a pronounced feminist approach, which denounces unfairness and demands social change. From this new point of view, some of the same issues presented in the first area are reintroduced and new themes appear: the urgent need for women's active involvement in society, the metaphysical quest, politics, social problems, sexual needs, and the struggle for personal identity. Literary techniques are more elaborate: the use of multiple narrative voices, parody, and humor. Language becomes direct and innovative.[23]

The third literary area not only uses many of the same themes but also transforms them into more complex issues that lend themselves to multiple interpretations and interdisciplinary analysis. Stories from this phase often draw from different literary genres and fields: poetry, drama, history, journalism, oral literature, and fable. Almost all of them use demystification as a means to subvert patriarchal institutions and traditional male mythology. This stage of development projects a deep metaphysical quest directed towards an almost constant inquiry into human relationships and into the spiritual and subconscious aspects of universal/female knowledge. The solidarity of women with other marginal elements of society is also apparent, as well as political commitment and the exploration of violence. The use of complex technical structures and linguistic codes is almost always present in these stories. It becomes very important to break away from traditional rhetoric and to use language on all possible levels of symbolic meaning through both the self-reflexive mode and intertextuality. These texts seek the reader's active participation, stress multiple narrators, humor, synthesis of opposition, ambiguity, female eroticism, innovative use of time and narrative space, and extremely individualistic characters.[24]

"The Judge's Wife" offers at least two possible readings. It may be read as entertainment: the unfolding, intriguing story of a man trying to avoid his predicted fate. Or it may be read on the feminist level: the weak, disadvantaged position in which a patriarchal society places women, and the personal power of a woman to challenge and change this position. These readings are not mutually exclusive, but rather complement each other. The omniscient narrator displays a light sense of irony and uses metaphorical analogies to demythicize male values while amusing the reader. The central plot is deceptively simple and presents the traditional marriage of a tough, older judge and his young, fragile wife. The wife exerts a positive influence on her husband, gradually converting him into a kinder human being. As a subplot, the narrator tells the story of a born outcast who managed to survive and win the respect of his fellowmen through the use of violence. The destinies of these three characters are surprisingly connected in a deadly game in which the locus of power moves from one character to another and finally acquires a humane meaning in which the ostensibly weakest character, the wife, proves to be the strongest. Her use of power, however, rejects the traditional hierarchical concept and acquires a new meaning of personal freedom. This story explores human relations at the primitive level of sexual attraction as well as on a more sophisticated level. The interaction of the central characters gradually emphasizes the history of women dependent upon male rules, and the difficulties they undergo in order to defend themselves and become the mistresses of their own fate.

"The Prize of Freedom" creates a world of legend and fable in which the unfolding clues of a moral lesson keep the narrative suspense alive. A rich imagination, combined with a healthy sense of humor, gives new insight into the meaning of freedom and teaches the importance of preserving one's own liberty against encroachment from the outside world. Freedom is a personal treasure not to be trusted to anyone's care, not even that of a friend. The story can also be interpreted on a sociopolitical level.

"A Passion for Donna Summer" presents the theme of racial discrimination in an innovative literary form. The structure is organized as a spontaneous monologue/stream of consciousness through which Colita/Dawn, the female protagonist, denounces discrimination of blacks in the Dominican Republic, New York City, and South Africa, while reviewing her own life. She is a poor black woman who realizes her own situation as a victim of society but finds herself incapable of overcoming the world of hostility around her. The constant use of the present tense, plus a rich exuberant language full of free association and ironic humor, gives movement to the mental action. The references to Donna Summer's music add a sensual, nostalgic lament to Dawn's monologue and set the narrative space and tone of the story.

"The Hunt" shares some thematic characteristics with "Perfecto Luna," a short story by Elena Garro also included in this volume." It underlines the implicit paradox of our concept of time in dealing with our perceptions of life and death, the finite and the infinite. In this story the vehicle of thematic expression is an art object: a tapestry hung in an antique store. The carefully detailed yet dynamic description of a still scene represented in an old tapestry, in contrast with scenes—also carefully portrayed—in which a man contemplates the tapestry, conveys movement to the static scene and to the plot, creating an impression of art within art, and reality within fiction. The increasing identification of the man with the scene portrayed in the tapestry evokes in him visions of an illusive experience that may have taken place in the past (perhaps in another life) in which he was either the hunter or the hunted. The variety of techniques used to evoke time, and the elusive connection between the scene in the tapestry and the scene in which the man is contemplating it, require the active participation of the reader and invite him/her to reflect on the mystery and the nature of time, art, and life itself.

"Mercedes-Benz 220SL" is marked by a sensual, metaphorical language. This story deals with many of the social problems experienced in Puerto Rico, particularly the indifference of the rich towards the poor, and the very few options offered to women by society. One of the central characters of "Mercedes-Benz 220SL" is a rich white woman who is a prisoner of the very circumstances that, on the one hand, ensure her physical survival but, on the other hand, bring about her spiritual death: an unhappy marriage, asphyxiating social rules, and her own ignorance. Ironically, she collaborates in her own oppression. The story exhibits a provocative avant-garde literary structure by fracturing time at different levels of narration and by using multiple narrative voices and a complex montage that demand the reader's constant involvement.

"The Wedding" presents one of the most difficult subjects of patriarchal pathology: incest. The story is told from the point of view of a third-person narrator, Fernanda, a friend of Elsa's, who is the object of her father's desire. Through subtle description and short interrupted dialogue, the narrator reveals the tragedy of a young woman and her mother. Both women try to regain their freedom in desperate ways: one through marriage, the other through suicide. The father maintains his social standing and reputation by declaring that his daughter is ungrateful and his wife is crazy. The story adopts a low-key poetic tone which, in contrast with the hidden violence that moves the plot, invites the reader to take a severely critical stand, and avoids a traditional sentimental response in which the reader often feels compassion for the aggressor's sickness.

"Perfecto Luna" depicts the elusive nature of the boundary between life and death through a narrator-protagonist who believes that he is alive, although the ending of the story suggests that he has been dead from the beginning. In a highly mysterious, although realistic, narrative space, the ambiguity of existence prevails beyond physical death. The "naïveté" and simplicity of the protagonist illustrate the idea that metaphysical anguish is apparent at all levels of human experience.

"Under the Yubayas in Bloom" presents the power structures and the functioning of an imaginary hierarchical male society, at a metaphorical level, by mixing parables, reality, and legend. This fiction explores the intellectual and sexual relationships of male prisoners. Women appear only in the parables that the "Ancient Master," the leader of a group of prisoners, uses in his discourses. Women have no identity of their own; they acquire it solely through men's interpretative versions. The story achieves a provocative intellectual dimension by questioning fundamental concepts of society, such as the value placed on male culture and education, and the idea of God as a pillar of a hierarchical system that supports the power of some individuals over others. Male spiritual and sexual needs are explored, and the use of sex as a ritual of power is denounced as an act that eliminates true emotional intimacy. The fact that the narrator-protagonist describes and interprets the world around him, while admitting that he understands neither that world nor the parables of the Ancient Master, allows the reader to interpret the text on several levels. The structure of this story centers on a main plot, presented by the narrator-protagonist and interpreted through five parables told by the Ancient Master, amplified by the prisoners' occasional dialogues. This structure allows maximum flexibility to the theme. The language is rich in symbolic meaning and labyrinthine descriptions that offer the reader a basis for multiple interpretations. Parody and irony play a fundamental role by adding a healthy, creative humor to the depth of thought presented in this story.

"Homelife" brings the dilemma of an average bourgeois housewife whose ambitions for a happy family life conflict with the political reality of her country, which demands a militant commitment from everyone. The dilemma is graphically illustrated by interpolating certain narrative fragments, which are intertwined throughout the protagonist's monologue/letter to her husband, now a political prisoner. The frequent fragmentation of the main level of narration visually expresses the breakdown of the protagonist's world: her husband is imprisoned, her son has been killed by the regime, and her daughter is in hiding underground after enduring jail and torture. This story questions the detached political attitude of the traditional housewife, yet it maintains profound respect for, and understanding of, all its characters.

"Adamastor" explores the mysterious labyrinth of human emotions and its links with social symbolic meaning. This story presents a male protagonist whose apparent extroverted, happy approach to life reverts to an introverted, intractable position by the end of the narration. The text strategically places several intertextual clues that connect the main plot with references from the Bible, the gigantic epic hero from Camoen's *Lusiads*, and an imposing painting of Saint George slaying the dragon. Playing with the meaning of these clues, the reader could imagine various possible explanations for the protagonist's behavior. Women characters are portrayed through the biased, often negative comments of the two central male characters, with one significant exception: a woman librarian unveils a piece of information to the protagonist which profoundly changes his view of himself.

Traditional gender constructs are at the core of this story, particularly one that emerges as the voice of the father. Internalized social meaning is embedded in its very fabric: plot, character development, imagery, narrative point of view. It is left to the reader to reflect upon the validity of these social constructs and to question the powerful role they play in the lives of the fictional characters and, by extension, in our own lives.

"Slide in, My Dark One, Between the Crosstie and the Whistle" is a nostalgic exploration of the love that Pancho, a railroad man, feels for his engine. It is also a metaphorical lament of a worker who loses his intimate relationship with his job to a highly technological society which alienates him from his identity. In long detailed descriptions of healthy sexual encounters between Pancho and his mistress, Teresa, the narrative suggests a comparison with Pancho's erotic feelings for his engine. The careful psychological descriptions of Pancho and Teresa lead the reader into a fascinating world of sensual spontaneity. The plot gradually reveals the history of a railroad company and the struggle of its workers for their rights. In so doing, it offers a critical reflection on management's disregard for human needs. The narrator uses ambiguity to provide a mysterious ending in which feelings of love and solidarity prevail over profit and power.

"The Immigrant" challenges the traditional meaning of the mother's role and opens it to new possibilities. The protagonist is a mature, strong, sensible woman who sustains a healthy, honest relationship with her son while, at the same time, playing the role of mother-lover, model-teacher to satisfy a young woman's needs and her own. The plot explores the sexual and emotional intimacy between two women and stresses the importance of sharing a significant experience with another human being. The literary structure is based on a complex montage technique, the use of alternating narrative voices, and an epistolary style. The story requires active participation from the reader in order to edit the narrative material and to expand the text to several levels of possible interpretation. Proclaiming the individual's right to intellectual and personal freedom, the story defies dogmas and traditional myths to assert the primacy of human dignity.

"Crickets and Butterflies," although traditional in structure, deals with a theme infrequently discussed: the abuse and commercial use of children in society. The story achieves a poetic harmony in balancing scenes of extreme cruelty with others in which human generosity keeps alive the hope for a better future.

Like many innovative feminist short stories of our time, "Up Among the Eagles" offers at least two possible readings. One, at the anecdotal level, describes the adventures of a foreign female among the strange inhabitants of a remote city in the mountains. Another possible reading offers a philosophical dissertation on the concept of time, as defined and practiced in Western culture, and an attempt to subvert it.

The central plot presents the reflections and daily chores of the protagonist in a world totally foreign to her identity, one in which she finds herself accidentally and is afraid to leave. The story explores the myths, rituals, and beliefs of these bizarre people who constantly manipulate time from the "heights" of the "mind" in order to deny old age and death. By analogy the reader discovers ironic similarities with patriarchal efforts to manipulate time through reason. The protagonist, on the contrary, accepts aging and death as part of the natural progression of time, which is perceived as energy and essence. She offers a feminist avant-garde vision that opposes one of the fundamental principles of patriarchal society, that is, the chronological or linear concept of time and its resultant dichotomies: man/woman, logic/intuition, life/death/heaven/earth. The protagonist concludes that this interpretation of the universe lacks authenticity because it fragments the whole. Past, present, and future form an integral whole which constantly re-creates itself; so she rejects the Cartesian division of mind and body and decides that to be is an eternal becoming, while "to be afraid of dying is to be already dead." The reader must decode the metaphorical clues of the narrative to understand the hidden demystifying message.

The use of humor and irony make "The Secret World of Grandmamma Anacleta" a marvelous piece of entertainment. The plot is full of surprises and double meaning as it creates an intriguing, capricious character: Grandmamma Anacleta, who seems to represent all the faults traditionally associated with elderly grandmothers and yet emerges as a unique personality fully capable of shaping her own destiny. The story questions the myth of old age, the dependency of women, and the meaning of power. It also challenges modern media to pay attention to real marvels of human achievement rather than to "brutality and pornography." Precisely because of its unusual theme, this story is extremely refreshing.

These selections make a significant contribution to the establishment of an authentic female identity through the process of deconstruction/reconstruction at various levels: language, learning how to reread, and subversion of traditional patriarchal mythology.

It is our hope that this volume will be a source of information on contemporary fiction by women writers and a means for discovering important similarities and variations between Latin American women authors and their counterparts elsewhere in the world. Finally, we invite all our readers—students, researchers, and those who read solely to take pleasure from literature—to enjoy the excitement of aesthetic (re)creation.

Notes

1. At that time two women's publications attempted to improve the situation: Raquel Chang-Rodríguez and Malva Filer, *Voces de Hispanoamérica: Antología literaria* (Boston: Heinle, 1989) and a collection of critical essays by Patricia Elena González and Eliana Ortega, *La sartén por el mango* (Río Piedras, Puerto Rico: Huracán, 1984).

2. In the 1980s three short-story anthologies by women writers were published in Spanish: (1) *Detrás de la reja* (Behind bars, 1980) by Celia Correas de Zapata and Lygia Johnson; (2) *Mujeres en espejo* (Women in the mirror, 1983) by Sara Sefchovich; and (3) *Puerta abierta: La nueva escritora latinoamericana* (Open door: The new Latin American woman writer, 1986) by Caridad L. Silva-Velázquez and Nora Erro-Orthmann.

3. The decade of the 1960s was characterized by a tremendous increase in the number and quality of publications by Latin American narrative writers, many of whom achieved an international reputation. Examples include Julio Cortázar, José Donoso, Carlos Fuentes, Gabriel García Márquez, and Mario Vargas Llosa. Because of the explosion of productivity during this period, critics called it the "Boom," a term commonly used today.

4. At that time only two English anthologies were devoted entirely to short stories written by Latin American women writers: *Other Fires* edited by Alberto Manguel (1986) and *Short Stories by Latin American Women: The Magic and the Real* edited by Celia Correas de Zapata (1990). There was also an excellent volume edited by Marian Arkin and Barbara Shollar titled *Longman Anthology of World Literature by Women, 1875–1977* (1989). It included a whole section on Spanish American women writers and an introduction by Marguerite Fernández Olmos.

5. For English translations of Latin American women authors, see the general bibliography at the end of this volume.

6. For publications dealing with Latin American women writers from 1991 to the present, see the general bibliography. When one compares volumes of literary history and anthologies of the same period that include men and women authors, it is apparent that women are still underrepresented.

7. See the preface in Raymond Leslie Williams, *The Postmodern Novel in Latin America* (New York: St. Martin's Press, 1995); and the introduction in Roberto González Echeverría, *The Oxford Book of Latin American Short Stories* (New York: Oxford University Press, 1997).

8. See Kathy S. Leonard, *Index to Translated Short Fiction by Latin American Women in English Language Anthologies* (Westport, Conn.: Greenwood Press, 1997); Naomi Lindstrom, *Women's Voices in Latin American Literature* (Boulder, Colo.: Lynne Rienner, 1989); and Susan Benner and Kathy S. Leonard, eds., *Fire from the Andes: Short Fiction by Women from Bolivia, Ecuador, and Peru* (Albuquerque: University of New Mexico Press, 1997).

9. For arguments concerning this topic, consult Dale Spender, *Women of Ideas (and What Men Have Done to Them)* (London: Ark, 1983); Susan Faludi, *Backlash: The Undeclared War Against American Women* (New York: Crown, 1991); and Ann Oakley and Juliet Mitchell, *Who's Afraid of Feminism? Seeing Through the Backlash* (New York: New Press, 1997).

10. For different views of Sor Juana's final decision to abandon her studies and devote herself entirely to religion, see: Octavio Paz, *Sor Juana Inés de la Cruz, o las trampas de la fe* (Mexico City: Fondo de Cultura Económica, 1982); Dorothy Schons, "Some Obscure Points in the

Life of Sor Juana Inés de la Cruz," *Modern Philology* 24 (1926): 41–62, and "Nuevos datos para la biografía de Sor Juana," *Contemporáneos* 9 (1929): 161–76.

11. We have translated titles of essays, short stories, and novels into English but have not italicized them unless they have been published in English.

12. Critics have debated the true nationality of Gómez de Avellaneda. Both Spain and Cuba claim her as their own.

13. Important writers that belong to the indigenist movement are Jorge Icaza, Alcides Arguedas, Ciro Alegría, José María Arguedas, Gregorio López y Fuentes, and Rosario Castellanos.

14. For a complete list of twentieth-century women fiction writers as of the date of publication, see Sara Sefchovic, *Mujeres en espejo*, vol. 1 (Mexico City: Folios, 1983), 25–43.

15. Doris Meyer, *Victoria Ocampo: Against the Wind and the Tide* (New York: George Braziller, 1979), 36.

16. Ibid., 35.

17. In 1923, Marta Brunet (1901–67), another Chilean writer, published the novel *Montaña adentro* (Deep in the mountain), in which she openly and shamelessly discussed seduction, among other themes.

18. Many of these writers' narrative works were successfully made into films: Manuel Puig, *The Kiss of the Spider Woman*; Gabriel García Márquez, *Eréndira*; Carlos Fuentes, *Old Gringo*; Mario Vargas Llosa, *The City and the Dogs*; Julio Cortázar, *Blow Up*.

19. In the last three decades feminist criticism of Hispanic and Lusophone literature has incorporated the belief that works by Latin American women writers can be studied productively by drawing on such American and European theoretical thinkers as Kate Millet, Adrienne Rich, Mary Daly, Helene Cixous, and Julia Kristeva. For pertinent feminist bibliography and related references on this subject, see Naomi Lindstrom, "Feminist Criticism of Hispanic and Lusophone Literatures: Bibliographic Notes and Considerations," in *Cultural and Historical Grounding for Hispanic and Luso-Brazilian Feminist Literary Criticism*, ed. Hernán Vidal (Minneapolis: Institute for the Study of Ideologies and Literature, 1989) 19-51.

20. For the study of testimonial literature, consult Elzbieta Sklodowska, *Testimonio hispanoamericano: Historia, teoría, poética* (New York: Peter Lang, 1992).

21. Elena Castedo, born in Spain and raised in Chile, writes in English, and her works have been translated into Spanish. Julia Alvarez, from the Dominican Republic, and Judith Ortiz Cofer, from Puerto Rico, both write in English. Marjorie Agosín, from Chile, and Rosario Ferré, from Puerto Rico, write in both English and Spanish.

22. Two short stories not included in this anthology, "El último verano" (The last summer) by Amparo Dávila and "La hija del filósofo" (The philosopher's daughter) by Elena Poniatowska, illustrate many of these characteristics.

23. The short story "Homelife" exhibits many of these characteristics. "Mercedes-Benz 220SL" and "A Passion for Donna Summer" deal with political and social problems. "Perfecto Luna" and "The Hunt" reflect an existential problem, and both make use of complex literary and stylistic techniques. All these stories are included in this anthology.

24. "The Immigrant," "Under the Yubayas in Bloom," and "The Judge's Wife" are the most representative stories in this area.

Beyond the Border

Isabel Allende

Isabel Allende is the best-known and most widely read woman writer from Latin America. Born in Lima, Peru, in 1942, Allende lived most of her adult life in Chile, until shortly after the fall of Salvador Allende's government. Trained as a journalist, she wrote her first novel, *La casa de los espíritus* (1982), while in exile in Caracas, Venezuela. When the English translation appeared in 1985 under the title *The House of the Spirits,* she became an immediate international success. The novel, which is set in an unnamed South American country, chronicles three generations of a family from the beginning of this century to the fall of the Allende government, as told by the extraordinary women of the del Valle-Trueba family. *The House of the Spirits* is constructed around that mixture of reality and fantasy that is sometimes termed "magical realism."

Since then, she has published four novels, a book of short stories, an autobiography, and a collection of short stories and recipes, all of which have been translated into several languages and many of which have been bestsellers in Australia, Europe, Latin America, and the United States.

In each of her novels Allende experiments with new themes, characters, and techniques while maintaining her gift as a storyteller. *De amor y de sombra,* (1984; *Of Love and Shadows,* 1987) deals with the disappearance of fifteen peasants in the Lonquén region under the Pinochet military regime; *Eva Luna* (1987; *Eva Luna,* 1988), the story of a storyteller, is a modern and almost picaresque narrative about a twentieth-century Scherezade who tells tales to survive in a politically unstable Latin American society; and *El plan infinito* (1991; *The Infinite Plan,* 1993) is the story of a young man raised in a Chicano barrio in Los Angeles. She gained much respect and praise for *Paula,* a book of memoirs dedicated to her daughter, who died in 1996. In her latest novel, *Hija de la fortuna* (1999; *Daughter of Fortune,* 1999) Allende narrates the life of a young woman in the nineteenth century who leaves Chile to pursue her lover in California during the gold rush.

One of Latin America's most versatile and prolific writers, Isabel Allende has enriched and developed contemporary Latin American narrative with her literary output.

The Judge's Wife

Nicolas Vidal always knew he would lose his head over a woman. So it was foretold on the day of his birth, and later confirmed by the Turkish woman in the corner store the one time he allowed her to read his fortune in the coffee grounds. Little did he imagine, though, that it would be on account of Casilda, Judge Hidalgo's wife. It was on her wedding day that Vidal first glimpsed her. He was not impressed, preferring his women dark haired and brazen. This ethereal slip of a girl in her wedding gown, eyes filled with wonder, and fingers obviously unskilled in the art of rousing a man to pleasure, seemed to him almost ugly. Mindful of his destiny, he had always been wary of any emotional contact with women, hardening his heart and restricting himself to the briefest of encounters whenever the demands of manhood needed satisfying.

Casilda, however, appeared so insubstantial, so distant, that he cast aside all precaution and, when the fateful moment arrived, forgot the prediction that usually weighed in all his decisions. From the roof of the bank, where he was crouching with two of his men, Nicolas Vidal peered down at this young lady from the capital. She had a dozen equally pale and dainty relatives with her, who spent the entire ceremony fanning themselves with an air of utter bewilderment, then departed straightaway, never to return. Along with everyone else in the town, Vidal was convinced the young bride would not withstand the climate, and that within a few months the old women would be dressing her up again, this time for her funeral.

Even if she did survive the heat, and the dust that filtered in through every pore to lodge itself in the soul, she would be bound to succumb to the fussy habits of her confirmed bachelor of a husband. Judge Hidalgo was twice her age, and had slept alone for so many years he didn't have the slightest notion of how to go about pleasing a woman. The severity and stubbornness with which he executed the law, even at the expense of justice, made him feared throughout the province. He refused to apply any common sense in the exercise of his profession, and was equally harsh in his condemnation of the theft of a chicken and of a premeditated murder. He dressed formally in black, and despite the all-pervasive dust in this godforsaken town, his boots always shone with beeswax.

A man such as the Judge was never meant to be a husband, and yet not only did the gloomy wedding-day prophecies remain unfulfilled, Casilda emerged happy and smiling from three pregnancies in rapid succession. Every Sunday at noon she would go to mass with her husband, cool and collected beneath her Spanish mantilla, seemingly untouched by the pitiless summer, as wan and frail looking as on the day of her arrival: a perfect example of delicacy and refinement. Her loudest words were a soft-spoken greeting; her most expressive gesture was a graceful nod of the head. She was such an airy, diaphanous creature that a moment's carelessness might mean she disappeared altogether. So slight an impression did she make that the changes noticeable in the Judge were all the more remarkable. Though outwardly he remained the same—he still dressed as black as a crow and was as stiff-necked and brusque as ever—his judgements in court altered dramatically. To general amazement, he found the youngster who robbed the Turkish shopkeeper innocent, on grounds that she had been selling the boy short for years, and the money he had taken could therefore be seen as compensation. The Judge also refused to punish an adulterous wife, arguing that since her husband himself kept a mistress, he did not have the moral authority to demand fidelity. Word in the town had it that the Judge was transformed the minute he crossed the threshold at home: that he flung off his gloomy apparel, rollicked with his children, chuckled as he sat Casilda on his lap. Though no one ever succeeded in confirming these rumors, his wife got the credit for his newfound kindness, and her reputation grew accordingly.

None of this was of the slightest interest to Nicolas Vidal, who as a wanted man was sure there would be no mercy shown him the day he was brought in chains before the Judge. He paid no heed to the talk about Doña Casilda, and the rare occasions he glimpsed her from afar only confirmed his first impression of her as a lifeless ghost.

Born thirty years earlier in a windowless room in the town's only brothel, Vidal was the son of Juana the Forlorn and an unknown father. The world had no place for him. His mother knew it, and so tried to wrench him from her womb with sprigs of parsley, candle butts, douches of ashes, and other violent purgatives, but the child clung to life. Once, years later, Juana was looking at her mysterious son and realized that, while all her infallible methods of aborting may have failed to dislodge him, they had nevertheless tempered his soul to the hardness of iron. As soon as he came into the world, he was lifted in the air by the midwife who examined him by the light of an oil lamp. She saw he had four nipples.

"Poor creature: he'll lose his head over a woman," she predicted, drawing on her wealth of experience.

Her words rested on the boy like a deformity. Perhaps a woman's love would have made his existence less wretched. To atone for all her attempts to kill him before his birth, his mother chose him a beautiful first name, and an imposing family name picked at random. But the lofty name Nicolas Vidal was no protection against the fateful cast of his destiny. His face was scarred from knife fights before he reached his teens, so it came as no surprise to decent folk that he ended up a bandit. By the age of twenty, he had become the leader of a band of desperados. The habit of violence toughened his sinews, but the solitude he imposed on himself for fear of falling prey to a woman lent his face a sad expression. As soon as they saw him, everyone in the town knew from his eyes, clouded by tears he would never allow to fall, that he was the son of Juana the Forlorn. Whenever there was an outcry after a crime had been committed in the region, the police set out with dogs to track him down, but after scouring the hills they invariably returned empty-handed. In all honesty they preferred it that way, because they could never have fought him. His gang gained such a fearsome reputation that the surrounding villages and estates paid to keep them away. This money would have been plenty for his men, but Nicolas Vidal kept them constantly on horseback in a whirlwind of death and destruction so they would not lose their taste for battle. Nobody dared take them on. More than once, Judge Hidalgo had asked the government to send troops to reinforce the police, but after several useless forays the soldiers returned to their barracks and Nicolas Vidal's gang to their exploits. Only on one occasion did Vidal come close to falling into the hands of justice, and then he was saved by his hardened heart.

Weary of seeing the laws flouted, Judge Hidalgo resolved to forget his scruples and set a trap for the outlaw. He realized that to defend justice he was committing an injustice, but he chose the lesser of two evils. The only bait he could find was Juana the Forlorn, as she was Vidal's sole known relative. He had her dragged from the brothel where by now, since no clients were willing to pay for her exhausted charms, she scrubbed floors and cleaned out the lavatories. He put her in a specially made cage which was set up in the middle of the Plaza de Armas, with only a jug of water to meet her needs.

"As soon as the water's finished, she'll start to squawk. Then her son will come running, and I'll be waiting for him with the soldiers," Judge Hidalgo said.

News of this torture, unheard of since the days of slavery, reached Nicolas Vidal's ears shortly before his mother drank the last of the water. His men watched as he received the report in silence, without so much as a flicker of emotion on his blank, lone wolf's face, or a pause in the sharpening of his dagger blade on a leather strap. Though for many years he had had no contact with Juana, and retained few happy childhood memories, this was a question of honor. No man can accept such an insult, his gang reasoned as they got guns and horses ready to rush into the ambush and, if need be, lay down their lives. Their chief showed no sign of being in a hurry. As the hours went by, tension mounted in the camp. The perspiring, impatient men stared at each other, not daring to speak. Fretful, they caressed the butts of their revolvers and their horses' manes, or busied themselves coiling their lassos. Night fell, but Nicolas Vidal was the only one in camp who slept. At dawn, opinions were divided. Some of the men reckoned he was even more heartless than they had ever imagined, while others maintained their leader was planning a spectacular ruse to free his mother. The one thing that never crossed any of their minds was that his courage might have failed him, for he had always proved he had more than enough to spare. By noon, they could bear the suspense no longer, and went to ask him what he planned to do.

"I'm not going to fall into his trap like an idiot," he said.

"What about your mother?"

"We'll see who's got more balls, the Judge or me," Nicolas Vidal coolly replied.

By the third day, Juana the Forlorn's cries for water had ceased. She lay curled on the cage floor, with wildly staring eyes and swollen lips, moaning softly whenever she regained consciousness, and the rest of the time dreaming she was in hell. Four armed guards stood watch to make sure nobody brought her water. Her groans penetrated the entire town, filtering through closed shutters and being carried by the wind through the cracks in doors. They got stuck in corners, where dogs worried at them, and passed them on in their howls to the newly born, so that whoever heard them was driven to distraction. The Judge couldn't prevent a steady stream of people filing through the square to show their sympathy for the old woman, and was powerless to stop the prostitutes going on a sympathy strike just as the miners' fortnight holiday was beginning. That Saturday, the streets were thronged with lusty workmen desperate to unload their savings, who now found nothing in town apart from the spectacle of the cage and this universal wailing carried mouth to mouth from the river to the coast road. The priest headed a group of Catholic ladies to plead with Judge Hidalgo for Christian mercy and to beg him to spare the poor old innocent woman such a frightful death, but the man of the law bolted his door and refused to listen to them. It was then that they decided to turn to Doña Casilda.

The Judge's wife received them in her shady living room. She listened to their pleas looking, as she always did, bashfully down at the floor. Her husband had not been home for three days, having locked himself in his office to wait for Nicolas Vidal to fall into his trap. Without so much as looking out of the window, she was aware of what was going on, for Juana's long-drawn-out agony had forced its way even into the vast rooms of her residence. Doña Castilda waited until her visitors had left, dressed her children in their Sunday best, tied a black ribbon around their arms as a token of mourning, then strode out with them in the direction of the square. She carried a food hamper and a bottle of fresh water for Juana the Forlorn. When the guards spotted her turning the corner, they realized what she was up to, but they had strict orders, and barred her way with their rifles. When, under the scrutiny of the small crowd, she persisted, they grabbed her by the arms. Her children began to cry.

Judge Hidalgo sat in his office overlooking the square. He was the only person in the town who had not stuffed wax in his ears, because his mind was intent on the ambush and he was straining to catch the sound of horses' hoofs, which would be the signal for action. For three long days and nights he put up with Juana's groans and the insults of the townspeople gathered outside the courtroom, but when he heard his own children start to wail he knew he had reached the bounds of his endurance. Vanquished, he walked out of the office with his three days' beard, his eyes bloodshot from keeping watch, and the weight of a thousand years on his back. He crossed the street, turned into the square, and came face-to-face with his wife. They gazed at each other sadly. In seven years, this was the first time she had gone against him, and she had chosen to do so in front of the whole town. Easing the hamper and the bottle from Casilda's grasp, Judge Hidalgo himself opened the cage to release the prisoner.

"Didn't I tell you he wouldn't have the balls?" said Nicolas Vidal, laughing when the news reached him.

His laughter turned sour the next day, when he heard that Juana the Forlorn had hanged herself from the chandelier in the brothel where she had spent her life, overwhelmed by the shame of her son leaving her to fester in a cage in the middle of the Plaza de Armas.

"That Judge's hour has come," said Vidal.

He planned to take the Judge by surprise, put him to a horrible death, then dump him in the accursed cage for all to see. The Turkish shopkeeper sent him word that the Hidalgo family had left the same night for a seaside resort to rid themselves of the bitter taste of defeat.

The Judge learned he was being pursued when he stopped to rest at a wayside inn. There was little protection for him there until an army patrol could arrive, but he had a few hours' start, and his motorcar could outrun the gang's horses. He calculated he could make it to the next town and summon help there. He ordered his wife and children into the car, put his foot down on the accelerator, and sped off along the road. He ought to have arrived with time to spare, but it had been ordained that Nicolas Vidal was that day to meet the woman who would lead him to his doom.

Overburdened by the sleepless nights, the townspeople's hostility, the blow to his pride, and the stress of this race to save his family, Judge Hidalgo's heart gave a massive jolt, then split like a pomegranate. The car ran out of control, turned several somersaults, and finally came to a halt in the ditch. It took Doña Casilda some minutes to figure out what had happened. Her husband's advancing years had often led her to think about what it would be like to be left a widow, yet she had never imagined he would leave her at the mercy of her enemies. She wasted little time dwelling on her situation, knowing she must act at once to get her children to safety. When she gazed around her, she almost burst into tears. There was no sign of life in the vast plain baked by a scorching sun, only barren cliffs beneath an unbound sky bleached colorless by the fierce light. A second look revealed the dark shadow of a passage or cave on a distant slope, so she ran towards it with two children in her arms and the third clutching her skirts.

One by one she carried her children up the cliff. The cave was a natural one, typical of many in the region. She peered inside to be certain it wasn't the den of some wild animal, sat her children against its back wall, then, dry-eyed, kissed them good-bye.

"The troops will come to find you a few hours from now. Until then, don't for any reason whatsoever come out of here, even if you hear me screaming—do you understand?"

Their mother gave them one final glance as the terrified children clung to each other, then clambered back down to the road. She reached the car, closed her husband's eyes, smoothed back her hair, and settled down to wait. She had no idea how many men were in Nicolas Vidal's gang, but prayed there were a lot of them so it would take them all the more time to have their way with her. She gathered strength pondering on how long it would take her to die if she determined to do it as slowly as possible. She willed herself to be desirable, luscious, to create more work for them and thus gain time for her children.

Casilda did not have long to wait. She soon saw a cloud of dust on the horizon and heard the gallop of horses' hoofs. She clenched her teeth. Then, to her astonishment, she saw there was only one rider, who stopped a few yards from her, gun at the ready. By the scar on his face she recognized Nicolas Vidal, who had set out all alone in pursuit of Judge Hidalgo, as this was a private matter between the two men. The Judge's wife understood she was going to have to endure something far worse than a slow death.

A single glance at her husband was enough to convince Vidal that the Judge was safely out of his reach in the peaceful sleep of death. But there was his wife, a shimmering presence in the plain's glare. He leaped from his horse and strode over to her. She did not flinch or lower her gaze, and to his amazement he realized that for the first time in his life another person was facing him without fear. For several seconds that stretched to eternity, they sized each other up, trying to gauge the other's strength, and their own powers of resistance. It gradually dawned on both of them that each one was up against a formidable opponent. He lowered his gun. She smiled.

Casilda won each moment of the ensuing hours. To all the wiles of seduction known since the beginning of time she added new ones born of necessity to bring this man to the heights of rapture. Not only did she work on his body like an artist, stimulating his every fiber to pleasure, but she brought all the delicacy of her spirit into play on her side. Both knew their lives were at stake, and this added a new and terrifying dimension to their meeting. Nicolas Vidal had fled from love since birth, and knew nothing of intimacy, tenderness, secret laughter, the riot of the senses, the joy of shared passion. Each minute brought the detachment of troops and the noose that much nearer, but he gladly accepted this in return for her prodigious gifts. Casilda was a passive, demure, timid woman who had been married to an austere old man in front of whom she had never even dared appear naked. Not once during that unforgettable afternoon did she forget that her aim was to win time for her children, and yet at some point, marveling at her own possibilities, she gave herself completely, and felt something akin to gratitude towards him. That was why, when she heard the soldiers in the distance, she begged him to flee to the hills. Instead Nicolas Vidal chose to fold her in a last embrace, thus fulfilling the prophecy that had sealed his fate from the start.

Translated by Nick Castor
(From *Cuentos de Eva Luna*, 1990)

Bibliography

Fiction by Isabel Allende

Afrodita: Cuentos, recetas, y otros afrodisíacos. New York: HarperCollins, 1997.

Aphrodite: A Memoir of the Senses. Trans. Margaret Sayers Peden. New York: HarperFlamingo, 1998.

La casa de los espíritus. Barcelona: Plaza & Janés, 1982.

Cuentos de Eva Luna. Buenos Aires: Sudamericana, 1990.

Daughter of Fortune. Trans. Margaret Sayers Peden. New York: HarperCollins, 1999.

De amor y de sombra. Barcelona: Plaza & Janés, 1984.

Eva Luna. Barcelona: Plaza & Janés, 1988.

Eva Luna. Trans. Margaret Sayers Peden. New York: Bantam, 1989.

Hija de la fortuna. Barcelona: Plaza & Janés, 1999.

The House of the Spirits. Trans. Magda Bogin. New York: Knopf, 1985.

The Infinite Plan. Trans. Margaret Sayers Peden. New York: HarperCollins, 1993.

Of Love and Shadows. Trans. Margaret Sayers Peden. New York: Bantam, 1987.

Paula. New York: HarperCollins, 1994.

Paula. Trans. Margaret Sayers Peden. New York: HarperCollins, 1995.

El plan infinito. Buenos Aires: Sudamericana, 1991.

"Rosa the Beautiful." [Selections from the novel *The House of the Spirits.*] Trans. Magda Bogin. *Women's Fiction from Latin America: Selections from Twelve Contemporary Authors.* Ed. Evelyn Picón Garfield. Detroit: Wayne State University Press, 1988. 317–37.

Salidas de madre. Santiago: Planeta Chilena, 1996.

"The Spirits Were Willing." Trans. Jo Anne Engelbert. *Lives on the Line: The Testimony of Contemporary Latin American Authors.* Ed. Doris Meyer. Berkeley: University of California Press, 1988. 235–42.

The Stories of Eva Luna. Trans. Margaret Sayers Peden. New York: Atheneum, 1991.

Essays by Isabel Allende

"Los libros tienen sus propios espíritus." *Los libros tienen sus propios espíritus.* Ed. Marcelo Coddou. Xalapa: Universidad Veracruzana, 1986. 15–20.

"La magia de las palabras." *Revista Iberoamericana* 51.132–33 (1985): 447–52.

"Writing as an Act of Hope." *Paths of Resistance: The Art and Craft of the Political Novel.* Ed. William Zinsser. Boston: Houghton, 1989. 41–63.

Criticism on the Works of Isabel Allende

Agosín, Marjorie. "Isabel Allende: *La casa de los espíritus.*" *Revista Interamericana de Bibliografía/Inter-American Review of Bibliography* 35.4 (1985): 448–58.

Agosín, Marjorie, and Cola Franzen. "Entrevista a Isabel Allende: Interview with Isabel Allende." *Imagine: International Chicano Poetry Journal* 1.2 (1984): 42–56.

Aguirre, María Elena. "Isabel y sus espíritus." *Carola* 9 (1984): 23.

Aguirre-Rehbein, Edna. "Isabel Allende's *Eva Luna* and the Act/Art of Narrating." *Criti-*

cal Approaches to Isabel Allende's Novels. Eds. Sonia Riquelme-Rojas and Edna Aguirre-Rehbein. New York: Peter Lang, 1991. 179–90.

Alegría, Fernando. Nueva historia de la novela hispanoamericana. Hanover, N.H.: Ediciones del Norte, 1986. 395–97.

Alvarez-Rubio, Pilar. "Una conversación con Isabel Allende." Revista Iberoamericana 60.168–169 (1994): 1063–71.

Amaya, Lyana, and Aura María Fernández "La deconstrucción y la critica feminista: Lecturas posibles de Cien años de soledad y La casa de los espíritus." Nuevo Texto Crítico 2.4 (1989): 189–95.

Antoni, Robert. "Parody or Piracy: The Relationship of The House of the Spirits to One Hundred Years of Solitude." Latin American Literary Review 16.32 (1988): 16–28.

Aronson, Stacey L. Parker, and Cristina Enríquez de Salamanca. "La textura del exilio: Querido Diego, Te abraza Quiela, Eva Luna, Crónica de una muerte anunciada." Chasqui 22.2 (1993): 3–14.

Avelar, Idelber. " La casa de los espíritus: La historia del mito y el mito de la historia." Revista Chilena de Literatura (Santiago) 43 (1993): 67–74.

Badra, Nadia F. "Una historia de amor desvela a Isabel." Gente 29 (1984): 3–4.

Bautista, Gloria. "De amor y de sombra." Discurso Literario (Asunción) 5.1 (1987):211–15.

———. "El realismo mágico en La casa de los espíritus." Discurso Literario (Asunción) 6.2 (1989): 299–310.

Borowski de Llanos, Haydee, Silvia Ferrari de Zink, and Mercedes García Saravi de Miranda. "'Lázaro,' 'Gardelito' y 'Eva': Tres nombres y una tradición." Actas del Tercer Congreso Argentino de Hispanistas "España en América y América en España." Eds. Luis Martínez Cuitino and Elida Lois. Buenos Aires: Instituto de Filosofía y Literaturas Hispánicas, 1993. 340–47.

Boschetto, Sandra M. "Dialéctica metatextual y sexual en La casa de los espíritus de Isabel Allende." Hispania 72.3 (1989): 526–32.

———. "Threads, Connections, and the Fairy Tale: Reading the Writing in Isabel Allende's La casa de los espíritus." Continental, Latin-American, and Francophone Women Writers. Vol. 2. Eds. Ginette Adamson and Eunice Myers. Lanham, Md.: University Press of America, 1987. 51–63.

Brown, Meg H. "The Allende/Mastretta Phenomenon in West Germany: When Opposite Cultures Attract." Confluencia 10.1 (1994): 89–97.

Cabrera, Vicente. "La ironía metaficticia e intertextual de Eva Luna." Literatura como intertextualidad. Ed. Juana Alcira Arancibia. Buenos Aires: Instituto Literario y Cultural Hispánico, 1993. 357–65.

———. "Modalidades textuales en La casa de los espíritus." Chasqui 20. 2 (1991): 36–45.

———. "Refracciones del cuerpo y la palabra de Eva Luna." Revista Interamericana de Bibliografía/Inter-American Review of Bibliography 42.4 (1992): 591–615.

Camacho-Gingerich, Alina. "La mujer ante la dictadura en las dos primeras novelas de Isabel Allende." Discurso (Asunción) 9.2 (1992): 13–25.

Campos, Jorge. "La casa de los espíritus, de Isabel Allende." Insula: Revista de Letras y Ciencias Humanas (Madrid) 38.435–36 (1983): 19.

Campos, René. "La casa de los espíritus: Mirada, espacio, discurso de la otra historia." Los *libros tienen sus propios espíritus.* Ed. Marcelo Coddou. Xalapa: Universidad Veracruzana, 1986. 21–28.

———. "El orden desenmascarador: *De amor y de sombra* de Isabel Allende." *Inti* 29.30 (1989): 197–205.

Canovas, Rodrigo. "Los espíritus literarios y políticos de Isabel Allende." *Critical Approaches to Isabel Allende's Novels.* Eds. Sonia Riquelme-Rojas and Edna Aguirre-Rehbein. New York: Peter Lang, 1991. 37–47.

Carullo, Sylvia G. "Fetishism, Love-Magic, and Erotic Love in Two Stories by Isabel Allende." Trans. James A. Dunlop. *Readerly-Writerly-Texts: Essays on Literature, Literary Textual Criticism, and Pedagogy* 3.1 (1995): 193–200.

Carvahlo, Susan de. "Escrituras y escritoras: The Artist-Protagonist of Isabel Allende." *Discurso (Asunción)* 10.1 (1992): 59–67.

Carvahlo, Susan E. "Narration and Distance in Isabel Allende's Novels and in *Cuentos de Eva Luna.*" *Antipodas (Auckland)* 6–7 (1994 95): 55 62.

Castillo de Berchenko, Adriana. "Algunas claves de la narrativa de Isabel Allende." *Ventanal (Perpignan, France)* 13 (1987): 37–49.

———. "La inversión de los tópicos: *El plan infinito* de Isabel Allende." *Etats-Unis Mexique: Fascinations et repulsions reciproques.* Ed. Serge Ricard. Paris: L'Harmattan, 1996. 151–62.

———. "Neruda en *La casa de los espíritus* de I. Allende." *Ventanal (Perpignan, France)* 6 (1983): 50–62.

———. "Los signos de la diferencia en Isabel Allende." *La narrativa de Isabel Allende: Claves de una marginalidad.* Eds. Adriana Castillo de Berchenko and Pablo Berchenko. Perpignan, France: Centre de Recherches Ibériques & Latino-Américaines, 1990 7–24.

Castillo de Berchenko, Adriana, and Pablo Berchenko, eds. *La narrativa de Isabel Allende: Claves de una marginalidad.* Perpignan, France: Centre de Recherches Iberiques & Latino Américaines, 1990.

Clancy, Laurie. "Isabel Allende's Dialogue with García Márquez: A Study in Literary Debt." *Antipodas (Auckland)* 6–7 (1994–95): 29–43.

Coddou, Marcelo. "La casa de los espíritus y la historia." *Literatura Chilena* 13.1–4 (1989): 89–100.

———. "Dimensión del femenino en Isabel Allende." *Los libros tienen sus propios espíritus.* Ed. Marcelo Coddou. Xalapa: Universidad Veracruzana, 1986. 29–53.

———. "Dimensión paródica de *Eva Luna.*" *La narrativa de Isabel Allende: Claves de una marginalidad.* Eds. Adriana Castillo de Berchenko and Pablo Berchenko. Perpignan, France: Centre de Recherches Ibériques & Latino-Américaines, 1990. 99–112

———. "Las ficciones de Isabel Allende." *Literatura Chilena: Creación y Crítica* 11.1 (1987): 11–12.

———. Introducción. "La casa de los espíritus: de la historia a la Historia." *Los libros tienen sus propios espíritus.* Ed. Marcelo Coddou. Xalapa: Universidad Veracruzana, 1986. 7–14.

———. "Para leer a Isabel Allende: Su vida en su obra." *Araucaria de Chile* 38 (1987): 125–36.

———, ed. *Los libros tienen sus propios espíritus.* Xalapa: Universidad Veracruzana, 1986.

Cohn, Deborah. "To See or Not to See: Invisibility, Clairvoyance, and Re-Visions of History in *Invisible Man* and *La casa de los espíritus*." *Comparative Literature Studies* 33.4 (1996): 372–95.

Colomines, Gabrielle. "Convergencias y divergencias: De Gabriel García Márquez a Isabel Allende." *La narrativa de Isabel Allende: Claves de una marginalidad*. Eds. Adriana Castillo de Berchenko and Pablo Berchenko. Perpignan, France: Centre de Recherches Ibériques & Latino-Américaines, 1990. 39–68.

Correas de Zapata, Celia. *Isabel Allende: Vida y espíritu*. Barcelona: Plaza & Janés, 1998.

Cortínez, Verónica. "La construcción del pasado en la *Historia verdadera de la conquista de la Nueva España* y *La casa de los espíritus*." *Hispanic Review* 59.3 (1991): 317–27.

———. "El pasado deshonroso de Isabel Allende." *Revista Iberoamericana* 60.168–69 (1994): 1135–41.

———. "*Paula*: Memorias en silencio." *Antipodas* (Auckland) 6–7 (1994–95): 63–75.

———. "Polifonía: Entrevista a Isabel Allende y Antonio Skarmeta." *Revista Chilena de Literatura* (Santiago) 32 (1988): 79–89.

Craft, Linda J. "Testinovela/Telenovela: Latin American Popular Culture and Women's Narrative." *Indiana Journal of Hispanic Literatures* 8 (1996): 197–210.

Cruz, Jacqueline, Jacqueline Mitchell, Silvia Pellarolo, and Javier Rangel. "Entrevista a Isabel Allende." *Mester* 20.2 (1991): 127–43.

Cruz, Johanna. "'Living On' and the Women of Isabel Allende's *House of the Spirits*." *Likha* (Philippines) 12.2 (1990–91): 1–9.

Crystall, Elyse, Jill Kuhnheim, and Mary Layoun. "An Interview with Isabel Allende." *Contemporary Literature* 33.4 (1992): 585–600.

del Valle-Manrique, María. "*La casa de los espíritus*: Transgresión de discursos." *Historia, ficción, y metaficción en la novela latinoamericana contemporánea*. Ed. Mignon Domínguez. Buenos Aires: Corregidor, 1996. 147–60.

Diamond-Nigh, Lynne. "*Eva Luna*: Writing as History." *Studies in Twentieth Century Literature* 19.1 (1995): 29–42.

Dolz-Blackburn, Inés, and Violeta Sulsona. "Isabel Allende a través de sus entrevistas." *Revista Interamericana de Bibliografía/Inter-American Review of Bibliography* 42.3 (1992): 421–30.

Dolz-Blackburn, Inés, George McMurray, Paul Rea, and Alfonso Rodríguez. "Interview with Isabel Allende." *Confluencia* 6.1 (1990): 93–104.

Dulfano, Isabel. "Polyphonous Narrators and Kaleidoscopic Procedures in Isabel Allende's *La casa de los espíritus*." *Chasqui* 23.1 (1994): 3–9.

Duplaa, Cristina. "La voz femenina frente al discurso patriarcal en *La casa de los espíritus*." *Foro Literario* (Montevideo) 11.11–18 (1989): 19–27.

Durán, Gloria. "Women and Houses—from Poe to Allende." *Confluencia* 6.2 (1991): 9–15.

Earle, Peter. "De Lazarillo a Eva Luna: Metamórfosis de la picaresca." *Nueva Revista de Filología Hispánica* (Mexico City) 36.2 (1988): 987–96.

———. "Literature as Survival: Allende's *The House of the Spirits*." *Contemporary Literature* 28.4 (1987): 543–54.

Eberenz, Rolf. "La imaginación como libertad: *La casa de los espíritus* de Isabel Allende." *Iberoamericana* [Frankfurt] 8.22–23 (1984): 102–8.

Engelbert, Jo Anne, and Linda Gould Levine. "The World Is Full of Stories: An Interview with Isabel Allende." *Review* 34 (1985): 18–20.

Erro-Peralta, Nora. "Isabel Allende." *Dictionary of Literary Biography: Modern Latin American Fiction*. Eds. William Luis and Ann González. Detroit: Bruccoli, 1994. 33–41.

Escudero, Javier. "Función de la prolepsis en las novelas de Isabel Allende." *Cuadernos de Aldeeu* 9.2 (1993): 191–203.

Espinosa-Jacome, José T. "Palinuro: Escultura del artista adolescente." *Bulletin Hispanique* (Talence, France) 99.2 (1997): 457–70.

Fischer, Amalia E. "De sus espíritus a los míos, Isabel." *Fem* 11.53 (1987): 38–40.

Foreman, P. Gabrielle. "Past-On Stories: History and the Magically Real, Morrison and Allende on Call." *Magical Realism: Theory, History, Community*. Eds. Lois Parkinson Zamora and Wendy B. Faris. Durham, N.C.: Duke University Press, 1995. 285–303.

Foster, Douglas. "Isabel Allende Unveiled." *Mother Jones* 13.10 (1980): 42–46.

Freixas, Ramón. "*La casa de los espíritus.*" *Quimera* (Barcelona) 28 (1983): 69.

Friedman, Mary Lusky. "Isabel Allende and the More than Reliable Narrator." *Explicación de Textos Literarios* 24.1–2 (1995–96): 57–63.

Galarce, Carmen J. "El discurso picaresco en *Eva Luna.*" *Revista Signos* (Valparaíso, Chile) 24.30 (1991): 27–31.

———. *La novela chilena del exilio (1973–1987): El caso de Isabel Allende*. Santiago: Universidad de Chile, 1994.

Galaz-Vivar-Welden, Alicia. "Chile en el discurso referencial de *La casa de los espíritus.*" *Narrativa hispanoamericana contemporánea: Entre la vanguardia y el posboom*. Ed. Ana María Hernández de López. Madrid: Pliegos, 1996. 265–76.

Galvez-Carlisle, Gloria. "El sabor picaresco en *Eva Luna* de Isabel Allende." *Mujer y sociedad en América*. Ed. Juana Alcira Arancibia. Westminster, Calif.: Instituto Literario y Cultural Hispánico, 1988. 105–15.

García-Johnson, Ronie Richelle. "The Struggle for Space: Feminism and Freedom in *The House of the Spirits.*" *Revista Hispánica Moderna* 67.1 (1994): 184–93.

García Pinto, Magdalena, ed. *Historias íntimas: Conversaciones con diez escritoras latinoamericanas*. Hanover, N.H.: Ediciones del Norte, 1988. 1–26.

Gary, Edith Dimo, and Claire Emilie Martin. "Entrevista con Isabel Allende." *Alba de América* 8.14–15 (1990): 331–43.

Gazarian Gautier, Marie-Lise. "Isabel Allende." *Interviews with Latin American Writers*. Elmwood Park, Ill.: Dalkey Archive Press, 1989. 5–24.

Gimbernat de González, Ester. "Entre principio y final: La madre/materia de la escritura en *Eva Luna.*" *Critical Approaches to Isabel Allende's Novels*. Eds. Sonia Riquelme-Rojas and Edna Aguirre-Rehbein. New York: Peter Lang, 1991. 111–24.

Glickman, Nora. "Los personajes femeninos en *La casa de los espíritus.*" *Los libros tienen sus propios espíritus*. Ed. Marcelo Coddou. Xalapa: Universidad Veracruzana, 1986. 54–60.

Gnutzman, Rita. "Tres ejemplos de escritura femenina en America Latina." *Letras de Deusto* (Bilbao, Spain) 19.44 (1989): 91–104.

Gómez, Jaime P. "La representación de la dictadura en la narrativa de Marta Traba, Isabel Allende, Diamela Eltit y Luisa Valenzuela." *Confluencia* 12.2 (1997): 89–99.

Gómez, Ruben L. "La maternidad en la obra de Allende: 'Una historia inacabable de dolor, de sangre y de amor.'" *Narrativa hispanoamericana contemporánea: Entre la vanguardia y el posboom*. Ed. Ana María Hernández de López. Madrid: Pliegos, 1996. 277–91.

Gómez-Parham, Mary. "Isabel Allende's *La casa de los espíritus* and the Literature of Matrilineage." *Discurso Literario* (Asunción) 6.1 (1988): 193–201.

Gordon, Ambrose. "Isabel Allende on *Love and Shadows.*" *Contemporary Literature* 28.4 (1987): 530–42.

Guardiola, Nathalie. "Elementos para una bibliografía crítica sobre la obra de Isabel Allende." *La narrativa de Isabel Allende: Claves de una marginalidad*. Eds. Adriana Castillo de Berchenko and Pablo Berchenko. Perpignan, France: Centre de Recherches Ibériques & Latino-Américaines, 1990. 113–35.

———. "El fenómeno Allende o la trayectoria de una marginal." *La narrativa de Isabel Allende: Claves de una marginalidad*. Eds. Adriana Castillo de Berchenko and Pablo Berchenko. Perpignan, France: Centre de Recherches Ibériques & Latino-Américaines, 1990. 25–38.

Handelsman, Michael H. "*La casa de los espíritus* y la evolución de la mujer moderna." *Letras Femeninas* 14.1–2 (1988): 57–63.

Hart, Patricia. "Magic Feminism in Isabel's *The Stories of Eva Luna*." *Multicultural Literatures Through Feminist/Poststructuralist Lenses*. Ed. Barbara Frey Waxman. Knoxville: University of Tennessee Press, 1993. 103–36.

———. *Narrative Magic in the Fiction of Isabel Allende*. Rutherford, N.J.: Fairleigh Dickinson University Press, 1989.

Helsper, Norma. "Binding the Wounds of the Body Politic: Nation as Family in *La casa de los espíritus.*" *Critical Approaches to Isabel Allende's Novels*. Eds. Sonia Riquelme-Rojas and Edna Aguirre-Rehbein. New York: Peter Lang, 1991. 49–58.

Herlinghaus, Hermann. "Una novela chilena-latinoamericana sobre *La casa de los espíritus* de Isabel Allende." *Lateinamerika* 21.1 (1985): 143–50.

Hernán-Gómez, Beatriz. "Ideal y frustración: Sobre algunos personajes masculinos de Isabel Allende." *Maschere: Le scritture delle donne nelle culture iberiche*. Eds. Susanna Regazzoni and Leonardo Buonomo. Rome: Bulzoni, 1994. 183–99.

———. "Las violencias circulares: Notas a *La casa de los espíritus.*" *Studi di letteratura iberoamericana offertia Giuseppe Bellini*. Rome: Bulzoni, 1984. 333–48.

Hoeg, Jerry. "The Social Imaginary/Symbolic: Technology and Latin American Literature." *Mosaic* (Winnipeg) 30.4 (1997): 95–108.

Huerta, Teresa. "La ambivalencia de la violencia y el horror en *La casa de los espíritus* de Isabel Allende." *Chasqui* 19.1 (1990): 56–63.

Invernizzi, Virginia, and Melissa Pope. "An Interview with Isabel Allende." *Letras Femeninas* 15.1–2 (1989): 119.

Jara, René. "Los límites de la representación, la novela chilena del golpe." *Para una fundación imaginaria de Chile: La obra literaria de Fernando Alegría*. Ed. Juan Armando Epple. Lima: Latinoamericana, 1987. 131–38.

———. "Narrativa chilena post-golpe: En las huellas de la esperanza." *Araucaria de Chile* (Santiago) 39 (1987): 109–17.

———. *El revés de la arpilla: Perfil literario de Chile.* Madrid: Hiperión, 1988. 232–36.

Jenkins, Ruth Y. "Authorizing Female Voice and Experience: Ghosts and Spirits in Kingston's *TheWomanWarrior* and Allende's *The House of the Spirits.*" *Melus* 19.3 (1994): 61–73.

Kapschutschenko-Schmitt, Ludmila. "Una expresión literaria de la condición exílica: *La casa de los espíritus* de Isabel Allende." *Literatura del mundo hispánico.* Ed. Juana Alcira Arancibia. Westminster, Calif.: Instituto Literario y Cultural Hispánico, 1992. 137–44.

Karrer, Wolfgang. "Transformation and Transvestism in *Eva Luna.*" *Critical Approaches to Isabel Allende's Novels.* Eds. Sonia Riquelme-Rojas and Edna Aguirre-Rehbein. New York: Peter Lang, 1991. 151–64.

Kason, Nancy M. "La voz no callada: El discurso del exilio en *De amor y de sombra* de Isabel Allende." *La nueva mujer en la escritura de autoras hispánicas: Ensayos críticos.* Eds. Juana Alcira Arancibia and Yolanda Rosas. Montevideo: Instituto Literario y Cultural Hispánico, 1995. 89–99.

Keck, Ray M. "Cide Hamete, Melquiades, Alba Trueba: Marco narrativo y tema en Cervantes, García Márquez, y Allende." *Crítica Hispánica* 18.2 (1996): 313–23.

Koene, Jacoba. "Entre la realidad y el sueño: La parodia como arma de subversión en 'Tosca' de Isabel Allende." *Literatura, historia, e identidad: Los discursos de la cultura hoy, 1994.* Mexico City: Universidad Autónoma Metropolitana, Azcapotzalco, Centro de Cultura Casa Lamm; Knoxville: University of Tennessee, 1996. 99–102.

Kovach, Claudia Marie. "Mask and Mirror: Isabel Allende's Mechanism for Justice in *The House of the Spirits.*" *Postcolonial Literature and the Biblical Call for Justice.* Ed. Susan VanZanten Gallagher. Jackson: University Press of Mississippi, 1994. 74–90.

Labinger, Andrea G. "La mujer y el poder de la palabra en la novelística de Isabel Allende." *Mujer y sociedad en América.* Ed. Juana Alcira Arancibia. Westminster, Calif.: Instituto Literario y Cultural Hispánico, 1990. 143–50

Lagos-Pope, Marie Inés. "*De amor y de sombra.*" *Latin American Literary Review* 15.29 (1987): 207–13.

Laurila, Marketta. "Isabel Allende and the Discourse of Exile." *International Women's Writing: New Landscapes of Identity.* Eds. Anne E. Brown and Marjanne E. Go, ooze. Westport, Conn.: Greenwood Press, 1995. 177–86.

Lemaitre, Monique J. "Deseo, incesto y represión en *De amor y de sombra* de Isabel Allende." *Letras Femeninas* 18.1–2 (1992): 31–37.

Levine, Linda Gould. "Isabel Allende y Carmen Martín Gaite: El mundo al revés." *Poder y Libertad* 13 (1990): 14–17.

———. "A Passage to Androgyny: Isabel Allende's *La casa de los espíritus.*" Eds. Carol Maier and Noel Valis. In the *Feminine Mode: Essays on Hispanic Women Writers.* Lewisburg, Pa.: Bucknell University Press, 1990, 164–73.

Levine, Linda Gould, and Jo-Anne Engelbert. "The World Is Full of Stories." *Review: Latin American Literature and Arts* 34 (1985): 18–20.

López-Calvo, Ignacio. "El discurso de la liberación en la novela de Isabel Allende." *Teología y pensamiento de la liberación en la literatura latinoamericana.* Ed. José Luis Gómez-Martínez. Madrid: Milenio, 1996. 143–56.

————. "Las premisas ideológicas de *El plan infinito* de Isabel Allende: El pensamiento de la liberación y el de Octavio Paz." Ed. Ana María Hernández de López. Madrid: Pliegos, 1996. 293–303.

López-Morales, Berta. "Language of the Body in Women's Texts." *Splintering Darkness: Latin American Women Writers in Search of Themselves.* Ed. Lucía Guerra-Cunningham. Pittsburgh: Latin American Literary Review Press, 1990. 123–30.

Lorente-Murphy, Silvia. "Isabel Allende: Una puerta abierta a la esperanza." *La escritora hispánica.* Eds. Erro-Orthmann, Nora and Juan Cruz-Mendizabal. Miami: Universal, 1990. 93–100.

Lucas-Dobrian, Susan. "El mito y la magia femenina en *La casa de los espíritus.*" *Hispanic Journal* 12.2 (1991): 305–24.

Magnarelli, Sharon. "Framing Power in Luisa Valenzuela's *Cola de lagartija (The Lizard's Tail)* and Isabel Allende's *La casa de los espíritus (The House of the Spirits).*" *Splintering Darkness: Latin American Women Writers in Search of Themselves.* Ed. Lucía Guerra-Cunningham. Pittsburgh: Latin American Literary Review Press, 1990. 43–63.

————. "*The House of the Spirits.*" *Latin American Literary Review* 14.28 (1986): 101–4.

Manguel, Alberto. "Conversation with Isabel Allende." *Queen's Quarterly* (Kingston, Canada) 99.3 (1992): 621–26.

Marcos, Juan Manuel. "*La casa de los espíritus.*" *Revista Iberoamericana* 51.130–31 (1985): 401–6.

————. "El género popular como meta-estructura textual del post-boom latinoamericano." *Monographic Review/Revista Monográfica* 3.1–2 (1987): 268–78.

————. "Isabel viendo llover en Barataria." *Revista de Estudios Hispánicos* (Río Piedras, Puerto Rico) 19.2 (1985): 129–37.

Marcos, Juan Manuel, and Teresa Mendez-Faith. "Multiplicidad, dialéctica y reconciliación del discurso en *La casa de los espíritus.*" *Los libros tienen sus propios espíritus.* Ed. Marcelo Coddou. Xalapa: Universidad Veracruzana, 1986. 61–70.

Martínez, Z. Nelly. "The Politics of the Woman Artist in Isabel Allende's *The House of the Spirits.*" *Writing the Woman Artist: Essays on Poetics, Politics, and Portraiture.* Ed. Suzanne Jones. Philadelphia: University of Pennsylvania Press, 1991. 287–306.

Matos-Freire, Susana. "Lo simbólico, real, e imaginario en *Eva Luna.*" *Cuadernos de Poética* (Santo Domingo) 5.15 (1988): 25–32.

McCallister, Richard. "Nomenklatura in *La casa de los espíritus.*" *Critical Approaches to Isabel Allende's Novels.* Eds. Sonia Riquelme-Rojas and Edna Aguirre-Rehbein. New York: Peter Lang, 1991. 21–35.

McCarry, Charles. "A Strip of Exposed Film: Isabel Allende, Charles McCarry, Marge Piercy, Robert Stone, Gore Vidal." *Paths of Resistance: The Art and Craft of the Political Novel.* Boston: Houghton, 1989. 67–87.

McMurray, George. "*Paula.*" *World Literature Today* 70.3 (1996): 671.

Medwick, C. "The Amazing Isabel Allende." *Vogue* March 1985: 506.

Meyer, Doris. "Exile and the Female Condition in Isabel Allende's *De amor y de sombra*." *International Fiction Review* (Fredericton, Canada) 15.2 (1988): 151–57.

———. " 'Parenting the Text': Female Creativity and Dialogic Relationships in Isabel Allende's *La casa de los espíritus*." *Hispania* 73.2 (1990): 360–65.

Minc, Rose. "'Para que no se borre el tiempo': Apuntes sobre *De amor y de sombra*." *Alba de América* 5.8–9 (1987): 181–88.

Montserrat Alas-Brun, María. "'Bolero': El 'kitsch' en *Eva Luna*." *Antipodas* (Auckland) 6–7 (1994–95): 45–54.

Moody, Michael. "Una conversación con Isabel Allende." *Chasqui* 16.2–3 (1987): 51–59.

———. "Entrevista con Isabel Allende." *Discurso Literario* (Asunción) 4.1 (1986): 41–53. Rpt. in *Hispania* 69.1 (1986): 149–51.

———. "Isabel Allende and the Testimonial Novel." *Confluencia* 2.1 (1986): 39–43.

Moore, Pamela L. "Testing the Terms: 'Woman' in *The House of the Spirits* and *One Hundred Years of Solitude*." *Comparatist* 18 (1994): 90–100.

Mora, Gabriela. "Las novelas de Isabel Allende y el papel de la mujer como ciudadana." *Ideologies and Literatures: A Journal of Hispanic and Luso-Brazilian Studies* 2.1 (1987): 53–61.

———. "Ruptura y perseverancia de estereotipos en *La casa de los espíritus*." *Los libros tienen sus propios espíritus*. Ed. Marcelo Coddou. Xalapa: Universidad Veracruzana, 1986. 71–78.

Morales Pina, Eddie. "Los códigos del relato '*De amor y de sombra*' de Isabel Allende." *Nueva Revista del Pacífico* (Valparaíso, Chile) 31–32 (1987): 120–51.

Morello-Frosh, Marta. "Discurso erótico y escritura femenina." *Coloquio Internacional: Escritura y sexualidad en la literatura hispanoamericana*. Eds. Alain Sicard and Fernando Moreno. Madrid: Centre de Recherches Latin Américaines/Fundamentos, 1990. 21–30.

Moya-Raggio, Eliana. "*De amor y de sombra*: Una aproximación a su lectura." *Acta Literaria* [Concepción, Chile] 16 (1991): 113–24.

Mujica, Barbara. "Isabel Allende: The Life Force of Language." *Americas* 47.6 (1995): 36–43.

Muñoz, Elías Miguel. "La voz testimonial de Isabel Allende en *De amor y de sombra*." *Critical Approaches to Isabel Allende's Novels*. Eds. Sonia Riquelme-Rojas and Edna Aguirre-Rehbein. New York: Peter Lang, 1991. 61–72.

Muñoz, Willy O. "Las (re) escrituras de *La casa de los espíritus*." *Discurso Literario* (Asunción) 5.2 (1988): 433–54.

Munro-Clark, Margaret. "An Interview with Isabel Allende: Love, Life and Art in a Time of Turmoil." *Antipodas* (Auckland) 6–7 (1994–95): 15–27.

Otero, José. "La historia como ficción en *Eva Luna* de Isabel Allende." *Confluencia* 4.1 (1988): 61–67.

Palaversich, Diana. "Skeletons in the Closet: Reading Sexuality in Allende's *La casa de los espíritus*." *Revista de Estudios Hispánicos* 232 (Río Piedras, Puerto Rico) (1996): 211–27.

Panjabi, Kavita. "*The House of the Spirits*: Tránsito Soto: From Periphery to Power." *Critical Approaches to Isabel Allende's Novels*. Eds. Sonia Riquelme-Rojas and Edna Aguirre-Rehbein. New York: Peter Lang, 1991. 11–20.

Perricone, Catherine R. "Genre and Metarealism in Allende's *Paula.*" *Hispania* 81.1 (1998): 42–49.

———. "Iconic/Metaphoric Dress and Other Nonverbal Signifiers in *De amor y de sombra.*" *Critical Approaches to Isabel Allende's Novels.* Eds. Sonia Riquelme-Rojas and Edna Aguirre-Rehbein. New York: Peter Lang, 1991. 83–96.

———. "*El plan infinito:* Isabel Allende's New World." *SECOLAS* 25 (1994): 55–61.

Pfeiffer, Erna. "La imagen de la madre en *La casa de los espíritus* de Isabel Allende dentro del marco del machismo latinoamericano." *Beitrage-zur-Romanischen-Philologie* 29.1 (1990): 65–70.

Piercy, Marge. "Active in Time and History: Isabel Allende, Charles McCarry, Marge Piercy, Robert Stone, Gore Vidal." *Paths of Resistance:The Art and Craft of the Political Novel.* Ed. William Zinsser. Boston: Houghton, 1989. 91–123.

Pinet, Carolyn. "Choosing Barrabas: Dog as Text and Text as Dog in Isabel Allende's *La casa de los espíritus.*" *Hispanófila* 123 (1998): 55–65.

Reina, Elena. "La historia: Aparecida en *La casa de los espíritus* de Isabel Allende: Un caso de imaginación dialógica." *La historia de la literatura iberoamericana:Textos delVigésimo sexto Congreso del Instituto Internacional de Literatura Ibero-americana.* Ed. Raquel Chang-Rodríguez y Gabriella de Beer. New York: Ediciones del Norte, 1989. 393–404.

Reisz, Susana. "¿Una Scheherazada hispanoamericana? Sobre Isabel Allende y *Eva Luna.*" *Mester* 20.2 (1991): 107–26.

Riquelme-Rojas, Sonia, and Edna Aguirre-Rehbein. "Conversando con Isabel Allende." *Critical Approaches to Isabel Allende's Novels.* Eds. Sonia Riquelme-Rojas and Edna Aguirre-Rehbein. New York: Peter Lang, 1991. 193–97.

———, eds. *Critical Approaches to Isabel Allende's Novels.* New York: Peter Lang, 1991.

Rivero, Eliana S. "Scheherezade Liberated: Eva Luna and Women Storytellers." *Splintering Darkness: Latin American Women Writers in Search of Themselves.* Ed. Lucía Guerra-Cunningham. Pittsburgh: Latin American Literary Review Press, 1990. 143–56.

Rodden, John. Ed. *Conversations with Isabel Allende.* Trans. Virginia Invernizzi and John Rodden. Austin: University ofTexas Press, 1999.

———. "'The Responsibility to Tell You': An Interview with Isabel Allende." *Kenyon Review* 13.1 (1991): 113–23.

Rodríguez, Mario. "*La casa de los espíritus.*" *Atenea* 448 (1983): 270–73.

———. "García Márquez/Isabel Allende: relación textual." *Los libros tienen sus propios espíritus.* Ed. Marcelo Coddou. Xalapa: Universidad Veracruzana, 1986. 79–82.

Rojas, Mario A. "*La casa de los espíritus* de Isabel Allende: Una aproximación sociolingüística." *Revista de Crítica Literaria Latinoamericana* 11.21–22 (1985): 205–13. Rpt. in *Los libros tienen sus propios espíritus.* Ed. Marcelo Coddou. Xalapa: Universidad Veracruzana, 1986. 91–99.

———. "*La casa de los espíritus,* de Isabel Allende: Un caleidoscopio de espejos desordenados." *Revista Iberoamericana* 51.132–33 (1985): 917–25. Rpt. in *Los libros tienen sus propios espíritus.* Ed. Marcelo Coddou. Xalapa: Universidad Veracruzana, 1986. 83–90.

Romero, Graciela. "Isabel Allende: Diez años de soledad." *Mundo* November 12, 1983: 28–29.

Roof, María. "Maryse Condé and Isabel Allende: Family Saga Novels." *World Literature Today* 70.2 (1996): 283–88.

———. "W. E. B. DuBois, Isabel Allende, and the Empowerment of Third World Women." *College Language Association Journal* 39.4 (1996): 401–16.

Rotella, Pilar V. "Allende's *Eva Luna* and the Picaresque Tradition." *Critical Approaches to Isabel Allende's Novels*. Eds. Sonia Riquelme-Rojas and Edna Aguirre-Rehbein. New York: Peter Lang, 1991. 125–37.

Rubilar, Luis, and Virginia Vidal. "Crónica e historia de medio siglo en una novela chilena." *Araucaria de Chile* 23 (1983): 187–93.

Schminovich, Flora H. "Two Modes of Writing the Female Self: Isabel Allende's *The House of the Spirits* and Clarice Lispector's *The Stream of Life*." *Redefining Autobiography in Twentieth-Century Women's Fiction: An Essay Collection*. Eds. Janice Morgan, Colette T. Hall, and Carol L. Snyder. New York: Garland, 1991. 103–16.

Shapiro, H. "Salvador's Niece Builds a House of the Spirits from the Ashes of Exile." *People Weekly* June 10, 1985: 145–46.

Shea, Maureen E. "Love, Eroticism, and Pornography in the Works of Isabel Allende." *Women's Studies* 18.2–3 (1990): 223–32.

Shields, E. Thomson Jr. "Ink, Blood, and Kisses: *La casa de los espíritus* and the Myth of Disunity." *Hispanófila* 33.3 (1990): 79–86.

Sklodowska, Elzbicta. "*Ardiente paciencia* y *La casa de los espíritus*: Traición y tradición en el discurso del postboom." *Discurso* (Asunción) 9.1 (1991): 33–40.

Smith, Amanda. "Publishers Weekly Interviews: Isabel Allende." *Publishers Weekly* May 17, 1985: 119–20.

Spanos, Tony. "Isabel Allende's 'The Judge's Wife': Heroine or Female Stereotype?" *Encyclia* 67 (1990): 163–72.

Stefanovics, Thomas. "*La casa de los espíritus*." *Lengua, literatura, civilización en la clase de español*. Eds. Karl Heinz Joppich and Wolfgang Hillen. Bonn: Romanistischer, 1986. 5–12.

Stone, Robert. "We Are Not Excuses: Isabel Allende, Charles McCurry, Marge Piercy, Robert Stone, Gore Vidal." *Paths of Resistance: The Art and Craft of the Political Novel*. Ed. William Zinsser. Boston: Houghton, 1989. 19–37.

Swanson, Phillip. "Tyrants and Trash: Sex, Class and Culture in *La casa de los espíritus*." *Bulletin of Hispanic Studies* (Edinburgh) 71.2 (1994): 217–37.

Talmor, Sascha. "The House of the Truebas." *Durham University Journal* 81.2 (1989): 309–12.

Tayko, Gail. "Teaching Isabel Allende's *La casa de los espíritus* (*The House of the Spirits*)." *College Literature* 20.3 (1993): 228–32.

Toledo-Renner, Eugenia. "Isabel Allende: La fórmula de una escritora." *Alpha* (Osorn, Chile) 9 (1993): 121–25.

Urbina, Nicasio. "*La casa de los espíritus* de Isabel Allende y *Cien años de soledad* de Gabriel García Márquez: Un modelo retórico común." *Escritura* (Caracas) 15.29 (1990): 215–28.

Uribe, Olga T. "La fuerza de la fantasía: Hacia una política de dislocación sexual en un episodio de *Eva Luna* de Isabel Allende." *Romance Language Annual* 7 (1995): 637–41.

Valdivieso, Teresa L. "Palabras sobre 'la palabra' de Isabel Allende." *Narrativa hispano-americana contemporánea: Entre la vanguardia y el posboom.* Ed. Ana María Hernández de López. Madrid: Pliegos, 1996. 305–21.

Velasco, María Mercedes. "Evolución femenina en *La casa de los espíritus* de Isabel Allende." *Literatura del mundo hispánico.* Ed. Juana Alcira Arancibia. Westminster, Calif.: Instituto Literario y Cultural Hispánico, 1992. 145–59.

Vidal, Gore. "The Agreed-Upon Facts: Isabel Allende, Charles McCarry, Marge Piercy, Robert Stone, Gore Vidal." *Paths of Resistance: The Art and Craft of the Political Novel.* Ed. William Zinsser. Boston: Houghton, 1989. 127–52.

Weaver, Wesley J. III. "La frontera que se esfuma: Testimonio y ficción en *De amor y de sombra.*" *Critical Approaches to Isabel Allende's Novels.* Eds. Sonia Riquelme-Rojas and Edna Aguirre-Rehbein. New York: Peter Lang, 1991. 73–81.

Zamudio, Alfredo. "Isabel Allende: A vivir con alegría." *Hoy* 385 December 1984: 31–33.

Zapata, Mónica. "Ley y transgresíon femeninas en *La casa de los espíritus.*" *La narrativa de Isabel Allende: Claves de una marginalidad.* Eds. Adriana Castillo de Berchenko and Pablo Berchenko. Perpignan, France: Centre de Recherches Ibériques & Latino-Américaines, 1990. 69–98.

Zinsser, William. Ed. *Paths of Resistance: The Art and Craft of the Political Novel: Isabel Allende, Charles McCarry, Marge Piercy, Robert Stone, Gore Vidal.* Boston: Houghton, 1989.

Lydia Cabrera

Lydia Cabrera (1900–1991) is generally regarded as Cuba's foremost female author of the twentieth century. She was born in Havana, Cuba, on May 20, 1900, and after completing her secondary school studies she left for Paris in 1922 to study painting, art, and Oriental culture. There she became acquainted with significant artists of that time, among them Teresa de la Parra, with whom she lived for several years. Although Cabrera traveled extensively and lived in exile from Cuba after 1960, her work has always focused on her native country.

A short-story writer and cultural anthropologist, Cabrera published her first book, *Contes negres de Cuba* (Black tales from Cuba), in Paris in 1936. This collection of twenty-one African Cuban tales, mostly of Yoruba origin, gained her immediate international recognition and was published in its original Spanish in Havana in 1940. Based on stories she heard in her childhood, it presents a rich portrayal of the language, customs, beliefs, and psychology of Cuba's black population. Her continuous interest in Afro-Cuban folklore produced other collections of short stories: *¿Por qué? . . . Cuentos negros de Cuba* (Why? Black tales from Cuba) published in Cuba in 1948. Three additional collections were published in the United States: *Ayapá. Cuentos de jicotea* (Ayapa: Turtle stories, 1971); *Francisco y Francisca: Chascarrillos de negros viejos* (Francisco and Francisca: Jokes by old blacks, 1976); and *Cuentos para grandes, chicos, y retrasados mentales* (Stories for the young, old, and mentally retarded, 1983).

Influenced by the great pioneer work of her brother-in-law, Fernando Ortíz, on black Cuban heritage, Lydia Cabrera distinguished herself by her devotion to the study of Afro-Caribbean (especially Afro-Cuban) culture. She published exceptional research on the Bantú, Ewe, and Yoruba religions, traditions, and languages, which also served as the foundation for her creative literary work.

Lydia Cabrera will long be remembered for bringing the rich African heritage in Cuban culture to light and for creating the finest examples of Afro-Cuban prose fiction.

The Prize of Freedom

Back when animals used to talk, were good friends with each other, and got along with man, the Dog was already a slave.

In that age of never rushing, of elastic hours, the Cat, the Dog, and the Mouse were inseparable, Cuba's best pals. They usually got together in the backyard of a large house along the plaza, in whose stained-glass windows, still not so long ago, reflections from the sea went to die. There, at the foot of a laurel—murdered eventually, along with its birds, by the new age—they chatted away the early evening.

Once the Mouse, who was big in the book business (he was a scholar), and the Cat were singing the praises of liberty and discussing at length the rights of all the sons of the earth, including those of the air and water. The Dog realized that he was a slave and it made him sad. The next day he went to see Olofi:

"Bada dide odiddcna!"[1]

and he asked him for a license to be free.

The old man, the oldest of the heavens, was at a bit of a loss. Narrowing his crafty eyes which saw everything in advance, and scratching behind his ear, he had serious doubts about whether he should accommodate the Dog. But at last, after shrugging his shoulders and shooting black spit out from behind his eyetooth—which is what he always did when he made a decision—he put his signature on a sheet of parchment and, with everything in order, gave the Dog the longed-for liberty license. That same night, the Dog, feeling very pleased with himself, showed it to his friends.

"Listen, pal, put it away in a safe place, and guard it like gold," advised the Cat when he said good-bye. And the Dog, thinking that in no other place could it be safer—not having pockets—tucked it away in his rear end. But the precious document, shut up in there, stung terribly. It caused a disturbing condition that got worse with time. He was forced to walk in a grotesque way, his back paws immodestly spread apart, and didn't dare make even the slightest gesture to express any feeling with his tail. Then all of a sudden he had an overwhelming need to scratch, which gave rise to a violent urge to run, to rub himself desperately against the ground without measuring the consequences of such an act; when, to his shame, these outbursts took place in public, they made absolutely everyone laugh. It was torture. Constant worry over losing the document occupied his thoughts day in and day out. The fear of some careless slip that might smudge the text made the Dog abstain from eating; and at last, not knowing which to choose, freedom or martyrdom, the Dog pulled out the document and gave it to his friend the Cat for safekeeping.

The Cat thought that exposing a liberty license to the elements, and to risky rooftop living, was a big responsibility. So he took it to the house of his friend the Mouse, whose roof was at least over his head. The Mouse had gone to buy cheese at a bodega. The Mousewife came to the door, and the Cat, having given her full instructions, entrusted her with the license. But the Mousewife was having labor pains. She grabbed the license, ripped it up, and made her nest.

Meanwhile the Dog had quarreled bitterly with his owner.

The Dog had said, "Give me another bone!"

The Master had replied, "I don't feel like it."

The Dog stood up to the man. The man was about to lift the whip.

"I need to eat much more because I am free!"

The man said, "You were born a slave. You will eat as much as I think! You are my slave!"

"No Señor, my Master, I am not your slave"—and his tail wildly confirmed the fact. "I have my liberty license."

"If that's so, show it to me immediately!"

The Dog went out to the backyard and called on the Cat.

"Hurry, my friend. My liberty license!"

The Cat called on the Mouse.

"My friend the Mouse, hurry! Your wife has our friend's liberty license"

The Mouse ran to his house. His wife was sleeping with seven little mice nestled among the pieces of parchment.

The Mouse ran back with a heavy heart, and whispered into the Cat's ear. The Cat put his paws on his head, and for the first time let out a "Hissss!" and jumped, claws bared, on the Mouse; this was also the first time that the Dog jumped on the Cat and sank his fangs into the nape of his neck.

With eyes of green fire, the Cat defended himself, claws on all four paws bared; it made for a cycle of howling, whacking, biting, and blood. The Mouse, since he was small, slipped away into his hole.

The Cat, bristling and battered, clambered up on the laurel; from one branch he reached the roof, and from the eaves he hissed, challenging the Dog, his back arched like a bow.

But the Dog went to lick the hand of his owner, throwing himself at his feet without further explanation.

Translated by Lisa Wyant
(From *Cuentos negros de Cuba*, 1940)

Notes

1. Get up, old man, get up!

Bibliography

Fiction by Lydia Cabrera

"Apopoito Miamá." *El cuento cubano: Panorámica y Antología*. Ed. Pedro Izquierdo Tejido. San José: Litografía e Imprenta LIL, 1983. 158–63.

Ayapá: Cuentos de jicotea. Zaragoza, Spain, and Miami: Universal, 1971.

"Babalú Ayé-San Lázaro. Mitos y leyendas. (Ilustraciones de Hernán García): Guanaroca. La Tatagua. La cabeza de Patricio. San Félix, número 13. El diablo y la mujer." *La enciclopedia de Cuba*. Vol. 6. San Juan and Madrid: Playor, 1974. 263–303.

"El baile de las cucarachas y las gallinas." *La enciclopedia de Cuba*. Vol. 6. San Juan and Madrid: Playor, 1974. 394.

"Boloya." *La enciclopedia de Cuba*. Vol. 6. San Juan and Madrid: Playor, 1974. 384.

"Un buen hijo." *Cuentos cubanos contemporáneos*. Ed. José Antonio Portuondo. Mexico City: Leyenda, 1947. 91–104.

"C'est arrivé." *Cuba: Nouvelles et contes d'aujourd'hui*. Paris: L'Harmattan, 1985. 35–37.

"Cholé la holgazana y su buena vecina Daraya." *La enciclopedia de Cuba*. Vol. 6. San Juan and Madrid: Playor, 1974. 388.

"Como a Jicotea la coronaron Rey." *La enciclopedia de Cuba*. Vol. 6. San Juan and Madrid: Playor, 1974. 386.

Contes negres de Cuba. Trans. Francis de Miomandre. Paris: Gallimard, 1936.

"Cuentos negros de Cuba." *Estudios Afrocubanos* 2 (1938): 58–71.

Cuentos negros de Cuba. Prologue Fernando Ortiz. Havana: La Verónica, 1940. Rpt. in Madrid: Ramos, 1972.

Cuentos para adultos niños y retrasados mentales. Miami: Ultra Graphics, 1983.

"Cundió brujería mala." *Selección de cuentos cubanos*. Havana: Editorial Nacional de Cuba, 1962. 29–37.

"Damas." *Journal of Caribbean Studies* 1.1 (1980): 1–2.

"Deux contes populaires." *Cuba: Nouvelles et contes d'aujourd'hui*. Paris: L'Harmattan, 1985. 35–37.

"El dueño de Ewe (Oluwa-Ewe)." *Memoire de l'Institut Français de l'Afrique Noire* (Paris) 37 (1963): 169–80.

"Eggüe o Vichichi finda." *Revista Bimestre Cubana* (Havana) 60 (1947): 42–120.

"Francisco y Francisca." *Caribe* 2 (1977). Rpt. in *Repertorio Latinoamericano* 5.40 (1979): 29.

Francisco y Francisca. Chascarrillos de negros viejos. Miami: Peninsular, 1976.

"El granito de arena." *La enciclopedia de Cuba*. Vol. 6. San Juan and Madrid: Playor, 1974. 383.

"The Hill Called Mambiala." Trans. Elizabeth Millet. *Contemporary Women Authors of Latin America: New Translations*. Eds. Doris Meyer and Margarite Fernández Olmos. New York: Brooklyn College Press, 1983. 147–57.

"Historia de Elewá Echeún y de lo que le aconteció con su hermano envidioso y Ekué Kekeré, la Jutía." *La enciclopedia de Cuba*. Vol. 6. San Juan and Madrid: Playor, 1974. 391.

"How the Monkey Lost the Fruits of His Labor." Trans. Mary Caldwell and Suzanne Jill Levine. *Other Fires: Short Fiction by Latin American Women*. Ed. Alberto Manguel. Toronto: Lester & Orpen Dennys, 1986. 200–5.

"La jicotea endemoniada." *Orígenes* (Havana) 7.24 (1948): 3–9.

"The Mire of Almendares." Trans. Evelyn Picón Garfield. *Women's Fiction from Latin America: Selections from Twelve Contemporary Authors*. Ed. Evelyn Picón Garfield. Detroit: Wayne State University Press, 1988. 19–22.

"Obbara Lies but Doesn't Lie." Trans. Suzanne Jill Levine and Mary Caldwell. *Contemporary Women Authors of Latin America: New Translations*. Ed. Doris Meyer and Margarite Fernández Olmos. New York: Brooklyn College Press, 1983. 147–57.

"Oyé Ogbó. Refranes y ejemplos. Como enseñaban a sus hijos los viejos lucumíes y taitas criollos. Refranes criollos. Refranes Abakuá. Refranes Lucumí (Yoruba)." *La enciclopedia de Cuba*. Vol. 6 San Juan and Madrid: Playor, 1974. 349–82.

¿Por qué? . . . Cuentos negros de Cuba. Havana: Colección del Chichorekú, Cabrera Rojas, 1948. Rpt. in Madrid: Ramos, 1972; Miami: Universal, 1993.

Pourquoi; nouveaux contes negres de Cuba. Trans. Francis de Miomandre. Paris: Gallimard, 1954.

"El sabio desconfía de su misma sombra." *Cuentos fantásticos hispanoamericanos*. Ed. Mignon Domínguez. Buenos Aires: Crea, 1980. 183–211.

"Se dice que no hay hijo feo para su madre." *El cuento cubano: Panorámica y Antología*. Ed. Pedro Izquierdo Tejido. San José: Litografía e Imprenta LIL, 1983. 149–55.

"Susudamba Does Not Show Herself by Day." Trans. José Piedra. *Scents of Wood and Silence. Short Stories by Latin American Women Writers*. Eds. Kathleen Ross and Yvette E. Miller. Pittsburgh: Latin American Literary Review Press, 1991. 55–66.

"Tatabisako." Trans. Evelyn Picón Garfield. *Women's Fiction from Latin America: Selections from Twelve Contemporary Authors*. Ed. Evelyn Picón Garfield. Detroit: Wayne State University Press, 1988. 23–27.

"La tesorera del diablo." *Puerta abierta: La nueva escritura latinoamericana*. Eds. Caridad L. Silva-Velázquez and Nora Erro-Orthmann. Mexico City: Joaquín Mortiz, 1986. 37–57.

"La tierra le presta al hombre y éste tarde o temprano, le paga lo que le debe." *El cuento cubano: Panorámica y Antología*. Ed. Pedro Izquierdo Tejido. San José: Litografía e Imprenta LIL, 1983. 156–57.

"Time Fights the Sun and the Moon Consoles the Earth." Trans. Suzanne Jill Levine and Mary Caldwell. *Review: Latin American Literature and Arts* 31 (1982): 15.

"Tres cuentos (El insomnio de un marinero, Romualdo Nalganes; ¡Se va por el río!)." *Escandalar* 3.2 (1980): 60–63.

"Turtle's Horse." *From the Green Antilles*. Ed. Barbara Howes. New York: Macmillan, 1966. 275–76.

"La virtud del árbol Dagame." *Antología del cuento en Cuba*. Ed. Salvador Bueno. Havana: Cincuentenario, 1953. 141–45.

"Walo-Wila." *From the Green Antilles*. Ed. Barbara Howes. New York: Macmillan, 1966. 277–79. Rpt. in *Longman Anthology of World Literature by Women, 1875–1975*. Eds. Marian Arkin and Barbara Shollar. New York: Longman, 1989. 376–77.

"Y así fue . . ." *El Tiempo:Página Literaria* (New York) January 18, 1970.

Essays by Lydia Cabrera

Anaforuana: Ritual y símbolos de la iniciación en la sociedad secreta Abakuá. Madrid: Cabrera Rojas, 1975. Rpt. in Miami: Universal, 1976.

Anagó, vocabulario lucumí (El Yoruba que se habla en Cuba). Havana: Colección del Chicherekú, Cabrera Rojas, 1957. Rpt. in Miami: Colección del Chicherekú, Cabrera Rojas, 1970.

Los animales en el folklore y la magia de Cuba. Miami: Universal, 1988.

"La Ceiba y la sociedad secreta Abakuá." *Orígenes* (Havana) 7.25 (1950): 16–47.

Consejos, pensamientos, y notas de Lydia E. Pinbán. Miami: Universal, 1993.

"Fragmentos de la obra de Lydia Cabrera: 'Ukano Mambre,' 'Cómo se prepara una nganga,' 'Taita Hicotea y Taita Tigre,' 'Arere Marekén,' 'Refranes de negros viejos,' 'Refranes abakúas.'" *La fiesta innombrable: Trece poetas cubanos*. Eds. Victor Manuel Mendiola and Luis Soto. Mexico City: El Tukán de Virginia, 1992. 105–14.

"Historia de un perro callejero y un gato casero." *Journal of Caribbean Studies* 3.1–2 (1982): 1–7.

"Iemanjá en Cuba." *Iemanjá e Suas Lendas*. Ed. Zora A. Seljan. Rio de Janeiro: Gráfica Record, 1967. 49–58.

"El Indísime Bebe la Mokuba que lo consagra Abakuá." *Lunes de Revolución* (Havana) March 30, 1959: 5–6.

Itinerarios del insomnio: Trinidad de Cuba. Miami: Cabrera Rojas, Peninsular Printing, 1977.

Koeko Iyawó, aprende novicia: Pequeño tratado de regla lucumí. (Pequeño tratado de Regla Lucumbí.) Miami: Ultra Graphics, 1980. Rpt. in Miami: Universal, 1996.

La laguna sagrada de San Joaquín. Photographer Josefina Tarafa. Madrid: Erre, 1973.

La lengua sagrada de los Nañigos. Miami: Cabrera Rojas, 1988.

"Más diablo que el diablo." *Vuelta* (Mexico City) 5.60 (1981): 7–9.

La medicina popular de Cuba. Miami: Ultra Graphics, 1984.

El monte. Havana: Colección de Chicherekú, Cabrera Rojas, 1954. Rpt. in Miami: Universal, 1975.

El monte. Trans. Morton Marks. New York: n.p., 1984.

El monte. Piante e Magia: Religioni, medicina, e folklore delle culture afrocubane. Trans. Laura González. Milano: Rizzoli, 1984.

"Notas sobre Africa, la negritud y la actual poesía Yoruba." *Revista de la Universidad Complutense* [Madrid] 24.95 (1975): 9–58.

Otán Iyebiyé, las piedras preciosas. Miami: Colección del Chicherekú en el exilio, Cabrera Rojas, 1970. Rpt. in Miami: Universal, 1970.

Páginas sueltas. Ed. Isabel Castellanos. Miami: Universal, 1994.

Refranes de negros viejos. Havana: Cabrera Rojas, 1955. Rpt. in Miami: Colección del Chicherekú en el exilio, Cabrera Rojas, 1970.

La Regla Kimbisa del Santo Cristo del Buen Viaje. Miami: Peninsular Printing, 1977. Rpt. in 1986.

Reglas de congo: Palo monte mayombé. Miami: Peninsular Printing, 1979.

"Religious Syncretism in Cuba." *Journal of Caribbean Studies* 10.1–2 (1994–95): 84–94.

"Ritual y símbolos de la iniciación en la sociedad secreta Abakuá." *Journal de la Societé des Americanistes* [Paris] 58 (1969): 139–71.

"El sincretismo religioso de Cuba. Santos, Orisha, Ngangas, Lucumís, y Congos." *Orígenes* (Havana) 36 (1954): 8–20.

La sociedad secreta Abakuá, narrada por viejos adeptos. Havana: Colección del Chicherekú, Cabrera Rojas, 1958. Rpt. in Miami: Colección de Chicherekú, Cabrera Rojas, 1970.

Supersticiones y buenos consejos. Miami: Universal, 1987.

Vocabulario Congo: (el Bantú que se habla en Cuba). Miami: Cabrera Rojas, 1984.

Yemayá y Ochún. Kariocha, Iyalorichas, y Olorichas. Notes on cover by Pierre Verger. Madrid: Colección del Chicherekú en el exilio, Cabrera Rojas, 1974. Rpt. in New York: Cabrera Rojas, 1980.

Criticism on the Works of Lydia Cabrera

Abella, Rosa. "Breve crono-bio-bibliografía de Lydia Cabrera." *En torno a Lydia Cabrera.* Eds. Isabel Castellanos and Josefina Inclán. Miami: Universal, 1987. 321–24.

Acosta Saignes, Miguel. "El monte de Lydia Cabrera." *Revista Bimestre Cubana* (Havana) /1 (1956): 286–87.

Alzola, Concepción T. "Lexicografía de los *Cuentos negros de Cuba*." *En torno a Lydia Cabrera.* Eds. Isabel Castellanos and Josefina Inclán. Miami: Universal, 1987. 204–11.

Anhalt, Nedda G. de. "Lydia Cabrera, la Sikuanekua." *Vuelta* (Mexico City) 11.125 (1987): 35–44, 45.

Arenas, Reynaldo. "Diosa instalada en el centro del poema." *En torno a Lydia Cabrera.* Eds. Isabel Castellanos and Josefina Inclán. Miami: Universal, 1987. 27–28.

Arocha, José Antonio. "Vislumbración de Lydia Cabrera." *Alacrán azul* 1.1 (1970): 6–7.

Ballesteros, Manuel. "Mi imagen de Lydia Cabrera." *En torno a Lydia Cabrera.* Eds. Isabel Castellanos and Josefina Inclán. Miami: Universal, 1987. 32–34.

Bascom, William. "Oba's Ear: A Yoruba Myth in Cuba and Brazil." *African Folklore in the New World.* Ed. Daniel J. Crowley. Austin: University of Texas Press, 1977. 3–19.

Ben-Ur, Lorraine Elena. "Diálogo con Lydia Cabrera." *Caribe* 2.2 (1977): 131–37.

Cacchione, Richard D. "Lydia Cabrera: The Evolution of a Legacy." *En torno a Lydia Cabrera.* Eds. Isabel Castellanos and Josefina Inclán. Miami: Universal, 1987. 325–35.

Campana, Mario. "Entre dioses festivos: El mundo afroamericano a través de Lydia Cabrera." *Quimera* (Barcelona) 134 (1994): 63–67.

Carpentier, Alejo. "Los cuentos de Lydia Cabrera." *Carteles* (Havana) 28.41 (1936): 40.

Castellanos, Isabel. "Abre kutu wiri ndinga: Lydia Cabrera y las lenguas afrocubanas." *En torno a Lydia Cabrera.* Eds. Isabel Castellanos and Josefina Inclán. Miami: Universal, 1987. 212–26.

————. "Lydia antes de París." *Linden Lane Magazine* 11.4 (1992): 10–13.

————. "Lydia Cabrera: A Pioneer." *Review: Latin American Literature and Arts* 52 (1996): 5.

Castellanos, Isabel, and Josefina Inclán, eds. *En torno a Lydia Cabrera.* Miami: Universal, 1987.

Conde, Carmen. "A Lydia Cabrera." *En torno a Lydia Cabrera.* Eds. Isabel Castellanos and Josefina Inclán. Miami: Universal, 1987. 35–36.

Cuervo-Hewitt, Julia. *Aché, presencia africana: Tradiciones yoruba-lucumí en la narrativa cubana.* New York: Peter Lang, 1988.

————. "In(ter)vención y (sub)versión de (E)Cue en *Tres tristes tigres.*" *La Chispa '95: Selected Proceedings.* New Orleans: Tulane University, 1995. 117–32.

De Armas, José R. "Carta no literaria a Lydia Cabrera." *En torno a Lydia Cabrera.* Eds. Isabel Castellanos and Josefina Inclán. Miami: Universal, 1987. 29–31.

De Costa-Willis, Miriam. "Folklore and the Creative Artist: Lydia Cabrera and Zora Neale Hurston." *College Language Association Journal* 27.1 (1983): 81–90.

Dopico-Black, Georgina. "Exhibitionism and Woman's Voice: Lydia Cabrera's 'El mono perdió el fruto de su trabajo.'" *Feministas Unidas* 13.2 (1993): 46-54.

Echerri, Vicente. "Trinidad de Cuba: El sueño insomme de Lydia Cabrera." *En torno a Lydia Cabrera.* Eds. Isabel Castellanos and Josefina Inclán. Miami: Universal, 1987. 73–79.

Escarpanter, José A. "La memoria como salvación: *Itinerarios del Insomnio. Trinidad de Cuba* de Lydia Cabrera." *En torno a Lydia Cabrera.* Eds. Isabel Castellanos and Josefina Inclán. Miami: Universal, 1987. 80–87.

Fernández, Wilfredo. "Puntos de vista." *Réplica* March 30, 1970: 16.

Fernández Marcané, Leonardo. "Semblanza de Lydia Cabrera." *En torno a Lydia Cabrera.* Eds. Isabel Castellanos and Josefina Inclán. Miami: Universal, 1987. 37–42.

Figueroa, Esperanza. "Lydia Cabrera: *Cuentos negros de Cuba.*" *Sur* (Buenos Aires) 349 (1981): 89–97.

————. "Tres vidas divergentes, Lydia, Enríquez y Carpentier." *En torno a Lydia Cabrera.* Eds. Isabel Castellanos and Josefina Inclán. Miami: Universal, 1987. 278–99.

Florit, Eugenio. "Medio siglo de *Cuentos negros.*" *En torno a Lydia Cabrera.* Eds. Isabel Castellanos and Josefina Inclán. Miami: Universal, 1987. 43–44.

Foster, David William. *Cuban Literature: A Research Guide.* New York: Garland, 1985. 122–24.

————. *A Dictionary of Contemporary Latin American Authors.* Tempe: Center for Latin American Studies, Arizona State University, 1975. 19–20.

Gallardo, Jorge Emilio. "Descubrir a Cuba en París." *La Nación:* (literary supplement; Buenos Aires) June 12, 1988: 2.

García Vega, Lorenzo. "Entrevistando a Lydia Cabrera." *Escandalar* 4.4 (1981): 80–86.

González, Celedonio. "Lydia Cabrera: Una vida eterna." *En torno a Lydia Cabrera.* Eds. Isabel Castellanos and Josefina Inclán. Miami: Universal, 1987. 45–47.

González, Manuel Pedro. "Cuentos y recuentos de Lydia Cabrera." *Nueva Revista Cubana* (Havana) 1.2 (1959): 153–61.

González, Reynaldo. "El monte nuestro de cada día." *Unión* (Havana) 10.3 (1990): 87–90.

Gordo-Guarinos, Francisco. "El negrismo de Lydia Cabrera visto con perspectiva de España." Congreso de literatura afro-americana: Homenaje a Lydia Cabrera. Florida International University, November 1976. Rpt. in Homenaje a Lydia Cabrera. Eds. Reinaldo Sánchez and José Antonio Madrigal. Miami: Universal, 1978. 25–30.

Granda, Germán de. "Un caso más de influencia canaria en Hispanoamérica (Brujería isleña en Cuba)." Revista de Dialectología y Tradiciones Populares (Madrid) 29.1–2 (1973): 155–62.

Greenfield, Charles. "Cuba's Matriarch of Letters: Lydia Cabrera." Nuestro 6.7 (1982): 13–15.

Gutiérrez, Mariela. "La armonía cósmica africana en los cuentos de Lydia Cabrera." Encuentro de la Cultura Cubana 4–5 (1997): 202–9.

———. El cosmos de Lydia Cabrera: Dioses, animales, y hombres. Miami: Universal, 1991.

———. Los cuentos negros de Lydia Cabrera: Estudio morfológico esquemático. Miami: Universal, 1986.

———. "Un gran personaje de Lydia Cabrera." En torno a Lydia Cabrera. Eds. Isabel Castellanos and Josefina Inclán. Miami: Universal, 1987. 88–94.

———. Lydia Cabrera: Aproximaciones mítico-simbólicas a su cuentística. Madrid: Verbum, 1997.

———. "Lydia Cabrera: Autora de cuentos negros." Las desobedientes: Mujeres de Nuesta América. Eds. María Mercedes Jaramillo and Betty Osorio. Bogota: Panamericana, 1997. 254–71.

———. "Rediscovering Lydia Cabrera's El monte, the Afro-Cuban Forest's Archive." Diaspora: Journal of Afro-American Studies 4.4 (1995). 158–74.

Guzmán, Cristina. "Diálogo con Lydia Cabrera." Zona Franca 24 (1981). 34–38. Rpt. in Repertorio Latinoamericano January–March 1985: 7–10.

Hasson, Liliane. "Lydia Cabrera en los Estados Unidos." En torno a Lydia Cabrera. Eds. Isabel Castellanos and Josefina Inclán. Miami: Universal, 1987. 95–104.

Hernández Miyares, Julio. "Lydia Cabrera: Presencia y significacion en las letras cubanas." Círculo 18 (1989): 129–32.

Hernández Travieso, Antonio. "Lydia Cabrera: Su originalidad y estilo." En torno a Lydia Cabrera. Eds. Isabel Castellanos and Josefina Inclán. Miami: Universal, 1987. 121–23.

Hiriart, Rosario. "Algunos apuntes sobre Cuentos negros." Vida Universitaria (Mexico City) 25.1298 (1976): 5–16.

———. Cartas a Lydia Cabrera (correspondencia inédita de Gabriela Mistral y Teresa de la Parra). Madrid: Torremozas, 1988.

———. "Dos cartas de Gabriela Mistral." Insula (Madrid) 36.415 (1981): 4, 10.

———. "En torno al mundo negro de Lydia Cabrera." Cuadernos Hispanoamericanos 359 (1980): 433–40. Rpt. in Américas 32.3 (1980): 40–42.

———. "La experiencia viva en la ficción: Lydia Cabrera e Hilda Perera." Círculo 8 (1979): 124–31.

———. "Lydia Cabrera: Perfil literario." Círculo 18 (1989): 133–39.

———. Lydia Cabrera: Vida hecha arte. New York: Eliseo Torres, 1978. Rpt. in Miami: Universal, 1983.

———. "Lydia Cabrera and the World of Cuba's Blacks." Américas 32.3 (1980): 40–42.

————. *Más cerca de Teresa de la Parra: Diálogos con Lydia Cabrera*. Caracas: Monte Avila, 1983.

————. "El tiempo y los símbolos en los *Cuentos negros de Cuba*." Congreso de literatura afroamericana: Homenaje a Lydia Cabrera. Florida International University, November 1976. Rpt. in *Homenaje a Lydia Cabrera*. Eds. Reinaldo Sánchez and José Antonio Madrigal. Miami: Universal, 1978. 31–43.

Inclán, Josefina. *Ayapá y Otán Iyebiyé de Lydia Cabrera*. Miami: Universal, 1976.

————. *En torno a "Itinerarios del Insomnio: Trinidad de Cuba" de Lydia Cabrera*. Miami: Peninsular Printing, 1978.

————. *Lydia Cabrera: Creación y poesía*. Miami: Peninsular Printing, 1981.

————. "Una polifacética y transformista historia de Lydia Cabrera." *Círculo* 22 (1993): 38–44.

————. "Tres criollas ejemplares." *En torno a Lydia Cabrera*. Eds. Isabel Castellanos and Josefina Inclán. Miami: Universal, 1987. 105–20.

Irizarry, Estelle, "Los hechos y la cultura en los Estados Unidos." *Nivel* (Mexico City) December 1976: 10.

————. "Lector y destinatario en dos libros de Lydia Cabrera." *En torno a Lydia Cabrera*. Eds. Isabel Castellanos and Josefina Inclán. Miami: Universal, 1987, 124–34.

————. "Lydia Cabrera, fabuladora surrealista." *The Contemporary Latin American Short Story*. Ed. Rose S. Minc. New York: Senda Nueva, 1979. 105–11.

————. "Review of *Lydia Cabrera: Vida hecha arte* de Rosario Hiriart." *Nivel* (Mexico City) March 31, 1979: 10.

Jiménez, Julio. "Review of *Lo ancestral africano en la narrativa de Lydia Cabrera* de Rosa Valdés-Cruz." *Hispania* 59.1 (1976): 181.

Jiménez, Onilda A. "Dos cartas inéditas de Gabriela Mistral a Lydia Cabrera." *Revista Iberoamericana* 53.141 (1987): 1001–11. Rpt. in *Hispamérica* 12.34–35 (1983): 97–103.

Josephs, Allen. "Lydia and Federico: Towards a Historical Approach to Lorca Studies." *Journal of Spanish Studies: Twentieth Century* 6 (1978): 123–30.

Labrador Ruiz, Enrique. "Calidad del destierro." *En torno a Lydia Cabrera*. Eds. Isabel Castellanos and Josefina Inclán. Miami: Universal, 1987. 53.

Lama, Sonia de. "Review of *Homenaje a Lydia Cabrera*." *Hispania* 63.1 (1980): 159.

León, Argeliers. "*El monte*, de Lydia Cabrera." *Nuestro Tiempo* 2.7 (1955): 15–16.

León, René. *Bibliografía sobre Lydia Cabrera*. N.p.: n.p., 1977.

Levine, Suzanne Jill. "A Conversation with Lydia Cabrera." *Review: Latin American Literature and Arts* 31 (1982): 13–15.

Lezama Lima, José. "El nombre de Lydia Cabrera." *Tratados en La Habana* Ed. José Lezama Lima. Havana: Universidad Central de las Villas, Departamento de Relaciones Culturales, 1958. 144–48. Rpt. in Buenos Aires: la Flor, 1969. 144–48.

Loret de Mola, Florinda Alzaga. "Lydia Cabrera: Una anécdota desconocida." *En torno a Lydia Cabrera*. Eds. Isabel Castellanos and Josefina Inclán. Miami: Universal, 1987. 25–26.

Madrigal, José Antonio. "El mito paradisíaco y la poesía afrocubana contemporánea." *Homenaje a Lydia Cabrera*. Eds. Reinaldo Sánchez and José Antonio Madrigal. Miami: Universal, 1978. 35–39.

Marks, Morton. "Exploring El monte Ethnobotany and the Afro-Cuban Science of the Concrete." En torno a Lydia Cabrera. Eds. Isabel Castellanos and Josefina Inclán. Miami: Universal, 1987. 227–45.

Menton, Seymour. Prose Fiction of the Cuban Revolution. Austin: University of Texas Press, 1975. 243–44.

Miomandre, Francis de. Introduction. Contes negres de Cuba de Lydia Cabrera. Paris: Gallimard, 1936. 9–15.

———. "Sobre El monte, de Lydia Cabrera." Orígenes (Havana) 39 (1955): 75–78.

Mistral, Gabriela. Siete cartas de Gabriela Mistral a Lydia Cabrera. Miami: Peninsular Printing, 1980.

Molloy, Sylvia. "Disappearing Acts: Reading Lesbian in Teresa de la Parra." ¿Entiendes? Queer Readings, Hispanic Writings. Ed. Emilie Bergmann. Durham, N.C.: Duke University Press, 1995. 2320–56.

Montero, Susana A. "La narrativa femenina cubana (1923–1958)." Cuadernos Hispanoamericanos 544 (1995): 19–42.

Montes Huidobro, Matías. "Itinerario del ebo." Círculo 8 (1979): 105–14. Rpt. in Studies in Afro-Hispanic Literature 2–3 (1978–1979): 1–13.

———. "Lydia Cabrera: Observaciones estructurales sobre su narrativa." Congreso de literatura afroamericana: Homenaje a Lydia Cabrera. Florida International University, November 1976. Rpt. in Homenaje a Lydia Cabrera. Eds. Reinaldo Sánchez and José Antonio Madrigal. Miami: Universal, 1978. 41–50.

Muriedas, Mercedes. "Lydia Cabrera: Su espacio y su tiempo." En torno a Lydia Cabrera. Eds. Isabel Castellanos and Josefina Inclán. Miami: Universal, 1987. 54–57.

Murphy, Joseph M. "Lydia Cabrera and La regla de Ocha in the United States." En torno a Lydia Cabrera. Eds. Isabel Castellanos and Josefina Inclán. Miami: Universal, 1987. 246–54.

Noulet, Edmond. "Lydia Cabrera." La Nouvelle Revue Française May 1936: 798.

Novás Calvo, Lino. "Los cuentos de Lydia Cabrera." Exilio (New York) 3.2 (1969): 17–20.

———. "El monte." Papeles de Son Armadans (Palma de Mallorca) 150 September 1968: 298–304.

Núñez, Ana Rosa. "Perfil de Lydia Cabrera." En torno a Lydia Cabrera. Eds. Isabel Castellanos and Josefina Inclán. Miami: Universal, 1987. 21–22.

Ochando-Aymerich, Carmen. "Antropoesía cubana: Lydia Cabrera." Quimera (Barcelona) 123 (1994): 8–9.

Ortiz, Fernando "Dos nuevos libros del folklore afrocubano." Revista Bimestre Cubana 42 (1938): 307–19.

———. "Lydia Cabrera (una cubana afroamericanista)." Crónica (Havana) 1.3 (1949): 7–8.

———. Prologue. Cuentos negros de Cuba. Havana: Nuevo Mundo, 1961. 9–12.

Ortiz Aponte, Sally. "La virtud del árbol Dagame, de Lydia Cabrera." La esoteria en la narrativa hispanoamericana. Ed. Sally Ortiz Aponte. San Juan, Puerto Rico: Universitaria, Universidad de Puerto Rico, 1977. 231–38.

Perera Soto, Hilda. "El aché de Lydia Cabrera." Congreso de literatura afroamericana:

Homenaje a Lydia Cabrera. Florida International University, November 1976. Rpt. in *Homenaje a Lydia Cabrera*. Eds. Reinaldo Sánchez and José Antonio Madrigal. Miami: Universal, 1978. 51–59.

———. "La Habana intacta de Lydia Cabrera." *Círculo* 13 (1984): 33–38.

———. *Idapo: El sincretismo en los cuentos negros de Lydia Cabrera*. Miami: Universal, 1971.

———. "Recordando a Teresa de la Parra con Lydia Cabrera." *Romances* 4 (1967): 64–98.

Picón Garfield, Evelyn. "Lydia Cabrera." *Women's Fiction from Latin America: Selections from Twelve Contemporary Authors*. Detroit: Wayne State University Press, 1988. 15–27.

Pita, Juana Rosa. "*Cuentos para adultos, niños y retrasados mentales* de Lydia Cabrera." *Vuelta* (Mexico City) 8.86 (1984): 35–36.

Portell Vilá, Herminio. "Los estudios africanistas en Cuba." *En torno a Lydia Cabrera*. Eds. Isabel Castellanos and Josefina Inclán. Miami: Universal, 1987. 313–17.

R. B. "Los negros en Cuba." *Índice de Artes y Letras* 127 (1959): 24.

Rexach, Rosario. "Lydia Cabrera, persona." *En torno a Lydia Cabrera*. Eds. Isabel Castellanos and Josefina Inclán. Miami: Universal, 1987. 65–67.

Rodríguez-Florido, Jorge. "La función del doble en los *Cuentos negros* y en *Porqué* . . ." Congreso de literatura afroamericana: Homenaje a Lydia Cabrera. Florida International University, November 1976. Rpt. in *Homenaje a Lydia Cabrera*. Eds. Reinaldo Sánchez and José Antonio Madrigal. Miami: Universal, 1978. 61–71.

Rodríguez Tomeu, Julia. "*Cuentos negros de Cuba*." *Cuadernos Americanos* (Mexico City) 7.2 (1949): 279–81.

Romeu, Raquel. "Lo cubano en el sincretismo de Lydia Cabrera." *Mujer y sociedad en América*. Ed. Juana Alcira Arancibia. Westminster, Calif.: Instituto Literario y Cultural Hispánico, 1990. 133–41.

———. "Dios, animal, hombre o mujer: Jicotea, un personaje de Lydia Cabrera." *Letras Femeninas* 15.1–2 (1989): 29–36.

Ruiz del Vizo, Hortensia. "Algunos aspectos del universo religioso y mental del negro en dos colecciones de cuentos de Lydia Cabrera." *En torno a Lydia Cabrera*. Eds. Isabel Castellanos and Josefina Inclán. Miami: Universal, 1987. 135–42.

———. "La función del monte en la obra de Lydia Cabrera." Congreso de literatura afroamericana: Homenaje a Lydia Cabrera. Florida International University, November 1976. Rpt. in *Homenaje a Lydia Cabrera*. Eds. Reinaldo Sánchez and José Antonio Madrigal. Miami: Universal, 1978. 73–82.

Sánchez, Reinaldo, and José Antonio Madrigal. *Homenaje a Lydia Cabrera* Miami: Universal, 1978.

Sánchez-Boudy, José. "La armonía universal en la obra de Lydia Cabrera." Congreso de literatura afroamericana: Homenaje a Lydia Cabrera. Florida International University, November 1978. Rpt. in *Homenaje a Lydia Cabrera*. Eds. Reinaldo Sánchez and José Antonio Madrigal. Miami: Universal, 1978. 83–92.

———. "A los cincuenta años de *Cuentos negros de Cuba*. *En torno a Lydia Cabrera*. Eds. Isabel Castellanos and Josefina Inclán. Miami: Universal, 1987. 143–54.

———. "Rev. of *Lo ancestral africano en la narrativa de Lydia Cabrera* by Rosa Valdés-Cruz." *Explicación de Textos Literarios* 5.1 (1976): 112.

Soto, Sara. *Magia e historia en los "Cuentos negros," "Por qué," y "Ayapá" de Lydia Cabrera*. Miami: Universal, 1988.

Torre, Guillermo de. "Literatura de color." *El sol* (Madrid) July 12, 1936: 5–11. Rpt. in *Revista Bimestre Cubana* 38 (1936): 5–11.

Valdés-Cruz, Rosa. "African heritage in folktales." *Actes du Septième. Congres de l'Association Internationale de Littérature Comparée* (Bieber, Stuttgart) (1979): 327–30.

———. *Lo ancestral africano en la narrativa de Lydia Cabrera*. Barcelona: Vosgos, 1974.

———. "Los cuentos de Lydia Cabrera: ¿Transposiciones o creaciones?" Congreso de literatura afroamericana: Homenaje a Lydia Cabrera. Florida International University, November 1976. Rpt. in *Homenaje a Lydia Cabrera*. Eds. Reinaldo Sánchez and José Antonio Madrigal. Miami: Universal, 1978. 93–99.

———. "Mitos africanos conservados en Cuba y su tratamiento literario por Lydia Cabrera." *Chasqui* 3.1 (1973): 31–36.

———. "El mundo del folklore en Lydia Cabrera: Su técnica narrativa." *En torno a Lydia Cabrera*. Eds. Isabel Castellanos and Josefina Inclán. Miami: Universal, 1987. 161–73.

———. "El realismo mágico en los cuentos negros de Lydia Cabrera." *Otros mundos otros fuegos: Fantasía y realismo mágico en Iberoamérica*. Ed. Donald A. Yates. Memoria del décimo sexto Congreso Internacional de Literatura Iberoamericana. East Lansing: Michigan State University Latin American Studies Center, 1975. 206–9.

———. "The Short Stories of Lydia Cabrera: Transpositions or Creations?" *Latin American Women Writers: Yesterday and Today*. Eds. Charles Tatum and Yvette Miller. Pittsburgh: Latin American Literary Review, 1977. 148–54.

Verger, Pierre. *Cuba: 196 photos de Pierre Verger*. [Preface and notes by Lydia Cabrera.] Paris: P. Hartmann, 1958.

———. "Lydia Cabrera a Quasi Iyaloricha." *En torno a Lydia Cabrera*. Eds. Isabel Castellanos and Josefina Inclán. Miami: Universal, 1987. 68–70.

Viera, Ricardo. "Arte visual en la palabra de Lydia Cabrera." Congreso de literatura afroamericana: Homenaje a Lydia Cabrera. Florida International University, November 1976. Rpt. in *Homenaje a Lydia Cabrera*. Eds. Reinaldo Sánchez and José Antonio Madrigal. Miami: Universal, 1978. 101–8.

Weis, Jasson. "Story of a Friendship: Teresa de la Parra and Lydia Cabrera in Europe." *Linden Lane Magazine* 16.1 (1977): 6–9.

Willis, Miriam DeCosta. "Folklore and the Creative Artist: Lydia Cabrera and Zora Neale Hurston." *College Language Association Journal* 27.1 (1983): 81–90.

Zaldívar, Gladys. "La fabulación poética de los *Cuentos negros de Cuba*." *En torno a Lydia Cabrera*. Eds. Isabel Castellanos and Josefina Inclán. Miami: Universal, 1987. 174–89.

———. *Lydia Cabrera: De mitos y contemporáneos*. Miami: Publicaciones de la Asociación de Hispanistas de las Americas, 1986.

Zambrano, María. "Lydia Cabrera, poeta de la metamorfosis." *Orígenes* (Havana) 7.25 (1950): 11–13.

Zielina, María del Carmen. "Lydia Cabrera." *La africanía en el cuento cubano y puertorriqueño*. Miami: Universal, 1992. 56–72.

Aída Cartagena Portalatín

DOMINICAN REPUBLIC

Aída Cartagena Portalatín (1918–94), the most important twentieth-century woman writer in the Dominican Republic, was born in Moca, Dominican Republic, in 1918. She graduated from the School of Humanities at the Autonomous University of Santo Domingo and did postgraduate studies in music and theory at the School of Fine Arts in Paris. She taught history of art, colonial art, and history of civilization at her alma mater in Santo Domingo and served as director of the Museum of Anthropology in the Dominican Republic.

She initiated her literary career in the early 1940s when she became part of the group of Dominican poets who were collaborating on the new literary journal *La Poesía Sorprendida* (Surprised poetry). Her first collections of poems were published during this period: *Del sueño al mundo* (From dream to the world, 1945), *Víspera del sueño* (Eve of the dream, 1945), and *Llámale verde* (Call it green, 1945).

In the 1960s Cartagena Portalatín began editing numerous literary journals and collections. Among the most important are *Revista de la Facultad de Humanidades* (Journal of the School of Humanities) and *Cuaderno Brigadas Dominicanas* (Dominican brigades notebooks), which published much of the clandestine literature produced during the dictatorship of Rafael Trujillo. A well-known critic, she traveled extensively in Central America representing her country. In 1977 she was invited to be a juror in the Casa de las Americas Prize in Cuba, and in 1980 she represented the Dominican Republic in the Congress of Women Writers in Puerto Rico.

A poet, short-story writer, novelist, and essayist, Cartagena Portalatín is the author of fourteen books. In both her prose and poetry, she celebrates her African descent and refers to her struggle as a woman living and writing in a male-dominated society. Her best-known book, *Escalera para Electra* (A staircase for Electra, 1970), was a finalist in the prestigious literary contest Biblioteca Breve of Seix Barral in 1969. In this novel she continues her struggle against racism and social injustice and her experimentation with literary form. Her writing is characterized by innovative use of language, cinematographic techniques, and symbolism.

A Passion for Donna Summer

Mommy used to call me "Colita," Colita García. But Mrs. Sarah registered me in the public school as "Dawn."

"I won't have you be known as 'Colita,'" she screamed. I felt like 'Colita' even if I was 'Dawn' to her. I'll never forgive Mrs. Sarah for nicknaming me Dawn so she can discriminate against me whenever she calls me laughingly and teasingly. No. Noo. And Noo! I'm not going to stay here with her, in her house, even though it's true she pays for my studies, that she tells everyone that I'm real talented. I'm fed up with her and the nuns at the school, Sister Tantina, long and skinny like Twiggy from TV, and Mother Superior, wise but who looks like Aldonza, Sancho Panza's wife. They carry on about theorems, and about the triangle and rectangle and what are parallel lines, and screw Colita-Dawn with punishments and telephone calls so that Mrs. Sarah attacks me like a machine gun. No. Noo. And Nooo, NO!

I said no. I don't like Mrs. Sarah, nor do I care about her beautiful house, and I am not going to get old inside her four walls like a tree destined to become charcoal. No, I'm not going to stay with her like a tree burning under a dog day sun. No, I'm not going to stay sad, head bowed, like leaves beaten by the thunder-rain storms, these walls surrounded by an evergreen lawn and some fruit trees. I don't accept that Dawn is "an intelligent little black girl," or that blacks amuse people, or that blacks with their jazz and rhythm make the world happy. I don't like it either when she tells me to go to the store and bring her Donna Summer's latest record. I hate when she says blacks ought to be good for something, it's a good thing they amuse whites. No. Noo. And noo. I like the unending music of Donna Summer, scratching, howling nonstop, falling like a vibrant exciting cascade. But it's for sure that Mrs. Sarah isn't going to keep me inside her exciting music box forever. What about jazz, what about boogaloo, what about ragtime or beguine? That stuff is not for the old bag. She thinks I could never leave. I'd love her to see how fast I'm walking to the bus stop, dragging this heavy bundle with my clothes and books. Here, driver, I'm getting off in Haina.

I walk around a bit, smelling the air from the sugar refineries. I sit in Candita's restaurant and have a very cold 7-Up. Hungry, that's what I am, so I move on to the Dwarf's where I drink a Pepsi and eat two rolls. I leave quickly. Donna Summer's music fills the shack and permeates the whole neighborhood. How I remember now that little unending cascade of meows of years ago. Donna's music and singing floats beyond the shack, the neighborhood; it's the same tune that excites and shakes Mrs. Sarah.

The hell with everything, here I am again exactly fourteen kilometers from the capital and away from Mrs. Sarah's house. It's seven o'clock at night. I enter the church and hide behind Saint Isidro's altar, the saint who takes away the rain and brings the sunshine. Let the saint hide me, so I won't be found. Saint, Saint, Saint, the streets are full of job seekers and beggars. La la la la laaa, ya ya ya ya yaaa.

Next to a wall of the Dwarf Bar a girl is rocking. Donna's voice gets louder as a lottery vendor turns up the volume on his radio. Donna's voice again fills the bar, the neighborhood, the town. I try to gather up my kinky hair. If I was born with it this way, that's how I'll keep it. What is really absurd is that they discriminate against me and then brag about my intelligence because I'm almost a high school graduate. No. Noo. And noo. No! It infuriates me to see that so many millions of whites enjoy Donna Summer, the little black girl who sings energetically. They get themselves into a frenzy over Armstrong, and later Makeba's music. They choose to ignore our history. What about jazz and all that rhythm and blues that's born so happily? Congratulations! No, if I were Donna Summer I would recall all the records from the store shelves, dance floors, cabarets, hotels, motels, and the high-class houses.

The sugar technician's wife from Ohio who suggested I come to New York persuaded me to start out as a housekeeper. Here, in their apartment, on the eleventh floor, I cook, wash, iron, and shop for them. I put up with nonsense from the grocery keeper, that Italian son of a bitch, who pulls my hair and calls me "ugly black girl," asking where I'm from and this and that. I put up with the gringo Mrs. who asks me: "Colita, why do you take so long?" Sometimes I tell her that the son of a bitch detained me, or that I stopped to see Giordano kill Manfredi with a knife (both wanted some dead neighbor who each thought should be taken to his funeral parlor, and the police very calmly announce: Giordano is dead).

I am going to have to mentally organize myself like in a list of classified ads.

1 : *"I've been told that this is the FreeWorld and yet here the gringo Mrs. exploits me like a slave."*

2 : *"I don't understand why the FreeWorld agrees with Exploitation."*

3 : *"Colita, you are so ignorant!"*

4 : *"I didn't know anything about monopolies but I now know that they control everything I buy."*

Policemen, policemen, policemen everywhere! One of them grabs my breast and I scream "jerk." I'm tired of seeing drunks, drug addicts, cops, and CIA agents all over the world. I'm tired of seeing unemployed classless guys letting tough cops beat them up like in the westerns. That's not manly, Dominican style. Is this the Free World, so overexploited, excessive? I'm going to go crazy. And no. Noo. And no!

I'm back at Mrs. Sarah's house, with her constant music, Donna Summer music with the same catastrophies, screaming at me all the time. And she screams and yells angrily when I read in the newspaper about the injustices that are committed against the blacks in South Africa. When I read about the lynchings in Soweto and Johannesburg, Steve Biko imprisoned in Pretoria. Mrs. Sarah grabs me by the hair and she screams "it's nonsense." Then she drags me by the hair to the record player where she turns up the volume as loud as it will go. I can't even hear myself crying now. Donna Summer, my dear little black girl, fill Mrs. Sarah's house with your voice and excite it with your rhythm.

Translated by Nora Erro-Peralta and Caridad Silva-Núñez.
(From *Tablero: Doce cuentos de lo popular a lo culto*, 1978)

Bibliography

Fiction by Aída Cartagena Portalatín

"La autopsia." *La cuentista dominicana*. Ed. Jenny Montero. Santo Domingo: Biblioteca Nacional, 1986. 174–77.

"Colita." *Anthology of Contemporary Latin American Literature, 1960–1984*. Eds. Barry J. Luby and Wayne H. Finke. London and Toronto: Associated University Press, 1986. 91–93.

"En Off." *Universo* 12 (1982): 117–23.

Escalera para Electra. Santo Domingo: Universidad Autónoma de Santo Domingo, 1970. Rpt. in Santo Domingo: Taller, 1975.

"El fuego de todos." *Universo* 10 (1980): 67–73.

"La llamaban Aurora (Pasión por Donna Summer)." *Puerta abierta: La nueva escritora latinoamericana*. Eds. Caridad L. Silva-Velázquez and Nora Erro-Orthmann. Mexico City: Joaquín Mortiz, 1986. 75–77.

Tablero: Doce cuentos de lo popular a lo culto. Santo Domingo: Taller, 1978.

La tarde en que murió Estefanía. Santo Domingo: Taller, 1983.

"Tête-a-tête con Teresa de Avila." *Universo* 6 (1978): 123–25.

Essays by Aída Cartagena Portalatín

"El cuento dominicano." *Narradores dominicanos· Antología*. Ed. Aída Cartagena Portalatín. Caracas: Monte Avila, 1969. 7–12.

———. *Culturas africanas: Rebeldes con causa*. Santo Domingo: Taller, 1986.

———. *Danza, música, e instrumentos de los indios de la Española*. Santo Domingo: Museo de Antropología, Universidad Autónoma de Santo Domingo, 1974.

———. "Del texto de *La brevísima relación de la destrucción de las Indias*." *Universo* 3 (1972): 57–76.

———. "Los Ginés de Santiago de los Caballeros en textos de Alejo Carpentier y Pedro Henríquez Ureña." *Universo* 2 (1972): 27–35.

———. "La literatura chicana." *Universo* 11 (1980): 49–63.

———. "Recordando a Neruda." *Universo* 5 (1974): 39–42.

Poetry by Aída Cartagena Portalatín

"Cómo llorar la muerte de una rosa," "Mi gozo y mi amargura," "Estación en la tierra," and "Una mujer está sola." *Diccionario enciclopédico dominicano (Sección antología poética)*. Santo Domingo: Biblioteca Nacional, 1988. 754–56.

Del desconsuelo al compromiso/From Desolation to Compromise: A Bilingual Anthology of the Poetry of Aída Cartagena Portalatín. Ed. Daisy Cocco de Filippis. Trans. Daisy Cocco de Filippis and Emma Jane Robinett. Santo Domingo: Taller, 1988.

Del sueño al mundo/Llámale verde. Santo Domingo: Ediciones de la Poesía Sorprendida, 1945. Rpt. in *La poesía sorprendida* (1943–1947). Santo Domingo: Cultural Dominicana, 1974. 1–21.

En la casa del tiempo. Santo Domingo: Universidad Autónoma de Santo Domingo, 1984.

"Estación en la tierra," "De entero cuerpo," "Henri Matisse," "Tarde en el parque," "Cómo llorar la muerte de una rosa," "El viento en el amor," "Tierra fuerte de agua viva," "Fiesta del regreso," "La casa," "2000 años después," "Tal vez inútil súplica," and "Otoño negro." *Antología panorámica de la poesía dominicana contemporánea, 1912–1962.* Ed. Manuel Rueda. Santiago: n.p., 1972. 227–39.

Llámale verde. Santo Domingo: Poesía Sorprendida, 1945.

Mi mundo el mar. Ciudad Trujillo: n.p., 1953.

Una mujer está sola. Ciudad Trujillo: La Española, 1955.

"Por otro requiem: Homenaje a Ernesto Cardenal." *Universo* 9 (1979): 105.

La tierra escrita. Santo Domingo: Brigadas Dominicanas, 1967.

"La tierra escrita: Elegía octava." *Lecturas dominicanas.* Eds. Carlos Fernández Rocha and Danilo de los Santos. Madrid: Playor, 1977. 64–65.

"Víspera de sueño," "Del sueño al mundo," "Cómo llorar la muerte de una rosa," "Asolador," "Una mujer está sola," and "Estación en la tierra." *Sin otro profeta que su canto: Antología de poesía escrita por dominicanas.* Ed. Daisy Cocco de Filippis. Santo Domingo: Taller, 1988. 75–85.

Víspera del sueño. Santo Domingo: Poesía Sorprendida, 1944.

La voz desatada. Santo Domingo: Brigadas Dominicanas, 1962.

Yania tierra; poema documento. Santo Domingo: Colección Montesinos, 1981.

Criticism on the Works of Aída Cartagena Portalatín

Acosta de Hess, Josefina. "La función de la intertextualidad en *Escalera para Electra.*" *Mujer y sociedad en América.* Ed. Juana Alcira Arancibia. Westminster, Calif.: Instituto Literario y Cultural Hispánico, 1990. 101–8.

Alcántara Almánzar, José. "Aída Cartagena Portalatín." *Estudios de poesía dominicana.* Santo Domingo: Alfa y Omega, 1979. 269–85.

Back, Michele. "'En tiempo oscuro': The Search and Discovery of Territory in the Life and Work of Aída Cartagena Portalatín." *Lucero* 6 (1995): 44–52.

Brown, Isabel Zakrzewski. "Autora en busca de expresión en *Escalera para Electra.*" *Cincinnati Romance Review* 12 (1993): 130–38.

De Filippis, Daisy Cocco. "Aída Cartagena Portalatín: A Literary Life. Moca, Dominican Republic, 1918–94." *Moving Beyond Boundaries. Vol 2: Black Women's Diasporas.* Ed. Carole Boyce Davies. New York: New York University Press, 1994. 227–36.

———. "Indias y trigueñas No Longer: Contemporary Dominican Women Poets Speak." *Cimarrón* 1.3 (1988): 133–50.

———. Introducción. *Del desconsuelo al compromiso/From Desolation to Compromise: A Bilingual Anthology of the Poetry of Aída Cartagena Portalatín.* Ed. Daisy Cocco de Filippis. Trans. Emma Jane Robinett. Santo Domingo: Taller, 1988.

Figueroa, Ramón. "Nacionalismo y el universalismo en *Escalera para Electra.*" *Areíto* 10.38 (1984): 41–43.

Guzmán, Catherine. "Onomatology in Aída Cartagena Portalatín's Fiction." *Literary Onomastics Studies* 10 (1983): 75–86.

Montero, Jenny. *La cuentista dominicana.* Santo Domingo: Biblioteca Nacional, 1986. 79–82.

Ramos, Emelda. "Hacia una narrativa femenina en la literatura dominicana." *Continental, Latin-American, and Francophone Women Writers*. Vol 1. Eds. Eunice Myers and Ginette Adamson. Lanham, MD: University Press of America, 1987. 167–75.

Rosario Chandelier, Bruno. "Aída Cartagena Portalatín." *Tendencias de la novela dominicana*. Santiago: Universidad Católica Madre y Maestra, 1988. 306–19.

———. "Swain o la observación creadora en Aída Cartagena Portalatín." *Ensayos críticos*. Santiago: Universidad Católica Madre y Maestra, 1982. 165–75.

———. "Técnica y temática en *Escalera para Electra*." *Ensayos críticos*. Santiago: Universidad Católica Madre y Maestra, 1982. 273–91.

Sosa, José Rafael, ed. *Mujer y literatura: Homenaje a Aída Cartagena Portalatín*. Santo Domingo: Universidad Autónoma de Santo Domingo, 1986.

Williams, Lorna V. "The Inscription of Sexual Identity in Aída Cartagena Portalatín's *Escalera para Electra*." *Modern Language Notes* 112.2 (1997): 19–31.

Lygia Fagundes Telles

Lygia Fagundes Telles, one of Brazil's best-known authors, was born in São Paulo, Brazil, in 1923 and spent her childhood in small towns, where her father was posted as a district attorney, police commissioner, and judge. After studying law at the University of São Paulo, she had a fruitful legal and public service career, although she has devoted most of her life to cultural and literary activities. Fagundes Telles served as vice president of the Brazilian Writers' Union and as president of the Brazilian Cinematique and is an active member of the Brazilian Academy of Letters.

Fagundes Telles has written five novels and more than a dozen collections of short stories. These stories exhibit tightly knit structures and a commitment to realism and aesthetic values, in combination with an indirect style and frequent use of myth, evocation, and ambiguity. While her short stories often deal with the complex corners of the human mind and with experiences that go beyond rational order, her novels portray women characters caught in conflict between the pursuit of self-fulfillment and the reality of established social codes. In her fiction she especially explores the themes of moral and economic adjustment of women to modern society in the urban atmosphere of São Paulo. Her most powerful works, such as *Giranda de Pedra* (1954; *The Marble Dance,* 1986), are concerned with women's sexuality.

In more recent years, she has adopted an experimental style, as in *As meninas* (1973; *The Girl in the Photograph,* 1982), her celebrated novel about three women whose experiences with drugs, sex, and violence are described within the context of a turbulent right-wing dictatorship. Her later works are characterized by a magical, supernatural quality.

Since the publication of her first volume of short stories, *Praia viva* (Living beach, 1944), and throughout her long, steady production over the years,

Fagundes Telles has collected numerous honors and prizes at home and abroad. Her literary career has been marked by a rare set of circumstances for a woman writer: the official recognition of intellectual and literary critics and the sustained interest in her works by the general public, which makes her one of the most popular writers in Brazil today.

The Hunt

The antique shop with its mildewed clothes and moth-eaten books smelled like a coffer in a sacristy. With his fingertips the man touched a pile of paintings. A moth took off and collided with a statue with chopped-off hands.

"A beautiful statue," the man said.

The old woman removed a hairpin from her bun and cleaned her thumbnail. She replaced the pin in her hair.

"It's a Saint Francis."

Then the man turned slowly to face the tapestry that covered most of the wall at the back of the shop. He drew closer. The old woman also drew closer.

"I see that you're really interested in it. A pity it's in such a condition."

The man's hand reached for the tapestry, but he didn't touch it.

"It looks much sharper today."

"Sharper?" replied the old woman, putting on her glasses. Her hand slid along its threadbare surface. "What do you mean—sharper?"

"The colors look brighter. Have you treated the tapestry with something?"

The old woman stared at him. Then, evasively, she turned her gaze on St. Francis with the chopped-off hands. The man looked as pale and bewildered as the statue.

"No, of course not. Why do you ask?"

"I notice some difference."

"No, I didn't treat it with anything. This tapestry wouldn't bear even the slightest brushing, can't you see? I think the dust is what's holding the fabric together," she added, once more removing the hairpin from her head. She turned it in her fingers, her expression thoughtful. She pouted.

"A stranger brought it here. He needed the money very badly. I told him that the fabric was much too damaged, that it wouldn't be easy to find a buyer, but he kept persisting. I hung it on the wall, and there it has remained. But it's been many years. And that young man has never shown up again."

"Extraordinary . . ."

The old woman couldn't tell whether the man was referring to the tapestry or to the incident she had just told him. She shrugged. She started cleaning her fingernails with the hairpin. "I could sell it to you, but quite frankly, I don't think it's worth anything. The moment we remove it, it will probably fall apart."

The man lit a cigarette. His hands shook. When, oh God, when had he witnessed this same scene? And where?

The tapestry depicted a hunt. In the foreground was a hunter with a taut bow aimed at a large clump of bushes. In the background, a second hunter peered into the trees of the thicket, but he was merely a blurred silhouette whose face was reduced to a faded contour. The first hunter looked powerful and independent, his beard turbulent like entangled serpents, his muscles tense, waiting for his prey to emerge before shooting the arrow.

The man was breathing with difficulty. His gaze roamed over the tapestry, which was the greenish color of a stormy sky. Defiling the moss-green of the fabric were some purplish black blots, which seemed to ooze out of the foliage, slide down the hunter's boots, and spread over the ground like some malignant liquid. The clump of bushes where the animal was hidden also displayed the same blots, which could have been either part of the design itself, or else the mere effect of time eating up the fabric.

"Today everything seems closer together," the man said in a lower voice. "It's as if . . . Don't you think it looks different?"

The old woman narrowed her eyes. She took off her glasses and put them on again.

"I can't see any difference."

"Yesterday it was impossible to tell whether or not he had shot the arrow."

"What arrow? Can you see any arrow?"

"That tiny dot on the bow."

The old woman sighed.

"But isn't that a moth-eaten hole? See how the wall already shows through; these moths just put an end to everything," she complained, stifling a yawn. Noiselessly she moved away in her woolen slippers. She gestured vaguely, "Make yourself at home; I'm having my tea."

The man dropped his cigarette. He slowly stubbed it out with the sole of his shoe. His jaws tightened painfully. He knew that thicket, that hunter, that sky—how well he knew them all, ah, how well! He could almost smell the scent of the eucalyptus trees, could almost feel the damp cold of the dawn nipping his skin; ah, that dawn such a long, long time ago. Oh God, when had he traversed that same path, when had he breathed in that same mist that descended densely from the green sky? Or did it rise from the ground? The hunter with the curly beard seemed to smile, perversely cunning. Could he have been that same hunter? Or had he been the companion over there, that faceless man peering into the trees? A tapestry character. But which one? He stared at the clump of bushes where the game hid. Nothing but leaves, silence and leaves plastered down in the shadows. But behind the leaves, behind the blots, he thought he could see the arched shape of the animal. He felt compassion for that panicky being waiting for an opportunity to proceed in its flight. Death so close! The slightest movement and the ruthless arrow . . . The old woman hadn't seen it. Nobody would be able to see the arrow reduced to a tiny worm-eaten dot, paler than a speck of dust suspended over the bow.

Wiping the sweat off his chin with the back of his hand, the man stepped backward. A certain peacefulness invaded him now that he knew he had participated in that hunt. But his was a lifeless peacefulness, one impregnated with those treacherous blots in the foliage. He closed his eyes. Could he have been the painter of the picture? Most of the ancient tapestries were reproductions of paintings, weren't they? He had painted the original picture and therefore could reproduce with his eyes closed the entire scene in its finest details: the configuration of the trees, the dark sky, the hunter with his unkempt beard, all muscles and sinews, aiming at the clump.

"But I hate hunting! Why do I have to be in there?"

He pressed the handkerchief to his mouth. The nausea. Ah, if only he could explain all this frightening familiarity, if he could at least . . . Could he have been a mere casual spectator, one of those people that watch and then move on? A likely hypothesis. Or else he might have seen the original painting; the hunt was nothing but a figment of his mind. "Before making use of the tapestry . . . ," he murmured, drying the spaces between his fingers with the handkerchief.

His head jerked backward as if someone were pulling him by his hair; no, he hadn't stayed outside. He had been in there, nailed to the scenario. And why did everything look sharper than yesterday, why were the colors stronger despite the dusk? Why was the fascination, now coming out from the landscape, becoming so vigorous and rejuvenated?

He left with his head bowed, his hands clenched into a fist inside his pockets. Almost panting, he stopped at the street corner. His body ached, his eyelids felt heavy. And if he tried to sleep? But he knew that he wouldn't be able to sleep, and he already felt sleeplessness following him in step with his shadow. He turned up the collar of his jacket. Was this cold real? Or was it the remembrance of the cold in the tapestry?

"How crazy! But I'm not crazy," and he smiled helplessly. That would have been the easy way out. "But I'm not crazy."

He wandered through the streets, went to a movie and soon left, then realized that he was standing before the secondhand shop, his nose flattened against the show window in his attempt to catch a glimpse of the tapestry way back in the room.

When he got home he threw himself on the bed and there he remained, his eyes wide-open, staring at the darkness. The old woman's tremulous voice seemed to come from the pillow, a disembodied voice wearing woolen slippers: "What arrow? I can't see any arrow." Intermingled with her voice, the murmuring of the moths, amidst giggles, was rising in a crescendo. The cotton in the pillow muffled the peals of laughter, interwoven into a greenish, tightly knit net, which became enmeshed in a fabric that had blots trickling down to the ornamental borders. He became entangled in the filaments and wanted to escape, but the ornamental border arrested him in its arms. Down, deep down in the pit he could see the serpents entangled into one greenish black ball. He touched his chin. "Am I the hunter?" But instead of a beard he felt a gory clamminess.

He woke up with his own scream reverberating in the dawn. He dried his sweat-drenched face. Ah, that heat and that cold! He wrapped the sheets around him. And if he had been the craftsman who wove the tapestry? Again he could see it, so sharp and so near that if he reached out his hand he would awaken the foliage. He clenched his fists. He would destroy it. It wasn't true that there was anything else in that abhorrent rag; it was nothing but a rectangle of cloth held together by dust. It would be enough to blow upon it, to blow upon it!

He met the old woman at the door of her shop. She smiled ironically.

"You made an early start today!"

"You might think it strange, but . . ."

"I don't think anything strange anymore. Come in, come in, you know the way."

"I know the way," he murmured, following her between the furniture. He stopped, nostrils flared. That smell of foliage and earth—where did that smell come from? And why was the shop becoming blurred and distant? Growing larger, only the tapestry was real, creeping down to the floor, up to the ceiling, its greenish blots swallowing up everything. He wanted to turn back, he clutched at a cupboard, he staggered, still resisting, and extended his arms toward the pillar. His fingers disappeared amidst the branches and slid down the trunk of a tree; it wasn't a pillar, it was a tree! He stared wildly about him: he had entered the tapestry, he was in the thicket, his feet heavy with mud, his hair soaked with dew. Around him everything was motionless, spellbound. In the silence of the dawn, not even the chirp of a bird or the rustle of a leaf. He bent over, gasping. Was he the hunter? Or the hunted? It didn't matter, it didn't matter. He only knew that he had to go on running without stopping through the maze of trees, hunting or being hunted. Or being hunted? He pressed the palms of his hands to his flushed face, and in the cuffs of his shirt he dried the sweat that was trickling down his neck. His cracked lips were bleeding.

He opened his mouth. He remembered. "No!" he cried out, plunging into a clump of bushes. He heard the arrow hiss as it penetrated the foliage.

"No," he moaned, falling to his knees, still trying to hold on to the tapestry. He rolled down, huddled up and livid, his hands firmly clutching at his heart.

Translated by Eloah F. Giacomelli
(From *Historias de desencontro,* 1958)

Bibliography

Fiction by Lygia Fagundes Telles

A Disciplina do amor: Fragmentos. Rio de Janeiro: Nova Fronteira, 1980. Rpt. in Rio de Janeiro: Nova Fronteira, 1981.

Antes do bailes verde. Rio de Janeiro: Bloch, 1970. Rpt. in Rio de Janeiro: Livraria J. Olympio, 1982.

As horas nuas. Rio de Janeiro: Nova Fronteira, 1989.

As meninas. Rio de Janeiro: José Olympio, 1973. Rpt. in Rio de Janeiro: José Olympio, 1981.

"Before the Green Ball." *Short Stories of the Americas.* Ed. Lygia Johnson. San Francisco: Compile-a-Text, 1974. Rpt. in *Women of Latin America: A Collection of Twentieth Century Short Stories.* Ed. Lygia Johnson. *Latin American Literary Review* 4.7 (Fall–Winter 1975): 121–25.

"La cacería." Trans. Lilia Osorio. *Revista de la Universidad Mexicana.* Nueva Época 39.25 (1983): 14–15.

Ciranda de pedra. Lisbon: Editorial Minerva, 1954. Rpt. in Rio de Janeiro: José Olympio, 1983.

"Depoimento." *Prismal/Cabral* 3–4 (1979): 135–39. Rpt. in *Journal de Letras* (Lisbon) 2.30 (1982): 7.

Dez contos escolhidos. São Paulo: n.p., 1984.

"La estructura de la pompa de jabón." Trans. Manuel Rodríguez Ramos. *Casa de las Américas* 27.159 (1986): 46–49.

Filhos pródigos. São Paulo: Livraria Cultura, 1978.

Gaby. Os sete pecados capitais. Rio de Janeiro: n.p., 1954.

The Girl in the Photograph. Trans. Margaret A. Neves. New York: Avon, 1982.

Histórias do desencontro. Rio de Janeiro: José Olympio, 1958.

Histórias escolhidas. São Paulo: Boa Leitura, 1964.

"Just a Saxophone." *One Hundred Years after Tomorrow: Brazilian Women's Fiction in the Twentieth Century.* Ed. Darlene J. Sadlier. Bloomington: Indiana University Press, 1992. 122–31.

Lygia Fagundes Telles. Seleção de textos, notas, estudos biográfico, histórico, e crítico, e exercícios. Montfeiro, Leonardo, and São Paulo: Abril Educacao, 1980.

The Marble Dance. Trans. Margaret A. Neves. New York: Avon, 1986.

Mistério ficções. Rio de Janeiro: Nova Fronteira, 1981. Rpt. in Rio de Janeiro: Nova Fronteira, 1981.

"New Fiction: Lygia Fagundes Telles." Trans. Jon M Tolman and Margaret A. Neves. *Review: Latin American Literature and Arts* 30 (1981): 65–70.

O cacto vermelho. Rio de Janeiro: Mérito, 1949.

O jardim selvagem. São Paulo. Martins, 1965 Rpt. in Rio de Janeiro: José Olympio and Civilizacao Brasileira Tres, 1974.

"The Objects." Trans. Eloah Giacomelli. *Mundus Artium* 14.1 (1983): 38–43.

Os melhores contos de Lygia Fagundes Telles. Ed. Eduardo Portella. São Paulo: Global, 1984.

Os mortos. Lisboa: Casa Portuguesa, 1963.

Praia viva. São Paulo: n.p., 1944.

Selecta de Lygia Fagundes Telles. Ed. Nelly Novaes Coelho. Rio de Janeiro: José Olympio, 1971. Rpt. in Rio de Janeiro: José Olympio, 1978.

Seminário dos ratos. Rio de Janeiro: Livraria J. Olympio, 1977.

"Tigrela." Trans. Eloah F. Giacomelli. *Seminario dos ratos*. 1977. Rpt. in *Mundus Artium* 11.1 (1979): 72–27. Rpt. in *Other Fires: Short Fiction by Latin American Women*. Ed. Alberto Manguel. Toronto: Lester & Orpen Dennis, 1986. 179–87.

Tigrela and Other Stories. Trans. Margaret A. Neves. New York: Avon, 1986.

"Trilogia da confissao." *Os dezoito melhores contos do Brasil*. Rio de Janeiro: n.p., 1968.

"The Truth of Invention." *Lives on the Line: The Testimony of Contemporary Latin American Authors*. Ed. Doris Meyer. Berkeley: University of California Press, 1988. 265–71.

Verao no aquário. São Paulo: Martins, 1963. Rpt. in Rio de Janeiro: José Olympio, 1980.

"The Wild Garden." Trans. Eloah F. Giacomelli. *Review* 36 (1986): 34–37.

"The Window." Trans. Eloah F. Giacomelli. *Branching Out* February–March (1976): 26–27, 47.

Essays by Lygia Fagundes Telles

"A linguagem da paixao." *Jornal de Letras* (Lisbon) 2.27 (1982): 21.

"Depoiment." *Jornal de Letras* (Lisbon) 2.30 (1982): 7.

Criticism on the Works of Lygia Fagundes Telles

Almeida, Sandra Regina Goulart. "Castration and Melancholia in Lygia Fagundes Telles's *As horas nuas*." *Romance Language Annual* 3 (1991): 339–43.

Angelini, Paulo Roberto Escudero. "A intertextualidade em dois contos femeninos." *Cuadernos de Lingüistica e Teoria da Literatura* 8 (1982): 107–15.

Araujo, Vagner Correia de. "Antes do baile verde." *Minas Gerais* [literary supplement.] 230 (1971): 7.

———. "As meninas, o novo romance de Lygia Fagundes Telles." *O Estado de São Paulo* [literary supplement] 9 (1973): 1.

Ataide, Vincente de Paula. *A narrativa de Lygia Fagundes Telles*. Curitiva: Escola Estrutural, 1969.

———. "Criacao e técnica." *Minas Gerais* [literary supplement] 312 (1972): 3.

———. "Noticias sobre Lygia Fagundes Telles." *Minas Gerais* [literary supplement] 243 (1971): 11.

Barbosa, Rolmes. "O drama da solidao humana." *Estado de São Paulo* [literary supplement] 771 (1972): 2.

Bella, Josef. "El arte de Lygia Fagundes Telles." *Nueva Narrativa Hispanoamericana* 5.1–11 (1975): 185–88. Rpt. in *Minas Gerais* [literary supplement] 2 (1974): 12.

Bianchin, Neila Roso. "Espelho, espelho meu: Uma leitura de *As horas nuas* de Lygia Fagundes Telles." *Travessia* (Florianopolis, Brazil) 21 (1990): 133–42.

Bins, Patricia. "Lygia Fagundes Telles Ontem, Hoje e Sempre: A Imortal." *Minas Gerais* [literary supplement] 20 (1985): 4.

Brown, Richard L. "Lygia Fagundes Telles: Equalizer of the Sexes." *Romance Notes* 32.2 (1991): 157–61.

Burgin, Richard. "*Tigrela and Other Stories*." *New York Times Book Review* May 4, 1986: 40.

Carelli, Mario. "'Je pars de la realité vers le magique.'" *La Quinzaine Litteraire* 484 (1987): 24–25.

Carvalho, Alfredo Leme Coelho de. "A densidade simbolica e sugestiva em dois contos de Lygia Fagundes Telles." *Mimesis: Revista de Letras* 3 (1977): 81–88.

Coelho, Neli Novais. "A linguagem criativa de Lygia Fagundes Telles." *Jornal de Letras* (Lisbon) 22 (1970): 44.

———. "Antes do Baile Verde." *Estado São Paulo* [literary supplement] 688 September 19, 1970: 1. Rpt. in *Minas Gerais* [literary supplement] 688 November 21, 1970: 1.

———. "Lygia Fagundes Telles." *Estado São Paulo* January 15, 1966: 1.

Coelho, Nelly Novaes. "Ligia Fagundes Telles: Romancista." *Coloquio/Letras* 27 (1964): 44–47.

Coronado, Guilhermo de la Cruz. "O odio caímico em Lygia e Unamuno." *C. Povo*, 4 191, 192 (1971): 10+.

Costigan, Lucia Helena. "Literatura e Ditadura: Aspectos da ficção brasileira pos-64 em alguns dos escritos de Lygia Fagundes Telles e de Nelida Piñon." *Hispanic Journal* 13.1 (1992): 141–51.

Coutinho, Edilberto. "Lygia Fagundes Telles: O aspero casco de uma arvore." *Correio da Manha* June 2, 1970: 3.

Dantas, Raimundo Sousa. "Lygia, no conto o itinerário de uma ficcionista." *Jornal de Brasil* January 30, 1971: 9.

———. "Originalidade de Ficcionista." *Leitura* 17 (1950): 20.

Duarte, José Afranio Moreira. "Antes do Baile Verde e Fundador (os contos de Lygia e a ficção de Nélida)." *Jornal de Letras* (Lisbon) 22 (1970): 41.

"Entrevista a Lygia Fagundes Telles." *Plaza: Revista de Literatura* 13 (1987): 1–11.

Faria, Otávio de. "A ficcionista Lygia Fagundes Telles." *Estado São Paulo* April 30, 1966: 6.

Ferreira, Edda. "As meninas e a maestria tecnica de Lygia Fagundes Telles." *Minas Gerais* [literary supplement] 13 (1976): 8–9.

Fischer, Almeida. "Contistas muitos e bons." *C. Povo* 142 August 15, 1970: 11.

Gomes, Duílio. "Antes do Baile Verde." *Minas Gerais* [literary supplement] April 15, 1972: 11.

Gorga Filho, Remi. "Lígia Fagundes Telles." *C. Povo* 88 July 12, 1969: 15.

Linhares, Temístocles. "Lygia Fagundes Telles e as duas edicoes de Antes do Baile Verde. A ultima fase da escritora." *Veinte dois diálogos sobre o conto brasileiro atual.* Rio de Janeiro: José Olympio, 1973. 109–16.

Lucas, Fábio. "A ficção giratoria de Lygia Fagundes Telles." *Travessia* (Florianópolis, Brazil) 20 (1990): 60–77.

———. "Contos fortes," *Temas literários e juizes críticos.* Belo Horizonte: Tendencia, 1963. 149–152. Rpt. in *Estado São Paulo* June 27, 1959: 3.

———. "Mistério e magia: Contos de Lygia Fagundes Telles." *Estado São Paulo* [literary supplement] September 5, 1970: 686. Rpt. in *A face visível.* Rio de Janeiro: José Olympio; São Paulo: Cons. Est. de Cultura, 1973. 143–46.

———. "O conto no Brasil mocerno." *O livro do seminário.* São Paulo: n.p. 1983. 103–64.

Magalhaes Junior, Raimundo. *Panorama do conto brasileiro.* 10 vols. Rio de Janeiro: n.p., 1959–61.

Malard, Letícia. *Escritores de literatura brasileira*. Belo Horizonte, Brazil: n.p., 1981.

Marques, Carlos Vaz. "Lygia Fagundes Telles-Sobre a indisciplina da vida." *Jornal de Letras, Artes, and Ideias* 9.365 (1989): 5–6.

Mautner Wasserman, Renata R. "The *Guerrilla* in the Bathtub: Telles's *As Meninas* and the Irruption of Politics." *Modern Language Studies* 19.1 (1989): 50–65.

Medina, Cremilda. "Lygia Fagundes Telles na eter na aventura do morro de duro." *Minas Gerais* [literary supplement] February 9, 1985: 8.

Melillo Reali, Erilde. "Missa do galo e variazioni sul tema: Sei riscritture di un racconto machadiano." *Annali Istituto Universitario Orientale* 25.1 (1983): 69–124.

Monfeiro, Leonardo. *Lygia Fagundes Telles: Selecao de textos, notas, estudos biográficos e crítico, e exercicios*. São Paulo: Abril Educacao, 1980.

Nascimento, Bráulio do. "Histórias do desencontro." *Jornal de Letras* 11 January 5, 1959: 114.

Paula, Everton de. "Lygia Fagundes Telles: 'O individuo tenta somar a forca dele a da sociedade comun, como um todo.'" *Minais Gerais* [literary supplement] 9 (1989): 5–6.

Pólvora, Hélio. "A intensidade do conto." *Jornal de Brasil* May 20, 1970: 2.

Pontes, Joel. "Unidade nas historias do desencontro." *Estado São Paulo* August 29, 1959. Rpt. in *O Aprendiz de Crítica*. Rio de Janeiro: INL, 1960. 108–15.

Rodrigues, Urbano Tavares. "Uma obra reflete São Paulo." *Estado São Paulo* May 28, 1972: 3.

Sharpe, Peggy. "Fragmented Identities and the Progress of Metamorphosis in Works by Lygia Fagundes Telles." *International Women's Writing: New Landscapes of Identity*. Eds. Anne E. Brown and Marjanne E. Gooze. Westport, Conn.: Greenwood Press, 1995. 78–85.

Silva, Antonio Manoel dos Santos. "Existencia e coisficação nos contos de Lygia Fagundes Telles." *Revista de Letras* (São Paulo) 26–27 (1986–87): 1–16.

Silva, Arguinaldo. "Um tratado sobre plantas carnívoras." *Globo* July 28, 1974: 7.

Silva, Vera Maria Tietzmann. *A metamorfose nos contos de Lygia Fagundes Telles*. Rio de Janeiro: Presença, 1985.

Silverman, Malcolm. "O mundo ficcional de Lygia Fagundes Telles." *Moderna Ficção Brasileira* Rio de Janeiro: Civilização Brasileira, 1981. 162–84.

Sobral, Patricia. "Lygia Fagundes Telles: Esperanca, pasargada, e vida literaria no Brasil." *Brasil-Brazil* 16 (1996): 85–95.

Stern, Irwin, ed. *Dictionary of Brazilian Literature*. Westport, Conn.: Greenwood Press, 1988. 337–38.

Tolman, Jon H. "New Fiction: Lygia Fagundes Telles." *Review* 30 (1981): 65-70.

Van Steen, Edla. "The Baroness of Tatui." Trans. Irene Matthews. *Review: Latin American Literature and Arts* 36 (1986): 30–33.

Xavier, Raul. "Uma contista maior. Antes do Baile Verde." *Jornal de Letras* 22 June 2, 1970: 239.

Rosario Ferré

Rosario Ferré is one of the most talented and versatile writers in Latin America today. Equally gifted as an essayist, novelist, short-story writer, and poet, she has also distinguished herself as a literary critic and journalist. Ferré was born in the city of Ponce, on the southern coast of Puerto Rico, in 1938, to one of the island's most prominent families. Her father, Luis Ferré, served as governor of the island from 1968 to 1972. She studied literature in Puerto Rico and the United States, and in 1987 she received a Ph.D. from the University of Maryland, writing her dissertation on the work of Julio Cortázar.

While still pursuing her studies at the University of Puerto Rico, she founded and directed a literary journal, *Zona de Carga y Descarga* (Loading and unloading zone, 1971–76), that was influential in bringing attention to the work of a new generation of artists. In 1976, she published her first book, *Papeles de Pandora* (*The Youngest Doll*, 1991). The book, which contains short stories and poems, has been considered something of a feminist manifesto for its critical portrayal of the dependent, marginal position of women in Puerto Rican society.

Ferré belongs to a group of writers whose work has introduced a new vision and another voice to the canon of Puerto Rican literature—a vision that encompasses not only the role of women in a patriarchal society but also Puerto Rico's status as a colonial society. In her narrative she combines her feminist concerns with the social and cultural problems of Puerto Rico. Her 1995 novel *The House on the Lagoon* caused quite an uproar in the Latin American literary community and especially in Puerto Rico since it was written and published in English first and subsequently in Spanish. In this work she chronicles the lives of a family and, by extension, the political upheavals in Puerto Rico, which, as territory of the United States, remains outside the mainstream of American society and politics but is still subject to its policies.

In her latest novel, *Eccentric Neighborhoods* (1998; *Vecindarios excéntricos*, 1998), also published first in English, she narrates the saga of two upper-class families: the Rivas de Santillana and the Vernets, through the eyes of one of its descendants, Elvira Vernet.

To date Ferré has produced a body of essays, novels, short stories, and poetry that places her at the forefront of the Puerto Rican literary scene.

Mercedes-Benz 220SL

The Mercedes is fantastic, Mom, don't you think so? Look how it fields the curves and sticks to the asphalt vrroom powerful the steering wheel responds to the touch of my fingertips through pigskin gloves they were a present from you so I could take the car out on its first spin, so my hands wouldn't slip over the grooves of the wheel that turn right and left at the slightest pressure from my fingers, the crossed lances on the hood flash chrome every-which-way, see the passersby in the rain looking at us, Mom, what a car, it feels like a tank the mudguards up ahead rolling rhinoceros, my family's always had big cars, Mom, the first Rolls Royce in San Juan was theirs, big as hope and poor as black, we've got to show them who runs this country, Mom, we've got too many people living on this Island, crowded together like monkeys, they like to smell each other's sweat, rub each other like bedbugs, that's what they like, a riot, how amusing, Mom, I never thought of our overpopulation problem that way before, that man's coming our way, Dad, he's right in front of us, careful, you'll hit him, a man was walking with his back to the car along the shoulder of the road, pressing with his thumb the golden disc of the horn that shone in the center of the elegant beige leather steering wheel, I love the touch of this wheel, squeezing the golden disc, it sounds just like the first trumpet in Das Reingold, Mom, but the man doesn't hear, doesn't get off the road until the last minute when he leaped sideways, the mudguards spared his head by an inch, he fell flat on his face in the ditch, I'll pick you off next time, you long-tailed monkey, next time you'll drop out of the trees, you're frightened, Mom, you're white as a sheet, it's because I'm thinking of the patrol car, Dad, it's for your sake, the hell with patrol cars, Mom, it's incredible that you should worry about them now, you still don't know who your husband is, this car is like a fortress, wherever we go it'll put us in the right, that's what I bought it for, Mom, what non-sense, do you think I work from eight to eight just to put fat on my ass? in this country power is the only thing that counts, Mom, don't you forget it.

He floored the pedal and shot off in a straight line, at least there's no traffic at this hour, Sunday morning is the best time to drive on this island's roads, the woman silently rubs the last beads of her rosary, I'm going to put the seat back to see if I can sleep a little, Dad, it's still dark and I'm a bit sleepy, these seats are really sexy, Mom, slipping his hand over the short, grey pile that yields to his fingertips, dolled up in your three-hundred-dollar alligator shoes and your nine-carat emerald-cut diamond ring, when I bought it you said it looked like an ice rink and I wanted to laugh, Mom, that's a good one, a ring as big as a skating rink, how you love to squander money, the stores and the church have me in the poor-house, but I don't complain, Mom, it's fine with me, you're every inch a lady and I couldn't manage without you.

He took his hand from the steering wheel and reached into the darkness to caress the forehead of the woman who slept at his side, I love you Dad, I said when I felt his hand on my face as I prayed again to the Holy Mother, you're like a little boy with a new toy, the truth is you work too hard, poor dear, you deserve a reward, it's not right to kill yourself working, only sometimes you make me suffer so with your lack of consideration like right now don't go so fast, Dad, the road is wet, the car could skid, you never pay attention, you never listen, it's just as if I were talking to myself, rubbing my arms because suddenly I feel cold, the trees shoot out from the sides forming a tunnel that is gobbling us up narrow-and-dark up ahead, wide-and-falling-on-us behind, we must be doing ninety, please, Dad, God forgive us and the Virgin protect us the wipers won't go fast enough to clear the huge raindrops, it's always been like this, since we got married twenty years ago he buys me everything, he's a good provider, but always the same deafness, I'm always at his side and always alone, eating alone, sleeping alone, once I looked at myself in the mirror, I opened my mouth, touched my palate with my finger to see if any sound came out, testing, one, two, three, my mouth formed the words for things, wood and hair, eye and lip, checking, the flow of breath, testing, one two three, but nothing came out, it was clogged up in there as if the opening were too small or the words too large, edges painfully jammed into the gums. I forced the words upward from the back of my throat but to no avail, it felt like I was touching a mute hole, I put my finger in deeper every time and then I looked at myself in the mirror and thought I was going crazy. Then my son was born and I could speak again.

She lay back in the seat and watched his profile outlined in darkness. The dashboard lights lit up his heavy features, his childlike smile. She closed her eyes and crossed her arms over her chest to rub her shoulders. And now she was alone again, because her son had left home after many angry disputes with his father. He said the business made him want to vomit, he was fed up with Dad's threatening to disinherit him, one morning I found a note on his bed, don't look for me, I'll come see you on Sundays. Of course we searched but he was always changing addresses until at last Dad got tired of shelling out money for private detectives and let him go to hell, he said, I'm not going to work my hide off just to waste thousands of dollars on detectives tracking out the likes of a prima donna who doesn't give a damn about money, raise crows and they'll pick out your eyes I've always said, and I wept but it was no use because deep down I knew Dad was right. Look at that road ahead of us Mom, it's all ours, if it weren't six o'clock Sunday morning it'd be packed full of cars, one on top of the other like monkeys, that's what they're like, the stink of apes, the stench of chimps, smooth, so smooth, the gas pedal to the floor, these Germans make cars as if they were tanks, Mom, no matter what it knocks off the steel body won't even dent, if it hits you it means a one-way ticket to kingdom come.

Standing before the kitchen sink, the girl picked up the cup from which she had just drunk coffee, and slid her finger over the blue roses of the porcelain. She turned on the hot water tap, squeezed the plastic bottle, and let three sluggish drops fall. She watched them slide slowly down the cup. The liquid, a raw green, reminded her of her fear, but when she let the water fill the cup it dissolved harmlessly in suds, spilling over the edge. She wiped the cup and dried it, feeling the glaze squeak clean under her fingertips, and then put it, still warm, on the table. She dried her reddened hands on her skirt and looked out through the kitchen window at the patio. In the grey light of dawn, the plants nodded at her under the rain as if they were wanderers that had lost their way. A mist was rising from the wet earth and the smell reminded her of when she was a child and used to bury things nobody wanted in the garden: a comb with missing teeth; a plastic swan with a ribbon around its neck, "Fernando and

María, Happiness Always," that her mother had brought back as a keep-sake from a wedding; a half-used lipstick; a thimble. I always enjoyed burying things nobody wanted so only I knew where they were. When it rains hard like now I remember it clearly, I see myself breathing the smell of the clods of earth that crumble between my fingers. Then when I went out for a spell in the garden, I'd walk over the buried things that only I knew were there. Now I stand over the little comb, I'd say to myself in a low voice, now I'm stepping over the wings of the swan, now over my old Easter bonnet, as if the power to remember every detail of the hidden objects somehow made me different from everyone else.

She left the kitchen sink and looked around at the half-furnished room. She had nothing to do so she began to pull out the bureau's half-empty drawers. She opened the almost empty closet and rattled the wire hangers together. It didn't bother her at all to have so few belongings; on the contrary, she welcomed the peace that an empty room brings. They usually sat on the floor at dinner and ate on a straw tatami which she kept scrupulously clean. In the mornings, before six o'clock, they would both do their Zen meditation together, sitting in lotus position with pistil straight backs and warbling like birds the mantra's sacred words. Then a soft ray of light fell on her hand and made her think of him. She realized she couldn't picture his face away from this place; he was part of the room itself, of the books, orderly, aligned on the table, of the little gas stove, of the faded bedspread covering the thin mattress which lay on the floor, of the bronze fish mobile that tinkled to the comforting beat of the rain against the window. Then she heard his knock on the door, ran to meet him, and embraced him. Should you go today? she asked, because look how it's raining, you're drenched. Yes; I agreed to go every Sunday.

If you go early we'll have Sunday to ourselves, I tell him. You should come with me, Mom has never met you and perhaps she'd come to like you, Dad might even forgive us both. No, it's better they don't meet me, let's leave it for now, I'll go with you as far as the house, as usual, and then I'll go. She looked out the window again, everything's so dark and still, the rain makes it seem like nighttime. Sunday mornings always seem end-less, people sleep forever behind closed doors. It's as though they grew roots under their sheets, or as if they lay with ears pressed against the windows, listening to the dry rasp of sunlight as it slowly climbs the walls.

The woman sat up in the car seat and tried to make out the silhouette of houses through the raindrops that spread a thick, transparent skin down the windshield. As they neared their own street she gave a sigh of relief, feeling the end of her travail near. She put away her rosary, shut her handbag, and let her body relax little by little, anticipating the moment when they would slow down, her hand on the handle to open the door, the car before their house at last. She saw him first, the dark figure zigzagging in the half-light of dawn trying to get out of the way of the car but trapped by the side of the building, it all happened in a fraction of a second. He came out of nowhere, his body swept by the curtain of rain which smothered everything. The mudguard hit with a thud and all of a sudden he was stuck to the hood, how awful, Dad, please stop, I told you we were going too fast, I begged you a hundred times, the body splayed across the hood, you have to get out and do something, Dad, you have to get out, shut up, for God's sake, you're driving me crazy, sitting side by side unable to think, looking at the rain that kept on falling as if nothing had happened, as if it wanted to rinse out the blood from the platinum surface, the grotesque shadow sprawled over the chrome trim like a mashed-up doll.

The low voice began again its endless string of swear words, crowded together like monkeys the better to smell the stink, the better to rut the stench, you can't even drive out at dawn on Sunday morning on this island without there being that thing crushed on top of the car, wiping the windshield from the inside as though nothing had happened, after all the world goes on perfectly ordered on this side of the glass, sitting comfortably on the grey pile, eyes glued to the windshield, telling himself that it was all right, nothing had happened which couldn't be fixed, his hand on the latch but unable to open the door.

The girl approached the car in the downpour, hair plastered to her face. She paused before the lighted headlights, useless now in the early morning light. They watched her from behind the windshield slide the body over the hood, struggling to support his weight against hers. Then she let the boy down slowly over the side, before stretching him out on the pavement. I lowered the window halfway and the rain splashed on my face, my mouth filled with water, what's going on? I screamed, what should we do, Dad? he lowered his window an inch and peered out, shut up you idiot, the whole neighborhood will hear you, that woman has taken charge of him now, she's sat him on the ground with his head on her lap, we'd better go, I'll leave her our name and address, how can we leave, Dad? the man is hurt, we can't leave him lying on the road in this downpour, don't argue with me, you're hysterical, we're not going to put him in the car and stain the new upholstery with all that blood. And so Dad scribbled something on a piece of paper, lowered his window an inch more to put out his hand, and let go of the note so that it fluttered to the side of the road.

He started the engine and backed up, the screeching tires began bearing down on the asphalt. Mom caressed the grey pile gently, as if trying to appease it. The upholstery, of course, how stupid of me not to think of it, so new, so soft, so alien to anything as disagreeable as a smear of blood, and she curled up in her bucket seat and began to pray. Thank you, oh God, for the protection, for the security, for the wonderful armor of a car around us, God forgive us and the Virgin protect us, one can't live without money, calming down little by little as they drove closer to home. She wiped her forehead, a nightmare, maybe it never happened, exhausted, anxious to lower herself into a hot tub, not to think about anything but the peaceful white ceiling over her room.

It had been raining all through lunchtime when the doorbell rang. I opened the door and recognized her immediately, she held the crumpled piece of paper in her hand. It fell apart as I tried to read it, "Contact us if we can be of help," next to the address of our house. She opened the door and I showed her the note. She turned white, as I knew she would when she saw me. Please wait here, Miss, I'll be right back. She half-closed the door and went in. My hands were in a sweat, Dad, I dried them on my skirt as I went to find you. I looked for you all over the house but you'd already left for the office. My husband's not here, Miss, can I be of help? please come in. I walked over the doorstep, let my feet sink in the carpet, and saw the stairway you had talked to me so much about, the handrail you used to slide down as a child as you burst through the door of the patio, the panes of glass in the living room window were blue and pink, just as you'd told me. Have a seat, Miss, please sit down. No, Ma'am, I'm not going to stay long. I looked out through the blue pane and saw you sitting next to the fountain in the garden, it's not fair, it's just not fair to see you all tinted in blue in the middle of the patio, playing a different game now where I can't reach you, where I can't be with you, swaying blue on the other side of the pane of glass, the water flowing hard and blue against your hands, your white face on my lap bleeding, stained by the rain that now gushes out of me too and I can't stop it, what's the matter, Miss? why, you're crying.

Are you the young lady who was with the stranger that awful night? I asked her, my hand trembling on the goose down pillow as I leaned curiously towards her. I wasn't sure it had really happened, it seemed like a nightmare, tell me, how is the boy? I've been so concerned about him. I felt terribly guilty for not having gotten out of the car to help you, for not having shared the unpleasantness, that's why my husband left that piece of paper with you, so you could get in touch with us and wouldn't think we were just common hit-and-runs. I'm sorry that at the moment my husband wasn't much help. He was so upset by the whole thing I almost had to take him to the hospital later, he was in such a state. He's a good man, Miss, I love him very much, and he suffers from terribly high blood pressure, I was afraid he'd have a heart attack that night. But it's different now. I'm sure we can help that poor boy, Miss. Were there hospital bills? Were there drug expenses? We'll pay for everything, I assure you. Only I'm curious to know why it took you so long to reach us, to get in contact with us, why didn't you come to see us the very next day? You'd have found friends to help you out, to take the boy to the best specialists, believe me, Miss, we want to help.

Thank you, Ma'am, but I didn't come here to talk about that. Then the accident wasn't serious, what a relief, Miss, thank God. My friend is dead, Ma'am, I wanted you to know that. He was buried two weeks ago; I took care of the arrangements myself. A simple coffin, a simple grave. There was no funeral that you may call as such; only a few friends and myself. He had no family. That's all. But it was my duty to tell you. The boy is dead and buried. Good-bye, Ma'am. You mean you're leaving, don't you want to explain what happened, Miss? Please wait until my husband returns, I'm sure he'll want to give you something, at least help out with some of the expenses of the burial, you can't leave like this without even telling us his name, Miss, we'd like to know that poor boy's name.

A few days later the girl stood once again in front of the kitchen window and turned on the hot water tap. It was Sunday, so she didn't have to go to work. She could spend the whole day thinking, remembering things. She squeezed the plastic bottle and let three drops of green liquid fall on her empty coffee cup. She watched the blue rose of the porcelain disappear under the soapsuds that rose to the edge. She knew that today the woman would wait again all day for her son, to no avail. She could almost see her leaning out the front door for the hundredth time, looking down the empty street at the short row of houses as the sun rose in the sky, making the walls seem more solid and heavily shadowed. She put her hand in the water and carefully rinsed out the cup and saucer. She could almost hear her say, I mustn't worry, this Sunday is like any other Sunday, he's just later than usual. For a while the girl went on looking through the window at the lush garden. The woman left the doorway and sat on the edge of her bed. There's no reason to get upset, he'll come next week if he doesn't come today, she said to herself out loud, as her eyes wandered to the bedspread. She patted the silk coverlet tenderly and thought of the expense of keeping a nice house. I just bought this coverlet a year ago and it already looks worn, there's no end to what a house will require, the redecorating is endless. After all, I made the right decision not to leave Dad, he keeps doing foolish things to scare me, like driving a hundred miles an hour down a highway, but it's not that he doesn't love me, it's just his way. All my friends envy me my husband because he's such a financial success, and this year, God willing, we'll make our usual trip to Europe. In Madrid I'll buy a Loewe suede coat for a bargain; and in Paris I'll visit Michel Swiss on the Rue de la Paix and Dior and Guerlain on the Place de la Victoire. And in addition to all that, I have him and he has me and we'll grow old together and never be alone. Young people want to be free and at the same time feel loved but they won't pay the price, life is hard, it's not a bowl of cherries, no, those who think life is a bowl of cherries have it all wrong. The girl opened the kitchen door and went out into the garden. She felt the ground with her feet and crouched down, burying her hands in the wet earth. She then began to reconstruct the memory of his face, his hands, his arms. She felt at peace. Now she was sure no one would ever discover where he had been buried.

Isn't it a splendid Sunday morning to go for a ride in our Mercedes, Mom, we haven't done this for a while and I just had it specially waxed. I had new hubcaps put on it and now it's sexier than ever, it shines in the dark like a chromium rhinoceros, just look at that highway up ahead, empty of cars and leading to kingdom come, it's just waiting for us, Mom, in this country there are so many people on the road you can't go for a ride anymore except at dawn on Sundays, that's the only time one can put one's head out the door and breathe. Now we can plan our trip to Europe in peace, Mom, tell me where you want to go.

First I have to tell you something, Dad, the strangest thing happened yesterday afternoon, a girl came to the house, she had a piece of paper in her hand, the very one you scribbled our address on under the rain the day that man threw himself under our car, it was definitely the same, I'm sure of it, I recognized your handwriting. You can't imagine what a time I had; she didn't complain, she didn't say more than ten words. She stood in the middle of the room and just stared at me for what must have been like fifteen minutes, until I began to think she was out of her mind. This girl wants something, I told myself. But I couldn't say anything, I just stood there in the middle of the room and stared back at her, begging all the saints to make you come back early from the office so you'd deal with her and let her know she couldn't blackmail us, that sort of thing doesn't go over with us because we have all the right friends in the right places. Still, I tried to be as civil to her as possible and kept asking her about the fellow, I was truly concerned and tried to learn all I could about the accident to see how we could help when the wretch cuts me short and tells me in an angry voice, the boy is dead, Ma'am. I buried him, just like that and nothing else, the boy is dead, I buried him, as if it were the most natural thing in the world to bury the dead yourself. I was struck absolutely dumb, unable to say a word. I felt as if a corkscrew or something were twisting into my left side and then was pulling hard. I had to sit down on the sofa, I felt so faint. She went on looking at me without a word for I don't know how long, and all I could do was sit there with that terrible pain in my chest.

But thank God I finally came to. I sat up on the sofa and told myself you're a fool, Mom, if you're going to let yourself be upset by what a stranger tells you. Life is always tragic and if you put it into your mind to save humanity you're sunk, give away what you have and you'll end up begging, we must all stand up and bear our cross. And just then I realized what the wretch was saying. That you had run over the fellow and killed him, that you were totally to blame. I flew at her in a rage, how dare you, you insolent wimp, you know me, Dad, I may complain and grumble, gripe and fume, but when I see you under fire I turn into a fiend. I could already see her coming at you with a charge of first-degree murder and a million-dollar lawsuit, my God, this world is full of swine. Your friend threw himself under the car, I was there, I saw it, I screamed back at her. I'll testify in any court and swear on any Bible to that fact. And I was still talking, setting things straight for her, when she turned her back on me and began walking towards the door and all I could do was stand there, watch her open it calmly and step out, with my mouth open and the words stuck in my throat. And then I sat down on the sofa with that thing twisting into my chest and thought I was going to die.

Don't let it bother you, Mom, you should have told me about it sooner, I would have made inquiries last night. If she shows up again at the house you mustn't open the door, if I'm not in tell the maid you can't talk to her, she can come see me at the office, I'll know how to deal with her. Forget about it for now, Mom, just look at the Mercedes go, watch it glide along the empty road purring like a car, its fenders shining in the dark like a chromium rhinoceros . . .

Translated by Claire B. Ashman and Rosario Ferré
(From *Papeles de Pandora*, 1976)

Bibliography

Fiction by Rosario Ferré

"El abrigo de zorro azul/The Fox Skin Coat." Trans. Rosario Ferré. *Mester* 15.2 (1986): 46–50.

La batalla de las vírgenes. San Juan: Universidad de Puerto Rico, 1993.

"La bella durmiente." *Ritos de iniciación.* Eds. Grinor Rojo and Cynthia Steele. Boston: Houghton, 1986. 147–211.

La caja de cristal. Mexico City: La Máquina de Escribir, 1978.

La casa de la laguna. Barcelona: Emecé, 1995.

La cucarachita Martina. Río Piedras, Puerto Rico: Huracán, 1990.

"El cuento de hadas." *Sin Nombre* (San Juan) 11.2 (1980): 36–40.

Los cuentos de Juan Bobo. San Juan: Huracán, 1981.

"El desengaño." *Hispamérica* 13.38 (1984): 67–72.

Las dos Venecias. Mexico City: Joaquín Mortiz, 1992.

Eccentric Neighborhoods. New York: Farrar, 1998.

"The Glass Box." Trans. Rosario Ferré and Kathy Taylor. *Massachusetts Review* 3.4 (1986): 699–711.

The House on the Lagoon. New York: Farrar, 1995.

"Juan Bobo va a oír misa." *Sin Nombre* (San Juan) 11.2 (1980): 41–42.

Maldito amor. Mexico City: Joaquín Mortiz, 1986.

"Maldito amor." *Novísimos narradores hispanoamericanos en Marcha, 1964–1980.* Ed. Angel Rama. Montevideo: Marcha, 1981. 307–18.

El medio pollito: Siete cuentos infantiles. San Juan: Huracán, 1976. Rpt. in San Juan: Huracán, 1977.

"Mercedes-Benz 220SL." *Puerta abierta: La nueva escritora latinoamericana.* Eds. Caridad L. Silva-Velázquez and Nora Erro-Orthmann. Mexico City: Joaquín Mortiz, 1986. 109–21.

La mona que le pisaron la cola. San Juan: Huracán, 1981.

La muñeca menor. San Juan: Huracán, 1980.

La muñeca menor/The Youngest Doll. Trans. Rosario Ferré. San Juan: Huracán, 1980.

Papeles de Pandora. Mexico City: Joaquín Mortiz, 1976. 2nd. ed. Mexico City: Joaquín Mortiz, 1979.

"Pico Rico, Mandorico." *Apalabramiento: Diez cuentistas puertorriqueños de hoy.* Ed. Efraín Barradas. Hanover, N.H.: Ediciones del Norte, 1983. 73–84. Rpt. in *Reclaiming Medusa. Short Stories by Contemporary Puerto Rican Women.* Ed. Diana Vélez. San Francisco: Spinster/Aunt Lute, 1988. 73–82.

"Pico Rico, Mandorico." *Reclaiming Medusa: Short Stories by Contemporary Puerto Rican Women.* Ed. and trans. Diana Vélez. San Francisco: Spinster/Aunt Lute, 1988. 64–72.

"El regalo." *Apalabramiento: Diez cuentistas puertorriqueños de hoy.* Ed. Efraín Barradas. Hanover, N.H.: Ediciones del Norte, 1983. 85–119.

"Sleeping Beauty." Trans. Rosario Ferré and Diana Vélez. *Reclaiming Medusa: Short Stories by Contemporary Puerto Rican Women.* Ed. Diana Vélez. San Francisco: Spinster/Aunt Lute, 1988. 34–63.

Sonatinas. San Juan: Huracán, 1989.

Sweet Diamond Dust. Trans. Rosario Ferré. New York: Ballantine, 1988.

Vecindarios excéntricos. Mexico City: Planeta Mexicana, 1998.

"When Women Love Men." Trans. Cynthia Ventura. *Contemporary Women Authors of Latin America: New Translations.* Eds. Doris Meyer and Margarite Fernández Olmos. New York: Brooklyn College Press, 1983. 176–85.

The Youngest Doll. Foreword by Jean Franco. Lincoln: Univerity of Nebraska, 1991.

"The Youngest Doll." Trans. Gregory Rabassa. *Kenyan Review* 2.1 (1980): 163. Rpt. *Reclaiming Medusa: Short Stories by Contemporary Puerto Rican Women.* Ed. Diana Vélez. Trans. Rosario Ferré and Diana Vélez. San Francisco: Spinster/Aunt Lute, 1988. 27–33. Rpt. in *Longman Anthology of World Literature by Women, 1875–1975.* Eds. Marian Arkin and Barbara Shollar. New York: Longman, 1989. 1055–58.

Essays by Rosario Ferré

"El acomodador—autor." *Escritura* (Caracas) 7.13–14 (1982): 189–209.

El acomodador. Una lectura fantástica de Felisberto Hernández. Mexico City: Fondo de Cultura Económica, 1986.

El árbol y sus sombras. Mexico City: Fondo de Cultura Económica, 1989.

"La cocina de la escritura." *Literatures in Transition: The Many Voices of the Caribbean Area: A Symposium.* Ed. Rose S. Minc. Gaithersburg, Md.: Hispamérica, 1982. 37–51. Rpt. in *Fem* 49 (1986–87): 36–42.

El coloquio de las perras. Río Piedras, Puerto Rico: Cultural, 1990.

"Una conciencia musical." *La escritora hispana.* Eds. Nora Erro-Orthmann and Juan Cruz Mendizábal. Miami: Universal, 1990. 7–15.

Cortázar: El romántico en su observatorio. Río Piedras, Puerto Rico: Cultural, 1991.

"Destiny Language and Translation, or Ophelia Adrift in the C & C Canal." *Women's Writing in Latin America.* Eds. Sara Castro-Klaren, Sylvia Molloy, and Beatriz Sarlo. Boulder, Colo.: Westview Press, 1991. 89–94.

"Entre Clara y Julieta: Dos poetas puertorriqueñas." *Revista Iberoamericana* 52.137 (1986): 999–1006.

"Felisberto Hernández: La vanguardia de un hombre solo." *La Gaceta del Fondo de Cultura Económica* (Mexico City) 185 (1986): 17–19.

"From Ire to Irony." Trans. Lizabeth Paravisini-Gebert. *Callaloo* 17.3 (1994): 900–904.

Memorias de Ponce: Autobiografía de Luis A. Ferré. Bogota: Norma, 1992.

"On Love and Politics." *Review: Latin American Literature and Arts* 37 (1987): 8–9.

Sitio a Eros: Trece ensayos. Mexico City: Joaquín Mortiz, 1980.

"S/Z: Una pregunta que responde y una respuesta que pregunta." *Texto Crítico* (Veracruz) 30 (1984): 7–12.

"The Writers Kitchen." Trans. Diana L. Vélez. *Lives on the Line: The Testimony of Contemporary Latin American Authors.* Ed. Doris Meyer. Berkeley: University of California Press, 1988. 214–27.

Poetry by Rosario Ferré

Fábulas de la garza desangrada. Mexico City: Joaquín Mortiz, 1982.

Criticism on the Works of Rosario Ferré

Acevedo, Ramón Luis. "Rosario Ferré." *Del silencio al estallido: Narrativa femenina puertor-riqueña.* Ed. Ramón Luis Acevedo. Río Piedras, Puerto Rico: Cultural, 1991. 131–36.

Acosta-Belén, Edna. "En torno a la nueva cuentística puertorriqueña." *Latin American Research Review* 21 (1986): 220–27.

Acosta-Cruz, María I. "Historia, ser e identidad femenina en 'El collar de camándulas' y *Maldito amor* de Rosario Ferré." *Chasqui* 19.2 (1990): 23–31.

———. "Historia y escritura femenina en Olga Nolla, Magali García Ramis, Rosario Ferré y Ana Lydia Vega." *Revista Iberoamericana* 59.162–63 (1993): 265–77.

Agosín, Marjorie. "Génesis de 'La bailarina,' un poema de Rosario Ferré." *Mairena* 13 (1983): 19–28.

Allemany-Valdez, Herminia M. "Las dos Rosarios frente al espejo: Castellanos y Ferré." *La otredad: Los discursos de la cultura hoy.* Ed. Silvia Elguea Vejar. Mexico City: Universidad Autonóma Metropolitana, 1997. 247–52.

———. "Galería de mujeres: Las mujeres en *Album de familia* y *Papeles de Pandora.*" *Presente y precedente de la literatura de mujeres latinoamericanas.* Ed. Luis Mario Cerda. Guadalajara: La Luciérnaga, 1994. 11–16.

Anzaldó González, Demetrio "Recorrer los hilos en el enlace con el otro a través del cuento hispanoamericano." *La seducción de la escritura: Los discursos de la cultura hoy.* Eds. Rosaura Hernández Monroy and Manuel F. Medina. Mexico City: n.p., 1997. 278–86.

Aponte Ramos, Lola. "Recetario para el novelar híbrido: Esmeralda Santiago y Rosario Ferré." *Nómada* (San Juan) 3 (1997): 33–37.

Apter-Cragnolino, Aida. "El cuento de hadas y la Bildungsroman: Modelo y sub-versión en 'La bella durmiente' de Rosario Ferré." *Chasqui* 20.2 (1991): 3–9.

———. "De sitios y asedios: La escritura de Rosario Ferré." *Revista Chilena de Literatura* 42 (1993): 25–30.

Arroyo, Elsa R. "Contracultura y parodia en cuatro cuentos de Rosario Ferré y Ana Lydia Vega." *Caribbean Studies* 22 (1988): 33–46.

Balseiro, Isabel. "Narrating Nation in Rosario Ferré's *Maldito amor.*" *Fissions and Fusions.* Eds. Lesley Marx, Loes Nas, and Lara Dunwell. Bellville, South Africa: University of the Western Cape, 1997. 96–98.

Barradas, Efraín. "Rosario Ferré, en *Fábulas de la garza desangrada.*" *Hispamérica* 11 (1982): 116–19.

Bilbija, Ksenija. "Rosario Ferré's 'The Youngest Doll': On Women, Dolls, Golems and Cyborgs." *Callaloo* 17.3 (1994): 878–88.

Binder, Wolfgang. "Entrevista con Rosario Ferré." *La Torre* (San Juan) 8.30 (1994): 239–53.

Birmingham Pokorny, Elba D. "(Re)writing the Body: The Legitimization of the Female Voice, History, Culture and Space in Rosario Ferré's 'La muñeca menor.'" *Confluencia* 10.1 (1994): 75–80.

Bush, Andrew. "Señalar las discrepancias: Rosario Ferré y Antonio Skarmeta hablan de Cortázar." *Revista de Estudios Hispánicos* (Rió Pigaras, Puerto Rico) 21.2 (1987): 73–87.

Bustos Fernández, María José. "Subversión de la autoridad narrativa en *Maldito amor* de Rosario Ferré." *Chasqui* 23.2 (1994): 22–29.

Castillo, Debra. "Surfacing: Rosario Ferré and Julieta Campos, with Rosario Castellanos." *Talking Back: Toward a Latin American Feminist Literary Criticism*. Ithaca, N.Y.: Cornell University Press, 1992. 137–84.

Castro-Klaren, Sara. "Unpacking Her Library: Rosario Ferré on Love and Women." *Review: Latin American Literature and Arts* 48 (1994): 33–45.

Cavallo, Susana. "Llevando la contraria: El contracanto de Rosario Ferré." *Monographic Review/Revista Monográfica* 8 (1992): 197–204.

Chaves, María José. "La alegoría como método en los cuentos y ensayos de Rosario Ferré." *Third Woman* 2.2 (1984): 64–76.

Cook, Jacqueline. "Bibliography on Rosario Ferré." *Chasqui* 22.2 (1993): 129–49.

Cornejo-Parriego, Rosalía. "Female Difference and Colonial Experience in Rosario Ferré's 'When Women Love Men.'" *Contemporary Literature in the African Diaspora*. Eds. Olga Barrios and Bernard W. Bell. Leon, Spain: Universidad de Salamanca, 1997. 115–21.

———. "Racialización colonial y diferencia femenina en 'Love Story' de Elena Poniatowska y 'Cuando las mujeres quieren a los hombres' de Ferré." *Afro-Hispanic Review* 16.2 (1997): 10–18.

Davis, Lisa E. "La puertorriqueña dócil y rebelde en los cuentos de Rosario Ferré." *Sin Nombre* (San Juan) 9.4 (1980): 82–88.

Erro-Peralta, Nora. "Identidad y creación en *The House on the Lagoon*." *La seducción de la escritura: Los discursos de la cultura hoy*. Eds. Rosaura Hernández Monroy and Manuel F. Medina. Mexico City: n.p., 1997. 176–81.

———. "Teaching Approaches to *Sweet Diamond Dust*." *Community College Humanities Review: [Special Issue]* (1996): 119–29.

Escalera Ortiz, Juan. "Perspectiva del cuento 'Mercedes-Benz 220SL.'" *Revista/Review Interamericana* 12.3 (1982): 407–17.

Fernández Olmos, Margarite. "Constructing Heroines: Rosario Ferré's cuentos infantiles and Feminine Instruments of Change." *Lion and the Unicorn* 10 (1986): 83–94.

———. "Los cuentos infantiles de Rosario Ferré, o la fantasía emancipadora." *Revista de Crítica Literaria Hispanoamericana* 14.27 (1988): 151–63.

———. "Desde una perspectiva femenina: La cuentística de Rosario Ferré y Ana Lydia Vega." *Homines* 8.2 (1984–85): 303–11.

———. "From a Woman's Perspective: The Short Stories of Rosario Ferré and Ana Lydia Vega." *Contemporary Women Authors of Latin America: Introductory Essays*. Eds. Doris Meyer and Margarite Fernández Olmos. New York: Brooklyn College Press, 1983. 78–90.

————. "Luis Rafael Sánchez and Rosario Ferré: Sexual Politics and Contemporary Puerto Rican Narrative." *Hispania* 70.1 (1987): 40–46.

————. "Respuestas anti-patriarcales en la narrativa puertorriqueña contemporánea." *Sobre la literatura puertorriqueña de aquí y de allá: Aproximaciones feministas*. Ed. Margarite Fernández Olmos. Santo Domingo: Alfa y Omega, 1989. 35–53.

————. "Rosario Ferré." *Spanish American Women Writers: A Bio-Bibliographical Source Book*. Ed. Diane Marting. Westport, Conn.: Greenwood Press, 1990. 165–75.

————. "Sex, Color, and Class in Contemporary Puerto Rican Women Authors." *Heresies* 4.3.15 (1982): 46–47.

————. "Survival, Growth and Change in the Prose Fiction of Contemporary Puerto Rican Women Writers." *Images and Identities: The Puerto Rican in Two World Contexts*. Ed. Asela Rodríguez de Laguna. New Brunswick, N.J.: Transaction Press, 1987. 76–88.

Figueroa, Armando. "Mujeres puertorriqueñas, una doble resistencia: Rosario Ferré." *Quimera* (Barcelona) 123 (1994): 22–23.

Fox-Lockert, Lucía. "El discurso femenino en los cuentos de Elena Garro y Rosario Ferré." *La escritora hispánica*. Eds. Nora Erro-Orthmann and Juan Cruz-Mendizábal. Miami: Universal, 1990. 83–91.

Franco, Jean. "Self-Destructing Heroines." *Minnesota Review* 22 (1984): 105–15.

García Pinto, Magdalena. "Rosario Ferré." *Historias íntimas: Conversaciones con diez escritoras latinoamericanas*. Hanover, N.H.: Ediciones del Norte, 1988. 67–96.

Gascón-Vera, Elena. "Sitio a Eros: The Liberated Eros of Rosario Ferré." *Reinterpreting the Spanish American Essay: Women Writers of the Nineteenth and Twentieth Centuries*. Ed. Doris Meyer. Austin: University of Texas Press, 1995. 197–206.

Gazarian Gautier, Marie-Lise. "Rosario Ferré." *Interviews with Latin American Writers*. Elmwood Park, Ill.: Dalkey Archive Press, 1989. 79–92.

Gelpí, Juan. "Apuntes al margen de un texto de Rosario Ferré." *La sartén por el mango: Encuentro de escritoras latinoamericanas*. Eds. Patricia Elena González and Eliana Ortega. Río Piedras, Puerto Rico: Huracán, 1984. 133–35.

————. "Especulación, especularidad y remotivación en *Fábulas de la garza desangrada* de Rosario Ferré." *La Chispa '85: Selected Proceedings*. Ed. Gilbert Paolini. New Orleans: Tulane, 1985. 125–32.

Gómes, Miguel. "De la ironía y otras tradiciones: Notas sobre el ensayo feminista latinoamericano." *Revista de Crítica Literaria Latinoamericana* 23.46 (1997): 235–53.

Gonzáles, Martha I. "El efecto liberador de la oposición oralidad/escritura en *Maldito amor* de Rosario Ferré." *Letras Femeninas* 23.1–2 (1997): 129–37.

Gosser-Esquilín, Mary Ann. "Textualidad y sensualidad compartidas en 'El regalo' de Rosario Ferré." *Alba de América* 11.20–21 (1993): 199–210.

Guerra Cunningham, Lucía. "Márgenes de la transculturación en la narrativa de Rosario Ferré." *La nueva mujer en la escritura de autoras hispánicas*. Eds. Juana Alcira Arancibia, Yolanda Rosas, y María Rosa Lojo. Montevideo: Instituto Literario y Cultural Hispánico, 1995. 59–65.

————. "Tensiones paradójicas de la femineidad en la narrativa de Rosario Ferré." *Chasqui* 13.2–3 (1984): 13–25.

————. "Transgresión del orden burgués en 'Cuando las mujeres quieren a los hombres' de Rosario Ferré." *Plural* (Mexico City) 4 (1985): 101–16.

Gutiérrez, Mariela. "La metafísica de la moral: Una visión lacano-kantiana del último rito en 'Isolda en el espejo' de Rosario Ferré." *Actas Irvine-92, Asociación Internacional de Hispanistas.* Vol. 2: *La mujer y su representación en las literaturas hispánicas.* Ed. Juan Villegas. Irvine: University of California Press, 1994. 212–19.

————. "Rosario Ferré y el itinerario del deseo: Un estudio lacaniano de 'Cuando las mujeres quieren a los hombres.'" *Revista Canadiense de Estudios Hispánicos* (Ottawa) 16.2 (1992): 203–17.

Gutiérrez-Mouat, Ricardo. "La 'loca del desván' y otros intertextos de *Maldito amor.*" *Modern Language Notes* 109.2 (1994): 283–304.

Handley, George B. "'It's an Unbelievable Story': Testimony and Truth in the Work of Rosario Ferré and Rigoberta Menchú." *Violence, Silence, and Anger: Women's Writing as Transgression.* Ed. Deirdre Lashgari. Charlottesville: University Press of Virginia, 1995. 62–79.

Hart, Patricia. "Magic Feminism and Inverted Masculine Myths in Rosario Ferré's 'The Youngest Doll.'" *Studies in Honor of María A. Salgado.* Eds. A. Bolden Millicent, Luis A. Jimenez, and Graciela Palau de Nemes. Newark: Juan de la Cuesta, 1995. 97–108.

Heinrich, María Elena. "Entrevista a Rosario Ferré." *Prismal/Cabral* 7–8 (1982): 98–103.

Heller, Ben A. "Landscape, Feminity, and Caribbean Discourse." *Modern Language Notes* 111.2 (1996): 391–416.

Hintz, Suzanne S. "An Annotated Bibliography of Works by and About Rosario Ferré: The First Twenty Years, 1970–1990." *Revista Interamericana de Bibliografía/Interamerican Review of Bibliography* 41.4 (1991): 643–54.

————. "The Narrator as Discriminator in (Auto)Biographical Fiction: Rosario Ferré's 'Vecindarios excéntricos.'" *Romance Language Annual* 7 (1995): 503–8.

————. *Rosario Ferré: A Search for Identity.* New York: Peter Lang, 1995.

————. "Rosario Ferré: The Vanguard of Puerto Rican Feminist Literature." *Revista de Estudios Hispánicos* [Río Piedras, Puerto Rico] 20 (1993): 227–32.

Jaffe, Janice A. "Translation and Prostitution: Rosario Ferré's *Maldito amor* and *Sweet Diamond Dust.*" *Latin American Literary Review* 23.46 (1995): 66–82.

Kaminsky, Amy. "Residual Authority and Gendered Resistance." *Critical Theory, Cultural Politics, and Latin American Narrative.* Eds. Steven M. Bell, Albert H. Le May, and Leonard Orr. Notre Dame, Ind.: University of Notre Dame Press, 1993. 103–21.

Lagos-Pope, María Inés. "Sumisión y rebeldía: El doble o la representación de la alienación femenina en narraciones de Marta Brunet y Rosario Ferré." *Revista Iberoamericana* 51.132–33 (1985): 731–49.

Levine, Linda Gould. "No más máscaras: Un diálogo entre tres escritoras del Caribe: Belkis Cuza Male—Cuba, Matilde Daviu—Venezuela, Rosario Ferré—Puerto Rico." *Literatures in Transition: The Many Voices of the Carribean Area: A Symposium.* Gaithersburg, Md., and Upper Montclair, N.J.: Hispamérica Montclair State College, 1982. 189–97.

Long, Sheri Spaine. "Entrevista breve con Rosario Ferré." *Mester* 15.2 (1986): 43–45.

López-Adorno, Pedro. "Coordenadas metafórico/feministas en Rosario Ferré." *Cupey* (Río Piedras, Puerto Rico) 4.1 (1987): 25–30.

López-Jimenez, Yvette. "La muñeca menor: Ceremonias y transformaciones en un cuento de Rosario Ferré." *Explicación de Textos Literarios* 11.1 (1982–83): 49–58.

———. "*Papeles de Pandora*: Devastación y ruptura." *Sin Nombre* [San Juan] 14.1 (1983): 41–52.

Martínez-Echezábal, Lourdes. "*Maldito amor*: Hacia una nueva hermenéutica de la historia." *La Torre* (San Juan) 3.11 (1989): 493–503.

———. "*Maldito amor*: Proyecto ideológico/proyecto textual." *Mujer y sociedad en América*. Ed. Juana Alcira Arancibia. Westminster, Calif.: Instituto Literario y Cultural Hispánico, 1990. 109–18.

Méndez-Clark, Ronald. "La pasión y la marginalidad en (de) la escritura: Rosario Ferré." *La sartén por el mango*. Eds. Patricia Elena González and Eliana Ortega. San Juan: Huracán, 1984. 119–30.

Méndez-Panedas, Rosario. "'Cuando las mujeres quieren a los hombres': El doble como metáfora de un mundo intratextual." *Symposium* 48.4 (1995): 311–17.

———. "La dama y la prostituta, la prostituta y la dama: La creación del doble literario en 'Cuando las mujeres quieren a los hombres' de Rosario Ferré." *Romance Language Annual* 7 (1995): 540–42.

Molinero, Rita Virginia. "El discurso irónico de un amor maldito en *Maldito amor* de Rosario Ferré." *Homines* 14–15.1–2 (1990–91): 275–78.

Mullen, Edward. "Interpreting Puerto Rico's Cultural Myths. Rosario Ferré and Manuel Ramos Otero." *Americas Review* 17.3–4 (1989): 88–97.

Muñoz, Willy O. "Rosario Ferré: Subestructuras patriarcales en 'La bella durmiente.'" *El personaje femenino en la narrativa de escritoras hispanoamericanas*. Madrid: Pliegos, 1992. 65–87.

Murphy, Marie. "Rosario Ferré en el espejo: Defiance and Inversions." *Hispanic Review* 65.2 (1997): 145–57.

Nichols, Elizabeth Gackstetter. "Loss and Abandonment: Rewriting the Myth of the National Romance in *Las dos Venecias*." *Osomayor* 4.10 (1997): 21–29.

Nitchinsky, Jill. "Madness and Colonization: Ferré's Ballet." *Revista de Estudios Hispánicos* (Río Piedras, Puerto Rico) 25.3 (1991): 103–28.

Norat, Gisela. "Del despertar de 'La bella durmiente' al reino patriarcal." *Linguistica y Literatura* (Medellín, Colombia) 15 (1989): 17–31.

Olazagasti Segovia, Elena. "Rosario Ferré y la re-visión de un texto medieval." *Torre de Papel* 4.2 (1994): 81–92.

Ortega, Julio "Rosario Ferré y la voz transgresiva." *Reappropiaciones: Cultura y nueva escritura en Puerto Rico*. Río Piedras, Puerto Rico: Universidad de Puerto Rico Press, 1991. 87–92.

Ortiz, Alejandra. "Los reflejos sobre una casa sobre la laguna." *Horizontes* (Ponce, Puerto Rico) 40.78 (1998): 127–33.

Paley Francescato, Martha. "Un cuento de hadas contemporáneo (envenenado) de Rosario Ferré." *Revista de Crítica Literaria Latinoamericana* 20.39 (1994): 177–81.

Paravisini-Gebert, Lizabeth. "Rosario Ferré." *Caribbean Women Novelists: An Annotated Critical Bibliography.* Westport, Conn.: Greenwood Press, 1993. 121–35.

Pérez-Marín, Carmen I. "De la épica a la novela: La recuperación de la voz en *Maldito amor* de Rosario Ferré." *Letras Femeninas* 20.1–2 (1994): 35–43.

———. "Estrategia emancipadora en 'Pico Rico Mandorico' de Rosario Ferré y *Goblin Market* de Christina Rosetti." *Plaza* 16 (1989): 64–69.

Perry, Donna. "Rosario Ferré." *Backtalk: Women Writers Speak Out.* Ed. Donna Perry. New Brunswick, N.J.: Rutgers University Press, 1993. 83–103.

Puleo, Augustus C. "The Intersección of Race, Sex, Gender and Class in a Short Story of Rosario Ferré." *Studies in Short Fiction* 32.2 (1995): 227–36.

———. "Nueva voz en el cuento puertorriqueño." *Cincinnati Romance Review* 12 (1993): 169–76.

Raymond, Kay E. "Eros and Revolution in Rosario Ferré." *Continental, Latin-American, and Francophone Women Writers.* Vol 4. Eds. Ginette Adamson and Eunice Myers. Lanham, Md.: University Press of America, 1997. 17–21.

Rinks Díaz, Gloria, and Elizabeth Sisson-Guerrero. "Rosario Ferré entre el inglés y el español: 'Let Oneself Become the Meeting Place of Both.'" *Dactylus* 16 (1997): 61–69.

Rivera, Carmen. "Porcelain Face/Rotten Flesh: The Doll in *Papeles de Pandora.*" *Chasqui* 23.2 (1994): 95–101.

Rivera de Alvarez, Josefina. *Literatura puertorriqueña: Su proceso en el tiempo.* Madrid: Partenón, 1983. 731+.

Rodríguez, Luis Julio. "De Puerto Rico a Nueva York: Protagonistas femeninas en busca de un espacio propio." *La Torre* [San Juan] 7.27–28 (1993): 577–94.

Roses, Lorraine Elena. "Las esperanzas de Pandora: Prototipos femeninos en la obra de Rosario Ferré." *Revista Iberoamericana* 59.162–63 (1993): 279–87.

Shaw, Donald L. "Three Post-Boom Writers and the Boom." *Latin American Literary Review* 24.47 (1996): 5–22.

Skinner, Lee. "Pandora's Log: Charting the Evolving Literary Project of Rosario Ferré." *Revista de Estudios Hispánicos* (Río Piedras, Puerto Rico) 29.3 (1995): 461–76.

Solá, María. "*Fabulas de la garza de sangrada* de Rosario Ferré: Contracanto del mito y la literatura." *Revista de Estudios Hispánicos* (Río Piedras, Puerto Rico) 20 (1993): 299–310.

———. "Habla femenina e ideología feminista en *Papeles de Pandora* de Rosario Ferré." *Alero* 1 (1982): 19–26.

Umpierre, Luz María. "Los cuentos ¿infantiles? de Rosario Ferré-estrategias subversivas." *Nuevas aproximaciones críticas a la literatura puertorriqueña contemporánea.* Ed. Luz María Umpierre-Herrera. San Juan: Cultural, 1983. 89–101.

———. "De la protesta a la creación: Una nueva visión de la mujer puertorriqueña en la poesía." *Imagine: International Chicano Poetry Journal* 2.1 (1985): 134–42.

———. "Un manifiesto literario: *Papeles de Pandora* de Rosario Ferré." *Bilingual Review: La revista bilingüe* 9.2 (1982): 121–28.

———. *Nuevas aproximaciónes críticas a la literatura puertorriqueña contemporánea.* San Juan: Cultural, 1983.

———. "Rosario Ferré *Sitio a eros: trece ensayos literarios.*" *Revista Iberoamericana* 49.123–24 (1983): 678–80.

Urrea, Beatriz. "El cuerpo femenino: Identidad(es) problematizada(s) en dos cuentos de Rosario Ferré." *Revista de Crítica Literaria Latinoamericana* 22.43–44 (1996): 279–300.

Vega Carney, Carmen. "El amor como discurso político en Ana Lydia Vega y Rosario Ferré." *Letras Femeninas* 17.1–2 (1991): 77–87.

———. "'Cuando las mujeres quieren a los hombres': Manifiesto textual de una generación." *Continental, Latin American, and Francophone Women Writers.* Eds. Eunice Myers and Ginette Adamson. Lanham, Md.: University Press of America, 1987. 183–93.

———. "Sexo y texto en Rosario Ferré." *Confluencia* 4.1 (1988): 119–27.

Vélez, Diana L. "Power and the Text: Rebellion in Rosario Ferré's *Papeles de Pandora.*" *MMLA: The Journal of the Midwest Modern Language Association* 17.1 (1984): 70–80.

Zapata, Miguel Angel. "Rosario Ferré: La poesía de narrar." *Inti* 26–27 (1987–88): 133–40.

Zee, Linda S. "Rosario Ferré's 'La muñeca menor' and Caribbean Myth." *Chasqui* 23.2 (1994): 95–101.

Lucía Fox

PERU

A professor at Michigan State University in the Department of Romance and Classical Languages, Lucía Fox teaches courses in Latin American culture, Chicano literature, and women's literature. Born and raised in Lima, Peru, she holds a bachelor of arts from San Marcos University (Peru), a master's from Washington University, and a doctorate from the University of Illinois.

Fox has distinguished herself as a creative writer and as a scholar in Latin American studies. She is the author of twenty-eight books, among them *Ensayos Hispanoamericanos* (Hispanic American essays, 1965); *El rostro de la patria en la literatura peruana* (The face of the motherland in Peruvian literature, 1970); *La odisea del pájaro* (The bird's odyssey, 1972); *Latinoamérica en evolución* (Latin America in evolution, 1974); *Women Novelists in Spain and Spanish America* (1979); *Formas/Forms* (1985); and *Chicanas, Their Voices Their Lives* (1989), which was made into a video. She has published two collections of short stories, *Constelación* (Constellation, 1978) and *En cierto lugar* (In a certain place, 1980), and has many unpublished short stories, including "The Wedding" (1988), which appears for the first time in this anthology.

Lucía Fox has won many prestigious awards and grants, such as the Michigan Council for the Arts Creative Grant (1981), the National Endowment for the Arts (1983), Palmas Magisteriales del Peru (1984), Woman Achiever Grant (1985), the Diana Creative Award (1986), Hispanic Educator of 1988, and the Rockefeller Grant (1989).

The Wedding

The twelve photographs were arranged in a circle on the floor of Otilia's room. She was sitting in the middle moving them as if they were tarot cards, repeating phrases that could have been an invocation, but which did not belong to any language that Fernanda, who was spying on her from the balcony, could understand. Fernanda had come to the wedding of Elsa, Otilia's daughter. Feeling a little dizzy from the champagne, Fernanda had gone to look for a bathroom in the enormous house. She had entered this room, and on seeing the lovely balcony that opened onto the garden, had stopped to rest in a rocking chair.

"I must have fallen asleep . . . but what's the time?" she said to herself when she awoke. She hadn't worn her watch, preferring to wear bracelets. When she spotted Otilia engaged in her ritual with the photographs, she decided not to leave her hiding place. Fernanda had always been fascinated by Otilia's strange beauty, which stood out even when she was with Elsa's friends from school.

Otilia began to make a large doll out of clothing that she took from a dresser. She stuffed it, then went to the closet to take out one of her husband's three-piece suits. Now clothed, the doll was almost done; the only thing lacking was for it to talk. Otilia looked it over with what appeared to be restrained vehemence, then ran to get a red tie which she wrapped around the neck of the doll. Taking it to the center of the circle, she began the movements of a dance, her feet barely touching the photographs. As Otilia and the doll moved together, it seemed to Fernanda that a handsome head now adorned the rag doll.

"I must be seeing things," thought Fernanda, feeling as if she were contemplating a miracle.

Then Otilia carried the doll to the bed, and covered it and herself with the bedspread. The ferocious, rhythmic movements under the bedspread indicated that Otilia and the doll were taking part in a passionate sexual interlude. Taking advantage of this, Fernanda tried to make her getaway, but when she heard the voices and footsteps of a group of people in the hall, she hid on the balcony once again in order to avoid questions.

When Fernanda felt at last that she could leave, once Otilia was no longer in the room, she began to tiptoe away, but had to run and hide once more because Elsa in her bridal gown had entered the room. Elsa went over to the bed, and when she discovered the doll began to tear it apart with a furious expression on her face, until there was nothing left of it but rags scattered across the bed. Then Elsa noticed the photographs and trampled them, kicking them in several directions. She went to the dressing table and, picking up a lipstick, wrote on the mirror: "Mama, where are you? I'm leaving. Elsa." She paused for a moment and with a sad expression looked at herself in the mirror. She dried the tears that her fury had caused her to shed and touched up her makeup a little before going out.

Fernanda began to reflect on the fact that she had shared a desk with Elsa during the last year of secondary school and that although they had known each other for years, this was the first time that Fernanda had had access to Elsa's personal life. She recalled one afternoon when the choir teacher, Miss Monone, had come to get the students, including Elsa, who were going to participate in the finals of the city choir contest. Since this was during study hall, nobody would bother the remaining students, who were expected to use the hour to catch up on their homework. Fernanda was counting on this fact to read Elsa's diary. It would be a good time to read it, with extreme care, paying attention to exactly where it was located so as to be able to put it back again. Fernanda remembered pulling out the diary and reading: "I'm Mama's baby and I'm ashamed of what's happening." Details followed but Fernanda concentrated more on the order of things. She found the entry in which Elsa first expressed anguish at her father's sexual intrusion into her body. "Yesterday Daddy got angry because I insisted on going with Mama on her monthly visit to the Romanian Center. He wanted me to stay home alone, but I knew what would happen . . . Daddy has threatened to kill himself if I talk."

Elsa's writing was scribbled, smudged perhaps by the tears that she must have shed in writing it. The entry was dated two years earlier. The most recent entries indicated the existence of young men whom Fernanda knew because they attended the neighboring boys' school. They would wait for the girls when school let out and accompany them to the city bus. These were the only moments that Elsa had met boys, since she was never permitted to attend her friends' parties nor leave the house after school without her mother.

Certain phrases of Elsa's diary stuck in Fernanda's mind: "Daddy came looking for me at school and found out that Ricardo is my boyfriend. He's threatened to kill him if I keep seeing him . . ." Fernanda knew the details of this scene since she had been with Elsa, Tita, and Ana that afternoon. The girls were with their respective boyfriends, but the couples never strayed too far from the group. Elsa had been dragged away by her father and shoved into his car. The next day Elsa had written, "He won't get away with this thing, even if it means that I have to kill him."

Fernanda felt that the diary simply confirmed what she had already suspected from bits and pieces of her conversations with Elsa. But now that she knew for sure, what should she do? Fernanda was paralyzed by confusion; she couldn't admit that she had read the diary because this would betray her friend's trust.

She could not tell Elsa about Otilia's strange ritual either.

Now, still in her hiding place, waiting for Elsa to leave her mother's room, Fernanda thought of her conversation with Elsa the day she had read her diary. Elsa had come back from choir practice. "It was a waste of time because we'll never win the contest. But we had a great time listening to the stories that Monone told us. She's not the greatest music teacher, but her stories are cute because they're so ridiculous."

"Haven't you ever wondered why Monone never got married?" asked Fernanda, trying to orient the conversation towards more confidential topics.

"Monone never got married because her parents wanted only the best for her, which is not the best," Elsa said, laughing. Fernanda noticed that Elsa made fun of the world; she, who was so pretty, had learned how to use irony.

"And aren't you afraid the same thing will happen to you? Your father is so protective that he doesn't let you come to our parties or even to our own class graduation," said Fernanda, knowing that Elsa would answer her directly.

"Daddy doesn't want to let me do certain things because he believes that he has power over me and over my Mama; but still, I'll find a boyfriend even more powerful than he is." Saying this, Elsa's face, normally beautiful, became sad and ugly.

Earlier on the day of Elsa's wedding Tita said: "Who would believe that Elsa would get married before us? When I got the invitation I almost fainted. We've hardly seen each other during summer vacation, getting ready for the university entrance examinations."

"What a surprise!" agreed Ana, who always got wind of everything and who felt the most betrayed.

"And who is Roberto Gonzalez?" asked Fernanda, who believed that the whole group should go to the university and not get married until they had careers.

"He's a lawyer and he works for an international company, General Motors. He's as old as my father. My uncle Alfredo says that he's real rich," said Tita.

"What I don't understand is why her father hasn't stopped it," said Fernanda, remembering the strict vigilance that Elsa was subject to.

"Her father went to the United States for medical treatment and that's all the time Elsa needed. She is eighteen now," said Ana, who seemed to know more details, probably because she had already put out feelers through her network of friends.

Now on Elsa's wedding day, everything had taken place in the strictest intimacy. The groom had brought only his closest relatives and two of his best friends. On Elsa's side the only ones in attendance were Otilia, who, having been a Romanian refugee, had no family in Lima, and two fellow refugees, who had been Elsa's godmothers at her baptism and confirmation. Elsa's three schoolmates were her only friends present. But the one who was conspicuously absent was "El señor Arturo," Elsa's father.

Later when Fernanda returned from Otilia's room, Ana, who was Fernanda's best friend, asked, "Where have you been all this time?"

"We've looked for you everywhere, you really disappeared," said Tita. "Elsa seems to be madly in love. Listen, the groom was 'almost' blushing at Elsa's public display of affection," she added.

Tita seemed to have enjoyed herself, judging from her rosy cheeks and the bride's bouquet in her hands. Both Ana and Tita had danced with Roberto's friends. Roberto himself seemed to be a nice guy, although too old for them.

"The angels fly in silence," said Ana in a moment of inspired eloquence.

"And I hope Elsa's father is struck by lightning," said Fernanda suddenly, separating herself from the group.

Two weeks later when Elsa returned from her honeymoon, a detective-lieutenant asked her to identify a suicide. Elsa recognized her mother even though the body had been in the gorge that was called Paradise of the Suicides of San Miguel for three days. Finally, the official notice of Otilia's death appeared in the paper. Fernanda went to express her condolences to Elsa, who seemed to have lost a lot of weight.

"Daddy abandoned Mama when he got back from the States and found out that my engagement to Roberto was serious. Poor Mama, she was so confused the day of my wedding. She must have felt like an accomplice. I could never explain to her what I was worried about."

"Maybe she guessed," said Fernanda in spite of herself.

"Yes, but Daddy goes around telling everybody that she was crazy and that if he didn't say anything before, it was to protect the family name."

"Have you seen him?" asked Fernanda.

"I don't ever want to see him again. He says that I'm a disobedient disgrace. What do you think?" Elsa asked Fernanda, who was finally going to reveal everything that she knew.

Unfortunately, Roberto's presence in the room interrupted the conversation.

Translated by Lucía Fox

Bibliography

Fiction by Lucía Fox

Un cierto lugar. Lima: Salesiano. 1980.

Constelación. East Lansing, Mich.: Shamballa, 1978.

"Detras del telón." *Puerta abierta: La nueva escritora latinoamericana.* Ed. Caridad L. Silva-Velázquez and Nora Erro-Orthmann. Mexico City: Joaquín Mortiz, 1986. 123–29.

Rueda. East Lansing, Mich.: Superspace, 1988.

Rueda dos. East Lansing, Mich.: Superspace, 1990.

Essays by Lucía Fox

"Amorours Fantasies." Trans. Andres Morales. *Americas* 39.1 (1987): 38–41.

Chicanas: Their Voices, Their Lives. Lansing, Mich.: Board of Education, 1989.

"La conciencia social andina en la obra de José María Arguedas." *Actas del Décimo Congreso de la Asociación de Hispanistas.* 3 Ed. Antonio Vilanova. Barcelona: Promociones y Publicaciones Universitarias, 1992. 601–10.

Cronistas y emancipadores. East Lansing, Mich.: La Nueva Crónica, 1996.

"Dicotomías culturales en José María Arguedas." *Discurso Literario* 4.2 (1987): 425–35.

"El discurso femenino en los cuentos de Elena Garro y Rosario Ferré." *La escritora hispánica.* Eds. Nora Erro-Orthmann and Juan Cruz Mendizábal. Miami: Universal, 1990. 85–91.

Ensayos hispanoamericanos. Caracas: García y Hermanos, 1965.

Feminist Centers in Lima, Perú. East Lansing. Mich.: La Nueva Crónica, 1988.

Grass-roots Feminist Organizations in Lima, Perú. East Lansing, Mich.: Women in International Development and Michigan State University, 1993.

Indian Visions. East Lansing, Mich.: La Nueva Crónica, 1997.

"Lima por fuera y por dentro." *The City in the Latin American Novel.* Ed. Bobby J. Chamberlain. East Lansing, Mich.: Michigan State University, 1980. 29–44.

Mitos en Hispanoamérica: Interpretación y literatura. East Lansing, Mich.: La Nueva Crónica, 1989.

Mujeres: Escritura y subversión. East Lansing, Mich.: La Nueva Crónica, 1995.

"Novelística femenina: Un esfuerzo de liberación." *Actas del Sexto Congreso Internacional de Hispanistas.* Eds. Alan M. Gordon and Evelyn Rugg. Toronto: University of Toronto, 1980. 269–72.

Perú: Escritura y subversión. East Lansing, Mich.: La Nueva Crónica, 1995.

El rostro de la patria en la literatura peruana. Buenos Aires: Continente, 1970.

Saga. East Lansing, Mich.: La Nueva Crónica, 1992.

"Silvina Ocampo's Fantastic Short Stories." *Monographic Review/Revista Monográfica* 4 (1988): 221–29.

Sor Juana de América. East Lansing, Mich.: La Nueva Crónica, 1995.

"Vida, pasión y muerte de Julia de Burgos." *Letras Femeninas* 16.1–2 (1990): 121–24.

Vida y creación. East Lansing, Mich.: La Nueva Crónica, 1993.
"Visión del paisaje andino peruano en José María Arguedas y Manuel Scorza." *Cuadernos de Aldeeu* 1.2–3 (1983): 337–45.
Visiones indias. East Lansing, Mich.: La Nueva Crónica, 1997.
Women Novelists in Spain and Spanish America. Metuchen, N.J.: Scarecrow Press, 1979.

Poetry by Lucía Fox

Aceleración Múltiple. Buenos Aires: Losada, 1969.
Assemblage. Lucía Fox in Translation. East Lansing, Mich.: Superspace, 1977.
Formas—Forms. East Lansing, Mich.: Shamballa, 1985.
Imágenes de Caracas. Caracas: García Hermanos, 1965.
Latinoamérica en evolución. Latin America in Evolution. East Lansing, Mich.: Superspace, 1974.
Leyendas de una princesa india—Legends of an Indian Princess. East Lansing, Mich.: Shamballa, 1979.
Lima en caos. East Lansing, Mich.: La Nueva Crónica, 1990.
Monstruos aéreos, terrestres, y submarinos. East Lansing, Mich.: Superspace, 1974.
Mosaicos. East Lansing, Mich.: Old Marble Press, 1974.
Mosaics. East Lansing, Mich.: Argonauta, 1974.
Múltiples. East Lansing, Mich.: Ghost Dance, 1969.
La odisea del pájaro. Bilbao: Empresas Editoras, 1972.
Preludios íntimos. Lima: Cóndor, 1945.
Redes. Barcelona: Carabela, 1968.
Tiempo atonal. East Lansing, Mich.: Ghost Dance, 1969.
Tragaluz. Los Angeles: La Frontera, 1967.

Plays by Lucía Fox

Ayer es nunca jamás. Lima: Salesiano, 1980.
El perfil desnudo. East Lansing, Mich.: Shamballa, 1978.
El riesgo de vivir. East Lansing, Mich.: La Nueva Crónica, 1992.
The Risk of Living. East Lansing, Mich.: La Nueva Crónica, 1991.
Sor Juana, the Tenth Muse. East Lansing, Mich.: Pachacamac, 1988.

Criticism on the Works of Lucía Fox

Agosín, Marjorie. "Lucía Fox: *Ayer es nunca jamás*." *Revista Iberoamericana* 48.120–21 (1982): 743–44.
———. "Rev. of *Women Novelists in Spain and Spanish America* by Lucía Fox-Lockert." *Revista Interamericana de Bibliografía/Inter-American Review of Bibliography* 30.4 (1980): 437.
Cain, Joan. "Rev. of *Women Novelists in Spain and Spanish America* by Lucía Fox-Lockert." *Journal of Spanish Studies;Twentieth Century* 8.3 (1980): 317–18.
Elissondo, Guillermina. "Lucía Fox." *Concerning Poetry* 17.2 (1984): 177–79.
Erro-Peralta, Nora. "Lucía Fox." *Alba de América* 12.22–23 (1994): 577–84.

Rojas-Trempe, Lady. "El brujo en 'La semana de colores' de Elena Garro." *Mitos en Hispanoamérica: Interpretación y literatura.* Ed. Lucía Fox-Lockert. East Lansing, Mich.: La Nueva Crónica, 1989.

————. "*El riesgo de vivir* de Lucía Fox: La dramatización de la violencia peruana." *La Escena Latinoamericana* 1.2 (1993) 14–17.

Werner, Flora M. "Introducción a la obra dramática de Lucía Fox." *Letras Femeninas* 5.1 (1979): 103–12.

Elena Garro

Elena Garro (1920–98) was one of the most innovative contemporary writers in Mexico. A choreographer, journalist, and dramatist, Garro is best known as a gifted narrator, whose novel *Los recuerdos del porvenir* (1963; *Recollections of Things to Come*, 1969) won the 1964 Xavier Villaurrutia Prize and was an early example of magical realism in Latin America.

She was born in Puebla, Mexico, on December 15, 1920, and spent much of her childhood in Iguala, Guerrero, the setting of her first novel. She attended the School of Philosophy at the National Autonomous University in Mexico, where she distinguished herself as the choreographer of the University Theatre. In 1937, after she finished her studies, she married the famous Mexican writer Octavio Paz, with whom she had a daughter, Helena.

Known for her championing of the powerless and downtrodden, Garro was identified as one of the instigators of the students' demonstration at the Plaza de Tlatelolco in 1968 and was placed under unrest. Shortly afterwards she left Mexico and lived in self-imposed exile in Paris until 1991, when she returned to Mexico.

Garro produced a rich body of literature, which can be divided into two distinct periods. In her earlier works, *Los recuerdos del porvenir* and *La semana de colores* (The week of colors, 1964), Garro explores the magical and the fantastic as they coexist with objective dimensions of reality. In these narratives she weaves the pre-Columbian Mexican tradition, especially its conception of cyclical time, with the history of her people to create a magical and mythical world. In her later fiction *Andamos huyendo Lola* (We are fleeing, Lola, 1980); *Testimonios sobre Mariana* (Testimonies about Mariana, 1981); *Reencuentro de personajes* (Reunion of characters, 1982); and *La casa junto al río* (The house by the river, 1983)—she focuses on the arbitrariness of power and the dangers of violence. She portrays the situation of women in exile who have escaped persecution in their countries of origin: their struggle to survive in poverty and isolation, and their inability to find a space for themselves in a male-dominated society.

Elena Garro's use of poetic language, original themes, intriguing characters, and, above all, her brilliant handling of unconventional narrative and psychological time make her a master of Latin American fiction. Although she lived most of her adult life in Spain and France, Garro's works retain the illusive quality of the fantastic that so characterizes Mexican art.

Perfecto Luna

It must have been about eleven-thirty when Perfecto Luna passed the last houses in town. At that hour everyone was asleep and no one heard him go by. Everything, thank God, had been simple: lifting the bars on the warehouse door, squeezing through the crack in the door, and going out into the dark street.

"So long as no one robs the warehouse and makes them think: 'That bastard Perfecto, he went in and stole everything there was in the store.'"

But what else could he have done? He wasn't about to give up his life to a prankster! Especially not once he had seen that all there was in the other world were cold gusts of wind. Now the only thing left for him to do was to run, erase the tracks he had left in town and on the roads, throw away his name and look for another one. Leave no trace of Perfecto Luna.

But what name? It wasn't so easy to stop being himself. Since he was little they had called him that. He had always been Perfecto Luna, the mason, the peon, the boy who knew how to do anything, because that's the way the boss had taught him to be. Now he had to forget what he had known and start all over again, so he could be someone else. It made him feel sad for himself: he had been so good-natured and obliging! But that's how life is: each person has his own luck, good or bad. He remembered his friends' names. Crisóforo Flores: there was no way he could call himself that; he would be stealing his friend's soul. Still, maybe he would have to. Crisóforo always went around so sure of himself, so happy, so carefree; he went around like Perfecto Luna had before. Domingo Ibáñez was risky, because that guy had sad nights. So was Justo Montiel; he might take to killing his friends.

He left the path and headed across the fields, in the direction of Actipan. That way, when they were all looking for him around San Pedro, he would be going about his business in Acetepec. He liked the market at Acetepec. As soon as he got there he was going to buy himself a good silk handkerchief and start looking for work. After all, he could do anything. It would take him all night to cross the field of acacia trees, but he was feeling safer. Who would be able to find his tracks in all those huisaches? He started hurrying and tripped on a rock. "Now you've done it, Perfecto Luna, you've messed up your toe!" he told himself out loud, to scare away the round silence that was surrounding him at that moment. It was better not to look; the countryside had become enormous. What was starting to happen is what had always happened, for the last five months: the silence would start to grow so big that it was useless to try to say anything. There, for centuries and centuries, not a single noise had been made. He had just said, "Now you've done it, Perfecto Luna, you've messed up your toe!" and yet he hadn't said it. The words had come out silently and stayed there, hanging on the tip of his tongue. He had to get a long ways away from Amate Redondo and from the Perfecto Luna that they were looking for; that's why they had stuck him into those round nights that lasted longer than the days. He stepped up his pace again. The layers of air divided; his nose was trapped in the empty space between two of them, and he could barely breathe. On the other hand, around his eyes and hair, the wind was blowing without blowing, lifting up his hair and turning it cold, so cold that it felt like thousands and thousands of ice cubes were puncturing his head. When would he finally get past that strange territory?

"I'll be Crisóforo Flores. I won't hang around here anymore, and I'll start having a good time with my friends again."

There in front of him, he saw a man crouched down, looking for something in the huisaches. He was stooped over close to the ground, trying to see in the dark. Perfecto Luna was pleased to run into someone in that solitude. The man was right there, two steps away, blocking his path. Out of courtesy he said good evening.

"Good evening," replied the stranger, without stopping his search.

"Are you looking for something?" asked Perfecto Luna politely, thinking that's how Crisóforo Flores would say it.

"Yes," answered the stranger in a plaintive voice. "And I can't find it."

"Can I help you, Sir?" offered Perfecto Luna, feeling more and more like Crisóforo Flores.

"If you would be so kind," responded the other man weakly.

Perfecto Luna crouched down to look for the lost object. It must be money, and the white man didn't want to say so, for fear he would be robbed. He could barely see amidst the shadows and the rocks. He peered curiously at the stranger's legs; it looked like he was wearing huaraches and a red cape. He seemed to move with difficulty, as if he were blind. He felt the ground around him laboriously, clinging to the rocks and bushes.

"Ay, Señor!" said Perfecto Luna, once again feeling as if the words were barely coming out of his mouth. The man paid no attention to him, but kept on searching, turning over rocks.

Perfecto Luna sat down on the ground, feeling discouraged.

"Ay, Señor, you wouldn't believe the things that have happened to me!" he went on, forgetting to be Crisóforo Flores. "Look what's left of me, just a pile of skin and bones!"

The confession did not move the stranger, who did not change his position.

"You know, I was Perfecto Luna until tonight!"

"Damn, I'm getting tired of all this looking!" the stranger complained.

"I'll help you in a minute," Perfecto offered, remembering that he was supposed to be the good-natured Crisóforo. He energetically threw himself into the hunt again. The stranger was a long ways off now; he could barely make out his red-and-white form searching among the huisaches. Perfecto Luna felt calm in his company. He thought, This is going to be my last unlucky night; starting tomorrow, when I'm Crisóforo Flores, no one will ever remember who I was.

"Sir!" he shouted optimistically, feeling like it was already the next day. "Do you believe in the dead?"

"In the dead?" the other man asked, surprised. His voice came from deep down.

"Yes, Sir, but not the dead incarnate, the other ones . . ."

"The other ones?" the stranger asked, pausing in his search.

"Yes, the other ones," Perfecto answered with aplomb, becoming Crisóforo Flores more and more. "Just imagine, I used to be Perfecto Luna, and I had to stop being him, all because of a dead man!"

"Ah!" responded the stranger.

"Did you come through Amate Redondo? You must have met Don Celso, the owner of the warehouse. Everything that I was, I owe to him. He taught me how to work, when I was Perfecto Luna. I must have been about five years old when I started running errands for him. I grew up with him, because I was an orphan at birth. 'See, Perfecto, this is how you plane wood. Stay here, Perfecto. Now that you know how much a measure of corn costs, you can ring it up here, on the cash register.' Because Don Celso has the only cash register in Amate Redondo. He's the only one who has worked at it, even though they say he steals grams from the kilos. And that's how I made a living, working, until Don Celso decided to build the famous annexes."

Perfecto Luna grew quiet. He remembered that, until that day, he had been very self-confident. Don Celso told him to demolish the huts that were behind the warehouse so he could build some houses like the ones in Mexico City. He came back with the hoe and started tearing down those shacks. How long did it take him to do the job? Let's say a month; and at the end of that month everything was cleared away. Until that day he had also been happy. What was missing? Nothing. He was treated well and had his friends' respect. No one wished him harm. It happened one April fourth, when Don Celso said to him, "Dig the ditches so we can lay the foundations." At about noon, as he was deepening the ditch, he found the dead man. It was an old dead body, because all that was left of him were bones. He could see him as if it was yesterday, glittering in the sun, with his arms crossed over his ribs. *He must have come to a bad end, because he doesn't have a head. Who could have killed him? Where can his head be?*

"Just imagine, Sir, his head was missing; someone must have chopped it off!" The stranger didn't say a word.

"The bad part, Sir, is that when I was Perfecto Luna I used to like to be wicked. 'Perfecto!' Don Celso's wife yelled at me, 'Come eat.' I put my blanket in the dead man's hole and went to dinner. I remember that, while they were heating up the tortillas, I was laughing inside."

"'What are you laughing at?' they asked me.

"'The only one who knows is me,' I said.

"And the only one who knew was me. After dinner I wrapped up the little bones in my blanket and took them to my room. 'You'll see, you goddamn dead man!' I said to him. The day came when I found myself making the adobe bricks . . . ," and Perfecto could once again picture himself stirring the dry leaves into the mud and whistling.

"'Look at that guy enjoying himself; I wish everyone worked like that!' Don Celso would say. And it was true, because as long as I was Perfecto

Luna, any old thing would make me happy. I remember that I was rolling a cigarette when the idea came to me. I went over to my room, took out a toe bone, and buried it in an adobe brick that I had put out in the sun to dry. 'Since they've done you the favor of burying you in pieces, I'm going to finish the job for you,' I said to him. I made a mark on the adobe, so I would know that a piece of his grave was there. Then I took out a rib and stuck it in another marked brick. And so on until I had used up all the little bones.

"'Hey, Don Celso, what happens to a dead man who's cut up in pieces?'"

"'He goes crazy, boy, looking for his pieces.'"

"'Ha, ha, ha.'" And I went to see my little graves, content. "How wonderful it is to be young and lighthearted, Sir!" Perfecto Luna said, sitting down again on the ground and looking around for the other man, who went about his business, paying no attention to him. Sadly, he thought that no one cared if he, Perfecto Luna, had been lighthearted, and that because of it, he had to stop being himself. He remembered how he began to build the houses: he carefully divided up the adobe bricks containing the bones among the different walls of the houses; not a space was left in the complex in which "the man with no head" wasn't buried. And he kept right on opening up windows, raising roofs, building doors, whistling and laughing to himself all the while.

"'Look, Perfecto, they turned out pretty; put a blue wash on them!' Don Celso said to me I used the brightest blue, Sir, to cheer up the white-washed burial site."

And he laughed again, in spite of himself, remembering. *I hope the Juárez family will come live here, and that during the night 'the man with no head' will grab their feet,* he had thought to himself, once the houses were finished. Don Celso told him to stand guard over them, so kids wouldn't go in there and write on the walls. They smelled new: like lime and mortar. The walls and the floor bricks were still damp; in all the rooms there was the presence of cleanliness, of something that hadn't been touched by people. Perfecto Luna took his shirts, his blanket and grass mat, and installed himself in one of the rooms. He was tired; he took off his huaraches, stretched out on the mat, and watched the night through the window. The sky was calm and clear and, from where he lay, he could see two stars shining. He shut his eyes halfway. *Who would have thought that he would do all that work all by himself!* He opened his eyes and looked proudly at his work of art: his gaze ran over the roof, walls, door, and rested on the window again. Underneath it, a little protrusion marked one of the tombs of "the man with no head." *Who darkened the night?* He felt around for the candle that he had left next to the mat. He stretched out his arm, which felt like it had become very short; the room, on the other hand, had grown enormously and the candle was a long ways off, beyond his reach. He resigned himself to the darkness. He opened his eyes wide, trying to make something out, any-thing, but the shadows grew more and more dense. *I think that's how people get scared.* He kept still. All at once he saw that the marker he had put on the adobe was shining. *It's the man with no head!* His heart started beating so hard that it seemed like he was being carried away by a rushing river. He felt like he was going deaf. The only thing left for him to do was to wait for morning. But the night stretched out into many nights. When day broke, he saw that his grass mat was damp with sweat.

"What's wrong with you, Perfecto? You look wild-eyed."

He didn't know what to answer. He barely tasted his coffee, thinking that it was going to get dark any time. Sadly, he sat down in the courtyard of the annexes, to watch the sun beating against the roofs.

"The day's just about over . . . ," he said with distress. He moved his mat and trinkets to the second room. Night returned and he went to bed, not daring to look out the window.

I am not going to look at the night anymore. And he squeezed his eyes tightly shut. A whirr of wings filled the room, beating as they went up and down the walls. They passed over his forehead and his body. He began to freeze. Which goddamn bone could be making that noise that he couldn't hear? And, that night, it lasted longer than the night before. He wanted to think about how to satisfy the dead man, but the wings were beating so fast that he could not formulate his thoughts.

"You caught a chill, Perfecto," they told him.

And he could not tell them about what had happened the night before with those cold wings. The sun set, but his knees were still frozen stiff. He didn't have time to warm himself up, because that day the sun hardly lasted any time at all. It seemed like the rooster had barely crowed, when he heard the hens settling onto their roosts to go to sleep. Completely disheartened, he moved his mat, blanket, and candle to the third room.

Goddam dead man, rest in peace and stop making trouble for me; I never hurt anyone!

He wrapped himself up in his cape so he wouldn't get cold, and closed his eyes so he wouldn't see the shadows surrounding him. From a corner of the room a whirlwind started; it hummed violently and perched next to his left ear. It entered his ear at high speed, deafening him.

Tell me, you blasted dead man, what do you want me to do for you? he would have liked to say, but the words stuck to his tongue. Then they wrapped around it, like they had wrapped up Anselmo's leg after he was cut up in a fight. Immobile, with his tongue tied, he endured the whirlwind that filled his body with cramps.

"It's morning . . . ," he said with difficulty, when he went into the kitchen to get some hot coffee.

"What's wrong with you, boy? Why are you talking that way? It sounds like the cat got your tongue."

And Perfecto Luna hung his head and thought that this day, too, would be over very soon.

"Don Celso, will you let Alambritos sleep with me?"

"What the hell, boy? What do you want him for? Is the bogeyman after you?"

He barely had time to grab Alambritos before night had already fallen. He tied the dog up with a long twine rope attached to the door latch in the next room, and lay down on the mat. He was getting skinny and his laugh had died on him! The darkness began to descend from the roof, like a thick black cloud that was out to crush him. *What do you want me to do for you, dead man? I can't undo the annexes, to unite your bones again.* He had just finished thinking that when he saw Alambritos come dragging himself along the ground, staying close to the floor like a sticker, to lie down next to him. A howl started to come out of Alambritos's new shape smashed flat like a sheet of paper. *It's true that you're here.* Perfecto Luna thought. *What do you want? I'll give you whatever you want if you'll just go away.* At that moment the layers of shadow fell on top of him like a heavy blanket and left him without thoughts. It was him that it wanted! All night he lay there under that black cover.

"Look, boy, your nose is smashed!" they said when they saw him come out of the room. His legs could barely support him.

"Don Celso, how long does a night last?"

"As long as every night."

Now the days were barely a streak of light between two immense nights. He didn't even have time to put on his huaraches and take them off again. Clothes began to wear out his body. What chances were there that he could go trim his mustache and hair! As soon as it dawned, there was the night back already! He didn't even have time to eat, and he was turning into skin and bones. He went from one room to another until he had worked his way through them all, and in every one of them he found the presence of the dead man waiting to pull him out of his skin. From where he crouched in a corner of the courtyard, he could hear Crisóforo playing the harmonica and singing with his friends in the distance. They were in the cantina, for sure. This realization sunk him deeper into sadness, since it meant that night was out there waiting for him.

"What's wrong with you, boy? If you keep on like this, it won't be long before you give up the ghost."

"Don Celso, let me sleep in the warehouse!"

That way "the man with no head" would wander, furious, through all the rooms without finding him, since he would be sleeping amidst the bunches of cinnamon and sacks of corn.

"Go ahead, but if you're doing it out of fear, you're not going to lose it there."

He moved his grass mat to the warehouse. It seemed like this night was falling more calmly. The warehouse was animated: the clients were having one last round of tequila; Don Celso was balancing his books; it smelled like alcohol and spices. He felt relieved. It struck ten o'clock and Crisóforo Flores, his friend, downed one last shot.

"See you around tomorrow, if you wake up, that is, 'cause you're looking more and more like a dead man . . ." And he went off confidently, with his hat cocked.

Don Celso told him good night. Perfecto Luna closed the warehouse doors, noting that they were well greased, then put up the bar that stretched from wall to wall, and lay down on top of the counter, leaving the gas lamp burning. With the light on, "the man with no head" wouldn't dare. With delight he breathed in the smell of lard, mixed with dust from the beans, and, feeling safe, he stretched out. A noise arose in the back room. He looked for the candle and matches, but they were in the pocket of his muslin shirt. The noise grew louder. It was wiser to not go see what was happening. Another noise echoed the first one: something was falling, falling endlessly, whistling softly. It sounded like two sacks of corn were emptying out their grain through a hole.

Now he's done it; the bastard is slitting open the sacks!

The whistling multiplied. All the sacks were spilling out at great speed. The back room was filling up with corn, he was sure of it. Cautiously, he peered in that direction: the doorway, filled with grain, was overflowing, and the corn was advancing into the store. Stunned, he looked around him. He was surrounded by sacks. Up above the exit door there were boards piled high with agave-fiber bags. At that moment the first sack opened up and the grain began falling silently, in a golden stream, onto the ground. Then a second sack was perforated, then a third, then a fourth, then the whole store rained corn from every wall. The space of the counter grew narrower. He saw that the street door, which he had barred so carefully, was being blocked, since the sacks above it were also being pierced. He got up as best he could and, taking long strides, burying himself in grain up to his thighs, he reached the door. With difficulty he lifted the bar and, with great effort, he managed to open the door a crack, sniff the night, and go out into the street.

"Right about now, Sir, I'd be back there buried in corn, and 'the sonofabitch with no head' would have me by the hair for the rest of eternity. But I got away from him. And I got away not just from Amate Redondo, but from Perfecto Luna, because when he looks for him, he isn't going to find him anymore. Now I'm Crisóforo Flores. That's what you call having a little presence of mind! Don't you think, Sir? That's why I was asking you if you believed in dead men, because before 'the man with no head' I didn't believe either."

"Ah!" answered the stranger from deep down. And he began straightening himself up, with difficulty.

"I'm going to help you look, now that I've told you the sad story of the man who was Perfecto Luna."

"Never mind!" answered the stranger, on his feet beside the narrator. The latter barely had time to see the faceless face of his new friend: the stranger's body ended at his shoulders.

"He was possessed by the devil!" said Don Celso the next day. "He spilled out all my corn and went and died out in the middle of the huisache field. Goddamn! And that Perfecto Luna seemed like such a good boy!"

Translated by Cynthia Steele
(From La semana de colores, 1964)

Bibliography

Fiction by Elena Garro

El accidente y otros cuentos inéditos. Mexico City: Seix Barral, 1997.

Andamos huyendo Lola. Mexico City: Joaquín Mortiz, 1980.

Busca mi esquela y Primer amor. Mexico City: Ediciones Castillo, 1996.

La casa junto al río. Mexico City: Grijalbo, 1983.

Un corazón en un bote de basura. Mexico City: Joaquín Mortiz, 1996.

"La culpa es de los Tlaxcaltecas." *Narrativa mexicana de hoy.* Madrid: Alianza, 1969. 75–93. Rpt. in *Cuentistas mexicanas siglo veinte.* Ed. Aurora M. Ocampo. Mexico City: Universidad Autónoma de México, 1976. 109–22.

"The Day We Were Dogs." Trans. Tona Wilson. *Contemporary Women Authors of Latin America: New Translations.* Eds. Doris Meyer and Margarite Fernández Olmos. New York: Brooklyn College Press, 1983. 186–91.

First Love and Look for My Obituary: Two Novels by Elena Garro. Trans. David Unger. Willimantic, Conn.: Curbstone Press, 1997.

"It's the Fault of the Tlaxcaltecas." Trans. Alberto Manguel. *Other Fires: Short Fiction by Latin American Women.* Ed. Alberto Manguel. Toronto: Lester & Orpen Dennys, 1986. 159–78.

"Perfecto Luna." *Puerta abierta: La nueva escritora latinoamericana.* Eds. Caridad L. Silva-Velázquez and Nora Erro-Orthmann. Mexico City: Joaquín Mortiz, 1986. 131–39.

"¿Qué hora es?" *Catorce mujeres escriben cuentos.* Ed. Elsa de Llarena. Mexico City: Federación Mexicana, 1975. 134–49.

Recollections of Things to Come. Trans. Ruth L. C. Simms. Austin: University of Texas Press, 1969. Rpt. in Austin: University of Texas Press, 1987.

Los recuerdos del porvenir. Mexico City: Joaquín Mortiz, 1963. Rpt. in Mexico City: Joaquín Mortiz, 1977.

Reencuentro de personajes. Mexico City: Grijalbo, 1982.

Revolucionarios mexicanos. Mexico City: Seix Barral, 1997.

La semana de colores. Xalapa: Universidad Veracruzana, 1964.

Testimonios sobre Mariana. Mexico City: Grijalbo, 1981.

"The Tiztla Robbery." *Americas* July 7, 1959: 21–25. Rpt. in *Mexican Life* 35.9 (1959): 20+.

"The Tree." Trans. Evelyn Picón Garfield. *Women's Fiction from Latin America: Selections from Twelve Contemporary Authors.* Ed. Evelyn Picón Garfield. Detroit: Wayne State University Press, 1988. 69–86.

Y Matarazo no llamó . . . Mexico City: Grijalbo, 1989.

Essays by Elena Garro

Memorias de España Mexico City: Siglo Veintiuno, 1992.

"Testimonios sobre Mariana." *Espejo* (Mexico City) 4 (1967).

Plays by Elena Garro

El árbol. Revista Mexicana de Literatura (Mexico City) 3–4 (1963): 10–31.

"The Dogs." Trans. Beth Miller. Latin American Literary Review 8.15 (1979): 68–85.

Felipe Angeles. Mexico City: Universidad Autónoma de México, 1979.

Un hogar sólido y otras piezas en un acto. Xalapa: Universidad Veracruzana, 1958. Rpt. in Xalapa: Universidad Veracruzana, 1983.

"The Lady on Her Balcony." Trans. Beth Miller. Shantih 3 (1976): 36–44.

La mudanza. La palabra y el hombre (Xalapa) 3.10 (1959): 263–74.

"Los perros." Revista de la Universidad de México (Mexico City) 21.7 (1965): 20–23.

"La señora en su balcón." Tercera antología de obras en un acto. Comp. Maruxa Vilalta. Mexico City: Colección Teatro Mexicano, 1960. 25–40.

"A Solid House." Evergreen Review 2.7 (1959): 62–74. Rpt. in Selected Latin American One Act Plays. Eds. Francesca Colecchia and Julio Matas. Pittsburgh: University of Pittsburgh Press, 1973. 20+.

Criticism on the Works of Elena Garro

Anderson, Robert K. "'El ahogado más hermoso del mundo' y Felipe Hurtado: Dos agentes de metamorfosis." Selecta 9 (1988): 102–6.

———. "La cuentística-mágico-realista de Elena Garro." Selecta 3 (1982): 117–21.

———. "Myth and Archetype in Recollections of Things to Come." Studies in Twentieth Century Literature 9.2 (1985): 213–27.

———. "La realidad temporal en Los recuerdos del porvenir." Explicación de Textos Literarios 9 (1980–81): 25–29.

———. "Recurrent Themes in Two Novels by Elena Garro." Selecta 11 (1990): 83–86.

Anderson Imbert, Enrique. "Elena Garro." Historia de la literatura hispanoamericana. Época contemporánea. Mexico City: Fondo de Cultura Económica, 1974. 400.

Arvizu-Hughes, Francisco. "Elena Garro, una escritora con dos ángulos." El Financiero Cultural December 30, 1996: 14A.

———. "La obra de Elena Garro, actual en Estados Unidos; Rhina Toruño." El Financiero Cultural December 31, 1996: 14A.

Avalos Facaci, Rafael. "El mundo maravilloso y alucinante de Elena Garro y Marcel Camus." México en la Cultura (Mexico City) 748 July 21, 1963: 8.

Balderston, Daniel. "The New Historical Novel: History and Fantasy in Los recuerdos del porvenir." Bulletin of Hispanic Studies (Edinburgh) 66.1 (1989). 41–46.

Bárcenas, Angel. "La dama boba." Revista Mexicana de Cultura (Mexico City) 889 April 12, 1964. 15.

Barry, John. "El lugar sin límites: El espacio como signo en Los recuerdos del porvenir." A Ricardo Gullón: Sus discípulos. Ed. Adelaida López de Martínez. Erie, Pa.: Publicación de la Asociación de Licenciados y Doctores Españoles en los Estados Unidos, 1995. 43–50.

Bartow, Joanna R. "Isolation and Madness: Collective Memory and Women in Los recuerdos del porvenir and Pedro Páramo." Revista Canadiense de Estudios Hispánicos (Ottawa) 18.1 (1993): 1–15.

Batis, Huberto. "*Los recuerdos del porvenir.*" La Cultura en México (Mexico City) 103 February 5, 1964: 18.

———. "*La semana de colores.*" La Cultura en México (Mexico City) 163 March 31, 1965: 16.

Bermúdez, María Elvira. "Dramaturgas." Diorama de la Cultura (literary supplement to Excelsior; Mexico City) April 5, 1959: 4.

———. "La novela mexicana en 1963." Diorama de la Cultura (literary supplement to Excelsior; Mexico City) January 19, 1964: 8.

Beverido Duhalt, Francisco. "Los perros de Elena Garro" Texto Crítico (Xalapa) 12.34–35 (1986): 118–35.

Biron, Rebecca. "Testimonio sobre Mariana: Representación y la otra mujer." Sin imágenes falsas, sin falsos espejos: Narradoras mexicanas del siglo veinte. Ed. Aralia López González. Mexico City: Colegio de México, 1995. 161–83.

Boling, Becky. "Tracking the Feminine Subject in Elena Garro's El rastro." Continental Latin-American and Francophone Women Writers. Vol 2. Eds. Ginette Adamson and Eunice Myers. Lanham, Md.: University Press of America, 1987. 7–14.

Bolívar, María Dolores. "Ascensión Tun en la tradición del discurso de la mujer en la América Latina." Nuevo Texto Crítico 2.4 (1989): 137–43.

Bonfils, Alicia de. La literatura Cristera. Mexico City: Instituto de Antropología e Historia, 1970.

Boschetto, Sandra. "Romancing the Stone in Elena Garro's Los recuerdos del porvenir." Journal of the Midwest Modern Language Association 22.2 (1989): 1–11.

Bradú, Fabienne. "Testimonio sobre Elena Garro." Señas particulares: Escritora. Mexico City: Fondo de Cultura Económica, 1987. 13–28.

Brushwood, John. Mexico in Its Novel. Austin: University of Texas Press, 1966. 52–53.

Bundgard, Ana. "La semiótica de la culpa." Sin imágenes falsas, sin falsos espejos: Narradoras mexicanas del siglo veinte. Ed. Aralia López González. Mexico City: Colegio de México, 1995. 129–48.

Callan, Richard J. "Analytical Psychology and Garro's Los pilares de Doña Blanca." Latin American Theater Review 16.2 (1983): 31–35.

———. "Elena Garro's El encanto tendajon mixto: The Magical Woman and Maturity." Crítica Hispánica 14.1–2 (1992): 49–57.

———. "El misterio femenino en Los perros de Elena Garro." Revista Iberoamericana 46.110–11 (1980): 225–31.

Cantón, Wilberto. "El teatro de Elena Garro: La poesía contra el absurdo." La Cultura en México (Mexico City) 191 October 13, 1965: 15.

Carballo, Emmanuel. "Elena Garro." Protagonistas de la literatura mexicana. Mexico City: Consejo Nacional de Fomento Educativo, 1986. 490–518.

———. "El mundo mágico de Elena Garro" Siempre (Mexico City) February 24, 1965: 15–16.

———. "La novela y el cuento." La Cultura en México (Mexico City) 151 January 6, 1965: 5.

———. "Todo es presente." La Cultura en México (Mexico City) 109 March 18, 1964: 19.

———. "La vida y la obra de Elena Garro." Sábado Unomásuno (Mexico City) January 24, 1981: 2–5.

Casey Reed, James, and Patricia Rosas Loátegui. "Valores tradicionales y tragedia en *Testimonios de Mariana* de Elena Garro." *Alba de América* 16.30–31 (1998): 165–78.

Castro, Dolores. "Los hechos y la cultura." *Nivel* 22 October 25, 1964: 12.

Catay. "Dos obras mexicanas . . . " *El Gallo Ilustrado: Literary Supplement to El Día* (Mexico City) 44 April 28, 1963: 4.

Chitwood, Shelley. "Woman's Struggle Against Tradition in Elena Garro's *La señora en su balcón*." *Romance Languages Annual* 2 (1990): 378–81.

Colchero-Garrido, María Teresa. "La originalidad y la excelencia narrativa en *Inés* de Elena Garro." *La seducción de la escritura: Los discursos de la cultura hoy*. Eds. Rosaura Hernández Monroy and Manuel F. Medina. Mexico City: n.p., 1997. 323–27.

Cortés, Eladio. "Felipe Angeles, Theater of Heroes." *A Different Reality: Studies on the Work of Elena Garro*. Ed. Anita K. Stoll. Lewisburg, Pa.: Bucknell University Press, 1990. 80–89.

Cypess, Sandra Messinger. "Dramaturgia femenina y transposición histórica." *Alba de América* 7.12–13 (1989): 283–304.

———. "The Figure of La Malinche in the Texts of Elena Garro." *A Different Reality: Studies on the Work of Elena Garro*. Ed. Anita K. Stoll. Lewisburg, Pa.: Bucknell University Press, 1990. 117–35.

———. "Titles as Signs in the Translation of Dramatic Texts." *Translation Perspectives* 2: *Selected Papers, 1984–1985*. Ed. Marilyn Gaddis Rose. Binghamton: Translation Research & Instruction Program, State University of New York at Binghamton, 1985. 94–104.

———. "Visual and Verbal Distances in the Mexican Theater. The Plays of Elena Garro." *Woman as Myth and Metaphor in Latin American Literature*. Eds. Carmelo Virgilio and Naomi Lindstrom. Columbia: University of Missouri Press, 1985. 44–62.

Dallal, Alberto. "Los recuerdos del porvenir." *Universidad de México* (Mexico City) 18.6 (1964): 31.

Dauster, Frank. "Elena Garro." *Historia del teatro hispanoamericano Siglos diecinueve y veinte*. 2nd ed. Mexico City: Andrea, 1973. 104–5.

———. "Elena Garro y sus *Recuerdos del porvenir*" *Journal of Spanish Studies: Twentieth Century* 8 (1980): 57–65.

———. *Ensayos sobre teatro hispanoamericano*. Mexico City: Secretaría de Educación Pública, 1975.

———. "Success and the Latin American Writer." *Contemporary Women Authors of Latin America: Introductory Essays*. Eds. Doris Meyer and Margarite Fernández Olmos. New York: Brooklyn College Press, 1983. 16–21.

———. "El teatro de Elena Garro: Evasión e ilusión." *Revista Iberoamericana* 30.57 (1964): 81–89.

Del Río, Pascal Beltran. "Cartas de Adolfo Bioy Casares a Elena Garro." *La Nación* (literary supplement; Buenos Aires) November 30, 1997: 1–2.

DiPuccio, Denise M. "The Merging of La(s) dama(s) boba(s)." *Gestos* 5.9 (1990): 53–63.

"Dos novelas mexicanas." *México en la Cultura* (Mexico City) 768 December 8, 1963: 3.

Duncan, Cynthia. "*La culpa es de los tlaxcaltecas*: A Reevaluation of Mexico's Past Through Myth." *Crítica Hispánica* 7.2 (1985): 105–20.

————. "An Eye for an 'I': Women Writers and the Fantastic as a Challenge to Patriarchal Authority." *Inti* 40–41 (1994–95): 233–46.

————. "Narrative Tension and Perpetual Subversion in Elena Garro's Short Fiction." *Letras Femeninas* 15.1–2 (1989): 11–21.

————. "The Theme of the Avenging Dead in 'Perfecto Luna': A Magical Realist Approach." *A Different Reality: Studies on the Work of Elena Garro.* Ed. Anita K. Stoll. Lewisburg, Pa.: Bucknell University Press, 1990. 90–101.

Durán, Manuel. "El premio Villaurrutia y la novela mexicana contemporánea." *La Torre* (San Juan, Puerto Rico) 13.49 (1965): 233–38.

Durán Rosado, Esteban. "Memorias del pueblo de Ixtepec." *Revista Mexicana de Cultura* (Mexico City) 879 February 2, 1964: 5.

Earle, Peter G. "*Los recuerdos del porvenir* y la fuerza de las palabras." *Homenaje a Luis Alberto Sánchez.* Ed. Robert G. Mead Jr. Madrid: Insula, 1983. 235–42.

Echeverría, Miriam B. "Texto y represión en '*Los perros*' de Elena Garro." *De la crónica a la nueva narrativa mexicana.* Eds. Merlín H. Foster and Julio Ortega. Mexico City: Oasis, 1986. 423–29.

Eldridge, Joan T. "Elena Garro, the Civil Rights Parodist." *Utah Foreign Language Review* (1991–92): 28–36.

Fernández de Ciocca, María Inés. "*Los recuerdos del porvenir* o la novela del tiempo." *Revista Interamericana de Bibliografía/Inter-American Review of Bibliography* 36.1 (1986): 39–51.

Foster, David William. *Dictionary of Contemporary Latin American Authors.* Tempe: Center for Latin American Studies, Arizona State University, 1975. 45.

Fox-Lockert, Lucía. "El discurso femenino en los cuentos de Elena Garro y Rosario Ferré." *La escritora hispánica.* Eds. Nora Erro-Orthmann and Juan Cruz Mendizábal. Miami: Universal, 1990. 85–91.

————. "Elena Garro: *Los recuerdos del porvenir* (1963)." *Women Novelists in Spain and Spanish America.* Metuchen, N.J.: Scarecrow Press, 1977. 228–40.

————. "The Meaning of Freedom in the Mexican Feminist Novel." *Sixth Conference of Ethic Studies.* LaCrosse: University of Wisconsin-LaCrosse, 1978.

Frisch, Mark. "Absurdity, Death, and the Search for Meaning in Two of Elena Garro's Novels." *A Different Reality: Studies on the Work of Elena Garro.* Ed. Anita K. Stoll. Lewisburg, Pa.: Bucknell University Press, 1990. 183–93.

Galli, Cristina. "Las formas de la violencia en *Recuerdos del porvenir.*" *Revista Iberoamericana* 56.150 (1990): 213–24.

Gallo, Martha. "Entre el poder y la gloria: Disyuntiva de la identidad femenina en *Los recuerdos del porvenir.*" *Sin imágenes falsas, sin falsos espejos: Narradoras mexicanas del siglo veinte.* Mexico City: Colegio de México, 1995. 149–60.

Galván, Delia V. "*Felipe Angeles* de Elena Garro: Sacrificio heroico." *Latin American Theater Review* 20.2 (1987): 29–35.

————. "Feminism in Elena Garro's Recent Works." *A Different Reality: Studies on the Work of Elena Garro.* Ed. Anita K. Stoll. Lewisburg, Pa.: Bucknell University Press, 1990. 136–46.

————. "Las heroínas de Elena Garro." *La Palabra y el Hombre* (Xalapa) 65 (1988): 145–63.

————. "Multiplicidad de testigos en *Testimonios sobre Mariana* de Elena Garro." *Deslinde* (Monterrey, Mexico) 11.35–36 (1992): 88–92.

————. *Las obras recientes de Elena Garro.* Querétaro, Mexico: Universidad Autónoma de Querétaro, 1988.

————. "El regreso del destierro y la pesquisa de Consuelo en *La casa junto al río* de Elena Garro." *Ensayos de literatura europea e hispanoamericana.* Ed. Félix Menchacatorre. San Sebastián, Spain: Universidad del País Vasco, 1990. 173–78.

García, Kay. "Comunicación y silencio en *Los recuerdos del porvenir* de Elena Garro." *Selecta* 11 (1990): 97–101.

García Barragán, Guadalupe. "El tema del cacique y la cuestión religiosa en *Bramadero* y *Los recuerdos del porvenir.*" Ed. Walter C. Kraft. *Proceedings: Pacific Northwest Conference on Foreign Languages.* Corvallis: Oregon University Press. 310–16.

García Ponce, Juan. "Poesía en voz alta." *Universidad de México* (Mexico City) 11.12 (1957): 29.

Gilabert, Joan. "Función del tiempo y la sensibilidad nostálgica en la autobiografía: *Memorias de España* (1937) por Elena Garro." *Chasqui* 26.1 (1997): 35–44.

Glantz, Margo. "*Andamos huyendo Lola:* El niño y el adulto se vuelven expósitos." *Sábado* (literary supplement to *Unomásuno*; Mexico City) May 23, 1981: 21.

González, José Ramón. "Estrategias discursivas y relato fantástico: Sobre 'La culpa de los tlaxcaltecas' de Elena Garro." *La Torre* (San Juan) 5.20 (1991): 475–88.

González Peña, Carlos. *Historia de la literatura mexicana: Desde los orígenes hasta nuestros días.* Mexico City: Porrúa, 1981. 325.

————. *History of Mexican Literature.* Trans. Gusta Barfield Nance and Florence Johnson Dunstan. Dallas: Southern Methodist University Press, 1968. 455.

Guillén, Pedro. "Cultura en México." *Revista Mexicana de Cultura* [Mexico City] 882 February 23, 1964: 2.

Gutiérrez de Velasco, Luzelena. "'El regreso a la otra niña que fui' en la narrativa de Elena Garro." *Escribir la infancia: Narradoras mexicanas contemporáneas.* Eds. Nora Pasternac, Ana Rosa Domenella, and Luzelena Gutiérrez de Velasco. Mexico City: Colegio de México, 1996. 109–25.

Hardin, Michael. "Inscribing and Incorporating the Marginal: (P)Recreating the Female Artist in Elena Garro's *Recollections of Things to Come*" *Hispanic Journal* 16.1 (1995): 147–59.

Johnson, Harvey L. "Elena Garro's Attitudes Toward Mexican Society." *South Central Bulletin* 40.4 (1980): 150–52.

————. "Elena Garro y el teatro de lo absurdo." *El teatro de Iberoamérica.* Mexico City: Instituto Internacional de Literatura Iberoamericana, 1966. 123–25.

————. "Papel de la mujer en la obra teatral de seis escritoras mexicanas." *Actas del Sexto Congreso Internacional de Hispanistas* (August 22–26, 1977). Eds. Alan M. Gordon and Evelyn Rugg. Toronto: Department of Spanish and Portuguese, University of Toronto, 1980. 443–45.

Jones, Julie. "Text and Authority in Elena Garro's *Reencuentro de personajes.*" *Canadian Review of Comparative Literature/ Revue Canadienne de Literature Comparee* (Edmonton, Canada) 18.1 (1991): 41–50.

Kaminsky, Amy. "Residual Authority and Gendered Resistance." *Critical Theory, Cultural Politics, and Latin American Narrative*. Eds. Steven M. Bell, Albert H. LeMay, and Leonard Orr. Notre Dame, Ind.: University of Notre Dame Press, 1993. 103–21.

Knapp, Bettina. "Elena Garro's *Recollections of Things to Come*: 'Exiles from Happiness.'" *Confluencia* 5.2 (1990): 69–77.

Landeros, Carlos. "Con Elena Garro." *Diorama de la Cultura*: (literary supplement to Excelsior; Mexico City) October 24, 1965: 3+.

———. "Con los recuerdos de Elena Garro." *El Día* April 9, 1964: 9.

Langford, Walter. *The Mexican Novel Comes of Age*. Notre Dame, Ind.: University of Notre Dame Press, 1971. 187–88.

Larson, Catherine. "The Dynamics of Conflict in *¿Qué hora es?* and *El duende*." *A Different Reality: Studies on the Work of Elena Garro*. Ed. Anita K. Stoll. Lewisburg, Pa.: Bucknell University Press, 1990. 102–16.

———. "Lope de Vega and Elena Garro: The Doubling of *La dama boba*." *Hispania* 74.1 (1991): 15–25.

———. "Recollection of Plays to Come: Time in the Theater of Elena Garro." *Latin American Theater Review* 22.2 (1989): 5–17.

Larson, Ross. *Fantasy and Imagination in the Mexican Narrative*. Tempe: Center for Latin American Studies, Arizona State University, 1977. 98–100.

Lemaitre, Monique J. "El deseo de la muerte y la muerte del deseo en la obra de Elena Garro: Hacia una definición de la escritura femenina en su obra." *Revista Iberoamericana* 55. 148–49 (1989): 1005–17.

León Vega, Margarita. "La experiencia del tiempo y del espacio en la novelística de Elena Garro." *Actas Irvine-92, Asociación Internacional de Hispanistas*. Vol. 2: *La mujer y su representación en las literaturas hispánicas*. Irvine: University of California Press, 1994. 205–11.

Lerín, Manuel. "Relatos desquiciantes." *Revista Mexicana de Cultura* (Mexico City) 926 December 27, 1964: 15.

Llarena, E. "Elena Garro: *La semana de colores*." *El Rehilete* 13 (1965): 61.

———. "*Recuerdos del porvenir*." *El Rehilete* 10 (1964): 49

———. *Teatro mexicano del siglo veinte*. Mexico City: Fondo de Cultura Económica, 1970. 57.

Maíz, Magdalena. "Una aproximación al paisaje cotidiano: Narrativa femenina mexicana." *Cuadernos de Aldeeu* 1.2–3 (1983): 347–54.

Marx, Joan. "The Parsifal Motif in *Testimonios sobre Mariana*: Development of a 'Mythological Novel.'" *A Different Reality: Studies on the Work of Elena Garro*. Ed. Anita K. Stoll. Lewisburg, Pa.: Bucknell University Press, 1990. 170–82.

McMahon, Dorothy. "Changing Trends in Spanish American Literature." *Books Abroad* 39.1 (1965): 15–20.

Méndez Ródenas, Adriana. "Tiempo femenino, tiempo ficticio: *Los recuerdos del porvenir* de Elena Garro." *Revista Iberoamericana* 51.132–33 (1985): 843–51.

Mendoza, María Luisa. "Naranja dulce y limón partido en el Teatro, de Elena Garro." *El Día* July 21, 1963: 4.

————. "El porvenir de los recuerdos." *El Día* January 13, 1964: 8.

Menton, Seymour. "Sin embargo: La nueva cuentista femenina en México." *Tinta* 1.5 (1987): 35–37.

Mercado, Enrique. "Elena Garro: Los fantasmas de la realidad, de la imaginación alegórica a la cotidianidad de la prosa." *La Cultura en México* (Mexico City) June 24, 1981: 2–7.

Meyer, Doris. "Alienation and Escape in Elena Garro's *La semana de colores*." *Hispanic Review* 55.2 (1987): 153–64.

Miller, Beth, and Alfonso González, eds. "Elena Garro." *Veintiséis autoras del México actual*. Mexico City: Costa-Amic, 1978. 199–219.

Mora, Gabriela. "*La dama boba* de Elena Garro: Verdad y ficción, teatro y metateatro." *Latin American Theater Review* 16.12 (1983): 15–22.

————. "*Los perros* y *La mudanza* de Elena Garro: Diseño social y virtualidad feminista." *Latin American Theater Review* 8.2 (1975): 5–14.

————. "Rebeldes fracasadas: Una lectura feminista de *Andarse por las ramas* y *La señora en su balcón*." *Plaza: Literatura y Crítica* 5–6 (1981–82): 115–31.

————. "A Thematic Exploration of the Works of Elena Garro." *Latin American Women Writers: Yesterday and Today*. Eds. Yvette E. Miller and Charles M. Tatum. Pittsburgh: Carnegie-Mellon, 1975. 91–97.

Mora, Juan Miguel. *Panorama del teatro en México*. Mexico City: Latinoamericana, 1970.

Mosier, Patricia M. "Protagonista y lector como detectives: Punto de vista en *La casa junto al río*." *Texto Crítico* (Xalapa) 13.36–37 (1987): 92–105.

Muncy, Michele. "The Author Speaks . . ." *A Different Reality: Studies on the Work of Elena Garro*. Ed. Anita K. Stoll. Lewisburg, Pa.: Bucknell University Press, 1990. 23–37.

————. "Elena Garro and the Narrative of Cruelty." *A Different Reality: Studies on the Work of Elena Garro*. Ed. Anita K. Stoll. Lewisburg, Pa.: Bucknell University Press, 1990. 147–58.

————. "Encuentro con Elena Garro." *Hispanic Journal* 7.2 (1986): 65–71.

Neglia, Erminio G. "La escenificación del fluir psíquico en el teatro hispanoamericano." *Hispania* 58 (1978): 884–89.

Ocampo de Gómez, Aurora M., and Ernesto Prado Velázquez. *Diccionario de escritores mexicanos*. Mexico City: Universidad Nacional Autónoma de México, 1967. 135–37.

Orenstein, Gloria. "Surrealism and Women: The Occultation of the Goddess: Elena Garro, Joyce Mansour, Leonora Carrington." *The Theater of the Marvelous Surrealism and the Contemporary Stage*. New York: New York University Press, 1975. 99–147.

Ostergaard, Ane-Grethe. "El realismo de los signos escénicos en el teatro de Elena Garro." *Latin American Theater Review* 16.1 (1982): 53–65.

Oviedo, José Miguel. "Notas a una (deprimente) lectura del teatro hispanoamericano." *Revista Iberoamericana* 37.76–77 (1971): 753–62.

Paley-Francescato, Martha. "Acción y reflexión en cuentos de Fuentes, Garro, y Pacheco." *Romance Quaterly* 33.1 (1986): 99–112.

Pertusa, Inmaculada. "Una aproximación a las realidades mágicas propuestas en el teatro de Elena Garro." *Explicación de Textos Literarios* 25.1 (1996–97): 105–15.

Piazza, Luis Guillermo. "México y el tiempo en tres novelas muy recientes." *Cuadernos del Congreso por la Libertad de la Cultura* 84 (1966): 108.

Portal, Marta. "Elena Garro." *Proceso narrativo de la revolución mexicana.* Madrid: Cultura Hispánica, 1977. 223–32.

Quemain, Miguel Angel. "La magia del espacio: Elena Garro." *Quimera* (Barcelona) 123 (1994): 26–27.

————. "El porvenir: Una repetición inanimada del pasado." *Reverso de la palabra.* Mexico City: El Nacional, 1996. 275–87.

Radchick, Laura. "Las memorias de Cronos en las manecillas de Dios." *Plural: Excelsior* (Mexico City) 204 (1988): 82–85.

"*Los recuerdos del porvenir.*" *Boletín del Centro Mexicano de Escritores* 11.2 (1964): 3.

Resnick, Margery, and Isabelle de Courtivron. *Women Writers in Translation: An Annotated Bibliography.* New York: Garland, 1984. 235.

Reyes, Mara. "Diograma teatral." *Diorama de la Cultura:* (literary supplement to Excelsior; Mexico City) April 28, 1963: 7.

Reyes Nevares, Salvador. "*Un hogar sólido.*" *México en la Cultura* (Mexico City) 517 February 8, 1959: 2.

————. "*Un hogar sólido de Elena Garro.*" *México en la Cultura* (Mexico City) 521 March 8, 1959: 2.

————. "El saldo de la novela: 1963." *La Cultura en México* (Mexico City) 99 January 8, 1964: 3.

Robles, Martha. "Tres mujeres en la literatura mexicana: Rosario Castellanos, Elena Garro, Inés Arredondo." *Cuadernos Americanos* (Mexico City) 246.1 (1983): 223–35.

Rojas-Trempe, Lady. "La alteridad indígena y mágica en la narrativa de Elena Garro, Manuel Scorza y Gioconda Belli." *Alba de América* 9.16–17 (1991): 141–52.

————. "El autorretrato de Elena Garro." *Alba de América* 9.16–17 (1991): 163–80.

————. "El brujo en *La semana de colores* de Elena Garro." *Mitos en Hispanoamérica: Interpretación y literatura.* Ed. Lucía Fox-Lockert. East Lansing, Mich.: Nueva Crónica, 1989.

————. "Dos escritores mexicanos dialogan sobre su teatro." *Alba de América* 8.14–15 (1990): 373–78.

————. "Elena Garro dialoga sobre su teatro con Guillermo Schmidhuber: Entrevista." *Revista Iberoamericana* 55.148–49 (1989): 685–90.

————. "El estado en *Las cabezas bien pensantes* de Elena Garro." *Revista Canadiense de Estudios Hispánicos* (Ottawa) 14.3 (1990): 597–605.

————. "Ex-patria-ción, locura y escritura en los cuentos de Elena Garro." *Escritos* (Puebla, Mexico) 8 (1992): 61–83.

————. "Historia narrativa de la conquista de los indígenas mexicanos: Elena Garro." *Literatura Mexicana* 3.1 (1992): 157–68.

————. "Las peripecias de la mirada del zapaterito de Guanajuato." *Alba de América* 11.20–21 (1993): 303–10.

————. "La ronda mágica y la palabra del deseo." *Lenguas, Literaturas, Sociedades: Cuadernos Hispánicos* 3 (1990): 137–48.

————. "Teatralización en la memoria de Elena Garro." Crítica de Teatro Latinoamericano 1 (1989): 135–41.

Rosas, Patricia. "Destiempo y nostalgia, Elena Garro y Los recuerdos del porvenir." Semana de Bellas Artes (Mexico City) October 29, 1980: 10–12.

Rosas Lopategui, Patricia. "Los espacios poéticos y apoéticos en Los recuerdos del porvenir de Elena Garro." Hispanic Journal 16.1 (1995): 95–108.

————. "El exilio y el baúl en Testimonios sobre Mariana: Una perspectiva psicoanalítica." Alba de América 9.16–17 (1991): 121–40.

————. "Un hogar sólido: Pieza existencial para un público mexicano." Alba de América 7.12–13 (1989): 221–31.

Rosas Lopategui, Patricia, and James Casey Reed. "El baúl receptáculo de la vida subconsciente y vehículo de la emancipación femenina en Testimonios sobre Mariana." La nueva mujer en la escritura de autoras hispánicas: Ensayos críticos. Eds. Juana A. Arancibia and Yolanda Rosas. Montevideo: Instituto Literario y Cultural Hispánico, 1995. 67–78.

Rosas Lopategui, Patricia, and Rhina Toruño. "Entrevista a Elena Garro." Hispamérica 20.60 (1991): 55–71.

Roses, Lorraine. "La expresión dramática de la inconformidad social en cuatro dramaturgas hispanoamericanas." Plaza: Literatura y Crítica 5–6 (1981–82): 97–114.

Rosser, Harry L. "Form and Content in Elena Garro's Los recuerdos del porvenir." Revista Canadiense de Estudios Hispánicos (Ottawa) 2 (1978): 181–95.

————. "Regional Reactions to Incursions from the Center: Yáñez, Garro, Mojarro." Conflict and Transition in Rural Mexico. Boston: Crossroads Press, 1980. 23–46.

Rubio de Lertora, Patricia. "Funciones del nivel descriptivo en Los recuerdos del porvenir." Cahiers du Monde Hispanique et Luso-Bresilien: Caravelle (Toulouse, France) 49 (1987): 129–38.

Salazar, Carmen. "In Illo Tempore. Elena Garro's La semana de colores." In Retrospect: Essays on Latin American Literature. Eds. Elizabeth S. Rogers and Timothy J.Rogers. York: Spanish Literature, 1987. 121–27.

San Pedro, Teresa Anta. "El acto de nombrar en el cuento de Elena Garro El día que fuimos perros." Explicación de Textos Literarios 19 1 (1990–91): 17–26.

————. "La caída de los 'dioses' en el cuento de Elena Garro 'El día que fuimos perros'." Monographic Review/Revista Monográfica 4 (1988): 116–26.

————. "El poder destructor de la palabra en la novela de Elena Garro Los recuerdos del porvenir." Explicación de Textos Literarios 23.1 (1994–95): 43–56.

————. "Suicida, fraticida, deicida, mujer en el cuento de Elena Garro 'El árbol.'" Narrativa hispanoamericana contemporánea: Entre la vanguardia y el posboom. Ed. Ana María Hernández de López. Madrid: Pliegos, 1996. 57–70.

Seligson, Esther. "In illo tempore (Aproximación a la obra de Elena Garro)." Revista de la Universidad de México (Mexico City) 29.12 (1975): 9–10.

"La semana de colores." Boletín Bibliográfico de la Secretaría de Hacienda y Crédito Público 311 January 15, 1965: 20–21.

Solórzano, Carlos. "El teatro de Elena Garro: Una nueva frescura literaria." *La Cultura en México* (Mexico City) 167 April 28, 1965: 18–19.

Sommers, Joseph. "*Los recuerdos del porvenir.*" *Books Abroad* 39.1 (1965): 68–69.

Stoll, Anita K. "*La casa junto al río* as Mythic Pattern for Growth and Change." *A Different Reality: Essays on the Works of Elena Garro.* Ed. Anita K. Stoll. Lewisburg, Pa.: Bucknell University Press, 1990. 159–69.

———. "*La casa junto al río* de Elena Garro y el gótico femenino." *Actas del Congreso de la Asociación de Hispanistas, 1–4.* Ed. Antonio Vilanova. Barcelona: Promociones y Publicaciones Universitarias, 1992. 1011–16.

———. "Elena Garro's /Lope de Vega's *La dama boba*: Seventeenth-Century Inspiration for a Twentieth-Century Dramatist." *Latin American Theater Review* 23.2 (1990): 21–31.

———. "The Old World Versus the New: Cultural Conflict in Four Works of Elena Garro." *Letras Peninsulares* 5.1 (1992): 95–106.

———, ed. *A Different Reality: Essays on the Works of Elena Garro.* Lewisburg, Pa.: Bucknell University Press, 1990.

Toruño, Rhina. "Del realismo mágico de *Los recuerdos del porvenir* al realismo social de *Y Matarazo no llamó.*" *Deslinde* 12.46–47 (1995): 36–39.

———. "*Un hogar sólido* by Elena Garro." *Latin American Theater Review* 2.1 (1968): 77.

———. "Protesta contra la opresión: Categorías medulares en la obra narrativa y dramática de Elena Garro." *Deslinde* 11.35–36 (1992): 93–95.

———. "*Reencuentro de personajes* de Elena Garro." *Sábado* (supplement to *Unomásuno*; Mexico City) August 2, 1997, 1035: 1–3.

———. "Sobre la vida desgarradora de Elena Garro." *Co-Latino Tres Mil: Cultural Supplement* (El Salvador) October 26, 1996: 6–7.

———. *Tiempo, destino, y, opresión en la obra de Elena Garro.* Lewiston, N.Y.: Mellen University Press, 1996.

———. "*Y Matarazo no llamó* . . . : Novela política y la última escrita por Elena Garro." *Boletín Letras Informa* 2.6 (1994): 9–14.

Umanzor, Marta A. *La visión de la mujer en la obra de Elena Garro: El árbol, Los recuerdos del porvenir, Testimonios sobre Mariana y La casa junto al río.* Miami: Universal, 1996.

Unruh, Vicky. "(Free)/Plays of Difference: Language and Eccentricity in Elena Garro's Theater." *A Different Reality: Studies on the Work of Elena Garro.* Ed. Anita K. Stoll. Lewisburg, Pa.: Bucknell University Press, 1990. 38–58.

Vázquez Amaral, José. "La novela de Luisa Josefina Hernández, Carlos Fuentes y Elena Garro." *El Gallo Illustrado* (Mexico City) 191 (1966): 2–3.

Vega, Hector Zetina. "Traducir la obra de Elena Garro a otras lenguas es ya una necesidad: Rhina Toruño." *Sol de Cuernavaca* July 13, 1997: 5D.

———. "Vida y obra de Elena Garro van profundamente entrelazadas: Entrevista con Rhina Toruño." *Sol de Cuernavaca* July 20, 1997: 5D.

Verwey, Antonieta Eva. *Mito y palabra poética en Elena Garro.* Mexico City: Universidad Autónoma de Querétaro, 1982.

Villaseñor, Raúl. "Libros." *Vida Universitaria* January 26, 1964: 7.

Winkler, Julie A. "Insiders, Outsiders, and the Slippery Center: Marginality in *Los recuerdos del porvenir.*" *Indiana Journal of Hispanic Literatures* 8 (1996): 177–95.

Woodyard, George. "The Theater of the Absurd in Spanish America." *Comparative Drama* 3.3 (1969): 183–92.

Zamora, Lois Parkinson. "The Animated Earth: American Books of the Dead by William Goyen, Elena Garro, and Juan Rulfo." *Mid-American Review* 13.1 (1992): 62–86.

Zendejas, Francisco. "El premio Villaurrutia de literatura." *Diorama de la Cultura* (literary supplement to *Excelsior*; Mexico City) March 1, 1964: 7.

Angélica Gorodischer

A short-story writer, novelist, and essayist, Angélica Gorodischer is the author of ten novels and several collections of short stories, but she is best known for her science fiction. She was born in 1928 in Buenos Aires and spent her early childhood immersed in books, which proved fundamental to her artistic development and her perception of the world. After studying at the University of Buenos Aires she moved to the city of Rosario, where she is a prominent cultural figure and activist. Gorodischer's first literary endeavor was a detective story titled "En verano a la siesta y con Martina" (In the summer, in the siesta, and with Martina). It appeared in the magazine *Vea y lea* (See and read) in 1964 and won her an award in the III Contest of Detective Short Stories.

Although she had a late start, her literary career has been steady and fruitful. She has cultivated a variety of narrative expressions, including several fabulous science fiction stories about the intergalactic adventures of a businessman named Trafalgar Medrano who converses with writers in cafes in Rosario, Argentina.

In 1973 Gorodischer's publication of the volume *Bajo las jubeas en flor* (Under the yubayas in bloom) marked a high point in her career. Its story titled "Los embriones de violeta" (The embryos of Violet) is considered the best Argentinian science fiction story of all time. This collection shows Gorodischer's brilliant mastery of stylistic complexities, as well as her extraordinary imagination, in presenting the reader a strange world in a familiar, everyday manner. A strongly developed sense of humor and vivid imagination characterize her short stories.

Gorodischer revealed her militant feminist side with the publication of *Mala noche y parir hembra* (Bad night and female birth, 1983), the most original, humorous, and complex narrative she has written to date.

Under the Yubayas in Bloom

I entered Sweet Memory of the Yubayas in Bloom Penitentiary an hour after having reached land. As I was the captain of the ship, they reserved for me the most rigorous punishment: they took my men to another prison, whose regimen was more benign, according to what I was given to understand, and I never saw them again. It was not that we had committed some terrible crime in disembarking there; it was not that they considered all foreigners dangerous outlaws. It was much simpler and, to use the appropriate word, more infernal.

Sweet Memory of the Yubayas in Bloom was an enormous, irregular building which rose up in the middle of a saltpeter plain. When the sun was high you couldn't look out because the reflection burned your eyes. I never got to know the entire establishment, and I can't say it was for lack of time. But it was a completely stupid building, of wood and stone: construction seemed to have been started in the central patio, which was paved with stones and surrounded with cells. Sitting in a corner, looking at it, I supposed that later they had built the other pavilions, one above the other, or touching at the vertices, or interconnecting, and that the old cells had been converted into offices and storage rooms. The result was a confusion of constructions of different shapes and sizes, put up in any way, in any place, and all highly disheartening. There were windows that opened onto other windows, stairways in the middle of a bathroom, passageways that led to a blind wall, galleries that at one time, perhaps, had dominated a space which later was outfitted with banisters and guardrails, doors that didn't open or that opened onto a wall, cupolas that had been converted into rooms one had to enter doubled over, contiguous rooms that adjoined in only a roundabout way.

But I am getting ahead of events. I had scarcely stepped foot on land when they arrested me, read me a long memorandum in which the charges were expounded, and took me to Sweet Memory of the Yubayas in Bloom. No one wanted to answer my questions as to the rest of the crew, as to whether there would be a trial, as to whether there could be a defense. No one wanted to listen to my explanations. I was simply taken prisoner. The iron gate at the entrance was lifted to let us pass, and my guardians handed me over to the Director of the prison, after a reading of the same memorandum. The Director said, "Aha!" and looked at me, I think, with scorn; no, no I don't think, I am certain. He pushed a button and two uniformed guards entered, with whips in their hands and pistols in their belts. The Director said take him away, and they took me away. It was that simple. They put me in a little room and told me to undress. I thought they were going to strike me, but I undressed anyway. What choice did I have? They did not strike me, however. After searching my clothes and taking my papers, pencil, handkerchief, watch, money, and everything, absolutely everything they found, they examined my mouth, ears, hair, navel, armpits, crotch, smiling, gesturing approvingly, and commenting favorably on the size, shape, and possibilities of my genitals. They laid me out on the floor, none too gently, spread my buttocks and toes, and again made me open my mouth. Finally they left off and held out pants and a shirt and nothing else and said, get dressed. "What about my clothes?" I asked. They threw everything in a corner, the money as well as the documents, and shrugged their shoulders. Let's go, they said. That was the first time I lost my bearings in the building. Not they: they made their way surefooted like elephants, slamming doors and navigating passageways in all tranquility. We ended up on the patio and there they left me.

Barefoot on the uneven paving stones, hurting everywhere but especially in the depths of my dignity, with a weight in my gut and another in my spirit, I looked at what there was to look at. There was an oval patio, enormous like an amphitheater and populated by groups of men dressed as I was. They too were looking at me. And now what do I do? I thought, and remembered beatings, tar and feathers, and worse things reserved for the initiate, and there I was barehanded. Against so many, I wouldn't have a chance. They left me alone only for a while. I tried to look like a hardened criminal, but I was riddled with fear. Finally one moved away from the others and came toward me: very young, with curly hair and his face swollen on the left side.

"One of my most ardent desires at this time," he said, "along with freedom and the forgiveness of my elders, is for your god to grant you many happy and peaceful hours, sire."

I should have answered, but I could not. At first I was dumbfounded, then I thought that this was the prologue to a cruel collective joke, and then that he was a homosexual with a curious way of insinuating himself. And then, no. The young man smiled and extended a welcoming arm.

"The Ancient Master sent me to ask if you would like to join us."

"Delighted," I said and started to walk.

But the young man remained planted there and clapped his hands.

"Did you hear?" he shouted at the top of his lungs to the prisoners in the enormous patio, "Did you hear? The foreign gentleman is delighted to join us!"

Here, I thought, is where the trouble starts. Again I was wrong; before long that would be the norm. After nodding their heads approvingly, the others paid us no further attention, and the young man took my arm and led me to the farthest corner of the patio.

We approached an ancient old man surrounded by ten or twelve men.

"They sent me," said the young man, speaking with difficulty, "because I am the youngest and can be expected to be indiscreet enough to ask anything of anyone, no matter how illustrious he may be."

Here's something, I concluded. At least I know that one mustn't go around asking about things.

"Welcome, worthy sire." The ancient old man had lifted his wrinkled face and toothless mouth, and spoke to me in a contralto. "Your god, from what I see, has accompanied you to this remote place."

I confess that I looked around, searching for my god.

Those who were squatting rose and made room for me. When they again crouched down, the kid waited until I followed suit and only then took his place.

Apparently I hadn't interrupted anything for they were all silent and remained so for a while. I wondered if they were waiting for me to say something, but what could I say if all that came to mind were questions and I was already aware that that wasn't done.

The ancient old man promptly said that the kind stranger must surely be hungry, and since I was the kind stranger I realized that the weight in my stomach was, in effect, hunger. The weight in my spirit, no, that didn't go away until I left Sweet Memory of the Yubayas in Bloom and not even then, completely. I said yes, that I was hungry but that I didn't want to bother anyone and only wished to know at what time meals were served. I hoped that I had spoken in accordance with their style and that that last hadn't sounded like a question. The ancient old man assented and said to no one in particular: "Bring something to restore the strength of the kind gentleman and companion, if already we may so refer to him."

Imitating as much as possible the head shaking of the others, I assented with a half-smile. My calves were hurting, but I remained squatting.

One of the group rose and left.

The ancient old man said, "Carry on."

And one of the squatting men began to speak, as though he were continuing a recently interrupted conversation.

"In my opinion, there are two types of numbers: those that serve to measure reality and those that serve to interpret the universe. These last need no connection to reality because they are not composed of units but of meanings."

Two others spoke at the same time:

"Superficially it may appear that there are only two classes of numbers. But I believe that there is an infinity of classes," said one.

"The number as such does not exist, but may be represented. But we must take into account that the representation of a thing is not the thing but that thing's void," said the other.

The ancient old man raised a hand and said that they couldn't keep talking if such confusion was to be the result. And while I tried to guess what was expected of me, if I should say something or not, and what that something might be, the one who had gone to get my food returned and I ate.

In a wooden bowl there was a bright red dumpling floating in a thick broth. With a spoon, also made of wood, I brought to my mouth something with a light seafood flavor, like well-done shellfish in a mild sauce that leaves a sour aftertaste. By the second mouthful it seemed tempting, and by the third, exquisite. By the time I realized that they were "solomantide" embryos cooked in their juice, I had already been eating them a good while and liked them and didn't care. The first day I scraped the bowl clean, and afterwards they brought me water. I was satisfied, very satisfied, and wondered whether or not I should belch. The tension between physical pressure and timidity resolved itself and since everyone smiled at me, I stayed calm. Already my feet had fallen asleep and were numb and my elbows were digging into my muscles, but still I held out. And they kept on talking about numbers. When someone said that numbers not only did not exist but did not exist as representations either, and moreover that they didn't exist in the absolute, another joined in to cast doubt on the existence of all representation, and from there the existence of all things, all beings, and the universe itself. I was sure that I at least existed. And then it began to get dark and turn cold. However, no one moved until the ancient old man said the day had ended, just as though he were God the Father, which made me remember my personal god, and I began to wonder where he had taken himself off to.

The ancient old man rose and so did the others and so did I. The other groups began to do the same. It was cold and my body ached. We walked slowly towards a door and went through. For the second time I lost my bearings. We went quite a way inside the building, passing through more complicated places, until we reached a large room with windows on one side, windows that at least looked out on an open space from which you could see the sky if you looked up, because on the other shorter wall—I don't know if I said that it was a vaguely hexagonal room—there were windows that looked out on a stone wall. There were mattresses on the floor, a large stove on one side, and doors, including one in a corner. The ancient old man pointed out a place and informed me that I would bed down there after washing. We washed in basins affixed to the floor and evacuated into holes beneath which you could hear water running. And upon returning, as when I discovered I was hungry, I discovered I was sleepy and decided to put off the problem of my future—which is to say my legal situation and my chances for escape—until the following day. But attentive as I was to the prisoners' customs, I waited to see what the others were doing, and the others were waiting for the ancient old man to lie down. Which unexpectedly he did on the floorboards and not on a larger or softer mattress that I had tried in vain to identify. Others also lay down and I did the same.

But it wasn't so easy to sleep. I was just about to drop off when again I had to resign myself to waiting, because all the others seemed to be talking at once. It occurred to me that they would be talking about me, understandably enough, and I surreptitiously opened my eyes for a look at their faces and again I was wrong. Like me, two others were stretched out and appeared to be sleeping. But the others were debating a difficult question, with the ancient old man as arbiter. After a while one of the men asked the ancient old man to pick three men because that night there were many. Many what, I thought, three what. I closed my eyes. When I opened them the ancient old man had picked three prisoners who silently undressed. I watched, careless of whether or not they saw me. One of the three was the kid with the swollen face. The others looked at the three nude men, touched them, and seemed to decide on one whom they set apart, in an orderly way, with neither haste nor anxiety, and I saw how they lay him down, how they took their pleasure and then moved back to give the next one a turn. The three allowed themselves to be done to with their eyes closed, with neither protest nor ecstasy, and the ancient old man remained stretched out on the wooden floor. When all were satisfied, each one lay down on his mattress, and the kid and the other two went into the bath; through the door I could hear water running. I fell asleep.

The next day I was awakened by shouting. Not the prisoners, of course, but the guards. They stood in the corner door, whips in their hands, pistols in their belts, screaming insults, *up you filthy garbage mongers you sons of bitches*, but they neither entered nor approached. The men got up, slapping on their clothes, it was hot there because the heat from the stove was trapped in the wood and stone, and many slept nude. I also got up. The guards left and we went off for ablutions and the ceremonies of the bath. I would have given anything for a cup of coffee, but led by the ancient old man we went to the patio, to the same spot we had been the day before. Everyone squatted around the ancient old man, and I decided to see what would happen if I sat cross-legged. Nothing happened, and so I remained, dreaming of a warm breakfast.

Before the ancient old man could say "carry on"—I would have bet anything he was about to say it—a man from another group approached and all the faces of our group, including my own, were lifted to look at him.

"May the new day be full of happy hours, meditation, and rest," said the newcomer.

The ancient old man smiled and said to someone: "Invite the kind companion to join us."

One of ours said: "We would be extremely pleased if you would agree to join us, kind companion."

The other answered, "I only come as I am sent by my Master, who requests permission of the Ancient Master that one of us, anxious to expand his vision of the world's wisdom, might spend several hours with all of you, understood of course that we will provide for his dietary and hygienic needs."

"Tell your kind companion," said the Ancient Master, "that we will be pleased for him to do so."

The man from our group who had spoken before repeated the message and the other man left, and in a little while the guest arrived and again an incomprehensible conversation about numbers began. I tried to understand a little, but it all seemed either very stupid or very profound, and besides, I was hungry.

I started to think about my problem—not hunger, which could wait— but how to get out of there. It was very clear that I would have to ask how to get an interview with the Director, but I didn't feel encouraged to ask questions because of what the kid with the swollen face had said. And thinking of him, two questions occurred to me. First, what had happened in the dormitory the night before. And second, how to make him my ally and have him help me when the chance arose. I glanced around but didn't see him. I turned halfway around and found him squatting to my right, a little behind me, nearly grazing me. Splendid, I said to myself, and waited for one of the frequent silences in the talk about numbers. When the others fell quiet, I turned, trying not to think of him crushed nude beneath the other men in the dormitory, and said to him:

"Something should be done about that tooth of yours."

He smiled at me as he had the day before, as though nothing had happened, and replied that his god would determine when the pain should end. I decided to pursue it. I answered that I could see that his god had determined that his pain should end, because I was the instrument designated to end it. He looked at me uncomprehendingly and I was afraid I had made a mistake. But within seconds his eyes were shining and it was plain that he had started out of happiness.

"All you have to do," I said, "is get me some tongs."

He nodded and went to kneel before the Ancient Master. There was a long conversation in which the kid asked permission and gave his reasons, and the ancient old man agreed and gave permission. The kid left, the guest looked at me in astonishment, as though I were a three-headed monster, and the disquisition on numbers or whatever came to a complete stop. I was still hungry and the Ancient Master began a parable.

"In faraway times," he started to recount, "there was a poor man who carved figures in order to subsist. But few bought them and with each one the carver grew poorer, so that each time the figures were less beautiful and less like the model. When the carver had gone some days without eating, the figures that came from his hands were frightful and no longer resembled anything. Then his god took pity on him and determined to make him such a prodigy that people would come from everywhere to behold him. And so he made the carved figures come to life. The carver was very frightened to see this, but then he thought: *The curious and the learned and people from faraway lands will come to see such a prodigy and I will be rich and powerful.* The beautiful figures carved in the days of poverty, but before the days of hunger, smiled and greeted him. But the monstrous figures threatened and grimaced at him meanly. The last one he had carved crawled toward him on its shapeless limbs, to devour him. Terrified, the carver begged for mercy in such a voice that again his god took pity on him and reduced the monstrous figures to ashes, keeping only the beautiful ones alive. And among these the carver discovered a most beautiful woman, whom he married and with whom he was happy for a time. He also grew rich from exhibiting his animated figures to the curious and the wise. But the woman, although made flesh by the carver's god, had kept her soul of wood, and so pitilessly tormented him for the rest of his life. He often begged, sobbing, that his figures be returned to inanimate life—even though he would lose his riches if he were freed of his wife. But this time his god did not want to listen to him."

I kept thinking about what it meant and what it might have to do with the kid's tooth. Obviously, everyone else had understood because they were smiling and nodding and looking at the Ancient Master and at me, but I couldn't make anything out of it and so I smiled without looking at anyone, and this time I hit it right. Everyone, except my stomach, seemed very happy.

Then the kid returned with the tongs. Wooden ones. Which he offered me. I was going to have to make do with them and I felt sorry for the kid. I took hold of the tongs and told him as gently as I could that in order for the tongs to work as an instrument of his god, I had to know his name. It had been weighing on me that I didn't know the kid's name.

"Which of my names?" he said.

Apparently there were questions that could indeed be asked. But the bad thing was that I didn't know how to answer him.

"The name I must use," came to me.

Again I had figured it right.

"Sadropersi," he said.

For me, he was always Percy.

"All right, Sadropersi, lie down on the floor and open your mouth."

I seemed to have stopped making mistakes and felt sure of myself.

He lay down and opened his mouth, not without first looking toward the Ancient Master, and I gestured to some of the others to hold down his arms, legs, and head. I had a terrible time of it but I pulled the molar. I had to go very slowly, wiggling it from side to side before pulling so as not to break the tongs. It must have hurt him like the tortures of hell. But not once did he move or cry out. Tears ran down his face and blood filled his mouth; I was afraid he'd suffocate on me, and from time to time I raised his head and made him spit. Finally I showed him the molar in the tongs, and they all sighed as though I had pulled a molar from each one of them.

The Ancient Master smiled and told another parable.

"A woman was cooking cakes in hot oil while waiting for her husband. But the oil ran out before all the dough was cooked. She went to one of her neighbors to get some oil, and was refused. She then went to another of her neighbors, who also refused her the oil to finish cooking the dough. Angered, the woman began shouting imprecations in her doorway, arousing the curiosity of passersby, until one of them shouted, 'Make your own oil and stop making a racket!' So the woman went out behind her house and cut the seeds of the zyminia plant, ground and pressed them in a piece of linen, in this way extracting the oil she needed. When her husband arrived, she presented him with two platters of cakes and said, 'These are made with oil bought from the store, and these others with oil I extracted from the zyminia plant.' The husband ate both platters and the cake cooked in the oil extracted by his wife tasted better in his mouth than the others."

Percy smiled more openly than the others, and so did I, nodding. After letting a little time go by, I would be able to ask him how to get to the Director. And while I was thinking of this and of my empty stomach, suddenly it was mealtime. There was no announcement—no bell, no call, no guards with whips, nothing.

But the Ancient Master stood up, and after him all the others, and we went towards one of the doors to the warm interior of the prison. After following the ancient old man through labyrinthine passageways, we reached the large dining room on the first floor. We went up and down so many stairways so many times that if someone had told me I was on the sixth floor, I would have believed it. But from the windows, you could see the ground floor, the eaves and balconies on the other floors, and the white plain beneath the sun. There were a lot of men cooking on stoves set up on the floor, and those of us arriving split up into groups and went towards one or another of the cookstoves. We all squatted around one, and the man cooking gave each of us a wooden bowl with the red broth, and we ate.

I saw that the others were doing what I wanted to do—asking for more—and when I finished my ration I asked for another. I drank a lot of water, and like the day before, was satisfied.

That day slipped by without further incident and the night was calm. Percy seemed happy and looked at me thankfully. There was no other meal during the day, but I wasn't hungry. With the problems of food and Percy's molar taken care of, I had to think about how I would get to the Director and what I would say when I saw him. But I was so tired by the time I lay down, that I fell asleep without planning anything.

The next morning there were the jailers' insults and yelling, which the prisoners took with the same indifference. Afterwards there was conversation on the patio, the meal, more conversation—always about numbers—and another night. I decided that the next day I would talk with Percy. But at that moment I needed something more urgent: I wanted to take a bath. Before we lay down I said to Percy:

"Sadropersi, dear friend." I was trying to learn, or at least imitate, the way the prisoners spoke. "I would like to bathe."

Percy became extremely upset.

"Bathe, sire?" He looked all around. "The gentlemen guards bathe us."

"You don't mean those brutes scrub our back with hair gloves?"

"The esteemed gentlemen guards" (it seemed I shouldn't have called them brutes) "fumigate, disinfect, and bathe the prisoners periodically, dear sire and companion."

"All right," I said. "When is the next fumigation, disinfection, and bath?"

But Percy didn't know. He figured it could be soon because the last session had taken place quite a while ago, and I had to make with ablutions in the washbasins.

That night also was calm and before falling asleep I pitied myself a little. Here I was, a discoverer of worlds, imprisoned in a ridiculous jail with a ridiculous name, among people who spoke in a ridiculous way, humiliated and not victorious, degraded and not exalted. And what could have happened to my ship and my men? And most important: How was I going to get out of there? And on reaching the end of these black thoughts, I fell asleep.

In the bathroom the next day I again took Percy aside and told him I had to see the Director.

"No one gets to see the Director, sire."

I refrained from cursing the Director's mother and Percy's mother at the top of my lungs.

"Tell me, kind Sadropersi, if someone started a riot, wouldn't they take him to see the Director?"

I was asking questions, too many questions, but that wasn't what Percy had picked up on.

"A riot, my fine foreign gentleman and kind companion! No one starts riots."

"I know, of course, that's clear. But in the theoretical and highly improbable case that I started a fight on the patio, wouldn't they take me to the Director to be punished?"

He seemed to be thinking it over.

Finally he said, "No one would fight with you, kind companion."

Damn you, Percy, I thought, and gave him a big smile. "Fine, fine, let's forget the question, it was academic."

He too smiled. "There is much to say in favor of the academies, illustrious sire."

He had called me illustrious—which was an honor—perhaps thinking back to his molar. With his face no longer swollen he was a handsome kid and one could see why they chose him for love. I felt truly upset. As for the enigmatic observation on academies, I let it pass, lest it occur to him to have changed, in my honor, the subject of numbers—to which I was already accustomed—to that of academies, about which I knew nothing. Of course I didn't know anything about numbers either, at least not the way they discussed them.

We sat on the patio until it was time to eat. We ate and returned to the patio, and the Ancient Master told another parable.

"In olden times, men were very poor for they kept losing their possessions, even the smallest and most insignificant, each time they moved from place to place. They brought only their wives and children and relatives, at least those who were able to walk. The very old stayed behind. And all because transport had not yet been invented. Men traveled empty-handed, lamenting the utensils and clothing left in the place they were leaving. But one man who had to move to a distant city had a wife he loved dearly. The woman was ill, unable to walk, and the man wept at the thought that he had to leave her. He went to the bed in which she lay and embraced her so forcefully he lifted her up. Surprised, he took a few steps with the woman in his arms, and then a few more steps, and then walked out of the house carrying the woman, and took to the road. People came out from everywhere to see him go by, and soon everyone understood that it was possible to take from one place to another as many things as one could carry. And then many were seen going from place to place carrying furniture, utensils, clothing, texts, jewelry, and ornaments. This went on a long time, with people traveling in all directions and the roads and byways packed with people showing one another what they were carrying, until everyone got used to it and a man carrying a sack in his arms no longer attracted attention."

Each time the ancient old man told a parable, I honestly tried to understand the meaning. But I never managed to get it. Neither did I get the one about the invention of transport, which seemed stupid to me, even though from time to time I remember it and again wonder if there might not be something important behind it.

That accursed night there was another assembly of men who wanted to fornicate, and I didn't lie down, I stayed with the others and apparently it attracted no one's attention. The Ancient Master again chose Percy and two others, not the same as the last time. The two immediately stripped, but Percy threw himself crying at the Ancient Master's feet begging that he let him be in the other group. Me, I don't know what came over me. I felt sorry for the kid, and it seemed shitty to sacrifice him twice in a row against his wishes, but at the same time I was glad because I desired him, and both things made me ashamed, my desire and my gladness.

The Ancient Master told him in his soft contralto that he was pardoning him because he was too young to distinguish between what was proper and improper, but that he, Percy, already knew that one wasn't allowed to appeal commands and that one had to bend to and obey orders. Percy then stopped crying and said yes, and the ancient old man said that he himself, as a special favor, would ask the others to allow Percy to be the object of their pleasure. At that I hated the old man, but the others seemed to think that what he said was just fine, even Percy, who smiled and said:

"Oh ancient, venerable, and eminent master, I beg you, as a special and undeserved favor, to allow my kind companions their enjoyment of my contemptible person."

The ancient old man allowed the filthy comedy to continue, as if it weren't decided, and Percy had to insist. I backed away, furious, and decided that I wouldn't take part in that business. But when Percy stripped and smiled at us, I drew close to him and carefully stayed behind him so he wouldn't see my face. When it was all over, I fell asleep, serene and sad.

I was already used to the wake-up routine, but that morning it seemed that the guards' insults were directed straight and personally at me. I almost wanted them to come at me with their whips and beat me. Not for having screwed Percy, but for feeling as happy about it as I did. Percy, on the other hand, treated me as he did every day, and I had to force myself to answer him naturally, and to look at him.

I had to distract myself, at any cost, I had to think of something else and feel something else. On the patio, while they were talking about numbers (I heard a good question that morning: Is it possible to construct another universe with different numbers, or to change the universe by changing the numbers?), I again thought about how to get out of there. Escape seemed the only possibility left, if Percy was to be believed, and why not believe him about no one getting to see the Director. But I was still going to try to open my heart to the Ancient Master. However much I despised him for what he had done to Percy, he still seemed to be the most important of the prisoners. I wondered why the ancient old man was there. For having corrupted young boys, surely. But Percy? These, of course, were the questions one wasn't supposed to ask.

After the meal, another man from another group approached to ask if he might greet the illustrious foreigner. I was already twice illustrious. After the customary formalities, the ancient old man gave permission and we exchanged greetings and good wishes. What he wanted, he didn't tell me. When I realized that he had a toothache, I had to tell him that I would look in his mouth. I found a big ugly hole in an upper molar. I told him I would pull it and he pronounced a string of good wishes and inevitably the Ancient Master told a parable.

"Long ago there was a man who had a multicorn with which he plowed his land. Later, when the time was right, he sowed and sat back to watch the tender plants grow, and when the time came he gathered a plentiful harvest. But one fatal day the animal fell ill, and when it wasn't getting better the man decided to kill it and sell its meat and wool, and did so. Then, not having a work animal, he himself pulled the plow to turn the earth, but the work went very slowly and delayed seeding and the harvest, which wasn't as plentiful as before. A neighbor, seeing him during those troubles, said, 'You should have been prudent and waited. The animal probably would have gotten well, and now you wouldn't be exhausted by work and impoverished by the lack of a good harvest.' Realizing that his neighbor was right, the man sat down at the edge of his field, and for a long time he wept and lamented."

What could be clearer? I said to myself. If the man hadn't killed the animal, two things could have happened. Either it would have gotten better, in which case it could have continued working the land with him, or it would have died, in which case he would have had to sell the meat and wool anyway. But apart from a superficial condemnation of hastiness, I didn't see what was so important there to arouse everyone's veneration. I let the question drop because the imminent tooth-pulling had made me the subject of discussion, and the ancient old man was explaining to my patient the crime I had committed.

"The honorable foreign gentleman disembarked on our land without first signaling with his ship lights and without turning three times in place," he said.

I felt obligated to defend myself on seeing the painful way the man with the decayed tooth was looking at me.

"In the first place," I said, "I didn't know that this land was inhabited. And in the second place, even if I had known, how could I have been acquainted with the protocol requiring lights and turns in place? What is more, no one brought me before a judge, nor allowed me to defend myself, which in my country would be considered a sure sign of barbarism."

Everyone was very serious and the Ancient Master told me that nature is everywhere the same—something with which I could agree or not, but which didn't enter into the case—and that pleading ignorance of a law didn't excuse one from not complying with it. I didn't punch him in the nose because Percy arrived with the wooden tongs, which permitted me to think a little and remember that I needed the old man's benevolence. Again I talked about names, which of my names, the one I would have to use, and the man with the decayed tooth told me he was named Sematrodio. I made him lie down and again went to work. It was harder than with Percy because the man's rotten molar was more firmly rooted, but in compensation there was less blood. Once more I had a rousing success and once more I was illustrious.

Luckily, that day there were no more parables, but at night the Ancient Master called me to him and after showering me with praise told me that perhaps my sentence would be short in view of my being a foreigner from a distant land—at the most, twenty years. I think I almost fainted. Twenty years! I'm sure I closed my eyes and slumped towards the floor.

"I understand your feelings," the ancient old man told me, "I will probably die here, since I have been accused, in all fairness, of improperly using two qualifying adjectives: two, you realize, during an official banquet." He sighed. "So, honorable foreigner and friend, I want to give you a souvenir to take back to your distant lands when you return to them."

From under his shirt he brought forth a pile of papers tied with string. I could think of only one thing: twenty years, twenty years, twenty years!

"This," the ancient old man was telling me, and I forced myself to listen, "is a copy of the *Code of What Is and Canon of Appearances*. Keep it, illustrious foreign gentleman, read it and meditate on it; I know it will provide you consolation, enlightenment, and support."

I took the papers. Twenty years, how was it possible? Twenty years! The ancient old man turned and closed his eyes, and I left and lay down, but slept little that night.

At dawn, in an effort to forget about the twenty years—a thought which kept me from planning an escape, or finding a way to see the Director, or doing anything that would get me out of there, let me search for my crew, get to my ship —I took out the Code and started leafing through it in the brilliant light that was streaming through the window. I understood it about as much as I did the ancient old man's numbers and parables. The Code was like a catalogue with explanations, but with no meaning whatsoever. I read it so many times, I remember it by heart: "The System organizes the world into three categories: In Front Of, Proximate, and Beneath. In the first are energy, insects, numbers, music, water, and white minerals. In the second are men, fruit, drawings, liquors, temples, birds, red metal, prophecy, and vegetables that grow in sunlight. In the third are food, animals with fur or scales, the word, sacrifices, weapons, mirrors, black metals, rope, vegetables that grow in shade, and keys." And so it went, full of enumerations, each more absurd than the next. At the end, precepts and poems, and at the very end a phrase about the string tying the papers given me by the ancient old man, in which case the papers would be the ideas. But all this wasn't important; my prospective sentence was. And thinking of my sentence, with the string-tied papers hidden under my shirt, I got up, left the patio, ate, and got through the rest of the day.

At night there was another council of men demanding to fornicate with someone. I feared for Percy and, instinctively, for myself. Yet I had to admit that I also experienced a certain happiness in seeing him chosen again. As it turned out, it occurred to the ancient old man to designate me, *me*, to play the woman for all the others . . . *me*! I was insulted, and told him that it mattered little to me what could and could not be done, that I was very macho and no one was going to take advantage of me. The ancient old man smiled and said a couple of stupid and pompous things: apparently to be chosen for this was a sign of deference, affection, and respect. I told him they could start respecting others because I wasn't about to let them respect me.

"Ah, honorable foreign friend and gentleman," said the ancient old man, "who then will feed you, give you shelter, take you into his group! Who will make life tolerable for you at Sweet Memory of the Yubayas in Bloom?"

Drop dead, I thought, and was about to answer: Percy. But I didn't of course, thinking of what would happen to the kid if I did. The ancient old man was waiting; I suppose he was waiting for me to drop my pants, which I didn't do. Instead, I took two steps and gave him the punch in the nose I'd wanted to give ever since the night he had forced Percy to submit himself to the others' pleasure. Blood ran down his face, and a heavy silence hung over the whole dormitory. The ancient old man told a parable, just like that, his lip split and his nose bleeding, and I listened, waiting for it to end so I could give him another punch in the nose.

"Long, long ago," he said, "there was a boy on the brink of becoming a man. When he reached the age where he needed a wife, he fell in love with a third cousin and wished to marry her. But his father had chosen his neighbor's daughter for him, in order to unite the two estates, and ordered the young man to obey him. The son turned a deaf ear to his father's words, and one night he stole his cousin away and escaped with her to the mountains. They lived happily, eating fruits and small birds and drinking water from streams, until his father's servants found them and brought them back to the house. There, with pomp and ceremony, was celebrated the wedding of the young man and the daughter of the father's neighbor. The third cousin was locked in a cage in the plaza, where she was exposed to public mockery."

That parable I certainly understood. And because I understood it, instead of again punching the ancient old man, I grabbed his neck and squeezed until it was broken. I let him lie there on the floor, in the same spot where he always slept, his face bloody and his head forming a right angle to his body. I yelled to the others: "Go to sleep!"

And they all obeyed me and went to their mats. I fell asleep instantaneously, and the next day was awakened not by the guards' insults, but by a deafening uproar. Everyone was running from one side to the other yelling, "Disinfection! Disinfection!" I saw a big group of guards come in, whips in hand. This time they used them: they hit out blindly, and men fled naked through the dormitory. As senselessly as the rest, I also ran. The guards immediately backed towards the door in the corner, and others came in carrying hoses. They overtook us with jets of ice-cold water— here was the bath I had been wishing for, exploding against our bodies and nailing us to the walls and floor. Then I saw that the only one not moving was the Ancient Master, and I remembered that I had murdered him, and why; the guards must have seen him at the same moment, because an order was given and the hoses stopped vomiting freezing water. One of the guards approached the old man's body, touched it so that the now black head wobbled from side to side, and shouted, "Who did this!"

I stepped forward. "I did."

I thought, if for not having signaled they sentence me to twenty years, now they'll shoot me instantly. I wasn't even afraid.

"Get dressed and follow us."

I put on my shirt and pants, grabbed the papers given me by the ancient old man, looked at Percy, and went with the guards.

At least I had gotten what I wanted; they took me to see the Director.

"I have been informed," he said to me, "that you killed a Master."

"Yes," I answered.

"Take him away," he told the guards.

Again they took me to the room where they had stripped, examined, and dressed me as a convict, and gave me back all of my things. At least I was going to die as a Captain and not a convict, as though that mattered. But it comforted me. I put the Code of What Is and Canon of Appearances in the right pocket of the jacket. We returned to the office of the Director.

"Foreign sire," he said to me, "you will be taken to your ship, and we pray you, return to your lands as quickly as possible. The action you committed has no precedent in our long history, and you will have to be so good as to pardon us and to understand when we tell you that it is impossible for us to keep any longer in one of our public establishments a person such as yourself. Good-bye."

"What about my men?" I asked.

"Good-bye," the Director repeated, and the guards took me away from there.

They took me to the ship. Motionless on a green plain, so different from the saltpeter surface on which Sweet Memory of the Yubayas in Bloom rises up, it seemed to be waiting for me. I gave her a military salute, which astonished the guards to no end, approached her, and opened the hatch.

"Good-bye," I also said, but they didn't answer. I didn't care, for I wasn't saying good-bye to them.

I looked around to see if my personal god was coming with me, and took off in the direction of Earth, with the sunlight of Colatino—as I myself had named the world I discovered—beating down on the fuselage and the countryside and the distant mountains. Good-bye, I said again, and began reading the Code of What Is and Canon of Appearances with particular attention to amuse myself on my solitary voyage home.

Translated by Marguerite Feitlowitz
(From Bajo las jubeas en flor, 1973)

Bibliography

Fiction by Angélica Gorodischer

Al Champaquí. Buenos Aires: Flor, 1985.

Bajo las jubeas en flor. Buenos Aires: Flor, 1973.

"Bajo las jubeas en flor." *Puerta abierta: La nueva escritora latinoamericana*. Eds. Caridad L. Silva-Velázquez and Nora Erro-Orthmann. Mexico City: Joaquín Mortiz, 1986. 141–59.

"La cámara oscura." *Doce mujeres cuentan*. Buenos Aires: La Campana, 1983. 157–74.

La casa del poder. Buenos Aires: Minotauro, 1983.

Casta luna electrónica. Buenos Aires: Andrómeda, 1978.

Cuentos con soldados. Santa Fe, Argentina: Club de Orden, 1965.

"Los embriones del violeta." *Los universos vislumbrados*. Buenos Aires: Andrómeda, 1978. Rpt. in *Lo mejor de la ciencia ficción latinoamericana*. Eds. Bernard Goorden and A. E. Van Vogt. Buenos Aires: Martínez de la Roca, 1982. 122–56.

Fábula de la virgen y el bombero. Buenos Aires: Flor, 1993.

Floreros de alabastro, alfombras de Bokhara. Buenos Aires: Emecé, 1985.

Jugo de mango. Buenos Aires: Emecé, 1988.

Kalpa Imperial. Buenos Aires: Minotauro, 1983.

Mala noche y parir hembra. Buenos Aires: La Campana, 1983.

"Man's Dwelling Place." Trans. Alberto Manguel. *Other Fires*. Ed. Alberto Manguel. Toronto: Lester & Orpen Dennys, 1986. 88–94.

Opus Dos. Buenos Aires: Minotauro, 1967.

Las pelucas. Buenos Aires: Sudamericana, 1968.

Prodigios. Barcelona: Lumen, 1994.

Las Repúblicas. Buenos Aires: Flor, 1991.

Trafalgar. Buenos Aires: El Cid, 1979. Rpt. in Rosario: Peregrino, 1984.

Essays by Angélica Gorodischer

"Borges y los judíos." *Confluencia* 8.1 (1992): 9–18.

"By the Light of the Chaste Electronic Moon." *Contemporary Argentinean Women Writers*. Eds. Gustavo Fares and Eliana Cazaubon Hermann. Gainesville: University Press of Florida, 1998. 65–78.

"Contra el silencio por la desobedien-cia." *Revista Iberoamericana* 51.132–33 (1985): 479–81.

"Las mujeres y las palabras." *Hispamérica* 13.39 (1984): 45–48.

"Narrativa fantástica y narrativa de ciencia-ficción." *Plural* (literary supplement to *Excelsior*; Mexico City) 188 (1987): 48–50.

"Palabras, mujeres, sombras. Peligros también." *Mujeres de palabras*. Ed. Angélica Gorodischer. San Juan: Universidad de Puerto Rico, 1994. 1–12.

"Poca paciencia y muchas pulgas." *Boca de dama: La narrativa de Angélica Gorodischer*. Eds. Miriam Balboa Echeverría and Ester Gimbernat González. Buenos Aires: Feminaria, 1995. 11–16.

"La puerta de Damasco." *Boca de dama: La narrativa de Angélica Gorosdicher.* Eds. Miriam Balboa Echeverría and Ester Gimbernat González. Buenos Aires: Feminaria, 1995. 151–55.
Técnicas de supervivencia. Rosario, Argentina: Municipal Rosario, 1994.

Essays by Angélica Gorodischer and Other Authors

Locas por la cocina. Buenos Aires: Biblos, 1997.

Criticism on the Works of Angélica Gorodischer

Bailey, Kay. "Reversión y apropiación del elemento folklórico en *Mala noche y parir hembra.*" *Boca de dama: La narrativa de Angélica Gorodischer.* Eds. Miriam Balboa Echeverría and Ester Gimbernat González. Buenos Aires: Feminaria, 1995. 69–87.

Balboa Echeverría, Miriam. "El contador y la emperatriz: La furiosa seducción del imperio." *Boca de dama: La narrativa de Angélica Gorodischer.* Eds. Miriam Balboa Echeverría and Ester Gimbernat González. Buenos Aires: Feminaria, 1995. 143–50.

———. "Poder, fabulación y memoria en tres novelas de Angélica Gorodischer." *Actas Irvine-92.* Vol. 2: *La mujer y su representación en las literaturas hispánicas.* Irvine: University of California Press, 1994. 196–204.

Balboa Echeverría, Miriam, and Ester Gimbernat González . *Boca de dama: La narrativa de Angélica Gorodischer.* Buenos Aires: Feminaria, 1995.

Berg, Walter Bruno. "La otredad del sexo: Escritura femenina en Gorodischer and Lispector." *Boca de dama: La narrativa de Angélica Gorodischer.* Eds. Miriam Balboa Echeverría and Ester Gimbernat González. Buenos Aires: Feminaria, 1995. 53–68.

Burgos, Fernando. "Retratos de la historia en el cuento posmoderno hispanoamericano: Luis Arturo Ramos y Angélica Gorodischer." *Palabra y el Hombre* (Xalapa) 92 (1994): 143–55.

Correa, Rafael E. "Angélica Gorodischer: Fabuladora de un país nuevo al borde de los ojos." *Boca de dama: La narrativa de Angélica Gorodischer.* Eds. Miriam Balboa Echeverría and Ester Gimbernat González. Buenos Aires: Feminaria, 1995. 95–106.

Dellepiane, Angela B. "Contar mester de fantasía o la narrativa de Angélica Gorodischer." *Revista Iberoamericana* 51.132–33 (1985): 627–40.

———. "Dos heroínas improbables en sendas novelas argentinas." *Actas del décimo Congreso de la Asociación de Hispanistas, 3.* Ed. Antonio Vilanova. Barcelona: Promociones y Publicaciones Universitarias, 1992. 573–83.

———. "La narrativa de Angélica Gorodischer." *Boca de dama: La narrativa de Angélica Gorodischer.* Eds. Miriam Balboa Echeverrría and Ester Gimbernat González. Buenos Aires: Feminaria, 1995. 17–40.

Eberle-McCarthy, Karen. "Worlds Within Argentine Women." *La escritora hispánica.* Eds. Nora Erro-Orthmann and Juan Cruz Mendizábal. Miami: Universal, 1990. 237–42.

Esplugas, Celia. "Angélica Gorodischer." *Hispamérica* 23.67 (1994): 55–59.

Fares, Gustavo, and Eliana Hermann. "Angélica Gorodischer, escritora argentina." *Hispania* 75.5 (1992): 1238–39.

Feitlowitz, Marguerite. "Angélica Gorodischer." *Bomb* 32 (1990): 58–60.

Ferman, Claudia. "Mujeres, cuento fantástico y ciencia ficción: Angélica Gorodischer, Interview." *Osamayor* October 4, 1997: 45–54.

Gandolfo, Elvio E. "Repúblicas dobles." *Boca de dama: La narrativa de Angélica Gorodischer.* Eds. Miriam Balboa Echeverría and Ester Gimbernat González. Buenos Aires: Feminaria, 1995. 88–94.

García Pinto, Magdalena. "Las posibilidades narrativas del viaje en *Jugo de mango.*" *Boca de dama: La narrativa de Angélica Gorodischer.* Eds. Miriam Balboa Echeverría and Ester Gimbernat González. Buenos Aires: Feminaria, 1995. 41–52.

Gimbernat González, Ester. "La aventura de la enunciación en *Jugo de mango* de Angélica Gorodischer." *El descubrimiento y los desplazamientos: La literatura hispanoamericana como diálogo entre centros y periferias.* Ed. Juana Alcira Arancibia. Westminster, Calif.: Instituto Literario y Cultural Hispánico, 1990. 133–42.

———. "La caótica prodigalidad: La creación del prodigio." *Boca de dama: La narrativa de Angélica Gorodischer.* Eds. Miriam Balboa Echeverría and Ester Gimbernat González. Buenos Aires: Feminaria, 1995. 129–42.

González, Gail. "De la forma a la ideología: Una lectura feminista del género de Raymond Chandler en una novela de Angélica Gorodischer." *Primeras jornadas internacionales de literatura argentina/Comparistica.* Ed. Teresita Frugoni de Fritzsche. Buenos Aires: Universidad de Buenos Aires, 1996. 393–400.

Lagmanovich, David. "Gandolfo, Gorodischer, Martini: Tres narradores jóvenes de Rosario (Argentina)." *Chasqui* 4.2 (1975): 18–28.

Lojo de Beuter, María Rosa. "Dos versiones de la utopía: 'Sensatez del círculo' de Angélica Gorodischer, y 'Utopía de un hombre que está cansado' de Jorge Luis Borges." *Mujer y Sociedad en América.* Ed. Juana Alcira Arancibia. Westminster, Calif.: Instituto Literario y Cultural Hispánico, 1988. 93–104.

Mathieu, Corina. "Feminismo y humor en *Floreros de alabastro, alfombras de Bokhara.*" *Letras Femeninas* 17.1–2 (1991): 113–19.

Mosier, M. Patricia. "Comunicando la transcendencia en *Trafalgar* por Angélica Gorodischer." *Foro Literario* (Montevideo) 9.15–16 (1986): 50–56.

———. "Communicating Transcendence in Angélica Gorodischer's *Trafalgar.*" *Chasqui* 12.2–3 (1983): 63–71.

———. "Women in Power in Gorodischer's *Kalpa Imperial.*" *Spectrum of the Fantastic.* Ed. Donald Palumbo. Westport, Conn.: Greenwood Press, 1988. 153–61.

Orgambide, Pedro, and Roberto Yahni. *Enciclopedia de la literatura argentina.* Buenos Aires: Sudamericana, 1970. 293.

Paris, Diana. "Discurso paródico, estética fantasy, y escritura del yo en tres cuentos de Angélica Gorodischer." *Boca de dama: La narrativa de Angélica Gorodischer.* Eds. Miriam Balboa Echeverría and Ester Gimbernat González. Buenos Aires: Feminaria, 1995. 107–28.

Souto, Marcial, comp. "Angélica Gorodischer." *La ciencia ficción en la Argentina: Antología crítica.* Buenos Aires: Eudeba, 1985. 91–98.

Urraca, Beatriz. "Angélica Gorodischer's Voyages of Discovery: Sexuality and Historical Allegory in Science Fiction's Cross-Cultural Encounters." *Latin American Literary Review* 23.45 (1995): 85–102.

Vásquez, María Esther. "Angélica Gorodischer: Una escritora latinoamericana de ciencia ficción." *Revista Iberoamericana* 49. 123-24 (1983): 571-76.

Sylvia Lago

Sylvia Lago was born in Montevideo, Uruguay, in 1932. She is a professor of literature at the University of the Republic in Montevideo and a literary critic for the newspaper *Brecha*. She has written several novels and collections of short stories, as well as numerous articles and essays that have appeared in several literary magazines and journals.

Her first novel, *Trajano* (Trajano, 1962), which deals with incest, won her awards from *Revista Número*. In her first two novels her style was simple, but by the mid-1960s she began to experiment with complex narrative techniques and a more dynamic use of language.

The short story "Días dorados de la señora Pieldediamante" (Golden days of Mrs. Diamondskin), published in the collection *La otra mitad* (Half of love, 1966), passionately denounces the use of women as sex objects. It won her both considerable praise and bitter criticism.

Lago's works clearly reflect her major concerns, which over the years have encompassed the social, the feminist, and the political. Her characters' personal lives are often eroded by unfair social and political circumstances. Many of her stories focus on the disadvantaged status of women in Uruguay and on the hypocrisy of gender roles in a patriarchal society.

Homelife

And outside, night kept falling.
Juan Rulfo, "Lluvina"

How are we to keep going, without understanding, picking our way blindly in this dark age.
Joaquin Giannuzzi

I think that it all began when we decided to buy the small sofas for the bedroom; the two lovely settees covered in brown brocade, with honey-colored flowers, which are still attractive there, next to the window, near the commode where—still—the crystal ashtray is lying, the one which your first patient gave you as a present. We had moved the baby to her own room from the room that she shared with Daniel. You saw that she was already getting too big to sleep in the same room with her older brother. And since you had finally made a nice fee—a sum which, as you said, a young doctor just starting out and concerned more about his profession than his income, practicing in a provincial city in the interior, could only expect to receive from very rich patients—we also decided to buy bedroom sets for the children.

The operation that you performed on don Olegario de la Sierra—the rancher suffering from a congenital intestinal disorder—brought you fame and fortune. When don Olegario had fully recovered, he wanted to pay his bill in person, and turned up one night at the house in his latest-model Cadillac. Apart from the check, as a token of his gratitude he brought us a roast suckling pig and a bottle of the best wine from his cellar.

That night we had a family supper. Daniel and the baby ate so much that they ended up with indigestion. You got up at the break of dawn to take care of them. Anyway, it had been a wonderful meal, lots of fun. You were so happy, so jolly—I remember that for dessert, on a fancy china tray, I served your favorite dessert, ambrosia. Yes, Miguel, I had made it myself, taking extra special care to get it just right: twelve beaten egg yolks, syrup, vanilla extract—I'd never use liquid extract, since it gives a bitter and vulgar taste—and three small cups of cognac.

"Doesn't Mom make wonderful desserts?" you said to the children, and immediately you reached out to me and put your arms around my waist. I felt your warmth on my skin, and the pressure of your right hand (the lancet and scalpel hand), so soft when you stroked me. I stood next to you while you stayed seated, sheltering your face against my breasts; you spoke again of money.

"OK, Rocío, finally you will be able to have a handsome sum to spend as you wish; get those sofas you like and the bedroom sets for the children."

Daniel, who was nine then, seized upon the climate of happiness, tinged with the rare aroma of wine, and the atmosphere of unusual luxury, and asked for the meccano set he had been longing for. To Susanna, I promised a doll; that cute MaryLou that said Mamá and which was on display, wearing an organza dress, in the window of the toy shop. With Susanna, I got the better of you that time. I said that we would buy her the doll before you would give her one of those mind games that you were crazy about. I always wanted our daughter to become a good housewife, attached to the home.

however, they came to get her at two in the morning and she didn't open her lips when they took her away, and I shouted, tell them no, that you have nothing to do with it, that your whole life is spent studying and doing household chores, that you know how to cook and knit and that you make your own clothes; but she endured the shoving and the manhandling with her lips pressed tight together and they took her away like that.

After supper, I put the children to bed. As usual, you took refuge in your study. When they had gone to sleep, I went to look for you, afraid that your habit of reading at night was taking too much of a hold over you. I wanted so much to be with you that night; I felt weightless, enveloped in a kind of ethereal happiness which made me feel tremendously light, ready to give myself completely, without any holding back.

"Rocío, the sea-nymph, the solitary and taciturn mermaid," you used to tell me at the beginning of our relationship, when we began to build our island: that drop of sunshine which I always dreamed was burning on the edge of our world.

I went into your study and pierced the gloomy depths of your reverie, without you particularly noticing it; above you there seemed to float an uneasy pall, which made me shiver.

his face suddenly aged, as if mourning had taken hold of it, the first time they allowed me to see him, when they brought him to the iron bars, and around his eyes there was that frightening dark ring, and inside his eye sockets, there were two burning stones which were his eyes. Somebody pushed him forward and when his trembling hands grabbed the bars, the iron bars screeched. Then, everything fell silent.

Even so, I spoke. I told you that I felt happy and that "the island was on fire." It was our language of lovers, Miguel, our private code. A metaphor like that should have made you break out of your private thoughts and give me a smile. But it didn't. I noticed that on the desk in front of you lay your newspaper, and that you had never even heard a word I said. Your voice sounded alien to me when, with your eyes fixed on the open page, you said, "It sounds like they have given them a real beating up north."

I was completely unaware of your train of thought, and I asked "Who?"

You gave me a disconcerting smile, and a look of astonishment, maybe of sorrow, came over your face. "It's incredible that there are so many people like you, sensitive, educated, who still refuse to face up to the realities of the world in which they are destined to live."

Or something like that you said. Later on I learned that Felipe was up north at the time. Of course, you feared for his safety. You didn't see fit, however, to share any of this with me.

That was the first cold underwater current that slid around the "island," like an icy shiver in the intimate water which we had filled with magnificent man-of-wars, rose-shelled snails, sea urchins you could touch, and multicolored coral reefs. We went to bed in silence, and made love with little enthusiasm. But I couldn't get to sleep that night. Sitting on the bed in the dark, I felt for the first time in my heart the full weight of that new sadness which was never again to leave me.

It was after receiving the payment from don Olegario de la Sierra that our family started to live a comfortable life. We didn't buy only the sofas and the furniture for the children, but also an elegant dining room set and a garden hammock, and for Christmas you gave me the aquarium. That aquarium is what I am looking at now, where a single fish with yellow fins is swimming in the murky slimy waters—in this room which we used to share, now that you're no longer here, there's nothing to be heard but an extended silence.

We went to the capital and picked out four varieties of fish. The gold-fish—remember the goldfish with glowing eyes whom we baptized Nero, making him the king of the fishbowl? So much, so much time has passed since then, Miguel—ten years have slid by since that summer—they are not so long, or at least they shouldn't be.

> time, endless, white, and smooth, on his adolescent face. What color, what color were his eyes? Grey with green reflections and gold specks? And wild alloy of lights, his pupils, where life was exploding. However, on the day they brought him home he was sleeping. I laid him down in his bed and his skin got pale, paler every minute. Only that flower, that purple petal where his teeth stuck out, was intense, each time more intense against the strange paleness, against his ashen face.

That February was the anniversary of our first meeting in the water, ten years before. So often we used to say that we belonged to the sea, Miguel. We met one summer, under the sign of Pisces; we met in the sea. A mer-maid sleeping on a rock is discovered and seduced by Poseidon, the King of the Ocean. Since that meeting, so many years have passed—I had fin-ished my exams and wanted to spend my holidays on a lonely beach. I chose one where in the sand, rough and burnt, wild plants were growing, drowning, near the shoreline. There were some bushes too, their branches submerged in the water which was dark brown near the shore, but clear farther out. Near the cliff, there was a floating raft. I would sunbathe there in the morning, and one day, swimming along, you found me. You emerged from the waves and your body was ablaze with the glare of the noonday sun. Silver-coated fish, your attendants, followed in your wake, and my eyes filled the air with other fish, winged and shining. I dove into the middle of this mirage; if you had dazzled a siren, I, in return, had attracted a god. I swam towards the reef and, as never before, I felt the power of the sea and of life in my body. When I stepped out, strings of algae were curling around my legs. You were waiting for me. Suddenly, we were surrounded by a sort of violent blue haze; in the distance, the beach was a yellow tongue, writhing in the heat of the sun.

"At last, you reached the white sand," you said, as you offered your hand to me. "Come up. Now that we've discovered this hill, we'll give it a name and it will belong to us."

I smiled into the mirage and triumphantly said, "It will be our island."

"Mermaid island," you said between the flashes of light that framed our dialogue and made it weightless. We were filled with a sort of innocent romanticism which signaled our discovery of each other, and which we would joke about together in the future. Your hand, wet and cold, stroked the skin of my arm.

"From now on, you agree to be the mermaid, right?" you asked.

I was hallucinating, Miguel; nobody can ever blame me for my innocence then. The world, life, was a surging wave breaking and building and breaking again against the reef. And the two of us rushed forward into its vortex.

Yes, ten years had passed since the perfect existence of the "island" and you wanted to commemorate the fact in the way that would please me most. After your celebrated cure of don Olegario, other relatives and friends of the la Sierra family started coming to you; almost immediately you operated on the gall bladder of his older sister, doña Adelaida, widow of a well to-do businessman of the region, who owned one of the largest properties in the whole departamento. We received an extraordinary sum of money and I suggested that we spend it right away. But at that time something strange was beginning to eat into you. Now I imagine that you were already keeping company with Felipe.

One evening, I went to the clinic and I found you there, gloomy and restless. You had finished your appointments and were smoking one cigarette after another. You told me that you had just seen a rancher from the border—you made it clear that he was "a smuggler"—who was suffering from a duodenal ulcer.

"He left me a check for four times what I asked." My surprised smile offended you. "Take it, then take it" you blurted out. "Keep on with your shopping and stuffing our house with junk!"

You were not being fair and I told you how I felt. You stood up, upset, looking out into the distance with flashing eyes, and you added, "I had better give it back, Rocío. I don't want people to start thinking that I'm a well-paid servant of the big landowners and swindlers of the region."

We had a quarrel. I argued that we had just begun to settle down, that we had hardly started to decorate our house and now you were sowing seeds of discord, based on absurd conflicts with your conscience.

You reproached me by saying, "Settling down, decorating; you just can't get beyond your world of petty personal ambitions, can you?"

That really hurt me; what harm could there be in wanting us to be comfortable, in wanting to decorate my home and in caring for my family's comfort? Would you rather I had spent my time outside, going to parties or gossiping with the neighbors? You begged me to understand your concerns, but you didn't try very hard to explain to me what they were. The truth was that we were still living in the time when we were following our bodies' appetites, Miguel, and our bed was still a place where we would patch things up. You used to love so much to look at me, naked, not moving, stretched out on the sheets which I myself had embroidered with flower patterns.

> naked, yes. She said that they had interrogated her naked, with her eyes covered, and I was horrified. I couldn't understand how she had stood all that, although she tried to explain to me that she had shielded herself with contempt. "You don't know, you don't realize, Mama, what strong weapons hatred and contempt can be." She was naked, smaller than me, and much thinner, her large beautiful eyes covered with bandages and cotton. Naked and defenseless, distant from us.

I couldn't come up with a better idea to celebrate our tenth wedding anniversary than to organize a holiday to the beach that summer. I chose a fashionable seaside resort. Doña Adelaida's money—"her precious gall stones," as you wisecracked—made it possible to rent a California-style beach house surrounded by gardens, with weeping willows and poplars and pines and grassy cliffs, and a beautiful swimming pool. Really, Miguel, today I'd say it was straight out of a fairy tale and its heroes were not really us. I remember the first morning of our holiday as a shining fantasy; you sprang from the diving board and I felt that you had changed yourself once more into a pagan god, and inside me the images of my readings of Homer flashed before me: "Swift-flying Miguel-Apollo descending from Olympus, Miguel-Hermes bestowing upon Earth his messages of eternal delight? Divine Poseidon floating on the surface of the water searching for his beloved Nereids? Rocío the nymph?"

"Rocío the mermaid" I called myself and I threw myself into the pool to surrender myself once more to you, my one and only god. I swam over to you and pressed my body to yours. We began to move gently, like a single creature, while a dazzling light falling from the sky splashed millions of stars upon us.

> Stars. They say that when he came to, after the injection they gave him to force him to confess, he too must have seen more and more lights, then later a smell of smoke which transformed the colors: sulphur-solid, green-mallow, or perhaps purple or violet . . . and black spots, then, which got larger and took shape next to him and gained their own voice. *Tell us your nickname. Speak, say your nickname.* And the hair they tore from Daniel's head, my Daniel; the autopsy determined that they first tore off his hair and they burned his skin and then they beat him until they broke him.

Toward the end of our stay, Felipe turned up at our beach house. He was younger than us, at least so it seemed; he looked like an unruly teenager, although he was quiet. His paleness struck me as odd.

"Haven't you been out in the sun during this marvelous summer?" I asked him before inviting him into the pool.

He smiled and answered ambiguously that he had been terribly busy, that he had recently arrived from abroad, things like that. I didn't take to him, Miguel, you know that. Even though he was always very polite with me, and so affectionate to the children. Susanna used to always climb onto his lap and kiss him. Daniel would follow him into the house, wanting him to go fishing or hunting. They went to the nearby mountains, carrying shotguns, and they brought down some pigeons

My God, how much time it took me to begin to figure them out.

You wanted Felipe to stay at the house until the evening before we returned home to the village. That night, we threw him a special dinner. We bought an excellent wine, I cooked a seafood stew and, of course, ambrosia.

"Food of the pagan gods," commented Felipe. "What a treat." Later, he assured us that the dessert was delicious. I didn't display any joy. I had become fond of the pampered life at the resort and it pained me to leave it—our shining pool, our garden, our bedroom with its windows open to the sea. All that would go up in smoke the next morning and it wasn't likely that, the next summer, someone else's precious gallstones, like doña Adelaida's, would pay for our holidays. After Felipe came, I felt that perhaps we would never again have such a summer as that one. But that whole place, that fleeting moment in the sun, was nothing but a mask concealing other purposes unknown to me.

I felt listless as I dressed for the "last supper." I chose a backless lamé dress (I had bought it in a shop on the main street of the resort town and hadn't yet worn it), gold earrings and bracelets. I put on my essence-of-violet perfume. It was my way of saying good-bye to that dream world, and I wanted to look like a queen, a queen of the night, magically wrapped in a silver web. However, my other table companions, Felipe and you (the children were tired and had already gone to bed), kept quiet and distant. I remember Felipe's smile when I showed up before the two of you; afterwards, I often spoke of it to you with bitterness. His was a sad, enigmatic smile which made me suddenly feel stripped of all my fictitious finery. Ridiculous, mute, alone . . . Ah! it was almost the same smile with which he appeared in the photo, in the newspapers years after when they announced that, after a confrontation with a squad of soldiers, they had beaten him in the street, right in the center of the city.

Forgive me, Miguel, but that night I think I hated Felipe. I don't know if it was because of his smile or because I had a feeling that he would be a sharp and relentless wedge which would split apart our "island," the bright, secluded island of my dreams, on the edge of the world. His smile had something magical in it, I see that now, it had the power to change the lamé of my dress into the wretched skin of a fish. I felt like a fish out of water, suffocating. He left that night in his red Volkswagen, and before he embraced you and me, he told me to kiss Susanna and Daniel for him; I felt that I was about to faint. You walked him to the gate of the beach house. It was dawn. I stayed on the porch, looking at you. My fingers trembled on my glass of cognac. You came back changed—transfigured even. Your features seemed to radiate an intense joy. I knew that your joy didn't belong to me, that he was the one who had caused it and that I couldn't share in it.

Maybe that's what made me provoke you in such an absurd way.

We were alone, relaxing on the deck near the pool. In silence, in front of you I undressed, with the intention of challenging you. The skin of the mermaid fell to my feet. Then your look ran over my body inch by inch, slowly, and it seemed to me that your eyes had become his. Felipe's eyes. And there was already nothing in your look but indifference—or perhaps sadness. Yes, maybe only sadness. I began to shake. You turned your eyes away from me and gazed out into the night, at the stars which glimmered in the dark; there was a shooting star, a point which flashed far away in the depths of the sky, whose bright gleam just barely gave me time to make a wish: that Felipe would never return.

You'll have to understand, you'll have to guess that the sentences between quotation marks in the letter are Susanna's. Also, I have tried to imitate her handwriting in those passages, so you'll recognize both the text and its meaning. I trust in your sagacity, Miguel, in your intelligence, which will remain lucid, I suppose, despite everything you have suffered. And what is happening with me, meanwhile? I shouldn't say it. However, often I think I'll go crazy if I don't tell you what is happening to me. My hours are dragging out nervously with all this lonely waiting. For now, day and night, I just stay seated in front of the aquarium, where there's only one fish left. I'm observing its movements as it glides along, and thinking about you, always thinking, trying to go deeper into areas that still remain incomprehensible.

Sometimes, she phones me; not her exactly, but a girlfriend who mentions the name of the Spanish dressmaker whom I was thinking of asking to make her wedding dress—the white dress of chiffon and lace which I dreamed of using for our daughter's wedding, Miguel. You see how deluded I was! Once I told her, "It's time for you to choose from among your suitors, Susanna, and think about getting married. I have even chosen the design of your dress, and I have planned out the ceremony." She smiled and I think that I detected a sparkle in her eyes, the same one as was in your eyes the night Felipe left, a mixture of tenderness and pity and a strange vitality . . . "I don't know if I'll ever get married, Mommy, but I know that if I do, I won't have to buy a wedding dress."

Undressed, yes, stripped. She will never wear a wedding dress. They interrogated her naked, they put her head into a tank of cold water, and on one occasion when they hooded her and they pulled her out, she had almost drowned, and her desperation to breathe made her inhale the dirty water that remained inside the hood. Of course: who could have imagined that a girl who resisted so much, a woman who was as fearless as a man, more than many, many men, would want to get married in a church wedding, in an elegant white gown.

Susanna's comrade, who has the same name as the Spanish dressmaker, tells me that everything is going along perfectly well, and that I shouldn't worry. And I continue to wait for her. Wondering why she doesn't come home if they didn't sentence her, Miguel. Waiting for her . . . stupid me! I don't want to think that, again, again, she chose the same adventure. On one occasion, I had stopped in front of a shop window in one of the downtown malls, looking at some beautifully embroidered tapestries, when she turned up in front of me, smiling; as if by magic she appeared and I blushed and immediately turned white; however, I couldn't bring myself to talk to her. She squeezed my arm and whispered in my ear, "Cheer up, Mama; you can see I'm doing fine." And into my hand she slipped the letter for you and quickly explained to me that I should insert her sentences between mine when I wrote to you, assuring me that you would understand. Afterwards, she disappeared into the crowd.

And yes, I think that you will understand, since you and she always understood each other. And also, you both got on with Daniel and, since they were children, she and Daniel with Felipe. At times, I imagine a disconcerting complicity to which you are not a stranger. At one time, I thought that I would never manage to understand you. I, the mermaid of your arms and of your desires, raised in the home, hidden away, shy; wanting only the flowers of my garden, our meals and our peaceful evenings. Suddenly, I was confronting another face of the world. Was Daniel the one who first showed me the wrong side of life? Or perhaps Felipe?

Felipe's face on the front page of the newspapers and the head-lines which called him the head of the *faciosos*; his broad forehead, his deep, searching eyes, full of conviction and power and harshness and tenderness and values which I didn't even know existed.

However, perhaps it wasn't Felipe, but Daniel, my own son. That time he had blazing eyes and you said that he hadn't been crying and I assured you that he had, that he'd cried the whole night over Felipe's death. Time passed and one day Daniel went away from us. That evening, I felt that my feet no longer were touching the ground, that under my feet there was a vacuum and that an evil force was drawing me towards Hell. Suddenly, I stopped seeing reality. I was blind and in my desperation I cried out for him not to leave, but he didn't reply. He turned to you, Miguel, "try to calm her," he said to you, "afterwards she'll understand." He left me, and I fell, lost, into your protective arms. The door closed quietly behind his large figure, behind his canvas satchel in which he had gathered—the following day I checked his closet—a few clothes. When they brought him to me, you were no longer at home. Only we two women were left. It was dawn. They said that he had died of a heart attack during an interrogation. Daniel, my Daniel, the healthiest and most lovely and well cared for of children . . . dead at nineteen of a heart attack. Who could believe them?

Do you remember when you supplied him with vitamin pills, vaccines, and tonics—because I had asked you so often, because I always wanted our children to be beautiful and strong—and you made fun of me, saying that you couldn't explain how a mermaid had given birth to a little bull? I don't know how you felt when they told you. When did you become aware that the autopsy had determined that it was death from a ruptured liver and immediate hemorrhaging? They had beaten him so much, Miguel, so much. Perhaps it's better if we never talk about this. Sometimes, I think that it would be better if, when you come home—because I know that they won't be able to keep you in prison, although they want to, because I know that if you helped the rebels by giving them medical assistance it is because you are, and always have been, an unselfish humanitarian doctor, ready to exercise your profession in the service of mankind. I think that it might be better if I am not here when you come home. Anyway, Miguel, I'm sure that you love me, that I was and always will be your mermaid, although the island has lost its fire and has sunk once and for all into a quagmire of bitterness.

At home, you will meet Susanna. You two can sit down and relax on the settee and chat. You were always such good company for each other. With her, also, you defeated me, although for a long time I thought I had won, at least in that battle. Since she was so obedient, she never objected to the fact that I taught her how to do household chores. I dreamed that she would choose the path I wanted for her—the life at home. Meanwhile, however, without my noticing it, she too was learning the other path, your path. That's why, on the many occasions I asked her to spend more time with me, sharing feminine chores, she smiled, and the shining spark would appear in her eyes: love-tenderness-pity-understanding, which, I see now, was Felipe's legacy to you and her.

You two will talk and go over the times you had with Daniel and Felipe.

But maybe, after all, it would be better if I were at home when you two come back to chat and smoke and recall what happened, what is happening; or that I don't disappear at the moment in which at last we will be together. The three of us will remain here, and we'll remember them. We'll have lunch, and I'll serve you coffee and sometime I'll approach you and I'll ask you to explain things to me. Probably some day I'll understand the truth in your eyes and your hands and in the eyes and hands of our children and in the eyes and hands of Felipe.

Translated by Ian Martin
(From Los últimos cuentos, 1972)

Bibliography

Fiction by Sylvia Lago

El corazón de la noche. Montevideo: Banda Oriental, 1987.

Detrás del rojo. Montevideo: Alfa, 1967.

"Días dorados de la señora Pieldediamante." *La mitad del amor.* Montevideo: Arca, 1966. Rpt. in *Narradores uruguayos.* Ed. Rubén Cotelo. Caracas: Monte Avila, 1969. 257–89.

Las flores conjuradas. Montevideo: Girón, 1972.

"Las horizontales." *La nueva narrativa.* Ed. Mercedes Ramírez de Rossiello. Montevideo: Centro Editor de América Latina, 1968. 57–65.

"Ninfas: Pasión y muerte." *Hispamérica* 7.22 (1979): 49–64.

"Los peces rojos." *Antología del cuento uruguayo.* Vol. 6: *Los Nuevos.* Montevideo: Banda Oriental, 1968. 73–82.

Quince cuentos para una antología. Eds. Fernando Gastón J. and Walter Rela. Montevideo: Zanocchi, 1984.

"Recibir al campeón." *Catorce cuentistas.* Havana: Casa de las Américas, 1969. 133. Rpt. in *El cuento uruguayo contemporáneo.* Buenos Aires: Centro Editor de América Latina, 1978.

Tan solos en el balneario. Montevideo: Feria del Libro, 1962.

"Tema de amor." *Cuentos de la revolución.* Ed. Mario Benedetti. Montevideo: Girón, 1972. 43–60.

Trajano. Montevideo. Alfa, 1962.

La última razón. Montevideo: Arca, 1968.

"Vida de hogar." *Los últimos cuentos.* Montevideo: Girón, 1972. 21–32.

"Vida de hogar." *Puerta abierta: La nueva escritora latinoamericana.* Eds. Caridad L. Silva-Velázquez and Nora Erro-Orthmann. Mexico City: Joaquín Mortiz, 1986. 161–71.

Essays by Sylvia Lago

Cuentos de ajustar cuentas; recopilación por Sylvia Lago. Montevideo: Trilce, 1990.

Días dorados: Días de sombra: Cuentos, 1965–1995. Montevideo: Grupo Editorial Planeta, 1996.

Eduardo Acevedo Díaz: El combate de la tapera. Montevideo: Técnica, 1976.

La flecha hacia el vacío: Introducción a la obra de Leopoldo Lugones. Montevideo: Universidad de la República, Facultad de Humanidades y Ciencias, 1988.

Essays by Sylvia Lago and Other Authors

Actas de la jornada de homenaje a Mario Benedetti. Montevideo: Universidad de la República, Facultad de Humanidades y Ciencias, 1997.

Actas de las jornadas de homenaje a Juan Carlos Onetti. Montevideo: Universidad de la República, Facultad de Humanidades y Ciencias, 1997.

Narrativa uruguaya de las últimas décadas (1960–1999): Las marcas de la violencia. Montevideo: Universidad de la República, Facultad de Humanidades y Ciencias, 1997.

Criticism on the Works of Sylvia Lago

Foster, David William. *Dictionary of Contemporary Latin American Authors.* Tempe: Center for Latin American Studies, Arizona State University, 1975. 57–58.

Rama, Angel. *La generación crítica, 1939–1969.* Montevideo: Arca, 1972. 198.

Rela, Walter. *Diccionario de escritores uruguayos.* Montevideo: Plaza, 1986. 197–99.

Shimrose, Pedro. *Diccionario de autores iberoamericanos.* Madrid: Ministerio de Relaciones Exteriores, 1982. 236.

Visca, Arturo S, ed. *Antología del cuento uruguayo.* Vol. 6: *Los nuevos.* Montevideo: Banda Oriental, 1968. 73–82.

Nélida Piñon

Nélida Piñon, one of the most outstanding writers of fiction in Brazil at this time, was born in Rio de Janeiro in 1937. Educated and trained as a journalist, she has worked for the newspaper *O Globo* and for the literary magazine *Cadernos Brasileiros*. In 1961 she published her first novel, *Guía-mapa de Gabriel arcanjo* (Guide-map of the archangel Gabriel), and has since produced eight novels, three collections of short stories, and numerous articles that have appeared in translation in seven languages as well as her native Portuguese.

In her first two novels—the second is *Madeira feita cruz* (The wooden cross, 1963)—Piñon explores philosophical and religious questions in a style that seems at once neobaroque and surrealistic. Piñon's later work contains diverse experiments in fictional technique and a more complex use of language.

The experimental quality of her prose and her preference for mythic themes result in stories that closely scrutinize basic human values in metaphoric terms, in the remarkable collection of short stories titled *Sala de armas* (Fencing room, 1973). Her semiautobiographical novel *A república dos sonhos* (1984; *The Republic of Dreams*, 1989) narrates the migration of a Galician family to Brazil and is widely regarded as her most important work to date.

The Brazilian writer has won the most coveted literary prizes, among them the prestigious Juan Rulfo Prize, considered the Nobel Prize equivalent for Latin American literature; the Gabriela Mistral Prize for Literature; and in 1997 she was elected president of the Brazilian Academy of Letters—the first woman ever to be selected for the post.

Adamastor

Adamastor was less than five feet tall. Women were his great weakness
even to the extent of taking them home when they didn't really appeal to
him. "They all look a little like Madonna," he once explained in order to
justify his devotion. He would buy them frocks and gaudy prints covered
with red roses and enhance their smile with gold fillings. He would play
them an old-fashioned samba on the record player and arrange regular
visits to a doctor for a checkup. Not a single woman had ever come to him
in a decent state of health. It was his destiny in life to rescue the afflicted,
he thought to himself as he shaved each morning.

And when they were back on their feet, with some money in their
purse saved from the tips that Adamastor deposited daily in the little plastic piggy bank by the bedside table, they would plan their escape. Sometimes, he could almost tell to the hour, the moment they had chosen.
Their furtive movements reminded him of tiny birds at play. But he never
tried to stop them and invariably took pity on them. After all, he himself
had spent years taking refuge in some city or other on the coast.

"Apart from men, who else needs to escape?" he frequently asked
himself, as he imagined his tiny frame weaving through gardens among
the fruit trees, attentive to the sounds of elfin intrigues. "Adamastor," he
would reply to himself in a loud voice.

No one had ever seen him weep or lament his lack of inches. For if
anyone suggested that he was a weakling, he would react at once, assuring
them with a broad grin: "What I possess is enough to convince anyone of
my manhood."

He opened a bar near the docks. This was a quarter of the city in which
he could prosper, for here the women whom he craved surged forth like
spray from the sea. And such was his dedication to the job that everyone
commented upon the atmosphere of contentment which reigned in that

establishment. "Forever and ever, amen," rejoined Adamastor, who became boastful when questioned about life in the dock area and the growing popularity of his bar.

Women and pederasts shouted after him in the street, "Take pity on
me, Adamastor." He would only smile, and say, "Sorting out the wheat
from the chaff," for his other great weakness was to quote from the Bible
at every possible opportunity. He had such a way with people that no one
could recall a single instance of him ever having quarreled with anyone.
"Only women enter into the esteem and space of my body," he would
claim.

Yet whenever anyone brought up the subject of the past, Adamastor
would coil up like a periwinkle and his skin became covered in goose
pimples which he tried to conceal by rolling down his shirtsleeves. His
reminiscences never went back farther than a few weeks. He confined his
conversation to the day's happenings, to the meal he had just eaten, to a
certain woman he had brought home that very week. And this behavior
became difficult to understand for it was common knowledge that Adamastor had led an adventurous life.

Adamastor looked after his friend João Manco as if he were an adopted
son. He made sure that he was well provided with women and rum, the
two main obsessions in João's existence. And Adamastor arranged these
benefits so discreetly that João not only became deeply attached to his
benefactor but carried all the gossip and information that Adamastor
needed in order to prosper.

The sailors from the ships always headed straight for Adamastor's bar,
dying of thirst and clamoring for women. The fame of Adamastor's bar
was such that his women were thought to be the most desirable of all. He
tolerated caressing and petting but barred anyone whom he found trying
to take liberties—not on moral grounds or because of any fear of the
police, as he was always at pains to remind his clients, for he had lost any
hope of respectability the day he decided to take on this business. He was
simply convinced that certain things should be restricted to the privacy of
one's bedroom.

Refusing to discuss the matter further, he would put on a grave expression and assume the posture of a sea captain. João Manco always backed
him up when he voiced this conviction. Desperate for female company,
the offending sailors found themselves obliged to leave the bar in the
middle of the night, protesting as they went: "We came here to spend the

night, Adamastor, so why turn us away?" They tried to make him see that food and drink were not enough and that what they needed most of all was a woman, a comfortable bed, and a welcoming home where they might enjoy sex at their ease. They finished up by persuading Adamastor that he had been too severe in forbidding them to relax like friends who had returned after a long absence.

To satisfy their needs he bought the house next door with direct access from the bar, and he brightened the place up with vases of flowers, some furniture, and cheerful curtains. A picture of Saint George slaying the dragon was hung prominently on the wall and the house even boasted vicuna mattresses, a gift from an Argentinian seaman who had enjoyed his stay so much that he had given Adamastor the mattresses, saying: "Please accept these and use them so that I shall recognize my home away from home when I return."

João supervised the bar's activities because Adamastor insisted upon decent behavior and only allowed one couple to use a room at a time. The room service itself was so meticulous that the guests often found towels embroidered with their initials, a refinement which moved some to tears.

Adamastor cautioned João that the facilities of the house were open to everyone with the exception of themselves, making it absolutely clear that they must not be seen frequenting the bedrooms—it was a question of formality. "We can enjoy our women elsewhere," he assured João. "If necessary, you can use my house."

After this conversation, João began to take full advantage of Adamastor's house, his bed, and any woman whom he happened to find there. When he discovered what was going on, Adamastor did not lose his temper with João, for he much preferred that his women should take up with someone whom he trusted.

The two men lived together in perfect harmony. Whoever dared to offend Adamastor knew that João Manco—whose surname (denoting lameness) did not imply any physical defect, for not only was his skin as smooth as that of any youth, but women fell in love with him at first sight—would roll up his sleeves, bare his teeth ferociously, and flex his muscular torso which matched the demeanor of a fighting cock. Adamastor felt proud of João at such moments, admiring as he did, "valor unto death."

Every day they shared breakfast at the same table and each morning Adamastor would greet him by inquiring: "And how is my friend today

. . . happy?" João would scratch his hairy chest and button up his trousers, concealing his underpants. He knew that Adamastor enjoyed these little rituals. "I asked God to send me a friend," he would reply, and "God sent you." Adamastor was struck by such delicate sentiments and the way in which this uninhibited young stud sought favors from God and then expressed his gratitude so spontaneously.

João's instinctive wisdom made Adamastor determined to look after the lad's future by willing him a piece of land, a little house, and medical insurance in case he should need it. For João could not stay here on land watching the stars forever with winter approaching and nothing to occupy him.

Adamastor would mount the platform behind the bar where, looking over the cash register, he could command a good view of the salon whenever he had something important to say. He had grown a moustache and his hair was so long that it crept under his shirt collar, his oriental features giving the impression that his hair was braided.

"And what about your future, my son?" João looked at him as if to say: "What are you talking about, old chap—some plant perhaps, some tree or sunflower?" Adamastor explained to João that it was common fate to all men to grow old. "One's energy was suddenly sapped up and disappeared, heaven knows where—perhaps even to Hell itself, where we shall all be reunited sooner or later. It all starts when one's teeth begin to fall out, the first unmistakable sign of encroaching frailty, so that we cannot say that we haven't been warned and should start making some preparations before it is too late. Our future means spending everything we have managed to save throughout our lifetime."

João became alarmed at all this wisdom. He trusted Adamastor completely in these matters and listened attentively before asking: "So the future comes with old age?" appealing to Adamastor's good nature. Both men laughed heartily. Adamastor found João's nonsensical quips irresistible, like the smell of rum on his breath and his habit of picking up women as if they were his private property. "If a man cannot tame a woman, Adamastor, what other animal can he hope to tame?"

Adamastor liked to think of himself as the captain of a great ship, gauging the direction of the wind under the threat of an impending storm. In the midst of these daydreams he invariably saved the ship at the eleventh hour because of some last-minute change of course. And should he ever lose his life in these adventures, it was never a question of cowardice or failure. In fact, he preferred the latter denouement, which came closer to his idea of a truly dramatic situation.

"Well now, young man. Do I buy you a house or don't I?"

João replied boldly: "Why should I want a house? Your home is my home, too, and your women are my women, because women don't really belong to anyone in particular and so long as you are alive I shall never go thirsty for want of rum."

Irritated by this flippant reply, Adamastor consulted his lawyer, explaining the situation.

"It's not that I need an heir because I don't have any fortune to dispose of, but what do you suggest I should do?"

"Is he a relative?" the lawyer inquired.

"He is as dear to me as a son, but he is only a friend." In the end he bequeathed him the bar, which was to pass into João's name after his death. He returned home exhausted after his interview and felt considerably older, like a tree without roots that suddenly rebels, following a different course from that originally ordained by nature. He did not intend to remain here forever caring for João, holding the same conversation morning after morning.

"Whoever tried to escape while holding the reins of power?" he asked himself with some feeling. Understanding was beginning to penetrate his life.

One day a sailor asked him outright: "Is Adamastor the name of some hero, or don't you know?" And others posed the same question until he began to feel haunted.

He said to João: "Look after things while I take a trip into town."

At the public library he tried to explain his query to the assistant so that there wouldn't be any misunderstanding: "I am not interested in education. All I want is a straightforward answer to a simple question: 'Who was Adamastor?'"

After some hesitation, she brought him a copy of Camoens's *Lusiads*, indicating those passages that refer to the epic's hero. "Would you like to read it?" she asked.

Adamastor was puzzled by the book, by the woman's tinted spectacles, and by the terrifying discovery that the hero Adamastor had been a giant, a fact which the librarian carefully emphasized as she looked him over from head to toe. Adamastor suddenly felt unpleasantly feverish, his body shaking with anger. For the first time in his life he could not understand why a man less than five feet tall should have been called Adamastor. A cruel joke had been played on him. And this was something that had not dawned on him before, for he had been living in all innocence for some considerable time. A joke, no doubt, on the part of his father, who had abandoned his mother when she became pregnant, leaving her not even enough money to buy food. He had been shown his father's farewell note many years later and had destroyed it immediately, certain of memorizing every single word of the message it contained: "Should the child be a boy, for reasons which I cannot explain, call him Adamastor."

And they baptized him Adamastor, respecting his father's wishes. And when he, too, ran away from home he only looked back once, for it struck him that this was a moment for shedding tears as other men had done before him.

"Every time they christen someone Adamastor, are they paying homage to the hero of Lusiads? he inquired, consulting the text in order to ascertain the truth.

"Is your name Adamastor?" the librarian asked him bluntly. To hide his embarrassment, he shook his head in denial.

"Adamastor is the name of my god-child, who is soon to be baptized. As you know, the Church can sometimes be awkward in these matters if one doesn't choose a saint's name."

He entered the bar crestfallen. He was now a dwarf on public exhibition. He took out his identity card and there he saw recorded: Four foot, eleven inches, and not an inch more. And him with the name of a giant. He didn't know on whom to vent his exasperation, for João was incapable of understanding his dilemma. João could never find any fault with Adamastor. Even were he to break a limb, upon coming to his assistance João in all probability would reassure him: "Adamastor you look better now than you ever did."

"Women are no good when it comes to confiding in someone," thought Adamastor aloud. "Women are foolish," he would say to compensate for his lack of height. And in the bar he would adopt an attitude of indignation and outrage, refusing to acknowledge even the most gracious compliment or politeness. Out of caution, he had taken to wearing a brown tie with a white suit.

João put up with his friend's silence, which had abruptly put an end to their customary banter each morning. He would slip quietly into the room in order not to disturb him.

"If it's a question of bumping off someone, I'll do the job for you. Just give me his name."

Even though wallowing in self-pity, Adamastor savored the idea of a man killing a complete stranger on a friend's behalf. And he mused to himself: "Only men are capable of such generosity. Women, on the other hand, are only good for sex." But he made no reply to João's offer.

He did not intend to bother João with his problem, but simply to tell him: "I have been deeply wronged by my father's perverse behavior. Don't forget that I am a man of the world and I can judge things quite impartially" . . . or to cry out that nature had bungled somewhere in his case. Since there was no mistaking the fact, someone must take the blame, he reflected sadly.

"Do you like my name?" he asked at the end. João nodded in the affirmative and said in a detached voice: "It's the name of a cowboy." Adamastor knew, however, he was no cowboy. There had been an Adamastor before him who had outclassed him so skillfully that his name had become immortalized in one of the world's great epics, such was the fame achieved by the other's devilish exploits. He would no longer be able to compete among men and now even women made him feel uncomfortable. He began to avoid them, fearing that they might start becoming intimate and bring about his ruin. And all those newspaper reporters who had once given him so much satisfaction making him feel important, he now carefully avoided, cowering behind the counter the moment he saw them approach.

"These clever types are a damn nuisance," he would mutter, surprising those who knew him to be vain and affected in his manner of speaking. He treated everyone with distrust and feared that they might unexpectedly embrace him or call out to him amidst laughter and taunts: "Well now, if it isn't the giant Adamastor!"

He had murdered the image of his father on innumerable occasions but that simply wasn't enough, just as changing one's city wasn't enough or assuming another name. The certainty of being Adamastor tortured him. He had to plead martyrdom in order to maintain his self-respect.

"Is it possible that I've been fated to play the cuckold?" he thought, recalling the perceptions which had caused him to forgive João Manco and others.

"What's troubling you, my friend?" João questioned him gently.

"One of these days, I shall go off in search of some new land. There is nothing here for me anymore." He was putting his friend to the test and tracing out the scar that he was about to inflict on the other's face—the symbol of love's revenge.

João dragged himself around the chair, rubbed his own belly, and practiced all the other little tricks that had once delighted Adamastor. "And what about my future?" he asked, anxious to please him.

Adamastor, ever susceptible to affection, reassured him: "What is mine is also yours. I was only joking. This time I intend to die right here."

He sat crouched behind the cash register in the hope that people would soon forget him. He no longer attended to the clients personally and kept out of their sight as much as possible. If any woman pestered him, he would severely rebuke her: "Is this all you women ever want?" The customers, as well as João, soon realized that Adamastor was a changed man. But they felt sorry for him. But they did not stop frequenting his bar. For who other than Adamastor offered them a house adjacent to the bar, gaily decorated with vases of flowers, and dedicated to the protection of Saint George.

Translated by Giovanni Pontiero
(From *Sala de armas*, 1973)

Bibliography

Fiction by Nélida Piñon

A casa da paixão. Rio de Janeiro: Francisco Alves, 1972.

A doce canção de Caetana. Rio de Janeiro: Guanabara, 1987.

A força do destino. Rio de Janeiro: Francisco Alves, 1978.

A república dos sonhos. Rio de Janeiro: Francisco Alves, 1984.

A roda do vento. São Paulo: Atica, 1998.

"Adamastor." Trans. Giovanni Pontiero. *Shantih* 3. 3 (1976): 20–23. Rpt. in *Contemporary Women Authors of Latin America: New Translations.* Eds. Doris Meyer and Margarite Fernández Olmos. New York: Brooklyn College Press, 1983. 235–40.

"Big-Bellied Cow." Trans. Gregory Rabassa. *Mundus Artium* 3.3 (1970): 89–96. Rpt. in *Short Stories by Latin American Women: The Magic and the Real.* Ed. Celia Correas de Zapata. Houston: Arte Público Press, 1990. 156–62.

"Bird of Paradise." Trans. Giovanni Pontiero. *Review: Center for Inter-American Relations* 19 (1976): 75–78.

"Bird of Paradise" and "The New Kingdom." Trans. Evelyn Picón Garfield. *Women's Fiction from Latin America.* Ed. Evelyn Picón Garfield. Detroit: Wayne State University Press, 1988. 268–77.

"Brief-Flower." Trans. Gregory Rabassa. *Contemporary Latin American Literature.* Eds. José Donoso and William Henkin. New York: Dutton, 1969. 309–16.

Caetana's Sweet Song. New York: Knopf, 1992.

Fundador. Rio de Janeiro: n.p., 1969.

Guía-mapa de Gabriel arcanjo. Rio de Janeiro: G.R.D., 1961.

"The Heat of Things." Trans. Gregory Rabassa. *Scents of Wood and Silence: Short Stories by Latin American Women Writers.* Eds. Kathleen Ross and Yvette E. Miller. Pittsburgh: Latin American Review Press, 1991. 159–62.

"House of Passion." Trans. Gregory Rabassa. *The Borzoi Anthology of Latin American Literature.* Vol 2. Ed. Emir Rodríguez Monegal. New York: Knopf, 1977. 393–98.

"I Love My Husband." Trans. Claudia Van der Heuvel. *Landscapes of a New Land: Short Fiction by Latin American Women.* Ed. Marjorie Agosín. Buffalo: White Pine Press, 1989. Rpt. in *Women's Writing in Latin America.* Eds. Sara Castro-Klaren, Sylvia Molloy, and Beatriz Sarlo. Boulder, Colo.: Westview Press, 1991. 72–77.

Madeira feita cruz. Rio de Janeiro: G.R.D., 1963.

"The Myth of Creation." Trans. Giovanni Ponitiero. *Lives on the Line: The Testimony of Contemporary Latin American Authors.* Ed. Doris Meyer. Berkeley: University of California Press, 1988. 306–11.

O calor das coisas. Rio de Janeiro: Nova Fronteira, 1980.

The Republic of Dreams. Trans. Helen Lane. New York: Knopf, 1989.

Sala de armas. Rio de Janeiro: Sabiá, 1973.

Tebas do mèu coração. Rio de Janeiro: José Olympio, 1974.

Tempo das frutas. Rio de Janeiro: José Alvaro, 1966.

Essays by Nélida Piñon

O pao de cada día. 1994.

"Quizás mi infancia fue una invención mía." *Alba de América* 12.22–23 (1994): 117–23.

Criticism on the Works of Nélida Piñon

Areas, Vilma. "Do Adamastor camoniano a 'Sala de armas' de Nélida Piñon." *Coloquio* 27 (1975): 32–39.

Castanon, Adolfo. "La casa de los destinos cruzados." *Vuelta* (Mexico City) 20.232 (1996): 57–60.

Coelho, Nelly Novaes. "*A casa da paixão* e as forcas primordiais da natureza." *Convivium* 16.3 (1973): 216–28.

———. "*A república dos sonhos:* Premio ficcao/84 APCA: Memoria, historicidade, imaginario." *Convivium* 28 (1985): 257–65.

———. "Nélida Piñon, premio 'Mario de Andrade.'" *Coloquio* 15 (1973): 74–77.

Costa, Horacio. "A margem de *A república dos sonhos* de Nélida Piñon." *Luso-Brazilian Review* 24.1 (1987): 1–15.

Costigan, Lucia Helena. "Literatura e ditadura: Aspectos da ficção brasileira pós-64 em alguns dos escritos de Lygia Fagundes Telles e de Nélida Piñon." *Hispanic Journal* 13.1 (1992): 141–51.

Fonta, Sergio. "Nélida Piñon: O papo." *Jornal do Livro* 260 (1973): 6.

Fuentes, Carlos. "Tras *La república de los sueños.*" *La Nación* [literary supplement] April 7, 1996: 1–2.

González Tosar, Luis. "Nélida Piñon ou a paixon de contar." *Grial: Revista Galega de Cultura* (Vigo, Spain) 28.105 (1990): 85–95.

Guimarães, Denise A. D. "Uma poética de autor: Leitura de um texto de Nélida Piñon." *Estudos Brasileiros* 5.9 (1980): 39–55.

Hinchberger, Bill. "Una narradora de mitos modernos." *Americas* 49.1 (1997): 40–45.

Igel, Regina. "Nélida Piñon." *Dictionary of Literary Biography: Modern Latin American Fiction.* Eds. William Luis and Ann González. Columbia, S.C.: Bruccoli, 1994. 237–46.

Issa, Farida. "Entrevista con Nélida Piñon." *Nueva Narrativa Hispanoamericana* 3.1 (1973): 133–40.

Lamar, Celita. "Nélida Piñon." *Contemporary World Writers.* London: St. James, 1993. 413–14.

Landers, Vasda B. "Interview with Nélida Piñon." *Belles Letres* 6 (1991): 24–25.

Lara, Cecilia de. "O 'indevassavel casulo': Uma leitura de *A república dos sonhos* de Nélida Piñon." *Revista do Instituto de Estudos Brasileiros* 27 (1987): 27–36.

Marting, Diane. "Female Sexuality in *A casa da paixão* by Nélida Piñon: A Ritual Wedding Song in Narrative." *Love, Sex, and Eroticism in Contemporary Latin American Literature.* Ed. Alun Kenwood. Melbourne: Voz Hispánica, 1992. 143–52.

McNab, Gregory. "Abordando a historia em *A republica dos sonhos.*" *Brasil/Brazil: Revista de Literatura Brasileira* 1.1 (1988): 41–53.

Milán, Eduardo. "Escribir un estado de alerta." *Revista de la Universidad de México* 36.3 (1981): 12–13.

Moniz, Naomi Hoki. "*A casa da paixão*: Etica, estéetica e a condição femenina." *Revista Iberoamericana* 50.126 (1984): 129–40.

———. *As viagens de Nélida, a escritora*. Campinas, Brazil: UNICAMP, 1993.

Moreira, Virgilio Moretzohn. "Apalo a vida [*A força do destino*]." *Jornal do Livro* 326 (1978): 2.

Norris, Nélida. "Conversando con Nélida Piñon." *Alba de América* 13.24–25 (1995): 519–28.

———. "La ilusión como prurito estético en *La dulce canción de Caetana* de Nélida Piñon." *Alba de América* 13.24–25 (1995): 375–85.

Nunes, Maria Luisa. "*A força do destino* by Nélida Piñon." *Revista Iberoamericana* 108–9 (1979): 712–16.

Ornellas, José. "El mundo simbólico y filosófico de *Madeira feita cruz* de Nélida Piñon." *Nueva Narrativa Hispanoamericana* 3.1 (1973): 95–102.

Paulino, María das Graças Rodrígues. "*Fundador*: A subversão do mito." *Cadernos de Lingüistica e Teoría da Literatura* 2 (1979): 71–75.

Pereira, Teresinha Alves. "Sobre un cuento de Nélida Piñon: 'Sala de armas.'" *Revista de Cultura Brazileña* 49 (1979): 118–20.

Pontiero, Giovanni. "Notes on the Fiction of Nélida Piñon." *Review: Center for Inter-American Relations* 17 (1976): 67–71.

Riera, Carmen. "Entrevista con Nélida Piñon: La vida es la literatura." *Quimera* (Barcelona) 54–55 (1986): 44–49.

Santos, Wendel. "Nélida Piñon." *Os tres reais da ficção; o conto brasileiro hoje*. Petrópolis, Brazil: Vozes, 1978. 135–42.

Schmidt, Rita Terezinha. "Un juego de máscaras: Nélida Piñon y Mary McCarthy." *Escritura* (Caracas) 16.31–32 (1991): 259–70.

Silverman, Malcolm. "*Quinze contos*: Some Revealing Narratives of Janio Quadros." *Romance Notes* 28 (1987): 143–47.

Spielmann, Ellen. "Um romance como espaco auto-reflexao literaria: Nélida Piñon, *A força do destino*." *Revista de Crítica Literaria Latinoamericana* 15.30 (1989): 209–19.

Tierney-Tello, Mary Beth. "Defiance and Its Discontents: Nélida Piñon's *A casa da paixão*." *Allegories of Transgression and Transformation: Experimental Fiction by Women Writing Under Dictatorship*. Albany: State University of New York Press, 1996. 29–77.

Vargas Llosa, Mario. "Palabaras de Mario Vargas Llosa en una presentación de un libro de Nélida Piñon." *Revista de Cultura Brasileña* 48 (1979): 81–91.

Elena Poniatowska

MEXICO

A well-known author and journalist, Elena Poniatowska is recognized as one of the most important writers in Mexico and is among the leading writers in Central and South America.

Poniatowska, the daughter of a Mexican mother and a Polish father, was born in Paris, France, in 1932 and immigrated to Mexico when she was nine years old. She studied in Mexico and the United States, and in 1954, after completing her education, she started working as a journalist for the prestigious newspaper *Excélsior,* later joining the staff of the magazine *Novedades.* She soon distinguished herself for her insightful interviews of leading Latin American, Spanish, and French artists, filmmakers, writers, and politicians.

Poniatowska achieved widespread recognition with the publication of two testimonial works: *Hasta no verte Jesús mío* (Until I see you again, Jesus, 1969) and *La noche de Tlatelolco: Testimonios de literatura oral* (1971; *Massacre in Mexico,* 1975). In *Hasta no verte Jesús mío,* she presents a first-person narrative fictional account of an adventurous peasant woman who, orphaned at an early age, wanders across Mexico working at an assortment of jobs: as a soldier in the Mexican Revolution, a fighter in the Cristero Wars, a factory worker, a servant, and a waitress. The book, based on conversations with Josefina Bórquez, whom Poniatowksa renames Jesusa Palancares, reveals the struggle of a working-class woman to survive, from childhood to old age, in Mexico.

In *La noche de Tlatelolco,* one of the most widely read books in Mexico, she chronicles the 1968 massacre of hundreds of people who gathered in the square of Tlatelolco to hear political protest speeches by students. Through the use of collage and the dramatic montage of the first-person account, Poniatowska vividly brings the reader into the horrifying event.

In *Tinísima* (1992), Elena Poniatowska recounts the life of Tina Modotti, the Italian militant and photographer, masterfully blending photographs and poetic prose: the visual and the written text.

Elena Poniatowska's works exhibit a continuous effort to give original expression to the silent voices of society. Whether writing about the violent attack of government forces on a popular demonstration in Tlatelolco square in 1968, recording the 1985 earthquake that devastated Mexico City, or denouncing the causes of the Indian rebellion in Chiapas, Elena Poniatowska is an eloquent and powerful witness to the sufferings and struggles of the Mexican people.

Slide in, My Dark One, Between the Crosstie and the Whistle

The tube of light perforates the night and the engine makes its way among the walls of trees, walls choked with inextricable vegetation. "Am I the one moving forward or is it the trees that are walking towards me?" the engineer asks himself, surrounded by the nocturnal density and the sugary smell of the tropics. Birds fly into the light, aim at the headlight, and are dashed to pieces. A moment before they die, their eyes are red. All night the engineer watches the birds die. The headlight also blinds the plants; it turns them white, and they only recover their opulence after it has passed and, up above, the dark masses of the mountains are once again sketched on the horizon. Pancho likes to stick his head out of the locomotive and see how, in the train's wake, everything comes back to life: the bushes of thick vegetation revive, transfigured, ghostly; they cross themselves, dazed by the light. Afterwards, the night swallows them up, immense and harsh like that army of trees that unfolds over hundreds of kilometers around them, with who-knows-what secret military strategy.

Meanwhile the intersecting flights of a thousand luminous insects cross the darkness of the sky; Pancho can even hear the death rattle of some animal caught in a trap and the occasional cry of a wounded bird. Fascinated, he thinks about the thousands of birds that fall on the tracks. Probably not even their little bones are left, their little bird bones, sticks, twigs; nothing is more fragile. The electric reflector weighs half a ton and illuminates half a kilometer in front of it; inside that white light the insects dance until dawn. (Camilo calls them "inseps.")

As it begins to turn light, the sounds of the night die down: the cicadas; the strangely human cries of the birds; the dark movements of the heavy, plant-covered ground; the secret, sinuous water, which is finally drowned in the swamp. Then Pancho, his senses overloaded, closes his eyes, sighs, leans back on the iron bench, brushes his strong hand over his face as if to wipe it off. All he manages to do is knock off his cap. He smooths his hair; it's time to go to sleep. Any minute now he will get off the locomotive to fall into any cot, the first one he can find, until night returns. Then, rested, he will once again climb onto his engine, his waking love, the river of steel that runs through his veins, his steam, his air, his reason for being on Earth, his only bridge with reality.

The nicest thing about Teresa, besides her ample flesh, was her prudence, or rather, her absolute incapacity for intrigue or malevolence. He would come home swearing a blue streak against the yard chief, saying that they were going to all get together to get rid of the sonofabitch, that the union was there for a reason, that . . . and Teresa, with her steady cow eyes, would respond calmly:

"Well, we'll see."

Never a judgement, never an unnecessary word. She would slowly shift her great passivity from the kitchen, to the bedroom, to the patio, and seemed to embrace everything. Nothing got to her, nothing altered her even temper.

Still, Pancho liked it when Teresa sat on top of him while they made love, he on his back in bed and she crouched over him, mounted on his chest, her legs encircling him, so enormous that Pancho couldn't see her face, smothered as he was by her stomach, her powerful thighs, but what sweet, what comforting asphyxiation. Pancho felt as satisfied then as he did before his engine's control panel. A dense happiness slid through him; the liquid metal that comes out of the foundry bubbled inside him, with the pure, white color of sunlight. Pancho went from the nocturnal plenitude on the tracks of the southwestern route, standing erect before the window of the locomotive, to the plenitude of his three-o'clock nap, when he reached out his hand to feel Teresa's thick, hot arm, and to draw her to him, to embrace that tender, soft *mole*, and to dive into her time and again, like the birds flinging themselves against the headlight time and again, their eyes red. They always made love around noon, with a diadem of sweat on Teresa's brow.

From the kitchen came the crackling of pork frying, covered with a lid so it wouldn't dry out, and Pancho's appetite would double. He would fuck sluggishly and go from one table to the other, barely taking time to put on his pajama bottoms. He would sit before the marrow broth that Teresa served him, a strap from her slip straying down her arm. She would eat too, gazing at his face while she flipped the tortillas on the *comal*, her arm outstretched. They would sop up their food, taking their time, sipping it, accumulating new sensations on their hot, agitated tongues, as if they were continuing and perpetuating the act of love. Many times, when he finished wiping his mouth with his hand, Pancho would again pull Teresa toward the disheveled, greasy bed. Afterwards they would remain in each other's arms, the nape of Teresa's sweaty neck against Pancho's shoulder, Pancho's wet organ fallen against Teresa's leg, so she could feel how the semen still trickled out. They would sink into sleep like that. But sometimes Teresa clung to Pancho's neck as if she were going to drown, as if she were on the verge of falling into the deepest part of the ocean, of her ocean, her own water. Then Pancho would desire her furiously for the dependency in her embrace and for that distracted expression in her round eyes.

At exactly six-forty he would say good-bye to her from the door, as Teresa would finally set about washing the dishes, cleaning up the kitchen. When Pancho would return from his run at six in the morning two days later, he would find her asleep. As he slipped under the sheets next to her, she would receive him with a murmur of acquiescence. In the course of the morning Teresa would abandon the bed; she would sweep, or "dustmot," as she called it, and do the ironing. Around two in the afternoon she would lie down next to him again, still dressed, to be within reach of his desire when he woke up.

"No, Pancho, this shouldn't be greased."

"You mean I shouldn't grease the bearings?"

"No, in a diesel engine all this work is automatic."

"And what about the joint pins, I don't grease them either?"

"No, everything's already done, see."

"But who does the engine maintenance?"

"She does her own maintenance, all by herself. A hydrostatic lubricator, run by steam, pressure, water, and oil, greases the cylinders. This diesel was built to make things easier for the people who operate it. All you have to do is drive."

Pancho looks uneasily at the engine; he doesn't recognize it, doesn't know how to get a hold on it. For the first time he feels out of place in a locomotive. Everything is hidden; the controls are contained inside a steel surface so shiny that it repels him. The yard up above also shines; the picture windows make the station look like a glass store.

"Nothing is like it used to be," he thinks, "nothing."

In the old days the dark *mole* of the locomotive would sprout up on the horizon, followed by its plume of smoke and, in less time than it takes a cock to crow, there it was, parked, blocking out the clarity of the morning with its blackness. It would enter, snorting its weariness, out of breath, and would settle in on the rails defiantly, with a screech of springs. Its triumphant panting would still echo through the station. The railroad men would climb off her and say good-bye or shout their hellos, overjoyed at coming home. As they got off, they would pat their engine, slapping her back as if she were a good old animal, caressing her with an open hand, ample caresses, trying to take in everything. Pancho would stay with La Prieta in the loading yard, cooling her down; he liked to hear the hammering that came from the workshop, cars, axles, and wheels, one, two, one, two, on top of the anvils, and the echoing in his ears, the purring of the lathes, as the whistle of the locomotive had once echoed. As the workmen straightened the old, arthritic track with bars, they would groan and yell as they tried to lift it: "Ahhhhhhh! Ooooooooooh! Ahhhhhhh!" It was as if they felt the rails' discomfort in their own bodies and were showing solidarity with them. And all of this amidst the even breathing of the boilers and the constant chugging of the air pistons.

As he would head off, feeling contented, king of the road, Pancho would tell the mechanic: "I'm leaving her in your hands; I'll be back in a while to take her for a spin." The trainmen would pass by cans of tar, piles of burlap; they would jump over the ballast with the heady joy of a traveler who recognizes his house; they would skirt around the empty containers, worn-out boxes, twisted iron, junk. It's true, everything wasn't clean; the ballast was covered with trash, with living things that were now charred, with loose chunks of carrion, with discarded tools, all the garbage that, ten thousand years from now, will be indistinguishable from organic and inorganic waste that time, or perhaps the sea, will pulverize into sand. An upside-down lantern dug into the earth, an abandoned cart displayed its guts, the trash was forming a mountain, but now the brightness of the tracks was driving Pancho crazy.

"So, this doesn't need to be greased?"

"No, Pancho, I told you it doesn't."

"OK, and what about La Prieta?"

"We're sending her to Apizaco. They'll run her on some short stretches."

"But why the hell didn't you tell me you were going to take her away?"

"No one was told, Pancho. The three-thousand-horsepower diesels arrived and we wanted to put them into service immediately."

"I was off yesterday, and you took advantage."

Just like Teresa. Treacherous, sneaky. One morning she wasn't there anymore. Afterwards a railroad worker told him that he had seen her get into a car, hoisted by a man's hand; he hadn't been able to get a look at the man, but he sure noticed how Teresa walked fast, without looking around her. At home the old, pot-bellied suitcase that the engineer always took with him was missing. For many days Pancho kept reaching out to take Teresa's thick arm and pull her towards him, until he finally decided to go to the station and escape into the dark chamber of his other woman, to take refuge in her womb which, even when stationary, seemed to be rocking, and to sleep curled up against the steel plate, telling her what he never told Teresa, "Prieta, my pretty little dark one, my darling, pretty Momma, Prieta, little railroad girl, you're my love, Prieta, you flirt," until his lips kept forming an *a*, the *a* of Prieta, that name pronounced like a charm against pain and abandonment. And now they come out with this business that La Prieta isn't there anymore either.

"When did they take her away?"

"Last night."

Pancho was at a section meeting at the very moment that La Prieta, slowly, sneakily, slid away along the rails, driven by another engineer.

"Who took her out?"

The superintendent is getting impatient. "Go ask in the office."

"I don't have anything to do with ink-shitters. They're not even railroad men."

"Man, it isn't like that; things are changing for the better. It's the new rules and regulations; the power of the railroad has to grow. It'll be good for us all. Anyway, thank your lucky stars that your locomotive isn't being sold as scrap iron to the United States. We're going to sell them almost three thousand cars that are in really bad shape."

"Fuck you."

Pancho turns around before the superintendent can respond. He walks away—he has always been a fast walker—and thinks, "If he catches up with me, we'll have it out right here." He almost wishes it would happen, but the other man doesn't come after him, no one follows him. He walks among the burning of the rails that flash in his eyes, waxing them, slicing them; he steps onto the ballast so he won't get tar on his shoes, and he remembers with what pleasure Teresa used to sweep the ground, even though she did it with a worn-out broom. He tries to retain the image, which begins to smear before him, but the heat seems to melt every-thing—signs, crossties, loading platforms, rivets—into a thick, grey gela-tin. The iron disintegrates; now it is just clumps of earth; yes, it is common dirt.

"If a train comes, fuck them; I'm not moving."

On a newly tarred wall a sign glitters: "Long live Demetrio Vallejo!" Pancho walks without stopping, the sun on his neck boring into his shoulders. It was a while back that he left Balbuena and passed under the bridge at Nonoalco; it was a while back that he entered the plains. Now there aren't even any crossing gates, not a single man sitting on the plat-forms, no one bent over kicking the gravel, no one playing with the sand, with the rocks that fall down onto the coal wagons; just a stray worn-out shoe, defeated like him, and over there, a caboose rotting in the sun. Now there aren't any guard towers or cranes. He thinks he hears the wailing of a brake shoe. "Goddamn, now I'm hearing voices." There isn't a single convoy of cars loaded with sulphur from the Isthmus of Tehuantepec, not a single convoy of salt. He has to go on, put one foot in front of the other, for who knows how many hours, until dusk, his throat dry. Anyway, he's used to it by now; he can put up with that and a lot more; he can put up with a helluva lot.

"I have to reach some station so I won't be stranded here in no-man's-land."

But since no house shimmers in the distance, Pancho leaves the rails and stretches out alongside the tracks, and there he sleeps like an angel, like a rock at the bottom of a well, like a dead man.

"You know, prices are getting to be sky-high."

When Teresa spoke it was to complain about the high cost of living. Otherwise she kept silent as she went from one chore to another. Only when she made love did she articulate words of love that started with m, "more," "mmm," slowly, softly, in a hoarse cooing, yes, that was it, a dove cooing, which Pancho always found gratifying. Precisely because of that moan, suddenly, in the middle of a meal, Pancho felt a piercing, an infinite desire to possess her. It was he who provoked that woman's moan, and on top of her, embracing her womb, he awaited the moment when it would begin, just as he waited for the instant La Prieta would begin back-stitching the plains with the clacking of her wheels on the tracks. When she ran quietly, sheathed in silence, he felt the same desire as when he mounted Teresa. He was the master of time, of all that darkness, of the blackness that his headlight penetrated; those shadows that he crossed over were conquered territory, lands owned by him, his booty; he had extracted them from the night. They warbled like Teresa, they flooded over him with their incredibly white, luminous masses; white like milk, thighs, breasts of night, almondlike fruits; skin that softly, tenderly enveloped him.

At first, Teresa had been more communicative. She had talked about her sister Berta, about how Berta used to hit her; about how once, when she couldn't delouse Teresa, she had shaved her head. Every so often she would complain to Pancho, "Hey, how come you never have anything to say?" And Pancho would mumble, "We railroad men are married to silence." That's why Teresa became quiet. Since she was only answered in monosyllables, little by little she stopped opening her mouth, spoke only when it was absolutely necessary, said only what came out in spite of her, beyond her control: that cooing, and the harping on sky-high prices.

"Pancho, get up, you sucker."

"Pancho!"

The shadows of two faces fall over him. Pancho rubs his eyes.

"We've been following you for hours. Come on, let's go."

El Chufas and El Gringo pull on him; El Chufas has already put his hands under his arms and lifted him up. "The hell you're going to stay here; let's get going."

El Gringo gets mad: "I'm on duty tomorrow, you sonofabitch. Come on, stop farting around."

"Hey, who asked you? You're the one that's farting around." Now it's Pancho who gets good and mad, so mad that he gets up. "I suppose I went looking for you guys? You're the ones who're fucking with me; I was just fine here."

El Chufas hasn't taken his hands out from under his arms, as if he's afraid Pancho will run away.

Pancho breaks loose violently, although all his anger is directed at El Gringo. "You go to hell!"

"Thatta way, Pancho, don't let anyone order you around."

"Who told you guys to come after me, huh? I didn't ask you."

"El Chufas started looking for you."

"So what the hell's with El Chufas? He doesn't give a damn."

"El Chufas saw you walking off along the track, mad as hell, and he hollered at you but you didn't turn around. That's why he got worried. Just forget it. We were in the loading yard . . . Come on, let's get out of here."

Without realizing it, Pancho has started walking alongside his buddies. It's been a long time since he has hung out with them. He didn't even go looking for them when Teresa left, didn't show his face at the cantina. Anyway, he had La Prieta, and that's where he went to sleep, cradled in the tremulous viscera that held him warmly, in the internal combustion of his own blood which demanded his recognition as the night advanced, to foresee her reactions, to guess the secret of her most hidden sounds, her tinklings, signals, and sighs. He wrapped his legs around her ardor, as Teresa used to imprison his, so that when they woke up they only had to turn over to be in each other's arms. He could predict her least convulsion: "Now she's going to shudder because the guys from the shop will come, and the hammer blows on the anvil will echo all through the steel plate. I'm going to feel the blows myself, here inside her. In a minute the boiler makers will come, along with the superintendent, and she'll soften up, happy." Before, Pancho had the habit of going to the cantina with his buddies, and when they shouted, "Wine for the men and water for the asses," he would belly up to the bar to guzzle his beer, then go to the house with the red light to dance with the broads who smell like rotten corn. But when Teresa came into his life, he no longer needed anything, not hell-raising, not clinging women from the cathouse. So long, Canicas, Camilo, Babalú, Gringo, Chufas, Luciano! Luciano had given his engine a name, too: "The Flirt," and he had her all dolled up, with her hanging trinkets and mirrors, her Virgin of Guadalupe, and even a picture of himself leaning out the window of the locomotive. Now that Pancho has had time to think about it, he feels kind of warm inside, walking with his friends, his buddies, his pals, who have come all this way to look for him, forgetting that he dumped them a long time ago.

"Climb into the caboose. Let's go have a cold one."

These fellows are good guys, really good guys.

"Pancho, a coupla beers'll do you good."

Pancho doesn't say yes or no.

"They're probably closed up already," says El Gringo.

"Well, let's go to Martita's."

Martita is a real hellcat. When the railroad men are out to party and everyone at the bar orders them out, "OK, you crazies, get going, it's time to call it a night, go sleep it off!" and a good cup of coffee is nowhere to be found, not even an eggnog or one last round, the front door of her house is always open. She doesn't mind climbing out of her hammock and waiting on them with her big, beautiful smile, a slow wave of light moving through her eyes, like a mother looking at her children, showing no favorites. No matter how wasted they might be, really out of it, hanging onto each other like they have been hanging onto the lampposts, like masts, feeling as if their ships are sinking, just seeing her raises their spirits. She immediately brings out the *mezcal* or makes a steaming pot of spiked coffee sweetened with condensed milk that comes gushing out of the can, and if they can pay her, fine, and if not, they'll drop by with the dough when they can. She brought the hammock from Juchitán, since she never could get used to sleeping in a bed: "It's the rocking I miss." "It's the rocking that keeps her in a good mood," the railroad men say. They always feel good as hell at Martita's house; their raw stomachs settle down and, even if they're sloppy drunk, she takes the edge off with her spiked coffee, so good for warming the belly. And none of this nagging or scolding them, none of that; Martita is beautiful, her eyes with those slow waves of light are beautiful. What more could you hope for in this goddamn life than to feel welcome, sheltered by the eyes of a woman who's happy to see you, what the hell more could you ask for, anyway? Pancho also stopped hanging out at Martita's when Teresa arrived.

"The superintendent wants to see you tomorrow," El Gringo says to him as they nurse their second cup of java.

"I already told him to fuck off."

"He said he wants to see you."

For the superintendent, Alejandro Díaz, Pancho is a real character. He even gets a kick out of watching him walk by with his grey hair and his slump shoulders, on his way to the section local, saying gravely, "Tomorrow at noon the strike begins, the two-hour work stoppage, because the deadline we gave management is past . . ." Alejandro Díaz is a company man. When he sees Pancho, he wishes he weren't, so he could hear him arguing in the assembly, see his strong, challenging gaze, the gaze of a free man, when all day long he's followed around by so many hangdog expressions. And he's only the superintendent. Imagine how many despicable expressions the president of the Republic must see! They say—but no one knows it for a fact—that Pancho once spoke at Section 19 in Monterrey, before an assembly of one thousand railroad men who believed in the Charro, Díaz de León. The first three speakers supported the Charro, and when Pancho Valverde got up to speak, everyone thought he would join them; but they were all taken aback when he said the Charro was a corrupt leader, out for the company, the government, and especially himself, his own petty self-interest. All those people knew that Pancho was a straight shooter, but still the assembly ended up divided. That was one of the biggest blows in Pancho's union career, but he never mentioned it. Sometimes in the cantina he remembers the assembly and murmurs, "It's no good, it's no good."

That's why the older guys respect Pancho and the younger ones want to be noticed by him, to make an impression on him. The superintendent feels the same way. Alejandro Díaz knows he doesn't count in Pancho's book, that the engineer would lay down his life for Timoteo, for Venancio, for Chon, for Baldomero, for El Gringo, for Camilo, for El Babalú, but not for him. For them he would. Alejandro Díaz has seen how Pancho demands compensation, fights for the retirees, stays up into the wee hours going over contracts, memorizing clauses, almost all of them in the company's favor, so he can shoot them down at the meeting. His "Shut up, you mother fuckers" is more effective in the assemblies than any reasoned argument; his fist hitting the debate table covered with cigarette burns is definitive; and the first thing you see in the presidium is his face, because of the intensity of his expression. It isn't even that he wants power; it's that Pancho is a friend of Timoteo the switch-engine worker, who is looking at him now, his stub resting on the table because he left his forearm trapped between two cars during one of so many maneuvers. And he is also a buddy of Venancio, a retiree who is starving to death inside the railroad car where he lives, even though his wife has hung geraniums in the windows. And he cares about Lenche the fireman, who these days shovels rancor instead of coal, and he likes Concepción, Chonito, who practically lives in the Temple of Noon, under the Nonoalco Bridge, on Luna Street, waiting for Roque Rojas—never mind Jesus Christ!—to take possession of his human form and free him from arthritis, old age, his breath smelling like slimy water, which tells him that his insides are rotting.

Pancho Valverde has never let himself get discouraged: "I speak up because I want to and because I can and because I've been giving 'em hell here for a lot of years." He peppers his allegations with sayings: "The fewer the burros, the more corncobs there are," "The shrimp that falls asleep gets carried away by the tide," "He who is an ox even licks the yoke." And Alejandro Díaz finds it amusing to associate Pancho's sayings with expressions like "gross national product" (We're the ones who are gross), "holidays" (He who is born to be an old pot can't even hope to become a sooty grill), "contractual" (There are no more railroad men with pocket watches and caps), and other wonderful sayings that Pancho has learned by heart in his many shifts as a warehouseman. "Come on, come on, don't start running around like a chicken with its head cut off." It was Pancho who started the initiative against the company men. Whatta we need with so many of them? What is that bunch of dolled-up accountants good for, those secretaries that totter around on their high heels like hens? Pancho said that, out of Pacific Railway's five hundred classified employees, the company men didn't even amount to fifty, and he called for at least twenty-three of them to be laid off, because he was here to tell you that they didn't do a damned thing. He identified the culprits, and two of them turned out to be sons of Benjamín Méndez, the manager. He said the eight thousand rail workers—now they were underfed and underpaid—were up to here with the bureaucracy, with so much dull paperwork. And naturally, the company didn't give in; it fired a lot of people.

But what a great fight Pancho put up, great even in the eyes of Alejandro Díaz, who intervened on Pancho's behalf so they wouldn't dismiss him, and he never even knew it. It's a helluva good fight, because Pancho pushes strikes but has always come out against acts of sabotage. He loves the trains too much to put up with a runaway engine, a crash; the least dent on his locomotive makes him flinch as if the blow were to his body. An attack on the track hurts him personally, like that time some bastard blocked the safety pedal on Train 6093, placing a plate of steel over the accelerator. He pulled the lever and the engine shot away at more than eighty kilometers an hour, heading straight for Train 9854, the Flirt, Luciano's engine, which was being moved around the yard. Luciano just about got it, but he took off the brakes and immediately jumped off his locomotive. He saved his own skin but not the Flirt's; she was transformed into a spine-chilling mountain of twisted metal. Months later, Luciano died of sadness.

At Luciano's side, Pancho had lived through strikes and other adventures. One time Luciano held tight to the driving shaft, trying to stop five runaway trains, and he only jumped off at the last minute, when he saw the wreck was imminent. Pancho used to sing, sitting on a crosstie, "Wherever I come / and wherever I go / the hen I don't take with me / I leave cackling." And the two of them would laugh, because when they were young they were both on the sign committee, and along with "Down with the company" and "Railroad workers with Vallejo," they used to write on the sides of the cars, in black tar, holding their sides and dropping the buckets, "What a rail I've got!" "I want to go clackety-clacketyclack with you," "Don't worry that the tunnel's dark, we'll slide in on the rail," "Just give me a good engine and I'll pull out all the stops," "Fuck you, Díaz de León," "Between the rails and between your legs, we make it from town to town," "Slide in, my dark one, between the crosstie and the whistle," "Onto a good caboose you can hook anything you want," and other delectable sayings that they drew with care, licking their lips, because they had just discovered women and the rails. Goddamn Luciano, one helluva guy, what a pal, he's like a brother to me, my man!

For Alejandro Díaz, the superintendent, it is painful to look at Pancho. The expression on his face is absolutely desolate; he looks like a dog without a master. Deep down inside, Alejandro Díaz would like to tell Pancho that, if his steam locomotive means so much to him, he will arrange for his transfer to one of the less-traveled routes, so he can keep driving it. But Pancho is one of the best engineers in the system, and now that his temples are turning grey and his face, which has always looked like a rail yard, is wrinkled, the company is taking away his engine to give him a diesel, one they just bought from the United States.

Instead of feeling proud, Pancho Valverde is suspicious. He wooed La Prieta—oh my Prieta!—because she was always finicky and you had to figure out how to treat her. He dressed her up; he bought her a bronze whistle, picking the deep tone himself: "Give me a whistle that sounds downright pretty for my Prieta, because I've got a three-star Prieta." On the days when it was his turn to take her out, he would arrive with the oil can, the cushion to protect him from the heat when the seat was on the sunny side, the heavy sweater for nighttime, the little suitcase, the hand mirror, the lantern. The other railroad men would laugh:

"Here comes Pancho with his trousseau for the honeymoon."

Actually, every run is the first night, the wedding night. Pancho installs himself in the seat, grabs the lever, and, while he transmits an order to her, caresses her. When the engine emits steam with the sound of a pressure cooker, Pancho also relaxes, and he tenses up like a cable when he puts on the brakes, when he checks on hills to see that the rail stops respond and brake, all of his concentration focused on keeping the cars in check. It's nice to hear the engines being hooked up; it's as familiar to him as the sound of a door closing!

Once they are out of the station, Pancho opens up the regulator all the way and speaks to his mount, to his iron mare, to his wide and powerful animal of fire; he strokes her with his hand, he acknowledges her: "OK, OK, Prieta, hold it Prieta, take it easy, take it easy, slow down, girl!" Camilo or Sixto or Supertino or Juan, whichever engineer's helper is on duty, is so used to Pancho's voice that he doesn't even listen. In fact, it puts him to sleep; it's a real drag, because Pancho doesn't like to share La Prieta with anybody. He leads her over the tracks almost as if he were dancing with her; his hand on her waist, the tips of his fingers on her side, they both sweep to the right, to the left, a two-step, dum dum, like someone running through the fields, over the ochre land, the brown dirt, the deep black soil that emerges from a swampy bed and approaches the track without respecting the fifteen meters on either side: the track's right-of-way. The land rolls down from the mountain to cuddle up against the track and penetrate the crossties. It pushes up the stones of the ballast, it nudges in everywhere, wheedling its way in, laughing at the train that runs along the wide track tooting and tooting and scurrying along.

Before noon, the sun begins to heat up; it flings itself against the metal, attacks the chimneys, crashes into the glass, turning it iridescent, heat against heat, fuel against fuel. Pancho shifts the cushion under his behind. Even the oil can is boiling. Threads of greasy sweat slide down from Camilo's railroad cap; Pancho's helper is sleeping while he cooks in his own juice, his mouth open like the chimney of the train, an oven of steam that also vanishes in thin air. From noon on, the towns around Veracruz are no longer towns, but rather corners of hell. When he stops at the stations, Pancho sees the burros hitched up, the tables that have been brought outside, the sausage blackened by flies, the lard under the table melting, and the little old woman who shades herself from the heat, covering her head and fanning herself with the fringe of her shawl, as if that could do any good. Those who approach the train observe it silently; the only ones who shout are the women vendors who go to the last cars, hawking their sandwiches of head cheese, their candies, their fruit-flavored water that is now lukewarm from the sun. In a little while they will take off again: "Come on, Prieta, pull hard, don't give out on me, because it's the last stretch."

Near the engine, a passenger in a threadbare suit says to another man who has just woken up: "You can't even feel this thing moving."

"That's because it doesn't move, it just inches along."

Pancho nearly talks back to that dandy; for a minute he considers sounding the alarm whistle just to give him a good scare, but self-discipline wins out. Pancho 's a good engineer for two reasons: first, because he's a good driver, and second, because he knows how to run his engine to get the most out of the steam and water. He could care less what the passengers say; they aren't aware that La Prieta is over twenty years old but is in better condition than almost any train. It is no accident that don Panchito, as the younger railroad men call him, goes with her to the shop to supervise her maintenance. The mechanics know her and take special care in examining all La Prieta's parts. Pancho himself paints her; he goes over her from head to tail so she won't get run down, she won't get mildewed, so not a single hinge will be forgotten, so each part will be oiled. When a young boy started working as his helper and saw the piles of black grease, he exclaimed, "What a filthy job!" Pancho replied, "Get out of here, you bum, you sonofabitch!" and he kept calling him a queer. The other railroad men followed suit, making fun of him, laughing and cursing; they themselves have grease up to their hineys, heavy, black, visceral grease, because it is what they use to cover the insides of the engine, rubbing it in, coaxing it into the smallest seams, ready to sing out gruffly, rounding off the angles with a thick, padded coat, lining the intestines of the locomotive with this new amniotic fluid that softens her and renders her docile. In the shop, grease has never been considered dirty; on the contrary, it's a blessing, and yet now the superintendent, Alejandro Díaz, begins lecturing him as if he had never been a railroad man: "With the diesel engine the work is cleaner, more technical; you won't get dirty anymore. Anyway, you're going to save God knows how many days that you spend lubricating the engine to death."

Pancho looks at him without comprehending. For him, manually lubricating the piston rods, taking them out of their axles, rubbing them over and over again, and putting them back, is a pleasure, a physical necessity.

"You'll see how fast you take to it, Pancho; it's just a matter of getting used to it."

Pancho shakes his head. "There are some of us who just don't get used to certain things."

"You'll see how much you're going to like it. Tomorrow we'll run the engine to Veracruz. You're going to take her out . . . hauling cement."

"To Veracruz?"

With this new, orange, stiff engine, Pancho doesn't speak. In the stations nothing has changed; there are the same rickety, flea-ridden benches; the same stalls selling toasted, dried beef; the same wobbly tables; the same swarms of flies; the same burros with their scar-lined backs. Still, it is as if Pancho, in his engineer's cab, is riding higher, more distant. He can't hear what the passengers say to him, their suits wrinkled from an overnight trip; nor can he hear the cries of the food vendors who lift their baskets up from window to window. During the night the cab didn't get hot; he didn't need his cushion or the oil can, and the second machinist slept soundly, used to Pancho's ways, and without threads of black sweat running down his face. Still, Pancho woke him up several times, feeling uneasy. "Come on, cuz I don't know how to do it in this one." With this one he's going to have to throw away the bridal trousseau; none of that is necessary, not even the little suitcase, because there in the corner is a locker where you can hang your jacket; you can adjust the air conditioning, so you don't even need a sweater, or a mirror, because the cab is full of rearview mirrors. Pancho keeps a suspicious silence and yet the diesel is so powerful, so noble in the upgrades, so good-natured, that the next day he is pleased with the notion of going with her to the shop for her checkup after the trip. "That's how I'll get acquainted with her," like with a new, three-thousand-horsepower love that one grows to admire, then care for; then it becomes that thing which makes one forget old flames, the Prietas, the Teresas. Who knows if it will happen, but it might.

The next morning, before Pancho goes into the shop, the yard boss tells him, "The engine has already been called in."

"Fine, I'll go in with her."

"No, a machinist is coming to get her in a few minutes."

"What do you mean?"

"That you leave her here and another driver will take her away."

"But it's just that I want to see how they get her ready for the next trip."

"On the next run you're going to take another 5409 out, not this one."

"What do you mean, another one?"

"That's right, any of the eight diesel engines that were bought in the United States. Those are the new rules. You leave her here and the shop takes care of her. Someone else will take this engine out. That's how it is now, like in the auto industry; engines are put through a process involving a lot of people. It's so we can speed up service."

Pancho pulls his cap down over his eyes. They're even taking that away from him! Watching, feeling how the engine molds to you, how she runs along memorizing the route, how she talks, after her own fashion, to ask for what she needs. Even that! Seeing how his hands begin to leave prints on the lever, on the regulator, hearing how the sound of his breathing infiltrates the steel plates day by day, until his warmth is transmitted to them. Even that, dammit!

"They're modern techniques; that's how the engineers have planned it, to save time."

Teresa also liked it when he caressed her little by little, softening her, carving her, coaxing his hand into her smallest seams to pull out her oil, her delicate juices. Then Teresa would open up, her thick legs far apart, forgetful of everything, and she would sway under his arm, her large, erect breasts pointing towards him, her sex twisted, liquid, a fruit of the sea, undone in his hands, whipped into foam, about to come. He liked waiting until the last minute so he could see her, listen to her changing rhythms, look at her open caldron-mouth full of saliva, her eyelids half-closed, her hands spread out over the sheets, the palms turned up, the fingers spread as wide as her oiled thighs which rose up in search of his hand. That's how he lubricated her, with her own flow, her own humors, until he had rendered her docile, until his hand was soaked and his arm was also soaked under her neck, while her head bobbed to the right, to the left, and her ample, sweaty buttocks also came and went in a wave that filled the bed with water. Only when her broad womb was shaken by spasms, only when the dove's cooing began, only then did Pancho penetrate Teresa, "Now, honey, now," and he wasn't inside of her five minutes before she had come in an avalanche of moans, of sobs, arching her back over and over again until she was fulfilled. Pancho sought the expression of satisfaction, never seen on her features except during lovemaking; that's why he couldn't stop looking pointedly at her until he saw her face relax, her mouth sucking gently like that of a newborn, the sucking, then the letting go, spilling over all her features. How glorious it was for him to see this big, panting woman, her eyes blank, unblushing, loose, the wide, bulky mountain now quiet, blind, then slowly coming back to life, drained, having given away all her fruits, one by one! Within the hour, Teresa would get out of bed, and just like that, without even going to the bathroom, she would go into the kitchen to light the fire. They would eat, then go back to bed filled with liquid murmurs, and he would mount her hurriedly because he had to go to work, and she would offer herself again, tender, whole, dry, good, what a good woman Teresa was, what goodness; she mended quickly, and he would start again, his hand groping, moving over her with familiarity, until his caresses drew out her water. Here? Lower? Lower? Tell me where, honey, here?

"I want to transfer to Apizaco."

"Don't be stupid, how could you possibly leave? Pancho, you'll lose your seniority, just for the hell of it."

El Gringo is getting mad. They call him El Gringo because of his blue eyes, but he's from the mountains in the state of Puebla.

"I'm going to talk to the superintendent in charge of Locomotive Power."

El Gringo is a seasoned man; he started working for the railroad as a laborer; then they promoted him from cleaner to fireman. "All we need now is for flies to be conductors!" But El Gringo had also been a stoker and a brakeman. He went all the way through the ranks: yard brakeman, foreman, yard boss, assistant to the general yard boss, and that was the end of the line, because the next position, that of general yard boss, the one who gives the orders in the terminal, is classified and he, like Luciano Cedillo Vásquez, would rather stay on this side of the curtain . . . of pesos. He knew the place inside and out. Just four months ago he had asked them to give him the rules and regulations for the diesels because these locomotives, which were much more powerful than the steam engines, went out with up to forty or fifty cars but used the same number of personnel, so a lot of railroad workers were laid off. El Gringo put up a fight because the engineer's helpers also had contracts, but he lost. What he never lost, not even in the slammer, was hope.

"You can get thirty thousand pesos out of the company when you retire."

"Don't bullshit me, what's the matter with you? How many retirees do you know who aren't starving to death?"

El Gringo slams his glass down on the table. "You can get up to forty thousand out of them."

If he weren't El Gringo, Pancho would tell him to get lost, but this old guy is prepared. El Chufas, a bit tipsy, laughs softly. El Gringo slams his glass down again and hollers at the bartender: "Where are the rest? We're going to accuse you of tortoise-ism." The bartender, peeved at seeing the glass in the air, is about to reply, "If you break it you buy it," but he thinks better of it.

"They took my little dark one away from me," says Venancio as he comes up to the tables. "But that doesn't mean I've looked down my nose at the new ones."

"Get out of here."

Pancho likes the taste of the first beer when it slides down his throat, sort of bitter and scratchy. With the back of his hand, El Chufas wipes the foam off his mustache. Only El Gringo downs it in one gulp, and then it's too late; he orders the others, and he's paying, so before his buddies have had time to finish theirs, they have new bottles in front of them.

"In those mountains, the track is just an opening in the forest."

"Around those parts," insists El Chufas, "the runs last for days, not just hours."

"And what about me?"

"That isn't an engine," Venancio retorts, "it's a chicken basket."

"Get out of here!" Pancho shouts again.

And this time Venancio gets up; anyway, he's finished his beer. "You and your engine get out of here."

Caritino sits down in the place that Venancio vacated; he orders a beer, leans back in the chair, and pulls his cap down over his face. He always does this. "I come here to relax," he explains. He only wakes up when the swinging starts, because he does like to join in a good fight.

In the warmth of the cantina, Pancho gives free reign to his memories, even more so now that he's feeling down in the mouth. He tells stories about the Brotherhood of Boiler Makers; about the Fraternity of Train Workers; about the struggle of 1945, which turned bloody; about Reza the foreman, who was fatally wounded by a bullet in the neck, right in the main railroad station; about his fellow yardmen. He speaks about past strikes that were invariably lost, about the Vigilance Committee that he once headed, and finally, at the very end, about how wonderful it is to stick your head out the window of La Prieta to feel the gusts of wind. And in a soft voice, he informs them: "Tomorrow I'm leaving for Apizaco."

El Gringo interjects, "As if we'd let you."

Caritino uncovers his face, his railroad cap tilted back, and he takes a long, slow drink of his beer. "If I were him, I'd leave too."

"You guys are against progress."

"Progress, my ass."

The next day Pancho didn't come in to work. The railroad workers thought he had gone off to Apizaco, that in a few days they would have news about him. The superintendent, Alejandro Díaz, personally asked the telegraph operator to let him know as soon as Pancho was seen, although in the mountains the telegraph operators have the irritating habit, especially in the out of-the-way stations, of turning off their machines and not transmitting orders. That's why there are so many train accidents.

A few days later, Alejandro Díaz learned that La Prieta wasn't parked at the platform of the Apizaco railway station, either. Since she was an old engine, he didn't report it immediately; that way the company wouldn't make a stink and they would have a few days to cover for Pancho, find him, send him word that he should stop acting like a fool.

"He's not going to be able to stay out long in that old coffeepot, and if he does, he'd better not have any illusions that we won't arrest him."

"What do you mean, arrest him? That rickety old heap of junk is going to die on him at the first stop. Haven't you seen her joints?"

At the cantina conjectures were flying: "Poor Pancho. That's what usually happens to old railroad men, they get a screw loose." "If Pancho hangs on to that lever, he's going to kill himself!"

The railroad company began sending messages that, at the first stop, Pancho should be informed that he was under arrest, that he was endangering the lives of the other people who used the minor routes. But not a single telegraph operator ever reported the arrival of La Prieta. At Buenavista, only El Gringo tried to organize teams to search the line from Apizaco to Huachinango. He even went along in the caboose, but he didn't see any engines; no locomotive that fit the description had taken in fuel; no grey-haired engineer had gotten off to load up on supplies. Either they were protecting him or he had met his maker.

The railroad company deduced: "He must have gone over into a ravine on his first run, vanishing without a trace." "He must be down at the bottom of the gorge." "But an engine with a man in it can't disappear just like that!" "A lot more than that disappeared in Rome, and who even remembers now!"

The strange thing is that, on many stretches of track, there were carbonized bats on the rails and ballast, as if a train had actually passed by and they, with their big eyes, had crashed into its headlight. Still, no station reported any engine; nothing, not a sound on the rails. After a few months had gone by, the dispatchers no longer received La Prieta's code among their orders, her distinctive markings, size, and dents, so they could recognize her. And if anyone did lay eyes on her, those who recognized her played dumb, because no one reported it to Buenavista.

From Apizaco to Huachinango, and among the villages high in the mountains, in the vicinity of Teziutlán, a rumor is spreading of a runaway engine that makes ghost runs, and at night you can hear how the engineer opens the steam valve and then the mountain echoes with a long lament, like the cry of a wounded animal, a deep, pained cry that cuts the mountains of Puebla in two. No one has seen her. But once a dispatcher who was starting out in a remote station in the Huasteca region, one of those stations where you never see a living soul and where they usually send rookies to be trained, amidst the dark abysses, sent a telegram that was read at Buenavista: "Slide in, my dark one, between the crosstie and the whistle." El Gringo, who was in the cantina at the time, heard about it, and was the only one who smiled. But since he didn't like to shoot the breeze anymore, he didn't offer any explanations. Nor did Alejandro Díaz, the company man.

Translated by Cynthia Steele
(From De noche vienes, 1979)

Bibliography

Fiction by Elena Poniatowska

"And Here's to You, Jesusa." Trans. Greogory Kolovakos and Ronald Christ. *Lives on the Line: The Testimony of Contemporary Latin American Authors.* Ed. Doris Meyer. Berkeley: University of California Press, 1988. 137–55.

"La borrega." *Cuentistas mexicanas siglo vigésimo.* Ed. Aurora M. Ocampo. Mexico City: Universidad Nacional Autónoma de México, 1976. 283–84.

Los cuentos de Lilus Kikus. Xalapa: Universidad Veracruzana, 1967. Rpt. in Mexico City: Grijalbo, 1982.

De noche vienes. Mexico City: Grijalbo, 1979. Rpt. in Mexico City: Grijalbo, 1983.

Dear Diego. Trans. Katherine Silver. New York: Pantheon, 1986.

La flor de lis. Mexico City: Era, 1988.

Hasta no verte Jesús mío. Mexico City: Era, 1969. Rpt. in Mexico City: Era, 1984.

"La hija del filósofo." *Puerta abierta: La nueva escritora latinoamericana.* Eds. Caridad L. Silva-Velázquez and Nora Erro-Orthmann. Mexico City: Joaquín Mortiz, 1986. 199–203.

Lilus Kikus. Mexico City: Los Presentes, 1954.

"Love Story." *Catorce mujeres escriben cuentos: Antología.* Mexico City: Federación Editorial Mexicana, 1975. 158–70. Rpt. in *Latin American Literary Review* 3.26 (1985): 63–73. Also rpt. in *Longman Anthology of World Literature by Women, 1875–1975* with trans. by Anne Twitty. Eds. Marian Arkin and Barbara Shollar. New York: Longman, 1989. 856–62.

"The Night Visitor." Trans. Catherine S. White-House. *Other Fires: Short Fiction by Latin American Women.* Ed. Alberto Manguel. Toronto: Lester & Orpen Dennis, 1986. 125–45.

Paseo de la Reforma. Barcelona: Plaza & Janés, 1996.

"La procesión." *Cuentistas mexicanas siglo vigésimo.* Ed. Aurora M. Ocampo. Mexico City: Universidad Nacional Autónoma de México, 1976. 281–82.

Querido Diego, te abraza Quiela. Mexico City: Era, 1978. Rpt. in Mexico City: Era, 1984.

"El recado." *Cuentistas mexicanas siglo vigésimo.* Ed. Aurora M. Ocampo. Mexico City: Universidad Nacional Autónoma de México, 1976. 285–86.

Tinísima. Mexico City: Era, 1992.

Essays by Elena Poniatowska

"Alusiones críticas al libro *Hasta no verte Jesús mío.*" *Vida Literaria* (Mexico City) 3 (1970): 22–24.

¡Ay vida no me mereces! Mexico City: Joaquín Mortiz, 1985.

Cartas de Alvaro Mutis a Elena Poniatowska. Mexico City: Alfaguara, 1998.

La casa en la tierra. Photos Mariana Yampolsky. Mexico City: INA-Fonapas, 1980.

"Diego estoy sola. Diego ya no estoy sola." *Frida Kahlo: La camera seducida.* Mexico City: La Vaca Independiente, 1992. 15–20.

Domingo Siete. Mexico City: Océano, 1982. Rpt. in Mexico City: Océano, 1983.

"Don't Go Away, I'm Going to Bring You Something." Trans. Deanna Heikkinen. *Goddess* of the Americas/La diosa de las Américas: Writing on the Virgin of Guadalupe. New York: Riverhead, 1996. 211–21.

"Las escritoras mexicanas calzan zapatos que les aprietan." Los Universitarios (1975): 4.

Fuerte es el silencio. Mexico City: Era, 1980. Rpt. in Mexico City: Era, 1983.

Gaby Brimmer. Mexico City: Grijalbo, 1979.

Guerrero viejo. Trans. Deanna Heikkinen. Photos Richard Payne. Houston: Anchorage, 1997.

"Hasta no verte Jesús mío." Vuelta (Mexico City) 24 (1978): 5–11.

"El hombre del pito dulce." Juchitán de las mujeres. Ed. Pablo Ortiz Monasterio. Photos Graciela Iturbide. Mexico City: Toledo, 1989. 11–26.

Introduction. Benita. By Benita Galeana. Pittsburgh: Latin American Literary Review Press, 1994. 11–21.

"Introduction and Essay." Mexican Color. Photos Amanda Seville Holmes. New York: Stewart, Tabori & Chang, 1998.

Juan Soriano, niño de mil años. Barcelona: Plaza & Janés, 1998.

"Un libro que me fue dado." Vida Literaria (Mexico City) 3 (1970): 3–4.

"La literatura de las mujeres en América Latina." Revista de la Educación Superior Asociación Nacional de Universidades e Institutos de Enseñanza Superior (Mexico City) 10 (1981): 23–25.

"Literature and Women in Latin America." Women's Writing in Latin America. Eds. Sara Castro-Klaren, Sylvia Molloy, and Beatriz Sarlo. Boulder, Colo.: Westview Press, 1991. 81–87.

Luz y luna las lunitas. Mexico City: Era, 1994.

"María Izquierdo, on Horseback."/"María Izquierdo a caballo." Trans. Deanna Heikkinen. The True Poetry: The Art of María Izquierdo. Ed. Elizabeth Ferrer. New York: Americas Society Art Gallery, 1997.

"Marta Traba o el salto al vacío." Revista Iberoamericana 51, 132–33 (1985): 883–97.

Massacre in Mexico. Trans. Helen R. Lane. Prologue Octavio Paz. New York: Viking Press, 1975.

"Memoria e identidad: Algunas notas histórico-culturales." Nuestra América frente al quinto Centenario. Mexico City: Joaquín Mortiz, 1989. 124–39.

"Mexicanas y chicanas." MELUS 21.3 (1996): 35–51.

"La muerte de Jesusa Palancares." La historia en la literatura iberoamericana. Eds. Raquel Chang-Rodríguez and Gabriela de Beer. Hanover, N.H.: Ediciones del Norte, 1989. 9–22.

Nada, nadie. Mexico City: Era, 1988.

La noche de Tlatelolco: Testimonios de historia oral. Mexico City: Era, 1973. Rpt. in Mexico City: Era, 1983.

Nothing, Nobody: The Voices of the Mexico City Earthquake. Trans. Aurora Camacho de Schmidt and Arthur Schmidt. Philadelphia: Temple University Press, 1995.

Octavio Paz: Las palabras del árbol. Barcelona: Plaza & Janés, 1998.

Pablo O'Higgins. Mexico City: Fondo de Cultura Económica, 1985.

Palabras cruzadas: Crónicas. Mexico City: Era, 1961.

"Introduction." México sin retoque. By Hector García. Mexico City: Universidad Nacional Autónoma de México, 1987.

"Introduction." *La raíz y el camino*. By Mariana Yampolsky. Mexico City: Fondo de Cultura Económica, 1985.

"Presentación al lector mexicano." *Se necesita muchacha*. Ed. Ana Gutiérrez. Mexico City: Fondo de Cultura Económica, 1983. 7–86.

Prólogo. *El libro de la invasión*. By Pedro Rivera and Fernando Martínez. Mexico City: Fondo de Cultura Económica, 1998.

Prólogo. *Un libro levemente odioso*. By Roque Dalton. Mexico City: La Letra, 1988.

Prólogo. *El primer primero de mayo*. Mexico City: Centro de Estudios Históricos del Movimiento Obrero Mexicano, 1976.

"A Question Mark Engraved on My Eyelids." Trans. Cynthia Steele. *The Writer on Her Work*. Ed. Janet Sternberg. New York: Norton, 1990. 82–96.

"Rosario Castellanos: Rostro que ríe, rostro que llora." *Revista Canadiense de Estudios Hispánicos* (Ottawa) 14.3 (1990): 495–509.

"Ser un escritor en México." *Literatura mexicana/Mexican Literature*. Ed. José Miguel Oviedo. Philadelphia: University of Pennsylvania Press, 1992. 10–21.

Las soldaderas. Mexico City: Era, 1999.

"Testimonios: Jesusa Palancares." *Fem* 4.24 (1982): 33–35.

"Testimonios de una escritora: Elena Poniatowska en microfóno." *La sartén por el mango: Encuentro de escritoras latinoamericanas*. Eds. Elena Patricia González and Eliana Ortega. Río Piedras, Puerto Rico: Huracán, 1984. 155–62.

Todo empezó el domingo. Drawings Alberto Beltrán. Mexico City: Océano, 1997.

Todo empezó el domingo. Mexico City: Fondo de Cultura Económica, 1963.

Todo México. Vol 1. Mexico City: Diana, 1991.

Todo México. Vol 2. Mexico City: Diana, 1994.

Todo México. Vol 3: *Gabriel Figueroa, La mirada que limpia*. Mexico City: Era, 1996.

Todo México. Vol 4. Mexico City: Diana, 1998.

Todo México. Vol 5. Mexico City: Diana, 1999.

El último guajolote. Mexico City: Cultura, 1982.

"El universo: Plaza pública." *Insula* (Madrid) 46.532–33 (1991): 9–11.

Play by Elena Poniatowska

Melés y Teléo. *Panoramas* 2 (1956): 135–299.

Works by Elena Poniatowska and Other Authors

Poniatowska, Elena, and Amy Conger. *Compañeras de México: Women Photograph Women*. Riverside: University Art Gallery, University of California, 1990.

Poniatowska, Elena, Iris H. W. Engstrand, and Richard Griswold del Castillo. *Culture y cultura: Consequences of the U.S.-Mexican War, 1846–1848*. Los Angeles: Autry Museum of Western Heritage, 1998.

Poniatowska, Elena, and Kent Klich. *Children of the Streets: Mexico City/Ninos de la calle: Cuidad de México*. Text by Elena Poniatowska. Photographs by Kent Klich. Syracuse: Syracuse University Press, 1999.

Poniatowska, Elena, and Carlos Monsivais. *EZNL: Documentos y comunicados; Crónicas de Carlos Monsivais y Elena Poniatowska*. Photos Paula Haro. Mexico City: Era, 1994–97.

Translations by Elena Poniatowska

Amor Poniatowska, Paula. *No me olvides.* Mexico City: Plaza & Janés, 1996.

Cisneros, Sandra. *La casa en Mango Street.* Cotrans. Juan A. Ascencio. New York: Vintage, 1994.

Criticism on the Works of Elena Poniatowska

Aguilera Garramuno, Marco Tulio. "Humor, erotismo y lenguaje en tres cuentistas latinoamericanas." *La Palabra y el Hombre* (Xalapa) 92 (1994): 178–84.

Aguilera Malta, Demetrio. "Elena y Alberto." *El Gallo Ilustrado* (literary supplement to El Día; Mexico City) 56 July 21, 1963. 4.

Alegría, Fernando, ed. *Nueva historia de la novela hispano-americana.* Hanover, N.H.: Ediciones del Norte, 1986. 426–28.

Alvarez, Federico. *"Todo empezó el domingo." La Cultura en México* 72 July 3, 1963: 20.

Amar-Sánchez, Ana María. "La ficción del testimonio." *Revista Iberoamericana* 56.151 (1990): 447–61.

———. "Las voces de los otros: El género de no-ficción en Elena Poniatowska." *Filología* 25.1–2 (1990): 161–74.

Aronson Parker, Stacey L., and Cristina Enriquez de Salamanca. "La textura del exilio: *Querido Diego, te abraza Quiela, Eva Luna, Crónica de una muerte anunciada." Chasqui* 22.2 (1993): 5–14.

Ascencio, Esteban. *Me lo dijo Elena Poniatowska: Su vida, obra, y pasiones contadas por ella misma* ... Mexico City: Ediciones del Milenio, 1997.

Balboa-Echeverría, Miriam. "Notas a una escritura testimonial: *Fuerte es el silencio* de Elena Poniatowska." *Discurso Literario* (Asunción) 5.2 (1988): 365–73.

Barbosa-Torralbo, Carmen. "*Querido Diego, te abraza Quiela." Notas y Estudios Filológicos* 7 (1997): 57–69.

Beer, Gabriela de. "La revolución en la narrativa de Campobello, Castellanos y Poniatowska." *Semana de Bellas Artes* (Mexico City) 165 January 28, 1981: 2–5.

Berry, John. "Invention, Convention, and Autobiography in Elena Poniatowska's *Querido Diego, te abraza Quiela." Confluencia* 3.2 (1988): 47–56.

Bruce-Novoa, Juan. "La búsqueda de la felicidad en 'De noche vienes.'" *Sin imágenes falsas, sin falsos espejos: Narradoras mexicanas del siglo veinte.* Ed. Aralia López González. Mexico City: Colegio de México, 1995. 379–92.

———. "Elena Poniatowska: The Feminist Origins of Commitment." *Women's Studies International Forum* 6.5 (1983): 509–16.

———. "Subverting the Dominant Text: Elena Poniatowska's *Querido Diego." Knives and Angels: Women Writers* in Latin America. Ed. Susan Bassnet. London: Zed Books, 1990. 115–31.

Bundgard, Ana. "Identidad e historicidad: Los discursos del amor y la memoria en *Querido Diego, te abraza Quiela." Sin imágenes falsas, sin falsos espejos: Narradoras mexicanas del siglo vigésimo.* Ed. Aralia López González. Mexico City: Colegio de México, 1995. 369–78.

Capistrán, Miguel. "La transmutación literaria." *Vida Literaria* (Mexico City) 3 (1970): 12–14.

Capote Cruz, Zaida. "Biografía y ficción: El desafío de Tinísima." *Sin imágenes falsas, sin falsos espejos: Narradoras mexicanas del siglo vigésimo.* Ed. Aralia López González. Mexico City: Colegio de México, 1995. 405–12.

Carballo, Emmanuel. "Elena Poniatowska una de las escritoras más auténticas de México." *La Cultura en México* 148 December 16, 1964: 18.

———. "*Lilus Kikus.*" *México en la Cultura* 294 November 7, 1954: 2.

———. "*Melés y Teléo.*" *México en la Cultura* 382 July 15, 1956: 2.

Cardoza, Lya de. "Un libro con duende." *La Cultura en México* 75 July 24, 1963. 18.

Cardoza y Aragón, Luis. "*Todo empezó el domingo.*" *El Día* 378 July 13, 1963: 9.

Carmona, Krista Ratowski. "Entrevista a Elena Poniatowska." *Mester* 15.2 (1986): 37–42.

Castellvi Demoor, Magda. "*Querido Diego, te abraza Quiela* o la escritura de un texto femenino." *Alba de América* 10.18–19 (1992): 261–71.

Cella, Susana Beatriz. "Autobiografía e historia de vida en *Hasta no verte Jesús mío* de Elena Poniatowska." *Literatura Mexicana* 2.1 (1991): 149–56.

Chavez, Daniel. "La no-alienación del yo femenino en *Querido Diego, te abraza Quiela* de Elena Poniatowska." *Dactylus* 14 (1995): 71–80.

Chevigny, Bell Gale. "The Transformation of Privilege in the Works of Elena Poniatowska." *Latin American Literary Review* 13.26 (1985): 49–62.

Chisholm, Kimberley Ford. "Searching for Singularity: Mother and Daughter Narration in Elena Poniatowska's *La 'flor de lis.'*" *Dactylus* 16 (1997): 99–121.

Christ, Ronald. "The Author as Editor." *Review* 15 (1975): 78–79.

———. "Los cuentos de *Lilus Kikus.*" *Recent Books in Mexico* 14.5 (1967): 5.

Chumacero, Alí. "*Todo empezó el domingo.*" *La Cultura en México* 69 June 12, 1963: 15.

Conde, Susana. "Belles Lettres Interview: Elena Poniatowska." *Belles Lettres* 7.2 (1991–92): 41–44.

Cornejo-Parriego, Rosalía. "Racialización colonial y diferencia femenina en 'Love Story' de Poniatowska y 'Cuando las mujeres quieren a los hombres' de Ferré." *Afro-Hispanic Review* 16.2 (1997): 10–18.

Corona, Ignacio. "Representación y estrategias retóricas en *Nada, nadie* de Elena Poniatowska." *Journal of Interdisciplinary Literary Studies* 8.1 (1996): 1–16.

Crespo de la Serna. Jorge J. "La hierba que crece: La ecuación Poniatowska-Beltrán." *El Día* December 3, 1963: 5.

"*Los cuentos de Lilus Kikus.*" *Recent Books in Mexico* 14.5 (1967): 5.

Davis, Lisa. "An Invitation to Understanding Among Poor Women of the Americas: *The Color Purple* and *Hasta no verte Jesús mío.*" *Reinventing the Americas: Comparative Studies of Literature of the United States and Spanish America.* Eds. Bell Gale and Gari Laguardia. New York: Cambridge University Press, 1986. 224–41.

Dever, Susan. "Elena Poniatowska: La crítica de una mujer." *Mujer y literatura mexicana y chicana: Culturas en contacto.* Vol 2. Eds. Aralia López-González, Amelia Malagamba, and Elena Urrutia. Mexico City: Colegio de México, 1990. 107–11.

Dimitriou, Agnes. "Entrevista con Elena Poniatowska." *Letras Femeninas* 16.1–2 (1990): 125–33.

Donoso Pareja, Miguel. "La caducidad del realismo." *Vida Literaria* (Mexico City) 3 (1970): 10–11.

Earl, Peter G. "El tema del sacrificio en obras de Fernando del Paso, Elena Poniatowska y Angeles Mastretta." *Literatura mexicana/Mexican Literature.* Ed. José Miguel Oviedo. Philadelphia: University of Pennsylvania Press, 1993. 34–43.

Epple, Juan Armando. "Las voces de Elena Poniatowska: Una entrevista." *Confluencia* 5.2 (1990): 127–29.

Ferman, Claudia. "México en la postmodernidad: Textualización de la cultura popular urbana." *Nuevo Texto Crítico* 4.7 (1991): 157–67.

Fernández Olmos, Margarite. "El género testimonial: Aproximaciones feministas." *Revista/Review Interamericana* 11.1 (1981): 69–75.

Flori, Monica. "El mundo femenino de Marta Lynch y Elena Poniatowska." *Letras Femeninas* 9.2 (1983): 23–30.

———. "Visions of Women: Symbolic Physical Portrayal as Social Commentary in the Short Fiction of Elena Poniatowska." *Third Woman* 2.2 (1984): 77–83.

Foster, David William. "Latin American Documentary Narrative." *Publications of the Modern Language Association* 99.1 (1984): 41–55.

Fox Lockert, Lucía. "Elena Poniatowska's *Hasta no verte Jesús mío.*" *Women Novelists in Spain and Spanish America.* Metuchen, N.J.: Scarecrow Press, 1979. 260–77.

Franco, Jean. " Rewriting the Family: Contemporary Feminism's Revisions of the Past." *Plotting Women: Gender and Representation in Mexico.* New York: Columbia University Press, 1989. 175–227.

Friedman, Edward. "The Marginated Narrator: *Hasta no verte, Jesús Mío* and the Eloquence of Repression." *The Antiheroine's Voice: Narrative Discourse and Transformations of the Picaresque.* Columbia: University of Missouri Press, 1987. 170–87.

Fuentes, Carlos. "Lilus Kikus." *Revista de la Universidad de México* 4.1–2 September–October 1954: 30.

Galindo, Carmen. "Vivir del milagro." *Vida Literaria* (Mexico City) 3 (1970): 8–9.

García, Kay S. "Elena Poniatowska." *Broken Bars: New Perspectives from Mexican Women Writers.* Albuquerque: University of New Mexico Press, 1994. 10–61.

———. "Elena Poniatowska: Search for the Voiceless." *A Dream of Light and Shadow: Portraits of Latin American Women Writers.* Ed. Marjorie Agosín. Albuquerque: University of New Mexico Press, 1995. 237–51.

García Flores, Margarita. "Entrevista a Elena Poniatowska." *Revista de la Universidad de México* 30.7 (1976): 25–30.

García Pinto, Magdalena. "Elena Poniatowska." *Historias íntimas: Conversaciones con diez escritoras latinoamericanas.* Hanover, N.H.: Ediciones del Norte, 1989. 173–98.

———. "Elena Poniatowska." *Women Writers of Latin America: Intimate Histories.* Trans. Trudy Balch and Magdalena García Pinto. Austin: University of Texas Press, 1991.

García Serrano, María Victoria. "Apropiación y agresión en *Querido Diego, te abraza Quiela* de Elena Poniatowska." *Letras Femeninas* 17.1–2 (1991): 99–106.

Gazarian Gautier, Marie-Lise. "Elena Poniatowska." *Interviews with Latin American Writers.* Elmwood Park, Ill.: Dalkey Archive Press, 1989. 199–216.

Gertel, Zunilda. "La mujer y su discurso: Conciencia y máscara." *Cambio social en México visto por autores contemporáneos.* Ed. José Anadón. Notre Dame, Ind.: University of Notre Dame Press, 1984. 45–60.

Gnutzman, Rita. "Tres ejemplos de escritura femenina en America Latina." *Letras de Deusto* 19. 44 (1989): 91–104.

Gold, Janet. "Elena Poniatowska: The Search for Authentic Language." *Discurso Literario* (Asunción) 6.1 (1988): 181–91.

———. "Feminine Space and the Discourse of Silence: Yolanda Oreamuno, Elena Poniatowska, and Luisa Valenzuela." In the *Feminine Mode: Essays on Hispanic Women Writers.* Eds. Noel Valis and Carol Maier. Lewisburg, Pa.: Bucknell University Press, 1990. 195–203.

González-Lee, Teresa. "Jesusa Palancares, curandera, espiritista o la patología de la pobreza." *Mujer y literatura mexicana y chicana: Culturas en contacto.* Vol. 2. Eds. Aralia López-González, Amelia Malagamba, and Elena Urrutia. Mexico City: Colegio de México, 1990. 93–97.

Groote, Sabine. "Al pie de la letra?: Translating Elena Poniatowska." *Reflections on the Conquest of America: Five Hundred Years After.* Eds. Willliam F. Forbes, Teresa Mendez Faith, Mary Anne Vetterling, and Barbara Wing. Durham: University of New Hampshire, 1996. 135–42.

Guerra, Cunningham. "Los margenes anticanónicos de la autobiografía de la pobreza en *Hasta no vente Jesús mío* de Elena Poniatowska." *Estudios sobre escritoras hispánicas en honor de Gendrgina Sabat-Rivers.* Ed. Lou Charnon. Deutsch. Madrid: Castalia, 1992. 113-27.

Hancock, Joel. "Elena Poniatowska's *Hasta no verte Jesús mío*: The Remaking of the Image of Woman." *Hispania* 66.3 (1983): 353–59.

Hjelm, Ruth. "El espejismo del amor en *Tinísima* de Elena Poniatowska." *Narrativa hispanoamericana contemporánea: Entre la vanguardia y el posboom.* Ed. Ana María Hernández de López. Madrid: Pliegos, 1996. 209–24.

Horno Delgado, Asunción. "Entrevista con Elena Poniatowska." *Confluencia* 7.2 (1992): 115–22.

Ibsen, Kristine. "Entrevista a Elena Poniatowska." *Literatura Mexicana* 2.4 (1997): 119–23.

Jaen, Didier T. "La neopicaresca en México: Elena Poniatowska y Luis Zapata." *Tinta* 1.5 (1987): 23–29.

Jorgensen, Beth Ellen. "Elena Poniatowska." *Escritoras hispanoamericanas: Una guía bio-bibliográfica.* Eds. Diane Marting and Montserrat Ordoñez. Bogotá: Siglo Veintiuno, 1990. 500–12.

———. "Elena Poniatowska." *Spanish American Women Writers: A Bio-Bibliographical Source Book.* Ed. Diane Marting. Westport, Conn.: Greenwood Press, 1990. 472–82.

———. "Framing Questions: The Role of the Editor in Elena Poniatowska's *La noche de Tlatelolco.*" *Latin American Perspectives* 18.3 (1991): 80–90.

———. "La intertextualidad en *La noche de Tlatelolco* de Elena Poniatowska." *Hispanic Journal* 10. 2 (1989): 81–93.

———. "Perspectivas femeninas en *Hasta no verte Jesús mío* y *La 'flor de lis.'*" *Texto Crítico* 14. 39 (1988): 110–23.

————. "Tinísima: Elena Poniatowska's Tina Modotti." Literatura mexicana/Mexican Literature. Ed. José Miguel Oviedo. Philadelphia: University of Pennsylvania Press, 1993.
22–33.

————. TheWriting of Elena Poniatowska: Engaging Dialogues. Austin: University of Texas Press,
1994.

Kaminsky, Amy. "Gaby Brimmer: A Life in Three Voices." Reading the Body Politic: Feminist
Criticism and Latin AmericanWomenWriters. Minneapolis: University of Minnesota Press,
1993. 60–76.

Kerr, Lucille. "Gestures of Authorship: Lying to Tell the Truth in Elena Poniatowska's
Hasta no verte Jesús mío." Modern Language Notes 106.2 (1991): 370–94.

Kostakowsky, Lya. "La entrevistadora entrevistada." México en la Cultura May 26, 1957: 5,
11.

Kuhnheim, Jill S. "Un nacionalismo internacional: Tinísima de Elena Poniatowska."
Literatura Mexicana 5.2 (1994): 469–78.

Kushigian, Julia A. "Transgresión de la autobiografía y el Bildungsroman en Hasta no
verte Jesús mío." Revista Iberoamericana 53.140 (1987): 667–77.

Lagos-Pope, María Inés. "El testimonio creativo de Hasta no verte Jesús mío." Revista Iberoamericana 56.150 (1990): 243–53.

Landeros, Carlos. "Con Elena Poniatowska." Diorama de la Cultura (literary supplement
to Excelsior; Mexico City) January 23, 1966: 3+.

Lara, Josefina. Diccionario bio-bibliográfico de escritores contemporáneos de México. Mexico City:
Instituto Nacional de Bellas Artes, 1988. 175–76.

Lemaitre, Monique J. "La identidad asumida y el texto subversivo en La 'flor de lis' de
Elena Poniatowska." Explicación de Textos Literarios 19.1 (1990–91): 27–37.

————. "Jesusa Palancares y la dialéctica de la emancipación femenina." Hispamérica
10.30 (1981): 131–35. Rpt. in Textuos. Mexico City: Oasis, 1986. 77–82.

López, Irma. "Tinísima: La (re)escritura del mito." Letras Femeninas 23.1–2 (1997): 149–
61.

López González, Aralia. "Dos tendencias en la evolución de la narrativa contempo-
ránea de escritoras mexicanas." Mujer y literatura mexicana y chicana: Culturas en contacto.
Vol 2. Eds. Aralia López-González, Amelia Malagamba, and Elena Urrutia. Mexico
City: Colegio de México, 1990. 21–24.

————. "Nuevas formas de ser mujer en la narrativa contemporánea de escritoras
mexicanas." Casa de las Américas (Havana) 31.183 (1991): 3–8.

López Negrete, Cecilia. "Con Elena Poniatowska." Vida Literaria (Mexico City) 3 (1970):
16–20.

Manjarrez, Héctor. "La indiscreción de Elena Poniatowska." Cuadernos Políticos 27
(1981). 102–14.

Marz, Joan F. "Palomas, parásitas y pecadoras: El eje femenino desde un punto de vista
social en La 'flor de lis' de Elena Poniatowska." Texto Crítico (Xalapa, Mexico) 2.3
(1996): 115–24.

Mattalia, Sonia. "Elena Poniatowska: Cuanto la ira ama." Quimera [Barcelona] 123
(1994): 52–53.

Matthews, Irene. "Women Watching Women, Watching." *Reinterpreting the Spanish American Essay: Women Writers of the Nineteenth and Twentieth Centuries.* Ed. Doris Meyer. Austin: University of Texas Press, 1995. 227–41.

Melo, Juan Vicente. "*Palabras cruzadas.*" *Revista de la Universidad de México* 16.8 (1962): 31.

Méndez-Faith, Teresa. "Entrevista con Elena Poniatowska." *Inti* 15 (1982): 54–60.

———. "Translation of an Interview with Elena Poniatowska." *Atlantis: A Women's Studies Journal /Journal d'Etudes sur la Femme* 9.2 (1984): 70–75.

Menton, Seymour. "Sin embargo: La nueva cuentista femenina en México." *Tinta* 1.5 (1987): 35–37.

Miller, Beth. "Elena Poniatowska." *Mujeres en la literatura.* Mexico City: Fleischer, 1978. 89–91.

———. "Interview with Elena Poniatowska." *Latin American Literary Review* 4.7 (1975): 73–78.

———. "Personajes y personas: Castellanos, Fuentes, Poniatowska y Sáinz." *Mujeres en la literatura.* Mexico City: Fleischer, 1978. 65–75.

Miller, Beth, and Alfonso González. "Elena Poniatowska." *Veintiséis autoras del México actual.* Mexico City: Costa- Amic, 1978. 299–321.

Monsiváis, Carlos. "A veinte años de La noche de Tlatelolco." *Semanal* (literary supplement to *La Jornada*; Mexico City) October 13, 1991: 20–29."

———. "Las palabras cruzadas de Elena Poniatowska"; "Mira, para que no comas olvido . . ."; "Las precisiones de Elena Poniatowska." *La Cultura en México* July 15, 1985: 2–5.

Monterde, Francisco. "Cuadro vivo del pueblo." *Vida Literaria* (Mexico City) 3 (1970): 3–4.

Morente, Javier. "Sala de lectura." *Diorama de la Cultura* (literary supplement to *Excelsior*; Mexico City) July 28, 1963: 4.

"Mujeres de México." *Nivel* 21 September 25, 1960: 1, 3.

Nagy, Silvia. "Palabras cruzadas: Dialoguismo e intertextualidad en *Querido Diego* de Elena Poniatowska." *Modalidades de representación del sujeto auto/bio/gráfico femenino.* Eds. Magdalena Maíz-Peña y Luis H. Peña. Mexico City: Facultad de Filosofía y Letras, Ciudad Universitaria, 1997. 243–54.

Noriega, Raúl. "El domingo nuestro de cada día." *México en la Cultura* 742 June 9, 1963: 8.

Ochoa, Sandy Gerardo. "De Lilus Kikus a Luz y luna, las lunitas." *Sábado* (literary supplement to *Unomásuno*; Mexico City) February 11, 1989: I, 3–4.

Ortega, Bertin. "La voz de los otros: Elena Poniatowska en busca de sí misma." *La seducción de la escritura: Los discursos de la cultura hoy.* Eds. Rosaura Hernández Monroy and Manuel Medina. Mexico City: n.p., 1997. 317–22.

Otero, José. "*Querido Diego, te abraza Quiela,* destrucción y reconstrucción de la personalidad: Lengua, estructura y símbolos del proceso." *Confluencia* 7.2 (1992): 75–8.

Pacheco, José Emilio. "Elena Poniatowska aporta, en sus incomparables crónicas, un espejo de la vida mexicana." *México en la Cultura* October 30, 1961: 3.

Palma, Martín. "Los silencios de Elena Poniatowska." *Revista de la Universidad de México* 13.5 (1959): 16–17.

Paul, Marcella L. "Letters and Desire: The Function of Marks on Paper in Elena Poniatowska's *Querido Diego, te abraza Quiela.*" *Continental, Latin American, and Francophone Women Writers.* Vol 2. Eds. Ginette Adamson and Eunice Myers. Lanham, Md.: University Press of America, 1987. 1–6.

Pérez Pisonero, Arturo. "Jesusa Palancares, esperpento femenino." *Mujer y literatura mexicana y chicana: Culturas en contacto.* Vol 1. Eds. Aralia López Gonzalez, Amelia Malagamba, and Elena Urrutia. Mexico City: Colegio de México, 1988. 221–29.

Pérez-Robles, Xiúhnel. "*La noche de Tlatelolco.*" *Cuadernos Americanos* (Mexico City) 177 (1971): 79–82.

Perilli, Carmen. "La increíble y triste historia de Angelina Beloff y de su amante desalmado." *Revista Chilena de Literatura* 50 (1997): 133–39.

Poot-Herrera, Sara. "Del tornasol de Lilus Kikus al tornaviaje de La 'flor de lis'." *Escribir la infancia: Narradoras mexicanas contemporáneas.* Eds. Nora Pasternac, Ana Rosa Domenella, and Luz Elena Gutiérrez de Velasco. Mexico City: Colegio de México, 1996. 59–80.

———. "La 'flor de lis,' códice y huella de Elena Poniatowska." *Mujer y literatura mexicana y chicana: Culturas en contacto.* Vol 2. Eds. Aralia López-González, Amelia Malagamba, and Elena Urrutia. Mexico City: Colegio de México, 1990. 99–105.

———. "Tina Modotti y Elena Poniatowska: Dos mujeres, un libro." *Sin imágenes falsas, sin falsos espejos: Narradoras mexicanas del siglo vigésimo.* Ed. Aralia López González. Mexico City: Colegio de México, 1995. 393–404.

———. "La voz de Jesusa Palancares, envoltura de su ser." *Mujer y sociedad en América.* Ed. Juana Alcira Arancibia. Westminster, Calif.: Instituto Literario y Cultural Hispánico, 1990. 71–84.

Portal, Marta. *Proceso narrativo de la revolución mexicana.* Madrid: Espasa-Calpe, 1980. 285–92.

Price, Greg. "Elena Poniatowska." *Latin America: The Writer's Journey.* London: Hamilton, 1990. 233–43.

Quemain, Miguel Angel. "Elena Poniatowska: La naturaleza del oficio." *Reverso de la palabra.* Mexico City: El Nacional, 1996. 392–405.

Radchik, Laura. "Las memorias de Cronos en las manecillas de Dios." *Plural* (literary supplement to *Excelsior;* Mexico City) 204 (1988): 82–85.

Reboreda, Aída. "Al terminar mi libro sobre Demetrio Vallejo haré una novela sobre mi mundo, la reacción: Poniatowska." *Unomásuno* October 5, 1979: 17.

Resnick, Margery, and Isabelle de Courtivron. *Women Writers in Translation: An Annotated Bibliography, 1945–1982.* New York: Garland, 1984. 243.

Richards, Katharine C. "A Note on Contrasts in Elena Poniatowska's *De noche vienes.*" *Letras Femeninas* 17.1–2 (1991): 107–11.

Río, Marcela del. "Todo empezó el domingo." *Diograma de la Cultura* (literary supplement to *Excelsior;* Mexico City) July 14, 1963: 3+.

Robles, Martha. "Elena Poniatowska." *La sombra fugitiva, escritoras en la cultura nacional.* Vol. 1. Mexico City: Universidad Nacional Autónoma de México, 1985. 343–65.

Rodríguez, Antonio. "Todo empezó el domingo." *El Día* August 16, 1963: 9.

Roses, Lorraine. "Entrevista con Elena Poniatowska." *Plaza: Literatura y Crítica* 5–6 (1981–82): 51–64.

Saltz, Joanne. "*Hasta no verte Jesús mío:* Testimonio de una mujer." *Mujer y literatura mexicana y chicana: Culturas en contacto.* Vol 1. Eds. Aralia López González, Amelia Malagamba, and Elena Urrutia. Mexico City: Colegio de México, 1988. 231–38

Schaefer, Claudia. "Updating the Epistolary Canon: Bodies and Letters, Bodies of Letters in Elena Poniatowska's *Querido Diego, te abraza Quiela* and *Gaby Brimmer.*" *Textured Lives: Women, Art, and Representation in Modern Mexico.* Tucson: University of Arizona Press, 1992. 61–87.

Scott, Nina M. "The Fragmented Narrative Voice of Elena Poniatowska." *Discurso* 7.2 (1990): 411–20.

Selva, Mauricio de la. "*Todo empezó el domingo.*" *Cuadernos Americanos* (Mexico City) 4 (1963): 283–84.

Shaw, Deborah. "Gender and Class Relations in *De noche vienes* by Elena Poniatowska." *Bulletin of Hispanic Studies* 72.1 (1995): 111–21.

———. "Jesusa Palancares as Individual Subject in Elena Poniatowska's *Hasta no verte Jesús mío.*" *Bulletin of Hispanic Studies* (Liverpool, England) 73.2 (1996): 191–204.

Shimrose, Pedro. *Diccionario de autores iberoamericanos.* Madrid: Ministerio de Relaciones Exteriores, 1982. 340.

Sklodowska, Elzbieta. *Testimonio hispanoamericano: Historia, teoría, poética.* New York: Peter Lang, 1992.

Sommer, Doris. "Taking a Life: Hot Pursuit and Cold Rewards in a Mexican Testimonial Novel." *The Seductions of Biography.* Eds. Mary Rhiel and David Suchoff. New York: Routledge, 1996. 147–72.

Starcevic, Elizabeth O. "Breaking the Silence: Elena Poniatowska, a Writer in Transition." *Literatures in Transition: The Many Voices of the Caribbean Area: A Symposium.* Ed. Rose S. Minc. Gaithersburg, Md.: Hispamérica, 1982. 63–68.

———. "Elena Poniatowska: Witness for the People." *Contemporary Women Authors of Latin America: Introductory Essays.* Eds. Doris Meyer and Margarite Fernández Olmos. New York: Brooklyn College Press, 1983. 72–77.

———. "Neglected by the Boom: So What Else Is New?" *Festschrift* 80–82.134 (1980): 103–9.

Steele, Cynthia. "La creatividad y el deseo en *Querido Diego, te abraza Quiela,* de Elena Poniatowska." *Hispamérica* 14.41 (1985): 17–28.

———. "Elena Poniatowska." *Hispamérica* 18.53–54 (1989): 89–105.

———. "Gender, Genre, and Authority: *Hasta no verte Jesús mío* (1969) by Elena Poniatowska." *Politics, Gender, and the Mexican Novel, 1968–1988.* Austin: University of Texas Press, 1992. 28–65.

———. "La mediación en las obras documentales de Elena Poniatowska." *Mujer y literatura mexicana y chicana: Culturas en contacto.* Vol. 1. Ed. Aralia López González. Mexico City: Colegio de México, 1988. 211–19.

———. "Testimonio y autoridad en *Hasta no verte Jesús mío* de Elena Poniatowska." *Revista de Crítica Literaria Latinoamericana* 18.36 (1992): 156–80.

Susti, Alejandro E. "Superposición discursiva en *Hasta no verte Jesús mío* de Elena Poniatowska: Medios masivos y corridos revolucionarios." *Torre de Papel* 6.3 (1996): 69–89.

Tatum, Charles M. "Elena Poniatowska's *Hasta no verte Jesús mío.*" *Latin American Women Writers:Yesterday and Today.* Eds. Yvette Miller and Charles M. Tatum. Pittsburgh: Latin American Literary Review, 1975. 49–58.

"*Todo empezó el domingo.*" *Cultura de Buenos Aires* 4.7 (1963): 92.

Torres, Juan Manuel. "Hasta el fin de la esperanza." *Vida Literaria* (Mexico City) 3 (1970): 15.

Tyler, Mary. "The Crack in the Facade: Social Aftershocks of Mexico's 1985 Earthquake." *Social and Political Change in Literature and Film* Ed. Richard Chapple. Gainesville: University Press of Florida, 1994. 83–91.

Valdés, María Elena de. "Elena Poniatowska: Identity and the Other as Myself." *The Shattered Mirror: Representations of Women in Mexican Literature.* Austin: University of Texas Press, 1998. 114–43.

Vargas, Margarita. "Power and Resistance in *De noche vienes* by Elena Poniatowska." *Hispanic Journal* 16.2 (1995): 285–96.

Vilches Norat, Vanessa. "Elena Poniatowska y el testimonio: La recuperación de todo Mexico." *Revista Interamericana de Bibliografía/Inter-American Review of Bibliography* 44.2 (1994): 283–89.

Volek, Emil. "Las modalidades del testimonio y *Hasta no verte Jesús mío* de Elena Poniatowska." *Literatura mexicana/Mexican Literature.* Ed. José Miguel Oviedo. Philadelphia: University of Pennsylvania Press, 1993. 44–67.

Volkow, Veronica. "Crónicas del silencio." *Revista de la Universidad de México* 36.4 (1981): 41–42.

Williams, Claudette. "Subtextuality in Elena Poniatowska's *Hasta no verte Jesús mío.*" *Hispania* 77.2 (1994): 215–24.

Young, Dolly J., and William D. Young. "The New Journalism in Mexico: Two Women Writers." *Chasqui* 12.2–3 (1983). /2 80.

Zielina, María. "La falsa percepción de la realidad en 'Cine Prado.'" *Mujer y literatura mexicana y chicana. Culturas en contacto.* Vol 2. Eds. Aralia López-González, Amelia Malagamba, and Elena Urrutia. Mexico City: Colegio de México, 1990. 87–91.

Armonía Somers

Armonía Somers (1914–94), pseudonym of the distinguished writer Armonía Etchepare de Henestrosa, was born in Pando, Uruguay. Before publishing her first novel in 1950, Somers had a long and outstanding career in education. She taught in Montevideo and was director of the National Museum of Education. She published widely in the field of education and was editor of several journals in Montevideo.

Somers's first novella, *La mujer desnuda* (The naked woman, 1950), caused a sensation in literary circles when it was published by the magazine *Clima*. Its overt sexual overtones were considered scandalous in the provincial Uruguayan society of the time.

Following *La mujer desnuda,* Somers continued to address the topics of sexuality, eroticism, and death in later works. From 1953 to 1988 she published five volumes of short stories and four novels. In her narratives, the Uruguayan author presents despairing men and women, seeking redemption from a useless, hopeless existence. These stories all treat common themes: violence, lack of communication, despair, death, desperation, and loneliness.

In recent years, Armonía Somers's production increased in quantity and quality. Her later works contain diverse experiments in fictional technique and a more complex use of language.

Somers was a rebellious writer whose originality clearly rests in her unusual presentation of themes—a blend of realism, fantasy, and absurdity—written in lyrical, symbolic, and poetic language. Her work is polemical, her style vigorous, with touches of humor and keen sarcasm.

The Immigrant

The letters that comprise the first part of this series, and to which I added others, titling them all THE IMMIGRANT, mostly appeared without heading and none of them had signatures.

The hastiness and the lack of style of the beginning letters can be explained by the place where they were written, the store that my mother managed for many years.

She was the protagonist of what follows, and that fact, according to certain theories of a man who looked very much like me physically (my estranged father), and whose portrait is connected to this case, should have forced me to destroy the documents, . . . I know, Father, it is not the moral of an island, but rather the social morality that commands. But it is also true that it has always rained like that night upon the naked flowers of this world, and it must be because of this that we still have a bit of courage left to continue living, to see how grace has not yet been covered by old dust in such a worn-out land like ours.

Juan Abel Grim
Collector and annotator of the letters

I

I am sending you this message with the elevator boy, the only person whom you can trust with minor tasks, in the event that you are fit for the job. I have been here for twenty years and the fact that I am the general manager has allowed me to catalogue the young people who make up the staff as if they were merchandise (you, too, and don't be offended). My intent is not to speak to you of matters that ought to be discovered on their own, but rather of others that place me under certain obligations to the person who has recommended you. And, as I do not want you to fail in this test and I am your supervisor, I ask you, please, to indicate to the elevator boy where I can meet you at the end of the day. And I hope that

my openness in pointing out your weaknesses on the job may be as help-
ful to you as I have promised your sponsor.

> Distinguished by temperaments, these strange, always hasty notes
> were exchanged from then on, all of them seemingly robbed from
> the hell that was the store within which my mother must have
> played a tremendous role for so many years. I remember her with
> awe as provoked by myth. She was feared and almost cruel to her
> poor trained ants. But, from the depths of that slavery, there rose a
> mist of admiration which sustained her tenuously above the vulgar-
> ity of the lower world, so much so that later, without her, everything
> disintegrated. That place grew to be what it is today, a place about
> which one would say, "I don't know if it was here or next door that
> I bought this . . ."

II

Forgive me, but I am going to use your system to confide in you that, after
your comments yesterday, I tried to find the image of the person who bore
my name, my face, my other personal attributes, in every mirror in the
store. And to what end? Because it was certain that each of the clumsy
gestures that you pointed out to me at our meeting at the bar—my way of
assaulting customers, intending to force a sale, my uncontrollable rage
when they withdrew without playing the game, and later, my tendency to
search out the display windows looking for freedom outside as if it had
been lost in some bad exchange—all this seemed to peel away from me
like the skin of an onion.

After the first transaction I began to follow you with ease. This—yes,
that one—no, careful. . . . And best of all: that no one suspects I am creating my own model, that the others know nothing of my process of self-
discovery. Tell me, even with a look: Am I doing well, do you approve?

> The manager then pushed to another aspect of the problem. With
> her chin held high she was, without a doubt, the proud woman I
> knew, and later this would explain many things to me.

III

No, my dear, nor is it necessary to exaggerate the way you did a moment ago. Better to let women of that special kind leave the way they came in, with their sparkling jewels, their chauffeur at the door, their four surnames. I couldn't wait, not even until later, to tell you that, in spite of everything, our dignity must continue to serve us. To retain a measure of pride, that is the secret. The very least of rights I granted myself from the start. Besides, it will always be your slim young waist that wins out over their midriff bulges, which seem to have taken revenge on an overload of gold. They are the wives of some of the present government officials, of certain industrialists and bankers who started out in the basement with brooms in their hands. Don't cater to them so much, all right? Even if it is to develop what you have called your "own process of self-discovery."

IV

Nevertheless I must tell you that I have failed today. I feel bad and don't think that I am cut out for this. It is true that you, the real you, could justify my misfortune of stepping into this place. But even with you here, I think I ought to leave. Yes, LEAVE, in capital letters. Just think, that lady who came in, asking so sweetly for the children's department, and whom I waited on, using all my imagination—almost able to see the light blue room, the plush bears on the shelves—took advantage, while waiting for the elevator, to show me the photo. She opened her purse, went through a mountain of things from which there rose a certain strange odor, and as I stood open-mouthed, took out a picture of a dog dressed in infant clothing. Then she turned into the real mother of that child and even seemed to sniff my side. I went to the ladies' room and vomited. After that I was not good for anything.

One day I may buy that perfume you use, in order to remember you; it was the only thing that managed to put me back together again. I walked by you, breathed in, and continued living. It is certain that you will come out of the bottle as soon as I take the cap off the one I buy. What is it called? I can't go on anymore, I can't . . .

V

My little one,[1] don't distract me with your perfumes today, I beg you. We have a directors' meeting to decide on certain purchases that must be made in Europe for the next season. In my experience, the important thing at this kind of meeting is to appear completely neutral to them, like a mechanical Store-Woman, so that no one can perceive anything other than this mechanism. I remain centered by using the technique of looking at myself in the mirror of the meeting room from time to time in front of their very noses. But what a pain, the bell is ringing now. Besides, a certain handsome young boy is coming your way. One who ought to smell of gasoline or of a leather jacket. Now you see that not everything in this world will smell of dog's breath. Ah . . . and at the moment when the young man takes out his wallet to pay, try to look more discreetly at the photos that shine under the plastic.

> How different the handwritings were. When I divided the letters to arrange them in their proper order, they began to seem like the same mosaic executed from two styles of craftsmanship.

VI

You toyed with me before the meeting, didn't you? Certainly I looked at the photo in your wallet the first day. But that's natural, I think. Many times I realize that, besides your well-hidden good nature, there must be other secrets in your life. And who was that boy in your photograph then? The same one who comes in sometimes, gives you a kiss that leaves all the girls' mouths watering, and leaves like he came, without buying anything.

Think for a moment that at the beginning I had considered myself a gem in this place for having arrived here with some knowledge in one subject or another, a membership card to a film club, certain other small things that made me think myself of another class. And that, later, I encountered something that dazzles (you), but which will never be able to illuminate what I want (you as well), your world, not the one of that Store-Woman you speak of, but the other where you probably have an armchair to forget all this, a bathroom with its little vials, a curtain that obeys you when the light bothers you. Here no one seems to know much about you. They respect you, they hate you, they envy even the length of your eyelashes and the quality of your hands. But they stop there. Would I have more rights? And why would I have them, in the end?

VII

Very good, that is how to do it. I watched you let that chance go by so that the customer would not notice the other girl's approach. The customer must be completely unaware of the internal quarrels over a better commission. But systems also exist to prevent someone from always beating us by a hair.

VIII

There is only one system I would like to master today, that of questions and their answers.[2]

IX

Unmanageable and delicious creature. It is obvious that the former will always be more important than the latter. And I have come to my desk solely to please you. Well then, it would seem that, while not as the manager of a large fashionable department store, but rather as a woman who inspects herself every once in a while in the mirror in the meeting room and sees that she is still attractive enough, I have always been vulnerable, in spite of my reputation as a tough woman. On another level of reality: my son, that young man who comes to give me a kiss and seems to stir up your coworkers when he walks near them.

I am forty and he is twenty. By simply comparing our ages, you will gather that he should not be considered only as my son, but also as the result of a fabulous moment in the life of a woman your own age, and, in time, the only thing that will remain when the ghosts retire. I live with him; he studies, smokes, muddies the apartment with dirty footprints, and gets telephone calls from various female voices. And, in addition to giving me silver cigarette cases which he buys with the money I give him on his birthday, he knows how to laugh like few people can.

I started here after that great misfortune which is usually reserved for us. Yours, I believe, was of an economic nature; mine was different.

But then everything began to fall into place again. The child smiled with his toothless mouth, the sky seemed to me to be small and pale then, the store always paid regularly, bakers know how to knead what they have in their hands, and foolish men what is between theirs. If life worked like the cord of the drapes that you spoke of, nothing would be necessary except a simple contract: pull softly so that nothing breaks. Are your questions answered now? Oh, I am sending you the perfume so that you do not waste your wages on little whims. Take note of its name: Violeta de Parma. We ought to have names like that, chosen. This one suits you well, therefore it will be yours.

> Perhaps at the moment of sending it, the manager crossed out a few final words of this letter. It would have been possible for me to have uncovered them with the techniques known today. But I preferred not to do so. Between that woman and me there has always been a silent, implicit respect for the other's decisions, whatever they may have been. Later I thought it best to put this little sales slip chronologically in tenth place; on the back it read:

X

I would like to see you one more time. But outside the city, far from here, for a fabulous weekend. Where, where?

> From now on, my mother will write only to me. Peace be with her delicate spoils. Whosoever looks to question her conduct will have to face me.

XI

. . . Then, my darling, upon surprising a certain farewell kiss you went into a state of shock which I did not know how to remedy; instead, I heightened it with my silence. Perhaps by putting together all these papers as best you can, you will be able to reconstruct it completely.

The girl who was embracing me when you got home came to return those crumpled notes that you are looking at right now, asking that I save or destroy them. She had just married a certain young proprietor of some spinning mills outside the city and decided to get rid of them. I certainly hope that you will repeat your rather melodramatic, "I want to know everything," from that day. In addition to that tone, which we have laughed at so much in others, I am bothered by the kind of strange fervor that has thrown you beyond your discreet respect for my affairs. I have always thought that if I protected you from the outside world, that would give you so much strength that you would not be interested in my affairs. You were my son, were you not? And, according to what we have always believed, you were a little different from the rest of humanity. Nevertheless, still being somewhat connected with the lies of the world, I repeat my question to you. Are you still in need of unlocking the door that swings open for each individual alone, and that, at times, not even that person himself can manage?

XII

Mother. After that first disconcerting episode, it occurs to me suddenly to imagine that nothing ever happened, that the pieces in our world will return to place normally without regard for the art of gluing things together so the seam may not even be noticed.

But, digging deeper, I also feel that I do not want this. The kind of gale wind that has risen to undo us is not contained by new glass, by righting the furniture, or by simply moving away to a new house.

I remember that one time, when I was a child, I asked you to give me nothing less than a beach. You laughed for a long time about my fantasies, and I, with the impotent expressiveness of a child my age, swore that someday I would have the eloquence to tell you my reasons. I am sure the moment has arrived. Certainly that which is strange will always be the unknown circumstance that awaits us. A boy desperate because he lacks the means to express himself. Later a man who is able to do so. And when does he discover it? The day his mother appears in the embrace of a young woman who is kissing her right on the lips and who then leaves in tears, moving away down the halls of the building.

That summer you were lying on the sand (right now I am thinking of how magnificent you have been at every age) when it occurred to me to draw a great circle around you, which would have you for its center. In those days I had just tried out my first bed, I was in school, and I was learning what it was like to increase the property of one's own body, to not be caught in a small crib with bars like a cage. The kind of restitution I paid you when I placed you within a vast expanse of sand surely penetrated other darker abysses. No one had the right to leave those grotesque footprints within our boundaries, like the tracks of those bears in the snow that appeared in my imagination and in your stories. In a word, I had raised boundaries around you, and I was as certain of their importance as all those who had invented them before me. But the same thing happened to me that had happened to them. In one of my comings and goings to the shore, I discovered the zone had been profaned by footprints, and that no one, not even you, knew it. I started to cry with all my might. Those very same bears ran to comfort me. I don't know what strange thing took the blame in the end. As always, the real enemy remained outside the story.

(Everything you write to me you can leave in my handkerchief drawer.)

XIII

Then there is no alternative, isn't that right? I must tell you that, on the day agreed upon after that very special "where," we left the city one weekend. You were studying with friends and I could tell that all of you were glad to see me go. I left the refrigerator full of enough food for an expedition and you, noticing my nervousness, sat down on that little crooked bench in the kitchen and rocked with laughter. In passing I must remember that your laughter, at that moment, had the same pitch as another's. You simply inherited it, that's all. To hear it was to bump into an echo delayed for many years, and from the kettledrums of death, no less. But I am unable to go on. I see that my nails need a touch-up or it will never be said that they shine perfectly.

XIV

Mother. The truth is that, because you mentioned something else, nails and other excuses aside, today I wouldn't have been able to follow the story of your departure from the city either. It is imperative that, before anything else, you tell me all of those things that make you stop, like a watch that suddenly would like to start marking time backwards. Because everything that hasn't been explained is also a kind of lie. And I am fed up with all that silence which offers nothing, which begins to seem dirty to me.

Until I was four I lived caught up by the idea of your paternity like the wooden doll belonging to Collodi's old man. At fourteen or fifteen, one prefers a certain rancor mixed with love, which one day appears to break loose from the root of those first hairs different from the rest which sprout from the body, from the first spot of acne, from the little shouts of pleasure drowned under the sheet. But twenty comes and no more miracles can be performed. One day the shadow, which threw itself between us like a dog, gets up and wants to search the house. This is the opportunity to open the locked cabinets, even though the keys have always been in sight. Now or never, then? And, in addition, all or nothing.

XV

Well then. Long and difficult again, like the stories you used to ask me for in the time of your private beach when the summer sun was the one to take the blame. (Now you see that I, too, have fresh memories.)

There are some photos and various press clippings in the bottom drawer of my dresser. There you will find the names and faces that may help you as you reflect on all this. I am not bothered by the slightly artificial response they may arouse in you. Your chain broke when you were conceived inside of me. But I am the one who has been unable to stir up those times without feeling as if my heart were in my hand. That, and we ought to talk one day of what that was, that is always there, completely alert. Sometimes I imagine it as a hidden monster, breathing, nourishing itself with the secret air of the boxes where it is kept. Passively, to be sure, but to the extent that every spring I take it out carefully. I fit it under my skin and I ought to explain it somehow, with reasons that people swallow with the same innocence that you swallowed those innocuous little pills that never did your sore throats any good.

My dearest. I certainly will never be able to forget that man. We loved each other with such splendor that I have often thought that might have been the very reason for our failure, especially when so many unimportant people can be seen, destined to laze nonchalantly in the best love seats. One night, in the clearing of a pine forest (your origin revealed) it suddenly occurred to us to project ourselves into space. But I don't know how many unknown planets we would have already explored, since in our case there was the constant renewal of situations, and every time we kissed we were suspended in a different sky. Nevertheless, the disaster was to be as great as our passion. In the depths of my soul a small childhood memory exists that I shall exchange for the one you have from the beach, and it may explain everything. A little friend my age, named Georgina, I think, the daughter of a poor woman, had taken a great liking to my sandals. One day, no longer able to resist her envious stares, I took them off and offered them to her. And she was going to take them when, as if stung by a familiar scorpion, she said she was going to ask her mother first and disappeared. I never saw her again. The woman, humiliated or incredulous, chose to keep me away from her daughter. I had to keep my sandals and everything I had not been able to give along with them.

Now you will undoubtedly understand the rest. Georgina may be used as a symbol. Georgina may well represent the blood with which one will have to learn that most people are frightened by everything that is too grand for them. (My treasure, what will your destiny in love be? How good we felt that day long ago within your boundaries on the beach . . .)

I didn't write for a few days. My father's face, imprisoned in the photos I found in that spot, a face which mine had badly duplicated, reflected an ironic smile at me from every mirror in the house. I began to understand maniacs. My dilemma burst forth from those mirrors in which my unknown rival was reflected in my very image. At times, especially when I shaved, I suffered a crazy urge to talk to him, man to man, to offer him a cigarette, to talk about my mother like two suitors who meet again once their lover has died. But mother was alive and beautiful. And besides, I had never met him before. It was then that I remembered the rest. Violeta, that Violeta de Parma. My mother was going to tell me about the famous weekend in an open and sincere letter, written with the warmth and the sound of whispered words.

XVI

And after all that, what about our Violeta de Parma?

For two or three days there was no answer in my handkerchief drawer. Until, opening it one morning with the caution of one carrying a birdcage, I found what I was looking for.

XVII

Ah, that's right we did begin with that. . . . And the name's not bad. Planning to indulge herself in a great feast, her first adolescent adventure, Violeta waited for me at the bus station on the agreed day.

Without her store uniform, and free of all the artifices I myself had transmitted to her, I could recognize in her a daring personality, perhaps the product of certain vicissitudes that had been confided to me second-hand, and which were as capable of drawing out her temerity as a green pasture would draw out a young mare. Like a diminutive pioneer she had already chosen a hotel and imposed conditions. Of course, without having any experience whatsoever, she was guided by a natural instinct to subordinate, to enforce the kind of obedience created by overpowering creatures even if they are the size of mere peas. Although such boldness did not allow her to completely control her trembling hands, which she often thought to cover up by going through her overnight bag.

That is how I allowed myself to be swept away, misleading her with a false air of submission. Because everything in her that seemed aimless, even when set off by the most intimate and exact desires, had a name for me, and it could only lead to one end. But here another avalanche overtakes me, yours. What will be the result of telling to you this long woven tale, which must still unravel before you come of age, if you yourself snatch from it Godiva's hair under which it is hidden from the world?

XVIII

Mother. In some notes written in your strange handwriting, which I found in the usual place, you remarked that that man, my father (to think that he is inside me like a tenant who has taken over the house), used to say that morality is a doubtful invention, because events that move us in society would not affect us if we were on a deserted island.

Very well. Whether on that famous deserted island or shouted out at a crowded rally, I am sure that your intuitive poetry will always be a formidable bully. Or do you really believe that before I knew the store's miseries, I had any realistic concept of that illuminated cave? No, you have never been a flesh-and-blood mother directing a crew of slaves that kills itself for a tiny commission, but instead you have been a kind of magical influence suspended over an unsteady sea which I have seen turn blue in your shadow and return to black in your absence. You have nurtured me with a strange milk, I think. And as I may have inherited my liking for integrity from you, I demand that you speak without fear on that island. At this point, you and I both realize that we have prolonged the preface more than necessary.

XIX

And how painful for the handkerchief drawer that you don't want to drop the subject, right?

The truth is that we finally arrived at a place that from the beginning I decided to call "I don't know where." It was deathly cold and they assigned us a room that seemed to have stored the cold, but with one advantage, its isolation along with other small rooms in the main wing of the building.

Forming part of the old section of the hotel, the room opened onto an uncovered patio with plants hung from the eaves and a windmill in the center. I know all this will sound cheap to you, because it bothers me too, as I write about it. But when an atmosphere is created in which we leave our mark, we can expect certain things to come to haunt our thoughts for the rest of our lives, like a postcard you can't throw away. Our blessed and good memory adheres like our skin to those landscapes in blue and green. They become ridiculous, and to merely remove them would end up hurting us as much as being skinned alive.

The place: wooded. Also a detail of no importance, but which suddenly, as I relive it, I come to realize controlled everything else. Because the wind which the trees[3] let loose upon us began to whip at the windows that faced north and then that initial tumult resolved itself by unleashing the rain which threatened to flatten the broken-down hotel.

There were two beds in the room. But someone to whom they have given the picturesque name of demon, perhaps to avoid having to name oneself when standing to be judged, began to stealthily say, "Join them, join them, God has given ardor to your flesh and no longer has the curiosity to spy on old houses like this one."

Meanwhile, removed from the situation and in a complete state of that last-minute fright which I had predicted, she watched me push the two beds together as she sat on the floor, imprisoned between the storm that raged without and the mystery within.

Frozen to the bone, and taking off only my shoes and my raincoat, I finally got under the covers. They smelled like an old closet, like something secondhand. But not even that could detract from their effectiveness, which was nothing more than old tenderness prostituted by so much human contact.

> We were going to have supper. From my room I listened to Mother rattling things around in the kitchen. For a moment, it seemed that the woman who had gone to bed in that hotel and the one who moved among the household objects were not the same. I needed my father to come in to occupy the void, to install himself with all his physical presence in the ambiguous air of the house.

Suddenly, and more because of my sighs of pleasure at being wrapped up in the covers than anything else, she began to undress decisively, throwing her clothes every which way, and jumped into bed beside me. Lastly she took off the only piece of clothing that she seemed to have left on to protect her life, a bra so small it made one laugh, and everything came into view. It was like finding two birds' eggs like those that are speckled and are always of an unknown species. I told her so and that prompted her to begin searching my body, which was still covered. She poked, I think she broke something, and suddenly I heard her say, choking on her words, "God, why they must be magnolias. This must be what perfumed the store, not Violeta de Parma . . ."

Her own voice shook her from her ecstasy, returning her to a reality that seemed to have momentarily abandoned her. From then on a kind of peasant terror began to overtake her, as if she had been discovered by all the simple women who had come before her.

"That isn't possible," she said, suddenly with her former vehemence. "It is necessary to die; better yet I would have died before being born, I died without having been born."

An impetus of destruction had possessed her, so strong it shook her from the bed and attempted to pull her onto the flooded patio. I managed to grab her at the door like a cat in a trance of madness, her hair and eyes electrified.

"Come on," I said to her, trying my luck with any banality, "they won't try us without legal counsel in the hotel's kitchen for this, nor do we have to fling ourselves out into the rain for sins that haven't been committed."

She let herself be led back to bed. She then looked at me with a velvety light which she saved for certain moments, and shading her eyes with her hands, she asked me to dim the lamp. I covered the ridiculous thing badly with a fashion magazine, and everything seemed to take on a normality that seemed a little suspicious.

"I am sorry," she said finally in a solemn voice, "I was giving a great deal of importance to doing things properly, the way books in a public library are catalogued. I came here because I wanted someone like you to caress me completely for the first time in my life. If you were a man, I would be here with you all the same. But the men I have known until now, including one, have provoked nothing in me, not even laughter. The day that one of them can at least do that, making me laugh so wholeheartedly that I twist and stretch over something he says or does to me, then I will come here with him to this same spot and I will give him whatever you may have left me."

Perplexed, I listened to this change in position, and for a moment it seemed to me that one lives prudently for many years so that someone else's madness can burst in one's face, like a stone that leaps off the road onto the windshield and shatters it to pieces.

She took advantage of my stupor then and leaped out of bed again, stopping to face me, framed in the bathroom door. She had the graceful and nervous body of a colt, but, not even in the dizziness all of that provoked, was it vulgar. We came from a decayed and shallow world. In exchange for that sordidness, she would only have needed a small basket on her hip for that miserable little room to have blossomed like a field sown with tulips.

"Well," she asked suddenly as if she were mocking me, leaving the doorway, "should we go to that rancid jury in the kitchen or not?"

The worn carpet, like the very earth that rocked us, brought her along slowly. I looked at her long-boned feet, the kind that seem to be searching for the floor as if they were dancing with every step. But those feet were the stem that supported the entire flower. And she radiated up from there, concentrating in her triangular field a heat more memorable than that of the famous world war.

Of course it was necessary to go to supper at a specific hour announced by the bell. We separated the beds again, admiring our great precaution, and left for the dining room, under the same raincoat.

All the details of our entrance to the dining room, and of our being seated at a table for two, seemed to be recorded on the eyes of the girl as if on virgin film. I saw her take the napkin off her plate, spread it over her knees and brush away the inevitable nocturnal fly with the same degree of inaugural importance with which she greeted the first guests who passed by, a mature pair who sat down at a nearby table. Then, with the same prolixity as that of a catalogue, she became interested in some pills that they took from the same bottle, letting the water they swallowed be heard in their stomachs.

"They must be the pills of boredom, see the effects?" I said, pretending to read the menu that was on the table. Cautious and silent until that moment, she let out a laugh which made everyone turn their heads.

"Delightful," she added in a low voice, "but over there are two who look like honeymooners. Might it occur to them to take pills someday?"

"The pills." I said absentmindedly to the waitress who came to serve us.

"What pills, madam?"

"Oh," I answered, feigning my carelessness badly, "one always thinks one is at home."

The woman looked at me with an air of secret complicity about my forgetfulness, and began to fill our plates.

It continued to rain in torrents. I thought of what this rain would be like, pounding on the door of room number . . .

"What number?" I asked Violeta, "do you remember it so we'll at least be able to get back to the room?"

She hadn't noticed it either. At that moment the young man on his honeymoon, who was in a bad mood because of the poorly lit room, threw the newspaper on the table, as if that were the only thing on his mind at that moment. The digestive process was in full gear. Every once in a while, Violeta put her knife and fork on the edge of her plate to listen to the concert of porcelain and metal that filled the air.

"Don't worry about the number," I told her, "you'll see how our door shines behind the curtain of water."

When we returned the twin beds were freshly made up, and it seemed that someone had sprayed more cold into the atmosphere.

Suddenly, while we were putting the beds back together the lock next door squeaked.

"Psst," I said, "it is an accident which can't figure into anyone's plans, we are going to live alongside them now."

"I hope that they are not the ones with the pills," added Violeta, getting under the covers this time without any problems.

The pacers went back and forth as if they were sinking into a floor of decayed boards. Then one was not heard anymore; the other, the woman, collapsed on the bed, sinking into it as if the bed was receiving an elephant.

"Hey, filthy loafer," one heard her shout suddenly, "do you have to forget to flush the toilet here too?"

"Always your healthy spirit of waste," the accused replied from a distance."

"Waste, with what we're paying? As if they didn't charge the price of gold even for the air we breathe in this frozen pigsty."

The water was heard running. The water bound for that dirty destiny and the free water outside had surrounded us in a circle. Impossible, then, to leave one or to fall into the other . . .

"Never, never," I heard her say meanwhile, lying next to me with as much tension as a cord that was about to break.

"What is that 'never,' what does it mean?"

"That nothing can ever come of this, never, not ever."

It was then that I had to help with words like a mother who resorts to the faucet when her child is slow about something else. Sometimes, who knows if today isn't the last time, it has occurred to me to evoke that unfolding of suggestions: "Alone you will be climbing a mountain whose peak you can't see (inventing the pain of scaling), and the more you bruise yourself, the more desperate you are to reach the top (but a scaling which, at the same time, would have a goal); it could be because of a black diamond that is buried there. The rest of the people shout and shout from below so that you'll lose hope and leave it just to them, but you, deaf, don't understand their evil language, and all of this so that in the end, when you reach the peak, you will understand that there is no such thing; rather there is deception so you will never forget that earth, the real earth, is in heaven."

There on the edge of midnight she found her diamond. I was going to note the exact time. I took the magazine off the lamp and I looked at my watch.

"Damn!" I whispered. "The crystal has fallen off and the hands have flown off, who knows where."

"And now," she asked breathlessly, "what will happen in the regimented store?"

A little laugh filled with sounds that interfered with our waves. It was almost a message substituted for a nose and an eye at the keyhole.

"How do you like that, two women," said the voice of the little man who conserved water, and who seemed plastered to our ears. "If one could still do that nowadays, at least try to do it; if you would let me try it, only . . . "

"Ugh," groaned the elephant woman, "how disgusting. That was all I needed to make everything complete. Give me the sleeping ones, they're in the big bottle."

A kind of amphibian sun finally began to filter through the crevices. Doubtlessly it had stopped raining, but I heard water falling, always more water. I opened the outside door a crack and I saw it. It was running down over the windmill, overflowing like a sort of liquid hair. Violeta, the color of her name, slept faceup between the reality of the room inside and my sleepwalking eyes which carried her to the mill.

I wrapped myself in my raincoat and went out to explore the park. I must have been out for an eternity, walking under the trees, sinking into dead leaves covered with mud. At times the sinister pines wanted to drive their needles into my shrouded heart, to return me to the moment that I told you about in the beginning, always those damned trees in my life, with their green signals on the firing line.

When I got back she was already dressed, seated on a suitcase, and crying silently. Outside one could hear some travelers preparing for the return trip. She continued to fuss, unaffectedly, but with the weight of solitary ruins.

And it was in that moment that it occurred to me to see her as I still do now, in the guise of a small, dirty, and ugly immigrant who has arrived from afar and still doesn't know if back home they think she is here, or if she really is here. She sat on her ordinary suitcase and, perhaps because she knew it was filled with dirt from her poor homeland, or because she feared the wealth of the new land, too attractive to be true, the immigrant looked at me suddenly, between her tears, and as the noise outside continued, said to me: "And now I want a diamond again, this time without attaining it, so that it will last my entire life. I am going to marry and I am afraid."

"You're going to do what? You're afraid of what?" I asked her, hastily, feeling all of that was too obscure for a final act.

"Of a wealthy man's poverty, speaking in a language that he doesn't understand. Of reaching the peak of the mountain and of still being alone when the black diamond appears . . . and of having to destroy it so that each person may possess his own in a different way."

Essay of Telepsychic Experience Violeta or the Immigrant—Mills with hair of water—Mother—Sand—Wind and Rain—Black Diamond—All or nothing —Georgina or Idiocy—The Monster with my face, nourished in a box.

These incoherent words appeared at the end, in my handwriting, that handwriting so lacking in blood stains, so inexperienced at the time.

Today I record the experiment of repeating them again and again, for the possible survivor named Georgina, who probably still walks barefoot. And for my unknown father's soul wandering through the pine forests, in search of the evaporated scent of love.

Juan Abel Grim

Collector and annotator of the letters

Translated by Anne Hohenstein
(From Muerte por alacrán, 1979)

Notes

1. In my handwriting "the boss was slowly yielding," J.A.G.
2. To challenge Mother, what courage . . . J.A.G.
3. At last I would find it said by someone else, that the wind comes from the trees! Only Mama and the child Chesterton could think of such a thing. J.A.G.

Bibliography

Fiction by Armonía Somers

"The Burial." Trans. Evelyn Picón Garfield. *Women's Fiction from Latin America: Selections from Twelve Contemporary Authors.* Ed. Evelyn Picón Garfield. Detroit: Wayne State University Press, 1988. 39–50.

La calle de viento norte y otros cuentos. Montevideo: Arca, 1963.

De miedo en miedo. Los manuscritos del río. Montevideo: Arca, 1965.

El derrumbamiento. Montevideo: Salamanca, 1953.

"El derrumbamiento." *Narradores uruguayos.* Ed. Rubén Cotelo. Caracas: Monte Avila, 1969. 149–70.

"El entierro." *Antología del cuento uruguayo.* Vol. 6: Los Nuevos. Ed. Arturo S. Visca. Montevideo: Banda Oriental, 1968. 11–26.

"The Fall." *Other Fires: Short Fiction by Latin American Women.* Ed. and Trans. Alberto Manguel. Toronto: Lester & Orpen Dennys, 1986. 9–23.

"The Immigrant." *Diana's Second Almanac.* Trans. Anne Hohenstein. Ed. T. Ahern. Providence, R.I.: Diana's Bimonthly Press, 1980. 4–35.

"La inmigrante." *Puerta abierta: La nueva escritora latinoamericana.* Eds. Caridad L. Silva-Velázquez and Nora Erro-Orthmann. Mexico City: Joaquín Mortiz, 1986. 205–22.

"Madness." Trans. Susana Hertelendy. *The Eye of the Heart: Short Stories from Latin America.* Ed. Barbara Howes. New York: Avon, 1973. 419–21.

Muerte por alacrán. Buenos Aires: Calicanto, 1979.

La mujer desnuda. Montevideo: Revista Clinia, 1950. Rpt. in Montevideo: Tauro, 1966. 2nd. ed. Montevideo: Arca, 1990.

"Plunder." Trans. Evelyn Picón Garfield. *Women's Fiction from Latin America: Selections from Twelve Contemporary Authors.* Ed. Evelyn Picón Garfield. Detroit: Wayne State University Press, 1988. 51–65.

La rebelión de la flor. Montevideo: Librería Linardi y Risso, 1988.

Un relato para Dickens. Montevideo: Arca, 1969.

Sólo los elefantes encuentran mandrágora. Buenos Aires: Legasa, 1983.

Todos los cuentos, 1953–1967. Montevideo: Arca, 1967.

Tríptico Darwiniano. Montevideo: Torre, 1982.

"The Tunnel." Trans. Evelyn Picón Garfield. *Women's Fiction from Latin America: Selections from Twelve Contemporary Authors.* Ed. Evelyn Picón Garfield. Detroit: Wayne State University Press, 1988. 31–38,

Viaje al corazón del día. Elegía por un secreto amor. Montevideo: Arca, 1986.

Essays by Armonía Somers

"Carta abierta desde Somersville." *Revista Iberoamericana* 58.160–61 (1992): 1155–65.

"Cuando el escándalo de *La mujer desnuda*." *Brecha* (Montevideo) November 16, 1990, 24.

Educación de la adolescencia: El adolescente de novela y su valor de testimonio. Mexico City: n.p., 1957.

Postscript. "Diez relatos a la luz de sus probables vivenciales." *Diez relatos y un epílogo*. Eds. Campodónico et al. Montevideo: Fundación de Cultura Universitaria, 1979. 113–54.

Criticism on the Works of Armonía Somers

Agosín, Marjorie. "'La mujer desnuda' o el viaje decapitado: Un texto de Armonía Somers." *Revista Interamericana de Bibliografía/Inter-American Review of Bibliography* 42.4 (1992): 585–89.

Ainsa, Fernando. "Armonía Somers y los lobos esteparios." *Tiempo reconquistado*. Montevideo: Geminis, 1977. 124–25.

Araújo, Helena. "Armonía Somers: 'El derrumbamiento,' 'Armonía y su Tríptico Darwiniano.'" *La scherezada criolla: Ensayos sobre escritura femenina latinoamericana*. Bogota: Universidad Nacional de Colombia, 1989. 75–81, 171–73.

———. "Escritura femenina: Sobre un cuento de Armonía Somers." *Cuéntame tu Vida* (Cali, Colombia) 5 (1981): 19–24.

———. "El tema de la violación en Armonía Somers y Griselda Gambaro." *Plural* (Mexico City) 15.179 (1986): 21–23.

"Armonía Somers: Los lobos esteparios." *Capítulo Oriental* (Montevideo) 33 (1968): 523.

Benedetti, Mario. "El derrumbamiento." *Número* (Montevideo) 5.22 (1953): 102–3.

———. *Literatura uruguaya siglo veinte*. Montevideo: Alfa, 1969. 205–9.

Biron, Rebecca E. "Armonía Somers 'El despojo': Masculine Subjectivity and Fantasies of Domination." *Latin American Literary Review* 21.42 (1993): 7–20.

Campodónico, Miguel Angel. "Homenaje a Armonía Somers: Diálogo con Miguel Angel Compodónico." *Revista de la Biblioteca Nacional* (Montevideo) 24 (1986): 45–61.

Clark, María B. "Desirous Fiction or 'El hombre del túnel' de Armonía Somers." *Romance Language Annual* 4 (1992): 404–10.

Cosse, Rómulo. "Armonía Somers: Monstruosidad y esplendor." *Fisión literaria: Narrativa y proceso social*. Montevideo: Monte Sexto, 1989. 49–66.

———. ed. *Armonía Somers, papeles críticos: Cuarenta años de literatura*. Montevideo: Librería Linardi y Risso, 1990.

Cousté, Alberto. "Armonía Somers, al este del paraíso." *Primera Plana* (Buenos Aires) 242 (1967): 52–53.

Erro-Orthmann, Nora. "Armonía Somers." *Spanish American Women Writers*. Ed. Diane Martin. Westport, Conn.: Greenwood Press, 1990. 493–500.

Erro-Peralta, Nora. "Armonía Somers." *Escritoras de Hispanoamérica*. Eds. Diane E. Marting and Montserrat Ordoñez. Bogota: Siglo Veintiuno, 1990. 523–30.

Espada, Roberto de. "Armonía Somers o el dolor de la literatura." *Maldoror* (Montevideo) 7 (1972): 62–66.

Figueira, Gastón. "*La calle del viento norte.*" *Books Abroad* (Summer 1964): 295.

Foster, David William. *A Dictionary of Contemporary Latin American Authors.* Tempe: Center for Latin American Studies, Arizona State University, 1975. 98.

Gandolfo, Elvio E. "Para conocer a Armonía Somers." *Clarín* January 1986: 1–3.

García Rey, José M. "Armonía Somers: Sondeo intuitivo y visceral del mundo." *Cuadernos Hispanoamericanos* (Madrid) (1985): 101–4.

Kantaris, Elia Geoffrey. "Disseminating Psychoanalysis: Armonía Somers." *The Subversive Psyche: Contemporary Women's Narrative from Argentina, and Uruguay.* Oxford: Clarendon Press, 1995. 82–132.

Moore, Charles B. "El papel del lector activo en 'La inmigrante' de Armonía Somers." *Chasqui* 26.1 (1997): 45–55.

Olivera-Williams, María Rosa. "'El derrumbamiento' de Armonía Somers y 'El ángel caído' de Cristina Peri Rossi: Dos manifestaciones de la narrativa imaginaria." *Revista Chilena de Literatura* (Santiago) 42 (1993): 173–81.

———. "Entre él y ella: J. C. Onetti y Armonía Somers desde sus cuentos." *Revista de Crítica Literaria Latinoamericana* 23.46 (1997): 211–24.

Penco, Wilfredo. "Armonía Somers: El mito y sus laberintos." *Noticias* (Montevideo) 3.82 (1979): 50–52.

Picón Garfield, Evelyn. "Armonía Somers." *Women's Voices from Latin America: Interviews with Six Contemporary Authors.* Detroit: Wayne State University Press, 1985. 29–51.

———. "La metatorización de la soledad: Los cuentos de Armonía Somers." *Revista de la Universidad Nacional* (Montevideo) 2.10 (1986–87): 25–30.

———. "Yo soplo desde el páramo (La muerte en los cuentos de Armonía Somers)." *Texto Crítico* (Xalapa) 3.6 (1977): 113–25.

Rama, Angel. *La generación crítica, 1939–1969.* Montevideo: Arca, 1972. 29.

———. "La insólita literatura de Somers: La fascinación del horror." *Marcha* (Montevideo) 1.188 (1963): 27–30.

———. "Raros y malditos en la literatura uruguaya." *Marcha* (Montevideo) 1319 (1966): 30–31.

Rela, Walter. *Diccionario de escritores uruguayos.* Montevideo: de la Plaza, 1986. 124–27.

Rodríguez-Villamil, Ana María. "Aspectos fantásticos en *La mujer desnuda* de Armonía Somers." *Río de la Plata* 1 (1985): 147–63.

———. *Elementos fantásticos en la narrativa de Armonía Somers.* Montevideo: Banda Oriental, 1990.

Romiti, Elena. "La aporía como signo de *Sólo los elefantes encuentran mandrágora.*" *Deslindes* (Montevideo) 1 (1992): 83–98.

Shimrose, Pedro. *Diccionario de autores iberoamericanos.* Madrid: Ministerio de Relaciones Exteriores, 1982. 405.

"Testimonio: Una gran escritora uruguaya (A.S.) habla para Rumbos." *Rumbos* (Montevideo) October 3, 1969: 8–9.

Varderi, Alejandro. "Armonía Somers: De la mujer y del amor, lo grotesco." *Monographic Review/Revista Monográfica* 7 (1991): 227–31.

Visca, Arturo Sergio. *Antología del cuento uruguayo: Los nuevos*. Montevideo: Banda Oriental, 1968. 11–26.

———. "El mundo narrativo de Armonía Somers." *Nueva antología del cuento uruguayo*. Montevideo: Banda Oriental, 1976. 260–63.

Zum Felde, Alberto. *Indice crítico de la literatura hispanoamericana*. Vol. 2: *La narrativa*. 2nd ed. Madrid: Aguilar, 1964. 501.

Gloria Stolk

VENEZUELA

Gloria Stolk (1918–79) was born in Caracas, Venezuela. She studied at the University of Paris, and at Smith College in the United States where she specialized in literature. She wrote poetry, short stories, novels, and literary criticism. In 1956 her novel *Amargo el fondo* (Bitter is the bottom) won her the Arístides Rojas Prize, the highest distinction given in Venezuela to a novelist.

For many years she wrote a column in the newspaper the *Caracas Nacional,* and she was a distinguished writer for several literary journals in Venezuela. While posted as ambassador of Venezuela to the Dominican Republic, she wrote her well-known short story collection *Cuentos del Caribe* (Short stories from the Caribbean, 1975). These stories reveal a profound respect for human dignity and a delicate equilibrium between the forces of good and evil in the world.

Gloria Stolk's literary and cultural efforts brought her considerable recognition and success; however, her personal life was marked by tragedy. She enjoyed several years of a loving marriage with children, but it ended abruptly with the tragic suicide of her husband. In 1979 Gloria Stolk also committed suicide in Venezuela.

Crickets and Butterflies

Because he had the soul of an explorer, Enriquillo turned out to be an inspired doctor. Beyond the suffering raw material he discovered the caged and sick spirit which took vengeance upon the flesh, or escaped by torturing it in order to divert its unbearable anguish. Enriquillo unmasked the hidden evil, using his eager and smiling goodness, and the patient felt his symptoms diminish, his body rejoice and become healthy, while at the same time his suffering spirit, which was fighting against life's implacability, was gradually letting go.

Enriquillo was not really a psychiatrist. It was enough for him to be a man with an insatiable human curiosity, a cheerful and silent discoverer of those islands that are men and women. Of their mountains and their springs, their dark places and their crystalline fountains. He would play at performing good deeds just as others play golf, for pure sport, and with a ferocity incomprehensible to those who watched him.

Thus, leaving the beautiful and hypocritical city, he came one day to that faraway village in the mountains. He arrived by sea. The sea brought him on its back of deep and rippled blue. He came to one of those scientific things—a conference or a lecture—and surprising everyone, even himself, decided to stay on. Up there, on the mountain, where the Yaque and the Jimonea Rivers flow, in a cool spot on the hot island, amongst stands of unexpected pine trees, the doctor pitched his solitary tent. He wanted to write, he wanted to reflect, to survey from above the route taken, to better spy what he needed. But soon he was interrupted in his intense contemplation of his interior landscape.

His fame had arrived with him, and timidly the sick began to approach him. The little girl who sang had now gone forever, and her sad mother could not bring her to Enriquillo so that the girl could be cured. The foreign woman who loved love with an insatiable passion could not bring herself to see him fortunately or unfortunately for both of them; but day after day God's humble creatures came to see him asking for his help to be relieved of their suffering: those sick from hunger who needed affection more than bread; children without fathers, or even worse, with false parents; women of the earth who seemed to be made of clay, kneaded with the sweat of ancestral desperation; men who emptied out their profound impotence in the face of life, with blind rage, drunk with poverty, and drugged with the fear of being alive.

It was a long line of pilgrims, an endless line, that would disappear with the night to form again when the sun came out. He attended to every one and, using few medicines and long talks, helped them slowly to live, which was tantamount to helping to cure them.

The druggists in the nearby towns ground out all the indignation of the world in their pestles. Except for three or four simple remedies, the doctor did not prescribe anything. The physicians from the nearby region also came up to see him without revealing who they were, pretending to be sick, and the diagnosis of their new rival amazed them.

"My friend, you don't have anything wrong with you," he said to one who was describing with a wealth of detail supposed symptoms that were bothering him.

He advised another one, who came with the same predicament to observe the new doctor on the sly, "Your problem is that you find yourself bothered by my presence here and that causes you to feel certain discomforts. Don't worry, for I'm not coming to compete with anyone, but rather to help wherever possible."

"And how do you know I'm a doctor?"

"I saw it in your eyes. You have a clinical eye," replied Enriquillo, laughing.

The witch doctor, Chilapa, who lived in a small cave in the surrounding area, did not come to see Enriquillo because a witch doctor does not like any doctor besides himself; but he cast all kinds of spells on him, sprinkled incense, and used other kinds of herbs so that he would leave. Small packages carefully tied up and filled with disgusting things would frequently appear at the doctor's door. He opened them carefully and declared in a loud voice: "Take them to Señor Chilapa's laboratory so he can analyze them."

Thus Chilapa remained calm. Enriquillo lived happily in that remote and beautiful place; by night he read and meditated, and by day he kept on conducting his necessary consultations, incapable as he was of rejecting the sick, even though they left him with little free time for contemplation. Sometimes he thought about going farther afield to a place that was really solitary, higher up on the steepest mountain peak.

One sunlit morning he saw a young woman followed by two children coming along the narrow, leafy path to his tent. The older one was a boy of about ten, with a dark and tormented face, and the other a girl, small and chubby with a faraway look in her eyes. Both, when seen at a glance, were far removed from ordinary reality, and had, at the same time, a vacant and anguished look on their faces.

The woman said to him simply: "I bring them here to you, Doctor. This one, Juan de la Cruz, has crickets in his head, and she, Lucinda, has butterflies. Don't you know it!"

"Crickets? Butterflies? Can you possibly mean that they have manias and strange ideas, that kind of thing?"

"No, Señor. Crickets, crickets. Crickets like those that go chirp, chirp. He has had them since he got back from down there. Her butterflies were already in her mind, it seems to me, but they have bothered her ever since he came to live in the house. Before that she didn't mention them, now she does."

The doctor bit his lips lightly.

"Are they your children?"

She laughed coquettishly.

"Those kids, so big? No, they're the late Lucrecia's children. I took them in and I said to my man, 'Our mother brought us up lovingly, and since Lucrecia my sister drowned during the flood, it's my turn to bring up her little ones.' My late mother, Minán, always said that loving is what counts the most in families. Because you see, Doctor, we are the daughters of good parents even though we're poor. Who has said that we poor people don't have manners or love for our fellow creatures. Oh, no!"

The young woman was talkative, but charming.

"Tell me briefly the story of the children before I go in to examine them."

"At the same time that the late Lucrecia died, the children's father lost the little bit of land he had, decided to go and look for work in the capital, and took the children with him. Around there he took up with another woman, and one day Juan de la Cruz ran away from home. His father searched for him, but didn't find him. I don't imagine he looked very hard for him, I say, because the woman was already pregnant and didn't want to have more than her own kids around. I learned about this and went to get the little girl and brought her here. She was chubby when I found her, yes, but half crazy as well. I think that already she had this thing with the butterflies. I brought her here, Doctor, because that woman had no love for the daughter of my dead sister. I noticed as soon as I saw her. It's a shame that the girl, who isn't ugly, is bewitched by that business of the butterflies. At first they weren't noticeable, Doctor."

"How is that?"

"Well, when he feels the crickets, right away she feels the butterflies that fly around inside her head. I go up to her and hear the noises that their wings make ever so softly."

"Do you believe that?"

"How am I not going to believe it? I hear them, ever so softly flying around in circles inside her head, and when they get stirred up, the child spends days not saying a word, looking at the ceiling; she doesn't sleep, not one wink, and eats without taking any notice of what she's eating. Listen to them, Doctor, ever so softly they go around and around her."

The doctor bent his face over the girl's and noticed that a very soft, almost inaudible whistle was coming out of her half-opened mouth.

"How do you do that?" he asked the girl suddenly, with notable kindness.

"I . . . I don't do anything," she countered defensively. "It's the butterflies. Here, Doctor." And she placed her chubby hands on her temples with a tragic gesture, while she looked at her brother, asking with her blank eyes for an approving glance.

"Now I see," said the doctor seriously. "And you, young man?"

"I, nothing. . . . It's the crickets . . . but not today. Today they are quiet," said the boy, blushing as he lowered his stern face.

The young woman continued to explain without a stop: "I took the girl to Señor Chilapa and he made her eat a live butterfly, a big one, one of those velvety ones, to see if the ones inside her would be frightened. Lucinda was sick for three days; she vomited up all her insides, and we thought she had been cured, but it came to nothing. After a few days, with the new phase of the moon the crickets came back, and the damned butterflies were flying around inside her. What she ate didn't make a bit of difference."

Enriquillo admired Chilapa's practical wisdom, although it was obvious that the boy's infectious influence was stronger. He focused his attention on the boy who was looking behind him because he wanted to leave.

"Tell me about the boy."

She raised her eyebrows to make a point, and speaking very softly, she said: "That one is certainly a really sad case, Doctor. He has never said anything to me about anything that happened to him since he fled from his father's house. You can't talk to him about that because he gets almost crazy with his crickets. One day when my husband and I insisted on his telling us, he had something like a dead fainting spell and we had to . . ."

"Aay! The crickets! Chirp, chirp . . . ," shouted the child suddenly, as if he had been overcome by a sharp pain while he looked with anguish at his aunt who was speaking softly to the doctor. He fell to the floor in a kind of attack, half real, half fake, which the doctor recognized at once as a hysterical trick to distract his attention.

"Didn't I tell you, Doctor? Look at that!"

They shook him, they threw water on his face, and soon he came to his senses.

"Juan de la Cruz, go to the patio and help the gardener water the lettuce. Go on, get out of here now." In a firm but gentle manner the doctor made him go to the vegetable garden, then continued with his questions: "How did you find him?"

"I didn't find him. I didn't have any idea where to look for him. Some people in a big car brought him. It seems that they had seen him a lot at the door of the three movie theaters in the capital. The lady used to give him some coins, and one day the gentleman began to talk to him, and they decided to bring him back to their home because he was smaller than the other street children and had an innocent face. The lady felt sorry for him. They intended to send him to school and he would help in the house and so on. He went off happily with them, but then the business of the crickets started, and he became a calamity case. Because the man didn't want to abandon him to roam around on the streets, he decided to bring him here to me. Good people, don't you think? Because they made that trip which was so long to bring him. The boy remembered the name of the town, and my name, and everything. He was about six when his late mother died, and his father took him away to the capital. What a bad time that was! There those crickets put themselves into his head, or was it that they were born inside him, eh, Doctor?"

"Let's see, Señora. To find that out, and other things as well, it would be best for the boy to remain here for the day. Let's ask him if he wants to."

First Juan de la Cruz said no, but ended up accepting the idea. At the same time he both wanted and did not want to be free of the crickets that were making him suffer horribly.

His aunt and Lucinda went back to the town and Enriquillo spent the rest of the day working in the garden and chatting nonchalantly with Juan de la Cruz.

He didn't clarify anything. The child was amiable, respectful, but laconic.

"I was around there, with some people," he said when Enriquillo questioned him about the time he spent away from his home. His face became contorted, nevertheless, when he mentioned the crickets.

"I can't see them, they're disgusting, and I have them inside of me. How revolting!"

The doctor let him be. They planted rosebushes in the garden and ate a seven-meat stew before Juan de la Cruz left.

"Come back whenever you feel like it," said the doctor over his shoulder.

"Could it be on Sunday, Señor? Your stew is very good and . . . I like talking with you."

A friendship was established between the two in which it was the doctor who would chat and tell stories about his childhood, about his studies, and other countries. The child listened, amazed.

"I would like to study too," he said once, "but with what? I have to work to help my aunt and uncle."

"If you are cured, if you get rid of the awful insects that bother you, maybe someone will want to pay for your studies."

"Do you think so, Doctor?" Mischievously, he let out a laugh. For the first time in years, a clear and childlike laugh. He had understood the veiled promise.

"Yes, I think so," said Enriquillo, looking him in the eyes, seriously, insistently, and the poor child, almost in a hypnotic trance, burst into tears, and sobbed: "I can't stand these crickets any longer, Doctor, I'm going to tell you everything, now, everything, everything."

But he had an attack. The most intimate part of him rebelled against confiding his secret, and that day, after he had recovered his senses, the doctor sent him home.

"Not yet, Juan de la Cruz. You will tell me another day." And the boy, again taciturn, said: "No, never, ever. It's too horrible."

"Then don't tell me. Come back another day when you are free."

"I'm not free, Señor. I'm not ever going to be, with these crickets!"

And sighing, he went off down the mountainside. When he returned some days later, the doctor had prepared a tiny cage made out of pieces of reeds.

"It's for the crickets," he told him.

And the boy laughed, before he remembered his anguish. "Yes, you believe they're nothing," he said in a resentful manner.

"I know they're not anything. They are a pretext that you give to confuse and punish yourself, and also, so as not to think about anything worse."

When he heard this, the boy began to tremble, shaking like a leaf, out of control in a full blown fit, and foaming at his twisted mouth.

"He cut off her hands, both of them, first one then the other. Ayyy! And I didn't say anything. I remained silent. I was very scared of him. He hit me hard several times on my head and it was then that the crickets entered my head. Ayy! Chirp, chirp . . ."

He rolled around on the ground and moaned. He was sweating copiously, and it seemed like he was about to die.

It was necessary to sedate him.

When he regained consciousness, Enriquillo said to him smiling: "Juan de la Cruz, you are cured."

"How is that, Señor, if I feel destroyed inside and with nothing in my head?"

"That's because the crickets are gone. They went away one by one. I saw them leave. They are gone forever. Do you see how it doesn't bother you to hear me talk about them?"

"That's true," said the child, vaguely surprised, and he closed his eyes as if falling into a stupor. After a little while he woke up, calmly.

"Listen to me, Juan de la Cruz. You aren't to blame anyway. Not at all. Do you understand me? The members of the gang that took you away were much stronger than you. You became a beggar for them, not for yourself; a thief perhaps, but for them, not because you wanted to. And the horrible thing that happened with the other child, you wouldn't have been able to avoid it."

"She was a tiny little girl like Lucinda, but smaller still; they found her walking alone in the countryside and they took her to the cave. One of the boys called her the butterfly, making fun of her, because she went around with her dress like this, as if it were wings, when they found her.

"They kept all of us in a dark cave, almost under the sea, on the coast, you know, almost without any food, and in the afternoon they would let us loose in the city so we could beg. They had threatened us that if we talked with the police or with anyone, they would kill all of us. They were very capable of doing it. The fat old man was very evil. He talked strangely. He wasn't from around here. He was the one who hit us, for everything, for nothing. Behind the ears, look."

"Yes, I had already noticed those scars."

"But the worst part was the day they took the little girl into the capital to beg, and afterwards they said that no one would give her money because she was chubby and healthy looking. One of the big men carried her in his arms and collected almost nothing. They waited a few days, looking in the newspapers, and because no one advertised for her, they decided to do that to her . . . what I told you about her hands. They got her drunk first so she wouldn't cry. She screamed a lot anyway. The noise of the sea covered her screams. On the rock . . . with a machete . . . I saw it, I saw it all, and I didn't go and tell the police. I got sick. Then the old man insulted me, threatened me, he was like a crazy man, and he hit me on the ear with a piece of iron. I fell down and fainted, but before that I heard the crickets and I saw inside myself with my eyes how they were getting themselves into my head. Dirty, disgusting things. Probably it was an idea of mine, like you say, but I felt them. Three days later I went out again onto the street. I was dying of hunger, and around there, on Guibia beach, where the shark bit the American's leg off last year, I started to beg.

"I brought lots of coins to the cave that night. And they gave me food too. I had the face of a dead man, believe me. That night when I lay down to sleep on my mattress, I heard the crickets again. At first they horrified me. Finally I became more or less accustomed. And now you say they've gone, Doctor?"

"Don't you believe it, Juan de la Cruz? Look how calmly you've spoken about all that."

"Yes, I believe it too. I don't feel them any more. Ah . . . Doctor, look, listen. I have to tell you something else. My crickets were real, but Lucinda's butterflies, those I put into her head so she would have something to tell her aunt as well. Lucinda reminded me of that other poor little girl, so I talked to her about the butterflies without telling her why, of course, and she began to feel them. Now they're going to leave her too, isn't that right, Doctor?"

"Yes, they will leave her easily, because they never existed. Just like your crickets. You don't need them any more to torment you, and for that reason they went away."

"Yes, Señor, I'm not afraid of them anymore. Now I've taken that weight off of me. Ah! . . . Doctor, excuse me. I'm very sleepy."

He gave a big yawn, was totally exhausted, and slept peacefully like an innocent child.

Translated by Brenda Segall
(From *Cuentos del Caribe*, 1975)

Bibliography

Fiction by Gloria Stolk

"Amargo el fondo." *Antología venezolana.* Ed. José Ramón Medina. Madrid: Gredos, 1962. 268–73.

Amargo el fondo. Caracas: Tipografía Vargas, 1957.

Angel de piedra. Caracas: J. Villegas, 1962.

Bela Vegas. Caracas and Madrid: Edime, 1953.

La casa del viento. Caracas: Arte, 1965.

Cuando la luz se quiebra. Caracas: n.p., 1961.

Cuentos del Caribe. Caracas: Monte Avila, 1975.

"Grillos y mariposas." *Puerta abierta: La nueva escritora latinoamericana.* Eds. Caridad L. Silva-Velázquez and Nora Erro-Orthmann. Mexico City: Joaquín Mortiz, 1986. 223–30.

Essays by Gloria Stolk

"Georgina inexistente y Juan Ramón Jiménez." *Repertorio Latinoamericano* 5.37 (1979): 7–8.

Manual de buenos modelos. Caracas: Instituto Nacional de Cultura y Bellas Artes, 1967; Santo Domingo: Listín Diario, 1973.

Poetry by Gloria Stolk

Cielo insistente. Caracas: Asociación de Escritores Venezolanos, 1960.

Rescate y otros poemas. Caracas: Tipografía Americana, 1950.

Criticism on the Work of Gloria Stolk

Aldariz, José R., ed. *Enciclopedia popular venezolana: Esto es Venezuela, 1987.* Caracas: Torre Phelps, 1988. 440–41.

Araujo, Orlando. ". . . Bela Vegas." *Papel Literario de El Nacional* (Caracas) January 28, 1954: 7.

———. *Narrativa venezolana contemporánea.* Caracas: Tiempo Nuevo, 1972. 233–37.

Calzadilla, J. "Amargo el fondo." *Revista Nacional de Cultura* 123 (1957): 145–46.

Cardozo, Lubio. *Diccionario general de la literatura venezolana.* Mérida, Venezuela: Centro de Investigaciones Literaria, Universidad de Los Andes, Facultad de Humanidades y Educación, 1974. 736–37.

C. D. "Amargo el fondo." *Papel literario de El Nacional* (Caracas) January 10, 1957: 7.

Medina, José Ramón. "Los miedos." *Revista Nacional de Cultura* 111 (1955): 180–81.

Paredes, Pedro Pablo. "Treinta y siete apuntes de crítica literaria." *Revista Nacional de Cultura* 111 (1955): 191–93

Pía P. y Beltran. "Amargo el fondo." *Cultura Universitaria* (Caracas) 63: 197–98.

Ramos Q., Elías A. *El cuento venezolano (1950–1970): Estudio temático y estilístico.* Madrid: Playor, 1979. 196.

R. P. "Tres libros de Gloria." *Papel Literario de El Nacional* (Caracas) August 26, 1954: 7.

————. "Versatilidad de Gloria Stolk." *Papel Literario de El Nacional* (Caracas) September 8, 1955.

Salazar Martínez, F. "Novela." *Papel Literario de El Nacional* 7.1 (1953): 3.

Telémaco. "Belas Vegas." *Papel Literario de El Nacional* 28.1 (1954): 7.

Tello, J. "Cuando la luz se quiebra." *Revista Nacional de Cultura* 148–49 (1961): 248–49.

Ungaro de Fox, L. "*América cuenta.*" *Revista Nacional de Cultura* 173 (1966): 146–47.

Luisa Valenzuela

ARGENTINA

Luisa Valenzuela is one of Argentina's most innovative and accomplished writers. Her revolutionary works have attracted the attention of many critics, who place it alongside the best contemporary prose fiction of such writers as Gabriel García Márquez and Julio Cortázar.

Born in Buenos Aires, Argentina, in 1938, the daughter of a well-known writer, Luisa Mercedes Levinson, Valenzuela began her literary career at the age of seventeen when she joined the staff of the newspaper *La Nación*. She wrote her first short story at eighteen and her first novel at twenty-one.

To date she has published five collections of short stories and six novels. Her writings reveal three thematic concerns: language, women, and politics. In several of her works she has given ironic, humorous, and often highly metaphorical accounts of the political and social events in her native Argentina during the last three decades.

In two of her most noted works, *Cola de lagartija* (1983; *The Lizard's Tail*, 1983) and *Cambio de armas* (1982; *Other Weapons*, 1985), Valenzuela examines male-female relationships against a backdrop of repression and terror.

Valenzuela's work is highly experimental. Her fiction is characterized by constantly shifting points of view, extensive use of metaphors, and wordplay. Often surrealistic, the structure of her work tends to be fragmentary and the imagery mythic and erotic.

Up Among the Eagles

You'll find what I tell you hard to believe, for who knows anything, nowadays, about life in the country? And life here on the mountains, up among the eagles. You get used to it. Oh yes, I can tell you. I who never knew anything but the city, just look at me now, the color of clay, carrying my pails of water from the public fountain. Water for myself and water for others. I've been doing it to eke out a living ever since the day I made the foolish mistake of climbing the path that borders the cliff. I climbed up and, looking down at the green dot of the valley below, I decided to stay here forever. It wasn't that I was afraid; I was just being prudent, as they say: threatening cliffs, beyond imagination—impossible even to consider returning. Everything I owned I traded for food: my shoes, my wristwatch, my key holder with all the keys (I wouldn't be needing them anymore), a ballpoint pen that was almost out of ink.

The only thing of any value I kept is my Polaroid camera; no one wanted it. Up here they don't believe in preserving images, just the opposite: every day they strive to create new images only for the moment. Often they get together to tell each other about the improbable images they've been envisioning. They sit in a circle in the dark on the dirt floor of their communal hut and concentrate on making the vision appear. One day, out of nothing, they materialized a tapestry of nonexistent colors and ineffable design, but they decided that it was just a pale reflection of their mental image, and so they broke the circle to return the tapestry to the nothingness from which it had come.

They are strange creatures; normally they speak a language whose meaning they themselves have forgotten. They communicate by interpreting pauses, intonations, facial expressions, and sighs. I tried to learn this language of silences, but it seems I don't have the right accent. At any rate, they speak our language when they refer to trivial matters, the daily needs that have nothing to do with their images. Even so, some words are missing from their vocabulary. For example, they have no word for yesterday or for tomorrow, before or after, or for one of these days. Here everything is now, and always. An unsatisfactory imitation of eternity like the tapestry I have already mentioned. Have mentioned? Oh yes, I'm the only one to use that verb tense; I may also be the only one who has any notion of conjugation. A vice left over from the world down there, knowledge I can't barter because no one wants it.

Will you trade me some beans for a notion of time? I went around asking the women in the marketplace, but they shook their heads emphatically. (A notion of time? They looked at me with mistrust. A way of moving on a different plane? That has nothing to do with the knowledge they are after.)

Who dares to speak of the passage of time to the inhabitants of this high place where everything endures? Even their bodies endure. Death neither decays nor obliterates them; it merely stops them in their path. Then the others, with exquisite delicacy—a delicacy I've seen them employ in connection with newly dropped kids or with certain mushrooms—carry the corpse beyond the rushing stream and with precise symmetry arrange it in the exact place it occupied in life. With infinite patience they have succeeded in creating, on the other side, a second town that obliterates time, an unmoving reflection of themselves that gives them a feeling of security because it is mummified, unmodifiable.

They only allow themselves changes in respect to the images. They grow, yes, they grow up and reach adulthood with only a suspicion of old age, remaining more or less the same until they die. In contrast, I discover with horror that I have a sprinkling of gray hairs, and wrinkles are lining my face; premature, of course, but who could keep her youth in this dry air, beneath such intense skies? What will become of me when they discover that time passes in my life, and is leaving its marks?

They are absorbed in other concerns, in trying to retain visions of what appear to be jeweled palaces and splendors unknown on this Earth. They roam around latitudes of awe while all I can do—and very infrequently and with extreme stealth at that—is take a photo of myself. I am down-to-earth despite living in this elevated land floating among clouds. And they say the altitude deranges those of us who come from sea level. But it is my belief, my fear, that they are the ones who are deranged; it's something ancestral, inexplicable, especially when they are squatting on their haunches, as they almost always are, looking inward in contemplation. I'm always looking outward, I search every road, almost nonchalantly nourishing my fear. They watch me go by carrying water, the pole across my shoulders and the two pails dangling from it, and I would like to think they do not suspect my fear. This fear has two faces, not at all like the one that kept me from returning after I had climbed the mountain. No, this is not a simple fear; it reflects others, and becomes voracious.

On the other hand, I am here, now. That now grows and changes and expands with time and, if I am lucky, will continue to evolve. I do not want them to be aware of this evolving, as I have already said, and even less do I want to be like them, exempt from time. For what would become of me if I kept this face forever, as if surprised between two ages? I think about the mummies in the mirror city, oh yes, absolutely, only mummies are unchanged by time. Time does not pass for the dead, I told myself one day, and on a different day (because I, if not they, am very careful to relate question to calendar) I added: nor does it pass for those who have no concept of death. Death is a milestone.

The inhabitants here, with their language of silence, could teach me the secrets of the immobility that so closely resembles immortality, but I am not eager to learn them. Life is a movement towards death; to remain static is to be already dead.

Sit here, little lady, nice and quiet here with us is one of the few things they consent to say to me in my own language, and I shake my head energetically (one more way of ensuring movement), and as soon as I am out of their sight, I begin to run like crazy along the neglected paths. More often than not I run up, not down, but either way, I don't want to get too far from the town, I don't want to stumble into the still city and find myself face-to-face with the mummies.

The secret city. I don't know it's exact location but I know everything about it—or maybe I only suspect. I know it has to be identical to this humble little clump of huts where we live, a faithful replica with the exact same number of bodies, for when one of them dies the oldest mummy is thrown into the void. It's noisy in the secret city. The noise announces its proximity, but it also serves a more basic purpose: scraps of tin, of every size and shape, hang from the rafters of the huts to scare away the buzzards. They are all that moves in the secret city, those scraps of tin to scare away the vultures, the only thing that moves or makes a sound. On certain limpid nights the wind carries the sound to where the living dwell, and on those nights they gather in the plaza, and dance.

They dance, but oh so slowly, almost without moving their feet, more as if they were undulating, submerged in the dense waters of sound. This happens only rarely, and when it does I feel an almost uncontrollable urge to join in the dance—the need to dance soaks into my bones, sways me— but I resist with all my strength. I am afraid that nothing could be more paralyzing than to yield to this music that comes from death. So that I won't be paralyzed I don't dance. I don't dance and I don't share the visions.

I have not witnessed a birth since I have been here. I know they couple, but they don't reproduce. They do nothing to avoid it, simply the stillness of the air prevents it. As for me, at this point I don't even go near men. It must be admitted that men don't come near me either, and there must be a reason, considering how often and how closely they approach almost anything else. Something in my expression must drive them away, but I've no way of knowing what it is. There are no mirrors here. No reflections. Water is either glaucous or torrential white. I despair. And every so often in the privacy of my cave, sparingly and with extreme caution, I take a new photo of myself.

I do this when I can't stand things any longer, when I have an overwhelming need to know about myself, and then no fear, no caution, can hold me back. One problem is that I am running out of film. In addition, I know perfectly well that if they find my photographs, if they place them in chronological order, two things can happen: they will either abominate or adore me. And neither possibility is to be desired. There are no alternatives. If they put the photos in order and draw the conclusions; if they see that when I arrived, my face was smoother, my hair brighter, my bearing more alert; if they discover the marks of time they will know that I have not controlled time even for a moment. And so if they find I am growing older, they won't want me among them, and they will stone me out of town, and I will have to face the terrifying cliffs.

I don't even want to think about the other possibility: that they will adore me because I have so efficiently, and so concretely, materialized these images of myself. Then I would be like stone to them, like a statue forever captive and contained.

Either of these two lapidary prospects should provide sufficient reason to restrain my suicidal impulse to take yet another photograph, but it doesn't. Each time, I succumb, hoping against hope that they will not be alerted by the glare of the flash. Sometimes I choose stormy nights; perhaps I conjure up the lightning with my pale simulacrum. At other times I seek the protective radiance of dawn, which at this altitude can be incendiary.

I make elaborate preparations for each of my secret snapshots, preparations charged with hope and danger, that is, with life. The resulting picture does not always please me but the emotion of seeing myself—no matter how horrible or haggard I appear—is immeasurable. This is I, changing in a static world that imitates death. And I feel safe. Then I am able to stop and speak of simple things with the women in the market and even understand their silences, and answer them. I can live a little longer without love, without anyone's touch.

Until another relapse, a new photo. And this will be the last. On a day with the sound of death, when the minimal activities of the town have come to a halt and they have all congregated to dance in the marketplace. That deliberate dancing that is like praying with their feet, a quiet prayer. They will never admit it, but I suspect that they count to themselves, that their dance is an intricate web of steps like knitting, one up, two backward, one to the right. All to the tinkling of the far-off tin scraps: the wind in the house of the dead. A day like any other; a very special day for them because of the sound that they would call music, were they interested in making such distinctions. But all that interests them is the dance, or believing they are dancing, or thinking of the dance, which is the same thing. To the pulse of the sound that floods over us, whose origins I cannot locate though I know it comes from the city of the dead.

They do not call to me; they don't even see me. It's as if I didn't exist. Maybe they're right, maybe I don't exist, maybe I am my own invention, or a peculiar materialization of an image they have evoked. That sound is joyful, and yet the most mournful ever heard. I seem to be alive, and yet . . .

I hide in my cave trying not to think, trying not to hear the tinkling; I don't know where it comes from, but I fear where it may lead me. With the hope of setting these fears to rest, I begin my preparations for the last photo: a desperate attempt to recover my being. To return to myself, which is all I have.

Anxiously, I wait for the perfect moment, while outside, darkness is weaving its blackest threads. Suddenly, an unexpected radiance causes me to trip the shutter before I am ready. No photograph emerges, only a dark rectangle that gradually reveals the blurred image of a stone wall. And that's all. I have no more film so I may as well throw away the camera. A cause for weeping were it not for the fact the radiance is not fading. A cause for uneasiness, then, because when I peer out I see that the blazing light is originating from the very place I wanted not to know about, from the very heart of the sound, from a peak just below us. And the radiance comes from millions of glittering scraps of tin in the moonlight. The city of the dead.

Spontaneously, I set forth with all my stupid photos, responding to an impulse that responds, perhaps, to a summons from the sonorous radiance. They are calling me from down there, over to the left, and I answer, and at first I run along the treacherous path and when the path ends I continue on. I stumble, I climb and descend, I trip and hurt myself; to avoid hurtling into the ravine I try to imitate the goats, leaping across the rocks; I lose my footing, I slip and slide, I try to check my fall, thorns rake my skin and at the same time hold me back. Rashly I pull ahead and it is imperative that I reach the city of the dead and leave my face to the mummies. I will place my successive faces on the mummies and then at last I'll be free to go down without fearing stone for I'll take my last photo with me and I am myself in that photo and I am stone.

Translated by Margaret Sayers Peden
(From *Donde viven las águilas*, 1983)

Bibliography

Fiction by Luisa Valenzuela

Antología personal. Buenos Aires: Instituto Movilizador de Fondos Cooperativos, 1998.

Aquí pasan cosas raras. Buenos Aires: Flor, 1975.

Bedside Manners. Trans. Margaret Jull Costa. London and New York: High Risk, 1995.

"The Best Shod" and "A Story About Greenery." Trans. Helen Lane. *Ms* 7.12 June 1979: 60–61.

Black Novel (with Argentines). Trans. Toby Talbot. New York: Simon, 1992.

"Blue Water-man." *Women's Fiction from Latin America: Selections from Twelve Contemporary Authors* Ed. Trans. Evelyn Picón Garfield. Detroit: Wayne State University Press, 1988. 281–87.

Cambio de armas. Hanover, N.H.: Ediciones del Norte, 1982; Mexico City: M. Casillas, 1983.

"The Censors." Trans David Unger. *City* 8 1.8 (1980): 8–10.

The Censors. Trans. Hortense Carpentier. Willimantic, Conn.: Curbstone Press, 1988.

Clara. Trans. Andrea G. Labinger. Pittsburgh: Latin American Literary Review Press, 1999.

Clara: Thirteen Short Stories and a Novel. Trans. Hortense Carpentier and J. Jorge Castello. New York: Harcourt, 1976.

Cola de lagartija. Buenos Aires: Brugera, 1983.

Como en la guerra. Buenos Aires: Sudamericana, 1977.

Donde viven las águilas. Buenos Aires: Celtia, 1983.

"The Door." Trans. N. T. Di Giovanni. *Mundus Artium* 7.2 (1974): 120–23.

"The Efficient Cat." Trans. Evelyn Picón Garfield. *River Styx* January 14, 1984: 87–89.

"Excerpts from *Strange Things Happen Here: Twenty-six Short Stories and a Novel.*" Trans. Helen Lane. *American Poetry Review* 8.2 (1978): 8–10.

"The First Feline Vision." Trans. Evelyn Picón Garfield. *Anatena* 48 (1983): 75–78.

"From *The Motive: A Novel in Progress.*" Trans. Cynthia Ventura. *Review of Contemporary Fiction* 6.3 (1986): 22–24.

El gato eficaz. Mexico City: Joaquín Mortiz, 1972.

"Generous Impediments Float down the River." Trans. Clementine Rabassa. *Contemporary Women Authors of Latin America: New Translations.* Eds. Doris Meyer and Margarite Fernández Olmos. New York: Brooklyn College Press, 1983. 245–49.

Hay que sonreir. Buenos Aires: Americana, 1966.

He Who Searches. Trans. Helen Lane. Elmwood Park, Ill.: Dalkey Archive Press, 1987.

Los heréticos. Buenos Aires: Paidós, 1967.

"'I'm Your Horse in the Night.'" *Women's Fiction from Latin America: Selections from Twelve Contemporary Authors.* Ed. Trans. Evelyn Picón Garfield. Detroit: Wayne State University Press, 1988. 311–14.

Libro que no muerde. Mexico City: Universidad Nacional Autónoma de México, 1980.

The Lizard's Tail. Trans. Gregory Rabassa. New York: Farrar, 1983.

"The Mask and the Word." Trans. Djelal Kadir. *World Literature Today* 69.4 (1995): 671.

"My Extraordinary Ph.D." *Review of Contemporary Fiction* 6.3 (1986): 7–8.

Novela negra con argentinos. Hanover, N.H.: Ediciones del Norte, 1990.

"On the Way to the Ministry." *You Can't Drown the Fire.* Ed. Alicia Partnoy. Pittsburgh: Cleis Press, 1988. 86–90.

Open Door. Trans. Hortense Carpentier et al. San Francisco: North Point Press, 1988.

Other Weapons. Trans. Deborah Bonner. Hanover, N.H.: Ediciones del Norte, 1985.

"Other Weapons." Trans. Deborah Bonner. *Women's Fiction from Latin America: Selections from Twelve Contemporary Authors.* Ed. Evelyn Picón Garfield. Detroit: Wayne State University Press, 1988. 288–310.

"Pantera Ocular." *El muro y la intemperie: El nuevo cuento latinoamericano.* Ed. Julio Ortega. Hanover, N.H.: Ediciones del Norte, 1989. 433–38.

"Papito's Story." Trans. David Unger. *City* 8 1.8 (1980) 66–68.

Realidad nacional desde la cama. Buenos Aires: Grupo Editor Argentino, 1990.

Simetrías. Buenos Aires: Sudamericana, 1993.

"Springtime." Trans. Evelyn Picón Garfield. *Formations* 3.1 (Spring 1986): 1–3.

"Strange Things Happen Here." Trans. Helen R. Lane. *Longman Anthology of World Literature by Women, 1875–1975.* Eds. Marian Arkin and Barbara Shollar. New York: Longman, 1989. 939–44.

Strange Things Happen Here: Twenty-Six Short Stories and a Novel. Trans. Helen Lane. New York: Harcourt, 1979.

Symmetries. Trans. Margaret Jull Costa. London: Serpent's Tail, 1998.

"Three Stories from *Strange Things Happen Here.*" Trans. Helen Lane. *Review, Center for Inter-American Relations* 24 (1979): 44–53.

Essays by Luisa Valenzuela

"April in Buenos Aires: Letter Without a Heading to Julio Cortázar." Trans. Edith Grossman. *Review of Contemporary Fiction* 3.3 (1983): 83–86

"Dangerous Words," "Dirty Words," "In Search of My Own Back Yard," and "Little Manifiesto." *Review of Contemporary Fiction* 6.3 (1986): 9–21.

"De la Manuela a la Marquesita avanza el escritor custodiado (o no) por los perros del deseo." *Revista Iberoamericana* 60.168–69 (1994): 1005–8.

"Escribir con el cuerpo." *Alba de América* 11.20–1 (1993): 35 40.

"The First Word." *Américas* 38.6 (1986): 3–4.

"Five Days That Changed My Paper." *Profession* (1991): 6–9.

"Los frutos del verano." *Hispamérica* 15 45 (1986): 83–85.

"I Was Always a Bit of a Rebel." *Artists in Exile.* Ed. Jane Katz. New York: n.p. 1982. 59–70.

"La geometría del sueño." *Los ochenta mundos de Cortázar.* Ed. Fernando Burgos. Madrid: EDI, 1987. 21–26.

"A Legacy of Poets and Cannibals: Literature Revives in Argentina." *Lives on The Line: The Testimony of Contemporary Latin American Authors.* Ed. Doris Meyer. Berkeley: University of California Press, 1988. 290–97.

"La mala palabra." *Revista Iberoamericana* 51.132–33 (1985): 489–91. Rpt. in *Repertorio Latinoamericano* 12.67 (1986): 8–9.

"Memories of the Past." *Dispatch* (New York) 6.2 (1988) 19–20.

"Mis brujas favoritas." *Theory and Practice of Feminist Literary Criticism.* Eds. Gabriela Mora and Karen S. Van Hooft. Ypsilanti, Mich.: Bilingual Press, 1982. 88–95.

"My Deadly Doctorate." Trans. Evelyn Picón Garfield. *Review of Contemporary Fiction* 6.2 (1986): 7–8.

"The Other Face of the Phallus." *Reinventing the Americas: Comparative Studies of the Literature of the United States and Spanish America.* Eds. Bell Gale Chevigny and Gari Laguardia. New York: Cambridge University Press, 1986. 242–48.

"Pandora ama el caos y la belleza." Ed. Nélida Piñón. *La Nación* [literary supplement] November 4, 1997: 3

"Peligrosas palabras." *Hispamérica* 15.45 (1986): 81–82.

"Pequeño manifiesto." *Hispamérica* 15.45 (1986): 82–83.

"Los porteños y sus literaturas." *Literature and Popular Culture in the Hispanic World: A Symposium.* Ed. Rose S. Minc. Upper Montclair, N.J.: Montclair State College, 1981.

"The Search, the Writer and the Land of No Evil." *Travellers' Tales, Real and Imaginary, in the Hispanic World and Its Literature.* Ed. Alun Kenwood. Melbourne: Voz Hispánica, 1993. 3–6.

"So Called Latin American Writing." Trans. Cynthia Ventura. *Critical Theory, Cultural Politics, and Latin American Narrative.* Eds. Steven M. Bell, Albert Le May, and Leonard Orr. Notre Dame, Ind.: University of Notre Dame Press, 1993. 209–11.

"Trying to Breathe." *The Writer in Politics.* Eds. William H. Gass and Lorin Cuoco. Carbondale: Southern Illinois University Press, 1996. 85–109.

"The Word, That Milk Cow." *Contemporary Women Authors of Latin America: Introductory Essays.* Eds. Doris Meyer and Margarite Fernández Olmos. New York: Brooklyn College, 1983. 96–97.

"Writing with the Body." *The Writer on Her Work: New Essays in New Territory.* Vol 2. Ed. Janet Sternburg. New York: Norton, 1991. 192–99.

Criticism on the Works of Luisa Valenzuela

Addis, Mary K. "Fictions of Motherhood: Three Short Stories of Luisa Valenzuela." *Romance Languages Annual* 1 (1989): 353–60.

Aínsa, Fernando. "Journey to Luisa Valenzuela's Land of Fear." Trans. David Draper Clark and Djelal Kadir. *World Literature Today* 69. 4 (1995): 683–90.

Alegría, Fernando. *Nueva historia de la novela hispanoamericana.* Hanover, N.H.: Ediciones del Norte, 1986. 342–45.

Angulo, Elsa B. de, and Dorothy S. Mull. "An Afternoon with Luisa Valenzuela." *Hispania* 69.2 (1986): 350–52.

Araujo, Helen. "Valenzuela's *Other Weapons.*" Trans. Rick McCallister. *Review of Contemporary Fiction* 6.3 (1986): 78–81.

Bach, Caleb. "Metaphors and Magic Unmask the Soul." *Américas* 47. 1 (1995): 23–27.

Bergero, Adriana J., et al. "Memoria y escritura, 'armas contra el olvido': Una entrevista con Luisa Valenzuela." *Mester* 22. 1 (1993): 89–102.

Bertelloni, María Teresa. "Eros como *iter* cognoscitivo: *Cambio de armas* de Luisa

Valenzuela." *Love, Sex, and Eroticism in Contemporary Latin American Literature*. Ed. Alum Kenwood. Melbourne and Madrid: Voz Hispánica, 1992. 13–21.

Bilbija, Ksenija. "El gran teatro del mundo (argentino): *Realidad nacional desde la cama* de Luisa Valenzuela." *La palabra en vilo: Narrativa de Luisa Valenzuela*. Eds. Gwendolyn Díaz and María Inés Lagos. Santiago: Cuarto Propio, 1996. 191–208.

———. "Maquillaje y escritura en 'Ceremonias de rechazo' de Luisa Valenzuela: Hacia un cuarto propio." *Inti* 43–44 (1996): 95–108.

———. "'La palabra asesino' de Luisa Valenzuela: La entrada en la lengua." *Confluencia* 8.1 (1992): 159–64.

Block de Behar, Lisa. "'Escribir sobre lo muy cercano (con perdón de toda analogía)'" *World Literature Today* 69.4 (1995): 740–44.

Boland, Roy C. "Luisa Valenzuela and *Simetrías*: Tales of a Subversive Mother Goose." *Antípodas* (Auckland) 6–7 (1994–95): 229–37.

———. *A Special Number in Honour of Sally Harvey: Rebelling in the Garden: Critical Perspectives on Isabel Allende, Cristina Peri Rossi, and Luisa Valenzuela*. *Antipodas* (Auckland) 6–7 (1994–95).

Boling, Becky. "'Cuarta versión': Implicit Subjects/Complicit Readings." *Hispanic Journal* 14.2 (1993): 105–15.

Burgos, Fernando. "Literatura a orillas del Mississippi: Diálogo con Luisa Valenzuela." *Confluencia* 8–9. 2–3 (1993): 157–78.

Burgos, Fernando, and M. J. Fenwick. "En Memphis con Luisa Valenzuela: Voces y viajes: Entrevista." *Inti* 28 (1988): 107–26.

———. "In and Around Memphis with Luisa Valenzuela: A Conversation." *River City* 9.1 (1989): 60–70.

Callejo, Alfonso. "Literatura e irregularidad en *Cambio de armas*, de Luisa Valenzuela." *Revista Iberoamericana* 51.132–33 (1985): 575–80.

Campello, Eliane T. A. "Romance and/or Arte de Narrar Femenino: *Novela negra con argentinos* de Luisa Valenzuela." The Sixteenth Louisiana Conference on Hispanic Language and Literature. *La Chispa '95: Selected Proceedings*. Ed. Claire Paolini. New Orleans: Tulane University, 1995. 59–70.

Case, Barbara. "On Writing, Magic, and Eva Perón: An Interview with Argentina's Luisa Valenzuela." *Ms* 12.4 (1983): 12–20.

Castillo, Debra A. "Appropriating the Master's Weapons: Luisa Valenzuela." *Talking Back: Toward a Latin American Feminist Literary Criticism*. Ithaca, N.Y.: Cornell University Press, 1992. 96–136.

Chaves Abad, María José. "Ahora me narro sola: Luisa Valenzuela." *Quimera* (Barcelona) 123 (1994): 60–61.

Christoph, Nancy. "Bodily Matters: The Female Grotesque in Luisa Valenzuela's *Cola de lagartija*." *Revista Hispánica Moderna* 48. 2 (1995): 365–80.

"*Cola de lagartija*." *Chasqui* 14. 2. 3 (1985): 77–79.

Cook, Alyce. "*Novela negra con argentinos* and the Move Toward Reconciliation." The Eighteenth Louisiana Conference on Hispanic Languages and Literature. Selected Proceedings. Ed. Claire Paolini. New Orleans: Tulane University, 1997.

Cook, Carole. "*Strange Things Happen Here: Twenty-six Short Stories and a Novel*." *Saturday Review* June 23, 1979: 80.

Corbatta, Jorgelina. "Metáforas del exilio e intertextualidad en *La nave de los locos* de Cristina Peri Rossi y *Novela negra con argentinos* de Luisa Valenzuela." *Revista Hispánica Moderna* 67.1 (1994): 167–83.

Cordones-Cook, Juanamaría. "*Como en la guerra*, en busca del otro." *Revista Canadiense de Estudios Hispánicos* (Ottawa) 16.2 (1992): 171–85.

———. "Humor negro y grotesco en *Cola de lagartija*." *Hispanófila* 110 (1994): 71–78.

———. "Luisa Valenzuela habla sobre *Novela negra con argentinos* y *Realidad nacional desde la cama*." *Letras Femeninas* 18.1–2 (1992): 119–26.

———. "*Novela negra con argentinos*, imagos de la guerra sucia." *La palabra en vilo: Narrative de LuisaValenzuela*. Eds. Gwendolyn Díaz and María Inés Lagos. Santiago: Cuarto Propio, 1996, 163–76.

———. "*Novela negra con argentinos*: The Desire to Know." *World Literature Today* 69.4 (1995): 745–50.

———. *Poética de transgresión en la novelística de Luisa Valenzuela*. New York: Peter Lang, 1991.

Cortázar, Julio. "Luisa Valenzuela." *Review: Latin American Literature and Arts* 24 (1979): 44.

Cox, Victoria. "Julio Cortázar y Luisa Valenzuela: Reflexiones en torno a la relación entre la escritura y el exilio." *Alba de América* 15. 28–29 (1997): 298–306.

———. "Political and Social Alienation in Valenzuela's *Novela negra con argentinos*." *Letras Femeninas* 23.1–2 (1997): 71–77.

Craig, Linda. "Women and Language: Luisa Valenzuela's *El gato eficaz*." *Feminist Readings on Spanish and Latin American Literature*. Eds. Lisa P. Conde and Stephen M. Hart. Lewiston, N.Y.: Mellen, 1991.

Dash, Robert C. "An Interview with Luisa Valenzuela." *Chasqui* 21.1 (1992): 101–5.

Davies, Catherine. "The Sexual Representation of Politics in Contemporary Hispanic Feminist Narrative." *Feminist Readings on Spanish and Latin American Literature*. Eds. Lisa P. Conde and Stephen M. Hart. Lewiston, N.Y.: Mellen, 1991.

De Feo, Ronald. "Two from Argentina." *Nation* 237.16 (1983): 239–42.

Díaz, Gwendolyn. "De Hegel a Lacan: El discurso del deseo en *Cambio de armas* de Luisa Valenzuela." *Revista Iberoamericana* 164–65 (1993): 729–37.

———. "Entrevista con Luisa Valenzuela." *La palabra en vilo: Narrativa de Luisa Valenzuela*. Eds. Gwendolyn Díaz and María Inés Lagos. Santiago: Cuarto Propio, 1996. 27–52.

———. "Estructuras caóticas en *Novela negra con argentinos* de Luisa Valenzuela." *La palabra en vilo: Narrativa de Luisa Valenzuela*. Eds. Gwendolyn Díaz and María Inés Lagos. Santiago: Cuarto Propio, 1996. 177–90.

———. "Politics of the Body in Luisa Valenzuela's 'Cambio de armas' and 'Simetrías.'" *World Literature Today* 69.4 (1995): 751–56.

———. "Postmodernismo y teoría del caos en *Cola de lagartija* de Luisa Valenzuela." *Letras Femeninas* [special commemorative issue, 1974–94] (1994): 97–105.

———. "El tango y otros simulacros: *Simetrías* y el postmodernismo." *Alba de América* 16. 3–31 (1998): 223–41.

Díaz, Gwendolyn, and María Inés Lagos. *La palabra en vilo: Narrativa de Luisa Valenzuela*. Santiago: Cuarto Propio, 1996.

Dolz-Blackburn, Inés. "El tratamiento del temor en *Cambio de armas* de Luisa Valenzuela." *Letras Femeninas* 18.1–2 (1992): 24–30.

Figueroa, Alvin Joaquín. "Feminismo y homosexualidad: Las voces de Luisa Valen-
zuela, Manuel Ramos Otero y Carmen Valle." *New Voices in Latin American Literature/
Nuevas voces en la literatura latinoamericana.* Eds. Miguel Falquez Certain, Pedro Monge
Rafuls, and Silvio Torres Saillant. New York: Ollantay, 1993. 175–85.

Forché, Carolyn. "Grasping the Gruesome." *Esquire* 100.3 (1983): 505–8.

Fores, Ana M. "Valenzuela's *Cat-O-Nine-Deaths.*" *Review of Contemporary Fiction* 6.3 (1986):
39–47.

Fulks, Barbara Pauler. "A Reading of Luisa Valenzuela's Short Story, 'La palabra
asesino.'" *Monographic Review/Revista Monográfica* 4 (1988): 179–88.

García-Moreno, Laura. "Other Weapons, Other Words: Literary and Political Recon-
siderations in Luisa Valenzuela's *Other Weapons.*" *Latin American Literary Review* 19.38
(1991): 7–22.

García Pinto, Magdalena. "Entrevista a Luisa Valenzuela." *Historias íntimas: Conversaciones
con diez escritoras latinoamericanas.* Hanover, N.H.: Ediciones del Norte, 1988. 215–49.

Garfield, Evelyn Picón. "Interview with Luisa Valenzuela." *Review of Contemporary Fiction*
6.3 (1986): 25–30.

———. "Luisa Valenzuela." *Women's Voices in Latin America: Interviews with Six Contemporary
Authors.* Ed. Evelyn Picón Garfield. Detroit: Wayne State University Press, 1985.
141–65.

———. "Muerte-Metamorfosis-Modernidad: *El gato eficaz* de Luisa Valenzuela." *Insula*
(Madrid) 35.400–401 March–April 1980: 17+. 23.

Gartner, Bruce S. "'Un regodeo en el asco': Cuerpos despedazados en *Cola de lagartija*
de Luisa Valenzuela." *La palabra en vilo: Narrativa de Luisa Valenzuela.* Eds. Gwendolyn Díaz
and María Inés Lagos. Santiago: Cuarto Propio, 1996. 79–111.

———. "'Un regodeo en el asco': Dismembered Bodies in Luisa Valenzuela's *The
Lizard's Tail.*" *Indiana Journal of Hispanic Literatures* 2, 2 (1994): 203–24.

Gazarian Gautier, Marie-Lise. "Luisa Valenzuela." *Interviews with Latin American Writers.*
Elmwood Park, Ill.: Dalkey Archive Press, 1989. 293–322.

———. "The Sorcerer and Luisa Valenzuela: Double Narrators of the Novel/Biogra-
phy, Myth/History." *Review of Contemporary Fiction* 6.3 (1986): 105–8.

Geisdorfer-Feal, Rosemary. "The Politics of 'Wargasm': Sexuality, Domination and
Female Subversion in Luisa Valenzuela's *Cambio de armas; Essays on Twentieth Cen-
tury Spanish American Fiction.* *Structures of Power.* Eds. Terry J. Peavler and Peter
Standish. New York: State University of New York Press, 1996. 159–88.

Geloven, Ineke van. "Entre modernismo y postmodernismo: *El gato eficaz* de Luisa
Valenzuela." *Alba de América* 12. 22–23 (1994): 271–78.

Gimbernat de González, Ester. "De cómo ejercitar la libertad: Dos obras de Luisa
Valenzuela." *Discurso Literario* (Asunción) 6.2 (1989): 405–21.

Glantz, Margo. "Luisa Valenzuela's *He Who Searches.*" Trans. Janet Perez. *Review of Contemporary Fiction* 6.3 (1986): 62–66.

Gold, Janet. "Feminine Space and the Discourse of Silence: Yolanda Oreamuno, Elena
Poniatowska and Luisa Valenzuela." *In the Feminine Mode: Essays on Hispanic Women
Writers.* Eds. Noel Valis and Carol Maier. Lewisburg, Pa.: Bucknell University Press,
1990.

Gómez, Jaime. "La representación de la dictadura en la narrativa de Marta Traba, Isabel Allende, Diamela Eltit y Luisa Valenzuela." *Confluencia* 12. 2 (1997): 89–99.

Gómez Engler, Raquel. "Borrón y cuenta nueva: Reflexión sobre el uso de las máscaras de belleza en un cuento de Luisa Valenzuela." *Alba de América* 3, 4–5 (1985): 123–28.

Grossman, Edith. "To Speak the Unspeakable." *Latin American Literature and Arts Review* 32 (1984): 33–34.

Guest, Victoria. *Reweaving the Violated Narrative: Strategies for Confronting the Discourse of Political Terror in Luisa Valenzuela's* The Lizard's Tail. Stanford, Calif.: Stanford University Press, 1990.

Gutiérrez-Mouat, Ricardo. "La alegoría nacional y Luisa Valenzuela." *La palabra en vilo: Narrativa de Luisa Valenzuela.* Eds. Gwendolyn Díaz and María Inés Lagos. Santiago: Cuarto Propio, 1996. 209–20.

———. "Luisa Valenzuela's Literal Writing." *World Literature Today* 69.4 (1995): 709–16.

Hart, Stephen M. "Is Women's Writing Spanish American Gender-Specific?" *Modern Language Notes* 110.2 (1995): 335–52.

Hernández, Ana María. "Luisa Valenzuela's *The Lizard's Tail.*" *World Literature Today* 58.2 (1984): 247.

Herron, Carol Olivia. "*The Lizard's Tail.*" *Womanews* 8.1–2: 239–40.

Hicks, Emily. "That Which Resists: The Code of the Real in Luisa Valenzuela's *He Who Searches.*" *Review of Contemporary Fiction* 6.3 (1986): 55–61.

———. "That Who Resists: The Code of Real in Luisa Valenzuela's *Como en la guerra* y Valenzuela: The Imaginary Body." *Border Writing: The Multidimensional Text.* Theory and History of Literature. Vol. 80. Minneapolis: University of Minnesota Press, 1991.

Hoeppner, Edward Haworth. "The Hand That Mirrors Us: Luisa Valenzuela's Re-Writing of Lacan's Theory of Identity." *Latin American Literary Review* 20.39 (1992): 9–17.

Josephs, Allen. "Sorcerers and Despots." *New York Times Book Review* October 2, 1983: 15+.

Kadir, Djelal. Ed. *Focus on Luisa Valenzuela. World Literature Today* [special issue] 69.4 (1995).

Kaminsky, Amy Katz. "Residual Authority and Gendered Resistance." *Critical Theory, Cultural Politics, and Latin American Narrative.* Eds. Steven M. Bell, Albert H. Le May, and Leonard Orr. Notre Dame, Ind.: University of Notre Dame Press, 1993. 103–21.

———. "Women Writing About Prostitutes: Amalia Jamilis and Luisa Valenzuela." *The Image of the Prostitute in Modern Literature.* Eds. Pierre L. Horn and Mary Beth Pringle. New York: Ungar, 1984. 119–31.

Katz, Jane. "I Was Always a Bit of a Rebel." *Artists in Exile.* New York: n.p., 1983. 59–70.

Kerr, Lucille. "Novels and 'Noir' in New York." *World Literature Today* 69.4 (1995): 733–39.

Lagos-Pope, María Inés. "Displaced Subjects: Valenzuela and the Metropolis." *World Literature Today* 69.4 (1995): 726–32.

———. "Mujer y politica en *Cambio de armas* de Luisa Valenzuela." *Hispamérica* 16.46–47 (1987): 71–83.

———. "Sujeto, sexualidad y literatura en 'Cambio de armas' y *Novela negra con argentinos* de Luisa Valenzuela." *La palabra en vilo: Narrativa de Luisa Valenzuela.* Eds. Gwendolyn Díaz and María Inés Lagos. Santiago: Cuarto Propio, 1996. 131–61.

Lauzen, Sarah E. "Strange Things Happen Here." Review 28. Latin American Literature and Arts. 28 (1981): 81–2.

Lertora, Juan Carlos. "El estatuto de la ficción en Cola de lagartija." Literatura Chilena: Creación y Crítica 11.3–4. 41–42 (1987): 12–13.

Logan, Joy. "Luisa Valenzuela and the Body Politic: Desire, Sexuality, and Political Transgression in Novela negra con argentinos and Realidad nacional desde la cama. Antípodas (Auckland) 6–7 (1994–95): 219–28.

———. "Southern Discomfort in Argentina: Postmodernism, Feminism, and Luisa Valenzuela's Simetrías." Latin American Literary Review 24.48 (1996): 5–18.

Lorente-Murphy, Silvia. "Aproximación a una definición del proceso militar en Argentina: Soriano, Viñas y Valenzuela." Confluencia 10.2 (1995): 94–103.

———. "Cambio de armas de Luisa Valenzuela: Una recuperación semántica." Alba de América 6.10–11 (1988): 117–28.

Maci, Guillermo. "The Symbolic, the Imagery and the Real in Luisa Valenzuela's He Who Searches." Trans. Janet Perez. Review of Contemporary Fiction 6.3 (1986): 67–77.

Magnarelli, Sharon. "Censorship and the Female Writer—An Interview-Dialogue with Luisa Valenzuela." Letras Femeninas 10.1 (1984): 55–64.

———. El discurso del cuerpo en el cuerpo del discurso: Hay que sonreir de Luisa Valenzuela." Mujer y sociedad en América. Ed. Juana Alcira Arancibia. Westminster, Calif.: Instituto Literario y Cultural Hispánico, 1988. 223–32.

———. "Framing Power in Luisa Valenzuela's Cola de lagartija (The Lizard's Tail) and Isabel Allende's La casa de los espíritus (The House of the Spirits)." Latin American Women Writers in Search of Themselves. Ed. Lucía Guerra Cunningham. Pittsburgh: Latin American Literary Review Press, 1990. 43–62.

———. "Gatos, lenguaje, y mujeres en El gato eficaz de Luisa Valenzuela." Revista Iberoamericana 45.108–9 (1979). 603–11.

———. "Humor and Games in El gato eficaz by Luisa Valenzuela: The Looking-Glass World Revisited." Modern Language Studies 13.3 (1983): 81–89.

———. "Juego/fuego de la esperanza: En torno a El gato eficaz de Luisa Valenzuela." Cuadernos Americanos (Mexico City) 247.2 (1983): 199–208.

———. "The Lizard's Tail: Discourse Denatured." Review of Contemporary Fiction 6.3 (1986): 97–104.

———. "Luisa Valenzuela." Spanish American Women Writers: A Bio-Bibliographical Source Book. Ed. Diane Marting. Westport, Conn.: Greenwood Press, 1990. 532–45.

———. "Luisa Valenzuela: Cuerpos que escriben (metonimicamente hablando) y la metáfora peligrosa." La palabra en vilo: Narrativa de Luisa Valenzuela. Eds. Gwendolyn Díaz and María Inés Lagos. Santiago: Cuarto Propio, 1996. 53–77.

———. "Luisa Valenzuela: From Hay que sonreir to Cambio de armas." World Literature Today: A Literary Quarterly of the University of Oklahoma 58.1 (1984): 9–13

———. "Luisa Valenzuela's Cambio de armas: Subversión and Narrative Weaponry." Romance Quarterly 34 (1987): 85–94.

———. "The New Novel/A New Novel: Spider's Webs and Detectives in Luisa Valenzuela's Black Novel (with Argentines)." Studies in Twentieth Century Literature 19.1 (1995): 43–60.

————. *Reflection-Refractions: Reading Luisa Valenzuela.* New York: Peter Lang, 1988.

————. "El significante deseo en *Cambio de armas* de Luiza Valenzuela." *Escritura: Revista de Teoría y Crítica Literarias* (Caracas) 16.31–32 (1991): 160–69.

————. "Simetrías: 'Mirror, Mirror on the Wall . . .'" *World Literature Today* 69.4 (1995): 717–25.

————. "The Spectacle of Reality in Luisa Valenzuela's *Realidad nacional (vista) desde la cama.*" *Letras Femeninas* 19.1–2 (1993): 65–73.

————. The Travelling Trope (The She Within): Metonymic Inversion in Luisa Valenzuela's *Como en la guerra. Travellers' Tales, Real and Imaginary, in the Hispanic World and Its Literature.* Ed. Alun Kenwood. Melbourne: Voz Hispánica, 1993. 181–87.

————. "Women, Discourse, and Politics in the Works of Luisa Valenzuela." *Antipodas* (Auckland) 6–7 (1994–95): 157–71.

————. "Women, Language, and Cats in Luisa Valenzuela's *El gato eficaz*: Looking-Glass Games of Fire." *The Lost Rib.* Lewisburg, Pa.: Bucknell University Press, 1985. 169–85.

Marcos, Juan Manuel. "Luisa Valenzuela: Más allá de la araña de la esquina rosada." *Prismal/Cabral* 11 (1983): 57–65. Rpt. in *De García Márquez al postboom.* Madrid: Orígenes, 1986. 83–90.

Martínez, Victoria. "In Search of the Word: Performance in Luisa Valenzuela's *Novela negra con argentinos.*" *Chasqui* 23.2 (1994): 54–65.

Martínez, Z. Nelly. "Dangerous Messianisms: The World According to Valenzuela." *World Literature Today* 69.4 (1995): 697–701.

————. "Entre el abismo y la Medusa: *Cola de lagartija* de Luisa Valenzuela." *La escritora hispánica.* Eds. Nora Erro-Orthmann and Juan Cruz Mendizábal. Miami: Universal, 1990. 101–7.

————. "*El gato eficaz* de Luisa Valenzuela: La productividad del texto." *Revista Canadiense de Estudios Hispánicos* (Ottawa) 4.1 (1979): 73–80.

————. "Luisa Valenzuela's *The Lizard's Tail* Deconstruction of the Peronist Mythology." *El Cono Sur: Dinámica y dimensiones de su literatura: A Symposium.* Ed. Rose S. Minc. Upper Montclair, N.J.: Montclair State College, 1985. 123–30.

————. "Luisa Valenzuela's 'Where the Eagles Dwell': From Fragmentation to Holism." *Review of Contemporary Fiction* 6.3 (1986): 109–15.

————. *El silencio que habla: Aproximación a la obra de Luisa Valenzuela.* Buenos Aires: Corregidor, 1994.

Marting, Diane. "Female Sexuality in Selected Short Stories by Luisa Valenzuela: Toward an Ontology of Her Work." *Review of Contemporary Fiction* 6.3 (1986): 48–54.

————. "Gender and Metaphoricity in Valenzuela's 'I'm Your Horse in the Night.'" *World Literature Today* 69.4 (1995): 702–8.

————. "Luisa Valenzuela." *Women Writers of Spanish America.* Westport, Conn.: Greenwood Press, 1987. 377–79.

————. "Sexuality in the Figural Mode: Luisa Valenzuela's *El gato eficaz.*" *El Cono Sur: Dinámica y dimensiones de su literatura.* Ed. Rose S. Minc. Upper Montclair, N.J.: Montclair State College, 1985.

Metzger, Mary Janell. "'Oedipal with a Vengeance': Narrative, Desire and Violence in

Luisa Valenzuela's 'Fourth Version.'" *Tulsa Studies in Women's Literature* 14.2 (1995): 295–307.

Morello-Frosch, Marta. "Discurso erótico y escritura femenina." *Coloquio internacional: Escritura y sexualidad en la literatura hispanoamericana.* Madrid: Centre de Recherches Latin America/Fundamentos, 1990.

———. "*Other Weapons*: When Metaphors Become Real." *Review of Contemporary Fiction* 6.3 (1986): 82–87.

———. "Relecturas del cuerpo en *Cambio de armas* de Luisa Valenzuela." *La palabra en vilo: Narrativa de Luisa Valenzuela.* Eds. Gwendolyn Díaz and María Inés Lagos. Santiago: Cuarto Propio, 1996. 113–30.

———. "The Subversion of the Ritual in *Other Weapons*." *World Literature Today* 69.4 (1995): 691–96.

Mull, Dorothy S. "Ritual Transformation in Luisa Valenzuela's 'Rituals of Rejection'." *Review of Contemporary Fiction* 6.3 (1986): 88–96.

Mull, Dorothy S., and Elsa B. de Angulo. "An Afternoon with Luisa Valenzuela." *Hispania* 69.2 (1986): 350–52.

Muñoz, Willy O. "'Cambio de armas' de Luisa Valenzuela: La aventura de la adquisición de la escritura ginocéntrica." *El personaje femenino en la narrativa de escritoras hispanoamericanas.* Madrid: Pliegos, 1992. 89–109.

———. "Del falogocentrismo a la escritura ginocéntrica: *Cambio de armas* de Luisa Valenzuela." *Antípodas* (Auckland) 3 (1991): 125–34.

———. "El lenguaje hembrico en 'Cambio de armas." *Antipodas* (Auckland) 6–7 (1994–95): 183–89.

———. "Luisa Valenzuela: Tautología lingüística y/o realidad nacional." *Revista Canadiense de Estudios Hispánicos* (Ottawa) 7.2 (1991): 333–42.

———. "Luisa Valenzuela y la subversión normativa en los cuentos de hadas: 'Si esto es la vida, yo soy Caperucita Roja.'" *La palabra en vilo: Narrativa de Luisa Valenzuela.* Eds. Gwendolyn Díaz and María Ines Lago. Santiago: Cuarto Propio, 1996. 221–16.

Niebylski, Diana C. "Humor, desamor y subversión en Luisa Valenzuela y Ana Lydia Vega." *Estudios Filológicos* (Valdivia, Chile) 30 (1995): 129–38.

———. "La palabra: Arma de doble filo en 'Cambio de armas.'" *Philologica* 68 (1994): 25–30.

———. "La que ríe último: Humor y subversión en Luisa Valenzuela y Ana Lydia Vega." *Estudios de literatura chilena e hispanoamericana contemporánea.* Ed. Eduardo Barraza. Osorno, Chile: Editorial Universidad de Los Lagos, 1996. 181–88.

———. "Rearmando a la mujer desarticulada: Estrategias de de(con)strucción y reconstrucción en *Cambio de armas*." *Mujeres: Escrituras y lenguajes (en la cultura latinoamericana y española).* Ed. Sonia Mattalia y Milagros Aleza. Valencia, Spain: Universidad de Valencia, 1995. 46–53.

Ordóñez, Montserrat. "Enigmas y variaciones: Luisa Valenzuela y Cristina Peri Rossi: En el límite de la crítica." Instituto Internacional de Literatura Iberoamericana XXIV Congreso. *La Crítica Literaria en Latinoamerica.* Stanford University, June 8–12, 1985. 97–106.

————. "Máscaras de espejos, un juego especular. Entrevista-asociaciones con la escritora argentina Luisa Valenzuela." *Revista Iberoamericana* 51.132–33 (1985): 511–19.

Paley Francescato, Martha. "*Cola de lagartija*: Látigo de la palabra y la triple P." *Revista Iberoamericana* 51.132–33 (1985): 875–82.

Panjabi, Kavita. "Physical Torture and Modes of Creative Expression: A Study of 'Cambio de armas' and 'Draupadi.'" *New Visions of Creation: Feminist Innovations in Literary Theory*. Eds. María Elena Valdés and Margaret R. Higonnet. Proceedings of the Thirteenth Congress of the International Comparative Literature Association, Tokyo, 1991. Tokyo: University of Tokyo, 1993. 85–94.

Parada, Andrea. "Metamorfosis del deseo femenino en 'Ceremonias de rechazo' de Luisa Valenzuela." The Sixteenth Lousiana Conference on Hispanic Language and Literature. *La Chispa '95: Selected Proceedings*. Ed. Claire Paolini. New Orleans: Tulane University, 1995. 281–90.

Perches, Ana. "El discurso hembrico de Luisa Valenzuela en *Cola de lagartija*." *Discurso femenino actual*. Ed. Adelaida López de Martínez. San Juan: Universidad de Puerto Rico, 1995. 111–20.

Perricone, Catherine R. "Valenzuela's *Novela negra con argentinos*: A Metafictional Game." *Romance Notes* 36.3 (1996): 237–42.

Potvin, Claudine. "Escribir con el cuerpo: *Novela negra con argentinos* de Luisa Valenzuela." *Antipodas* (Auckland) 6–7 (1994–95): 205–17.

Pye, Geralyn. "Political Football: Sports, Power and Machismo in Luisa Valenzuela's *The Lizard's Tail*." *Studies in Latin American Popular Culture* 13 (1994): 115–27.

Resnick, Margery. "*Other Weapons*." *New York Times Book Review* October 6, 1985: 38.

Reyes-Tatinclaux, Leticia. "Luisa Valenzuela." *Dictionary of Literary Biography: Modern Latin American Fiction Writers*. Vol 13. Ed. William Luis. Detroit: Gale Research, 1992. 303–12.

Rojas Trempe, Lady. "Apuntes sobre *Cambio de armas* de Luisa Valenzuela." *Letras Femeninas* 19.1–2 (1993): 74–83.

Rotella, Pilar V. "Similia Similibus Curantur: *The Lizard's Tail and the Writer's Tail*." *Narrativa hispanoamericana contemporánea: Entre la vanguardia y el posboom*. Ed. Ana María Hernández de López. Madrid: Pliegos, 1996. 127–39.

Rubio, Patricia. "La fragmentación: Principio ordenador en la ficción de Luisa Valenzuela." *Literatura Chilena: Creación y crítica* 13–14 (1989): 63–71.

————. "Fragmentation in Luisa Valenzuela's Narrative." *Salmagundi* 82–83 (1989): 287–96.

Sabino, Osvaldo R. "Los nombres y los gatos: Luisa Valenzuela y sus siete libros." *Alba de América* 1.1 (1983): 155–66.

Saltz, Joanne Carol. "Luisa Valenzuela's *Cambio de Armas*: Rhetoric of Politics." *Confluencia* 3.1 (1987): 61–66.

Santos Febres, Mayra. "Los juegos del yo: Antidotos contra la censura en 'Cuarta versión' de Luisa Valenzuela." *Revista de Estudios Hispánicos* (Río Piedras, Puerto Rico) 20 (1993): 311–22.

Sauter, Silvia. "Liberación de y reencuentro con 'lo otro' en *Cambio de armas*." *Chasqui* 27.2 (1998): 89–105.

Shaw, D. L. "The Narrative Strategy of 'La palabra asesino.'" *Antipodas* (Auckland) 6–7 (1994–95): 173–81.

Sheppard, R. Z. "Where the Fiction Is 'Fantástica.'" *Time* March 7, 1983: 78–82.

Stavans, Ilán. "Autumn of the Matriarch?" *Nation* March 6, 1995: 316–19.

Tanner, Stephen L. "Reality by the Tail." *Chronicles of Culture* 8.12 (1984): 10–13.

Tobin, Patricia. "Voices in the Silence." *Review* 76 18 (1976): 78–80.

Tompkins, Cynthia. "Aporias resultantes de la deconstrucción del sujeto en: *Como en la guerra* de Luisa Valenzuela, *Son vacas, somos puercos* de Carmen Boullosa y *Las andariegas* de Albalucía Angel." *Torre de Papel* 7.3 (1997): 148–65.

———. "La construcción del subalterno en *Homerica latina*, de Marta Traba y *Libro que no muerde* y *Donde viven las águilas*, de Luisa Valenzuela." *Confluencia* 8.1 (1992): 31–37.

———. "La posmodernidad de *Como en la guerra* de Luisa Valenzuela and Cortázar." *Nuevo Texto Crítico* 4.7 (1991): 169–96.

Trevizan, Liliana. "Luisa Valenzuela: Los riesgos de una versión plural y democrática." *Confluencia* 12.1 (1996): 93–105.

Tyler, Joseph. "Tales of Repression and 'desaparecidos' in Valenzuela and Cortázar." *Romance Languages Annual* 3 (1991): 602–6.

Umpierre, Luz María. "Luisa Valenzuela: *Cola de lagartija*." *Revista Iberoamericana* 51.130–31 (1985): 430–32.

Vázquez, María Esther. "De Nueva Delhi a Oklahoma." *La Nación* (literary supplement; Buenos Aires) March 5, 1995: 2.

———. "La realidad nacional desde la sátira." *La Nación* (literary supplement; Buenos Aires) December 23, 1990: 2.

Wilson, S. R. Rev. of *Aquí pasan cosas raras*. *Latin American Literary Review* 9.18 (1981): 67–69.

———. Rev. of *Cambio de armas*. *Latin American Literary Review* 12.24 (1984): 82–84.

Young, Richard A. "Detective Novels and Argentinians in Luisa Valenzuela's *Novela negra con argentinos*." *Antipodas* (Auckland) 6–7 (1994–95): 191–203.

Rima Vallbona

COSTA RICA

Rima Vallbona was born in San José, Costa Rica, in 1931. She attended the university in her native country and later in France, Spain, and the United States, where she completed her doctorate degree at Middlebury College. She has resided in Houston, Texas, for many years with her family, where she established the Spanish department of St. Thomas University, serving as its first chair. Since 1964 Vallbona has been a professor of Spanish literature in the United States, at the Universities of St. Thomas, Houston, and Rice University.

Related to her academic interest, Vallbona has published two bodies of literary criticism: *Yolanda Oreamuno* (1971) and *La obra de Eunice Odio* (The works in prose of Eunice Odio, 1981). She has written three novels, as well as six collections of short stories and numerous children's stories. Her short-story volume titled *Mujeres y agonías* (Women and agonies, 1982) was awarded the SCOLAS Prize. She has also won such important prizes as the Jorge Luis Borges Short Story Award (Argentina, 1977).

Rima Vallbona's novels and short stories reflect a deep feminist commitment and a continuous exploration into new levels of women's concerns. In her narrative she questions the established roles and norms, and women's demands for freedom in the modern world. Some of her characters break new ground as they replace traditional patriarchal myths with vibrant, joyful women's experiences and unique achievements in self-fulfiment.

The Secret World of Grandmamma Anacleta

Lying shipwrecked in the oceanic immensity of her baroque bed, framed by its twisted, leaf-covered columns, beneath the sheets and the fluffy feather comforter was the tiny, insignificant form to which nonagenarian Grandmamma Anacleta had shrunk. Seen from the vantage point of my ten years, and perhaps because of the lack of a better perspective, Grandmamma Anacleta was just a little heap of bones and corrugated skin. For many years she had spent her days lying still, moving her lips insistently, as if she were talking to herself. No matter how hard we tried, none of us could decipher the infinite mumbling that issued from her lips. At first, with the very patience of Job, we tried to communicate with her, straining to understand her incessant muttering. Little by little we began to give up until the day came when she mattered so little to us that we paid more attention to the TV, to the radio, or even to the putt-putt of the lawn-mower. To compensate for our indifference and to feel less guilty, we bought her a Walkman, a blessed modern apparatus that performed the amazing miracle of conclusively silencing Grandmamma Anacleta's jabbering and cleared away the lowering clouds of our guilt!

After that, we only reacted when she installed herself anew in our daily reality by filling the whole house with her booming rusty voice. Even today, in that distant memory, it seems incredible to me that that little heap of bones and skin was so powerful that it even caused the ever-present glass of water to vibrate on the bedside table. We all shook when that terrible rusted voice began to shout, "I want the bedpan right this minute! Water, a glass of ice water! Come straighten my sheets! Why doesn't anybody answer? Do you all think I'm just painted on the wall?" She spent her time making innumerable impertinent demands, like a captain at the head of his army, whenever she darned well felt like it, whenever it pleased her majesty to emerge from the silence of the sheets.

Her loud, rusty voice issued forth from the interminable baroque bed like a powerful projectile aimed unswervingly at each of us: it went straight through my body and was converted into remorse in the marrow of my conscience, asking if it were not my duty to ceaselessly weep over that tiny body lying like a useless rag on the bed, whose soul only joined it to become a great, despotic voice.

For Mamma, Grandmamma Anacleta's great, rusty voice was an indefinite sentence to remain by her side reading out loud to her: at first, only the Holy Scriptures, but to our surprise, she began to demand not only the usual classics, but also the more recent authors. However, they had better be substantial, because if they weren't, she would tear the books from Mamma's hands and furiously hurl them against the wall.

"Shitty writers who make fools of us by passing off a syrup of well-placed, dressed-up fancy words in order to cover up their emptiness! To hell with those imbeciles and their sleight-of-hand literature who fill our minds with nonsense! 'Straw, straw, straw,' as Unamuno said. They ought to learn from Goethe, Kafka, Hemingway, Borges, McCullers, Rulfo or Kundera . . . , now those are real writers! And what masterful writers!" Truly Grandmamma Anacleta gave us a hard time with the reading and my poor mother, although she enjoyed the books and the comments on them, stayed in a highly nervous state because when she least expected it the tyrannical voice would boom from the sheets, cursing the author, or some character, or Mamma, who from sheer fatigue would doze off as she read.

"I can't believe that at your age you're tired! Look at me, nearly a century old and I'm still alert! You people today are such delicate little touch-me-nots, with no spirit at all." It didn't even occur to Mamma to answer because Grandmamma Anacleta didn't listen to anyone and even less to her own daughter.

Grandmamma's big voice was a command that immediately made Norma, a good Samaritan-type grandchild, full of efficiency, race towards the heap of bones and corrugated skin and then the machine-gun orders burst from the bed: "Bring me the bedpan because I have to pee and take away the washbasin and towels because you've already bathed me enough, don't be messy, child, and fix this damned bed for me because it is my only refuge and my kingdom all day long, and today you're going to season the mashed potatoes the way I like them and add onions to the meat, oh, and I want caramel pudding for dessert, have Chela make it so I won't get diarrhea, and you fix me a watercress salad, yes, watercress and don't come to me saying it's not the season for watercress because that is what I want and that's that, but bring me the gown that I keep locked in the dressing table, here, unlock it and bring it on the double, because I'll catch cold lying here naked, hurry up, you little brat, just because I'm here shriveled up in this bed everybody thinks I'm a burden and no longer good for anything and they're wrong, remember that tomorrow is my ninetieth birthday and in this house I represent the voice of knowledge and experience."

We all believed that too, even Dad, because she always, before something happened, was psychic enough to foresee it and to forewarn us:

"Tell Anselma not to marry that fortune hunter because she'll have a hard time of it, very hard," she declared, but no one paid attention and Anselma, the eldest, married the fortune hunter, who in fact only wanted the shelter of the family to squander everything that fell into his hands and to spend his time doing absolutely nothing.

"Don't be a fool, don't buy that lot because the real estate agent is a con man and he'll cheat you."

And she was right; at the end of a year we'd lost lock, stock, and barrel since the lots that Dad bought were invented by the supersalesman in a part of the universe that never existed. That is what Grandmamma Anacleta was like, a little fistful of skin and bones, with a booming, rusty voice that shook the house and its inhabitants, and a clear and prescient mind when it suited her highness to take a hand in our affairs, because when it didn't suit her, even if we begged her, she stubbornly kept silent. Oh, I almost forgot that added to her foresight was her knowledge, up to the minute, of the news of the day. So well informed was she that when she deigned to speak, she referred to Gorbachev as if he were her neighbor, and even went so far as to affirm that she was becoming pro-Russian, if not downright Marxist, for she was always raving about the wastefulness of capitalism, while she rose up as the number one defender of the proletariat; she commented with exactness on the extermination of the rain forests of Brazil; on starvation in Africa; on the Panama Canal and its history. Moreover, she kept track of how many goals had been made by

Maradona, Pele, and who knows what other famous soccer players. It was from my grandmother that I learned Virginia Woolf had said that for a woman to write novels and short stories she should have two things: money and a room to herself.

"A vain hope, because men always take away both rights from us so they can continue being our lords and masters" was her repeated and disconsolate litany. "Have you noticed that there are hardly any women composers in the music world? You could count them on your fingers. Have you ever heard of Ida Doukosky? Of course not! There's a reason, there's a reason. . . . Music makes itself felt through its sound, while the pen glides silently across the paper when women secretly, as if they were committing a mortal sin, defy men with their books."

We knew the Walkman transistor, whose earphones were always plugged into her ears like a pair of leeches, was the source of her abundant knowledge, because she never wanted a newspaper nor condescended to look at television: "Save me, Lord, from those two nuisances; they are the enemies of progress, truth, and human aspirations." As she spoke, she crossed herself as if she were frightening away the devil.

Marcos was the one who had the idea of giving her two bowling balls for her birthday. They were jet black, as shiny as the entrance hall that Chela polished every day with the very persistence of Sisyphus. Dying laughing at our joke and imagining Grandmamma Anacleta's amazement when she saw them, we put them in a box which we wrapped with pretty baby pink paper and tied with a ribbon of the same color.

"Be careful, Sonia, don't get too close to Grandmamma Anacleta, because in one of her fits, her hands may get as strong as her voice. Wham! She'll throw the balls at you and knock you out flat with one blow. Watch out, I'm warning you, Sonia, don't forget!" Marcos advised me with the protective air of a big brother. I was touched and thanked him, because I was always climbing up on the mattress or on the edge of the bedframe.

"Can you imagine, Marcos, as weak and skinny as I am, how the bowling balls would flatten me? A cockroach would look big by comparison!"

We were so overcome by our irrepressible laughter that we couldn't even tie the bow on the gift. The next day, the birthday, was one long party for us as we anticipated the effect of our joke.

However, much to our surprise—of course, we waited to give her the bowling balls until the end of the festivities since we didn't want to take any risks before eating our share of the enormous cake with ninety candles that sparkled like little stars, and the strawberry ice cream that made our mouths water—well, I said to our surprise, those bony little arms with their parchmentlike skin took the package as if it didn't weigh much. Marcos and I looked at each other in bewilderment, wondering if instead of the bowling balls, we had by mistake put some light object in the box; but there could be no doubt, we both knew perfectly well what was inside. We had an even greater surprise, for when we had moved well out of reach of any sudden destructive fit of fury, she opened the gift and her face lit up as if at that moment she were contemplating the Holy Grail and that present were the end of an interminable quest.

"Well! This is exactly what I wanted. How did you guess if I never told you?"

All of us who were present thought that her words were a pretense to hide her chagrin at our naughtiness. Nonetheless, it amazed us, because she *never, never*, as long as I could remember, had ever hidden anything. That's the way she was and we had suffered her and loved her just as she was up to then.

Following the bowling ball episode, my mother was freed from the enslavement of reading beside the big baroque bed. Foibles of the human race: Marcos as well as I joyfully believed we had done Mamma a favor, until we began to think that she missed the routine of reading, because so often she would come into Grandmamma Anacleta's room and would ask her if she didn't want her to read something.

"The devil and all the demons in hell! Didn't I tell you I'm not interested anymore in all those wordy, inept writers who were clogging my spirits? For me, the moment for action has arrived. <u>ACTION</u>, un-der-lined and in capital letters, I'm telling you."

We all looked at each other wondering what she meant about the "moment for action." To tell the truth we had utterly no idea, until one sunny morning when the scent of orange blossoms perfumed the air, and her voice, now clear, rang through the house like church bells on Easter: "Norma, bring me the black pants and jacket with the red blouse so I can dress to go out."

To go out? How, when for twenty years she had been confined to the big baroque bed and hadn't left it even for her most elemental needs? We all feared that this was an evident sign that she was about to die and wanted to go to the other world all dressed up in style.

"May I ask where you plan to go, Grandmamma Anacleta?" asked Norma hesitantly, afraid the answer would be that she was dying. But she just said "Stop asking questions, you silly child. Bathe me and be quick about it because I want to go out right away."

We couldn't believe it! She jumped out of the big baroque bed with agility and dressed herself with no help from anyone. Then we all thought with one mind that that tiny old lady who seemed so fragile had been torturing and enslaving us all that time for the purpose of keeping us under her thumb; to be that agile and to work out her long-term plan, she must have been exercising for years. At that instant we understood the sound of footsteps and movement we had heard in her bedroom late at night when the rest of the house was silent and sleeping. We had even thought that there was a ghost in that room and we called the priest to exorcize it. Now I understood why grandmother was breaking up with laughter under her sheets while the priest sprinkled the walls and furniture with holy water and Latin phrases.

"Where's the bowling alley? You, Marcos, drive me in your Volkswagen to the bowling alley."

"But Grandmamma Anacleta, what are you going to do at the bowling alley?"

"Are you batty or do you just act that way? What does anybody do at a bowling alley—why, bowl, of course, you impudent young pup! Didn't you and your sister give me a pair of bowling balls for my ninetieth birthday? Well, did you think that I, Anacleta Gutierrez del Castillo, was going to let them gather dust when they were the best present I've ever gotten in my life? That would be ridiculous! Come on, brat, let's hurry to the bowling alley. You'll see that your grandmother will set a world record and the news will be the sensation of the day. Don't you believe it's necessary to fill the world with marvels to rid it of all the brutality and porno that are everywhere? Besides, imagine the double triumph, since I'm a woman, and all woman, and old, old, old. Can't you see the huge headlines in the newspapers that would broadcast to the four corners of the earth: 'NINETY-YEAR-OLD GRANDMOTHER, WORLD BOWLING CHAMPION?'"

Translated by Bertie Acker
(From *Los infiernos de la mujer y algo más* . . . , 1992

Bibliography

Fiction by Rima Vallbona

"Ame en Peine." Trans. Juliette Decreus. *Fer de Lance* (France) 115–17 (1981): 33–37.

"El árbol de chumico." *Letras Femeninas* 1 (1975): 20–21. Rpt. in *Posdata* (San José) January 1976: 6.

El arcangel del perdón. Buenos Aires: Universitarias, 1990.

"Augusto discípulo de Pitágoras." *SUMMA-Revista de Cultura e Información* 3 December 1987: 93–100.

"Bajo pena de muerte." *Ancora* (San José) 220 August 15, 1976: 4–5.

Barajas de soledades. Barcelona: Rondas, 1983.

"Beto y Betina." *Zona Franca* 18 (1980): 44–47.

"Bien au-déla de la chair." Trans. Juliette Decreus. *Fer de Lance* (France) 103 (1979): 14–17.

"Los buenos." *Análisis* 84 (1983): 24–25.

"Cementerio de camiones." *La Nación* (San José) March 29, 1969: 31–32.

"The Chumico Tree: A Modern Tale." *Nimrod—Latin American Voices* 18.1 (1973): 62–63. Rpt. in *Five Women Writers of Costa Rica* with trans. by Nuri Vallbona. Ed. Victoria Urbano. Beaumont, Tex.: Lamar University Printing, 1978. 113–14.

"Con los muertos al cinto." *Letras Femeninas* 7.2 (1981): 29–35.

Cosecha de pecadores. San José: Editorial Costa Rica, 1988.

"Cosecha de pecadores." *Ancora* (San José) part 1, October 20, 1985: 1D–4D; part 2, October 27, 1985: 3D–4D.

"Desde aquí." *Garcín—Libro de Cultura* 3 (1981): 56–59.

"Día de tinieblas." *La República* (San José) January 1976: 6.

Flowering Inferno: Tales of Sinking Hearts. Trans. Lilian L. Tagle. Pittsburgh: Latin American Review Press, 1994.

"El hondón de las sorpresas." *Revista Chicano-Riqueña* 4 (1980): 35–37. Rpt. in *Ancora* (San José) June 7, 1987. 3D.

"L'Imposteur." Trans. Juliette Decreus. *Fer de Lance* (France) 99 (1977): 27–30.

"El impostor." *El Urogallo* (Madrid) 34–35 (1975): 54–58.

"Infame retorno." *Cultura* 73 (1984–85): 49–57.

Los infiernos de la mujer y algo más . . . Madrid: Torremozas, 1992.

"Iniciación." *Cuaderno Literario Azor* 37 (1983): 49–50. Rpt. in *Puro Cuento* 7 November–December 1987: 46.

"El juego de los grandes." *Letras femeninas en América*. Montevideo: Asociación de Literatura Femenina Hispánica, 1981. 163–69.

"Libelo de repudio." *El Gato Tuerto* (Miami) (Summer 1987): 8.

"Los males venideros." *Alba de América* 2–3 (1984): 221–27.

"Más allá de la carne." *Foro Literario* (Montevideo) 3 (1978): 17–17. Rpt. in *Ancora* (San José) March 22, 1987: 4D.

"Mientras el niño Dios duerme en almohadones de raso." *Foro Literario* (Montevideo) 8.13 (1985): 9–12.

"El monstruo de las cosas." *Maize* 5.1–2 (1981–82): 62–64.

Mujeres y agonías. Houston: Arte Público Press, 1982.

Mundo, demonio, y mujer. Houston: Arte Público Press, 1991.

"El muro." *La Costa de Oro* 21 (1982): 14–15. Rpt. in *Ancora* (San José) March 22, 1987: 1D–2D.

"El nagual de mi amiga Irene." *La Palabra* 1–2 (1983): 151–57.

"Les Noces d'argent de Pénélope." Trans. Juliette Decreus. *Fer de Lance* (France) 101–2 (1978): 13–18.

Noche en vela. San José: Editorial Costa Rica, 1968. Rpt. in San José: Editorial Costa Rica, 1984.

"Parable of the Impossible Eden." Trans. Nuri Vallbona. *Five Women Writers of Costa Rica.* Ed. Victoria Urbano. Beaumont, Tex.: Lamar University Printing, 1978. 121–23.

"Parábola del amor imposible." *El Cuento—Revista de Imaginación* (Mexico City) 75 (1977): 136–38.

"Penélope en sus bodas de plata." *Foro Literario* (Montevideo) 5 (1979): 15–20. Rpt. in *Puerta abierta: La nueva escritora latinoamericana.* Eds. Caridad L. Silva-Velázquez and Nora Erro-Orthmann. Mexico City: Joaquín Mortiz, 1986. 259–65.

"Penelope's Silver Wedding Anniversary." Trans. Nuri Vallbona. *Five Women Writers of Costa Rica.* Ed. Victoria Urbano. Beaumont, Tex.: Lamar University Printing, 1978. 115–20. Rpt. in *Clamor of Innocence—Stories from Central America* with trans. by Barbara Paschke. San Francisco: City Lights, 1988. 26–32.

Polvo del camino. San José: Lehmann, 1971.

"Una rosa al viento." *La Nación* (San José) March 29, 1969: 32–33.

La salamandra rosada. Montevideo: Geminis, 1979.

Las sombras que perseguimos. San José: Editorial Costa Rica, 1983.

"Tierra de secano." *Letras Femeninas* 1 (1983): 80–83.

Tormy, la prodigiosa gata de Donaldito. San José: Mesén, 1997.

"Le Tréfonds de la surprise." Trans. Juliette Decreus. *Fer de Lance* (France) 111–12 (1980): 12–14.

"Una vez más Caín y Abel." *Ancora* (San José) January 31, 1988: 1D+.

Essays by Rima Vallbona

"Alegorización de la realidad dominicana en *Al final del arcoiris. Káñina* (San José) 8.1–2 (1984): 67–76.

"Alma en pena." *Woman of Her Word—Hispanic Women Writers. Revista Chicano-Riqueña* [special issue] 3–4 (1983): 122–26.

"Amparo Dávila," "Catalina de Erauso," "Eunice Odio," and "Yolanda Oreamuno." *Women Writers of Spanish America: An Annotated Bio-Bibliographical Guide.* Ed. Diane E. Marting. Westport, Conn.: Greenwood Press, 1987. 109–11, 124–25, 281–83, 284–85.

"Análisis ideológico de la poesía costarricense." *Ancora* (San José) November 24, 1985: 1D, 4D. Rpt. in *Cuadernos de poética* (Santo Domingo) 9 May–August 1986: 45–53.

"La antipoesía de Virginia Grutter." *Troquel* (San José) 1, 2 June 1977: 16–17.

"Ausentemente presente." *La Nación* (San José) June 5, 1969: 58+.

"Bibliografía de y sobre Yolanda Oreamuno." *Alba de América* 4–5 (1985): 415–29.

"Búsqueda de Minerva En los ritos de las palabras." *Hasta ahora.* Ed. Cándido Gerón. Santo Domingo: Editorial Santo Domingo, 1987. 129–34.

"Búsqueda de Minerva en los ritos de las palabras." *Minerva: en el temor de las mudas paredes.* Ed. Cándido Gerón. Santo Domingo: Editorial Santo Domingo, 1983. 45–49.

"Los conventos coloniales como espacios liberadores y de creación artística para la mujer." *Revista de Filología y Lingüística de la Universidad de Costa Rica* [San José] [supplement] 1 (1995): 7–23.

"Costa Rica." *Handbook of Latin American Literature.* Comp. David William Foster. New York: Garland, 1987. 191–202.

"Divagaciones sobre Nihil." *La Nación* (San José) July 2, 1967: 8

"Edward Albee: El arte y el público." *Índice* 248 (1968): 32–33.

"Erotismo, remembranzas tropicales y misterios en *María la noche* de Anacristina Rossi." *Mujer y sociedad en América.* Westminster, Calif.: Instituto Literario y Cultural Hispánico, 1988. 117–35.

"El escritor en Hispanoamérica." *Información* (Houston) part 1, May 1981: 11; part 2, June 1981: 14.

"Espinas y laureles del quehacer literario en Hispanoamérica." *Protestas, interrogantes, y agonías en la obra de Rima de Vallbona.* Vol 3: *La mujer en la literatura hispánica.* Westminster, Calif.: Instituto Literario y Cultural Hispánico, 1997. 343–83.

"Estructuras narrativas en los cuentos de Yolanda Oreamuno." *Evaluación de la literatura femenina de Latinoamérica.* San José: Universitaria Centroamericana—EDUCA, 1987. 27–42.

"Estudio valorativo de la obra de Eunice Odio." *Revista Atenea* (Puerto Rico) 1–2 (1985): 91–101.

"Eunice Odio: Rescate de un poeta." *Revista interamericana de bibliografía/Inter-American Review of Bibliography* 31.2 (1981): 199–214.

"Hispanic Literature at the Secondary Level." *Bulletin* 4.2 (May 1975): 4–5.

"A Homeless Writer." *Five Women Writers of Costa Rica.* Beaumont, Tex.: Lamar University Printing, 1978. 44–50, 111–23.

"Humor carnavalesco en los cuentos del salvadoreño Jorge Kattan Zablah." *Confluencia* 6.2 (1991): 149–55.

"Jean Peytard et la Methode Semiotique dans l'Enseignement de la litterature." *Ça Parle...Hommage au Professeur Jean Peytard (articles/temiognages).* Middlebury, Vt.: Ecole Francaise, Middlebury College, 1986. 97–100.

"Julieta Dobles: De la poesía íntimista al lirismo trascendental." *Alba de América* 10.18–19 (1992): 273–88.

"Loreina Santos Silva en el umbral de la soledad." *Ancora* (San José) part 1, March 6, 1988: 2D–3D; part 2, March 13, 1988: 3D–4D.

"María la noche—Erotismo, remembranzas tropicales y misterio." *Ancora* (San José) March 9, 1986: 2D+.

"La mujer conquistadora: La Monja Alférez doña Catalina de Erauso." *Ancora* (San José) October 28, 1984: 1+.

"La mujer guerrera." *Ancora* (San José) February 9, 1986: 2. Rpt. April 20, 1986: 2D+.

"La mujer pobladora." *Ancora* (San José) December 1, 1986: 2+.

"Las mujeres en los conventos del Nuevo Mundo." *Garcín—Libro de Cultura* (Montevideo) part 1.5, March–October 1982: 35–37; part 2.6, November –December 1982: 46–49. Rpt. in *Ancora* (San José) part 1, August 12, 1984: 2; part 2, August 19, 1984: 2–3.

"La Musa de Guatemala." *Ancora* (San José) June 8, 1986: 2D.

La obra en prosa de Eunice Odio. San José: Editorial Costa Rica, 1981.

"Octavio Paz: Prosa en movimiento." *Káñina* (San José) 6.1–2 (1982): 60–66.

"La palabra ilimitada de Eunice Odio: *Los elementos terrestres.*" *Los elementos terrestres. Eunice Odio.* Ed. Rima Vallbona. San José: Editorial Costa Rica, 1984. 11–36.

"El populismo pictórico de Mario González." *Ancora* (San José) November 2, 1986: 1D–3D.

"Por los pasillos de Jorge Luis Borges." *Insula* (Madrid) 274 (1969): 4.

"Rima (Gretel Rothe) de Vallbona." *Alba de América* 11.20–21 (1993): 69–78.

"*La ruta de su evasión* de Yolanda Oreamuno: Escritura proustina suplementada." *Revista Iberoamericana* 138–39 (1987): 193–217.

"El tiempo en siete relatos de Alejo Carpentier." *Troquel* (Costa Rica) 2.13 August 1977: 5–11; part 2, *Troquel* (Costa Rica) 2.14 September 1977: 22–28.

"Trayectoria actual de la poesía femenina en Costa Rica." *Káñina* (San José) 2.3–4 (1978): 15–29.

"Trayectoria actual de la poesía femenina en Costa Rica." *Káñina* (San José) 5.2 (1981): 18–27.

Yolanda Oreamuno. San José, Costa Rica: Ministerio de Cultura, 1972.

"Yolanda Oreamuno: El estigma del escritor." *Cuadernos Hispanoamericanos* 270 (1972): 1–27.

Poetry by Rima Vallbona

"En el mar de la nada." *La Urpila* 23–24 (1986): 11

"Nanita triste." *La Urpila* 4–5 September 1981–January 1982: 5–6.

"Perpetua búsqueda." *La Urpila* 22 (1985): 11.

Poesía compartida—quince poetas latinoamericanos de hoy. Montevideo: Urpila, 1983. 48–50.

"Tu voz de mar." *International Poetry.* Ed. Teresnika Pereira. Boulder, Colo.: International Writers Association, University of Colorado, 1987. 113.

Criticism on the Works of Rima Vallbona

Acevedo Leal, Anabella. "La búsqueda de los espacios propios: Un acercamiento a *Mundo, demonio, y mujer.*" *Protestas, interrogantes, y agonías en la obra de Rima de Vallbona. Vol 3: La mujer en la literatura hispánica.* Eds. Juana Alcira Arancibia and Luis A. Jimenez. Westminster, Calif.: Instituto Literario y Cultural Hispánico, 1997. 335–42.

Acker, Bertie. "*Mujeres y agonías de Rima de Vallbona*." *SCOLAS Bulletin* 6.2 (1982–83): 1–2.

———. "Revelación y hermetismo en *Mujeres y agonías:* Los nuevos cuentos de Rima de Vallbona." *Análisis* 80–81 June–July 1983: 41–42.

———. "Rima de Vallbona: Dos novelas y muchos enigmas." *Protestas, interrogantes, y agonías en la obra de Rima de Vallbona.* Vol. 3: *La mujer en la literatura hispánica.* Eds. Juana Alcira Arancibia and Luis A. Jimenez. Westminster, Calif.: Instituto Literario y Cultural Hispánico, 1997. 135–42.

Agosín, Marjorie. "*Mujeres y agonías.*" *Third Woman* 2.1 (1984): 114–15.

Aldaya, Alicia J. R. "*La obra en prosa de Eunice Odio.*" *South Central Bulletin* 1–2 (1983): 30. Rpt. in *Letras Femeninas* 9.2 (1983): 60.

———. "Three Short Stories by Rima Vallbona." *Five Women Writers of Costa Rica.* Trans. Eduardo C. Bejar. Beaumont, Tex.: Lamar University Printing, 1978. 124–27.

Amber, Angeles. "*Las sombras que perseguimos.*" *La Religión* (Caracas) November 10, 1985: 5.

Amoretti-Hurtado, María. "Rima de Vallbona: Entre la permanencia y el exilio." *El descubrimiento y los desplazamientos: La literatura hispanoamericana como diálogo entre centros y periferias.* Ed. Juana Alcira Arancibia. Westminster, Calif.: Instituto Literario y Cultural Hispánico, 1990. 95–105.

———. "La morada interior y sus espectros." *Revista de Filología y Linguistica de la Universidad de Costa Rica* [supplement] 1 (1995): 89–107.

Andrist, Debra D. "Reversiones y reversos de Rima de Vallbona: 'Beto y Betina.'" *Revista de Filología y Lingüística de la Universidad de Costa Rica* [supplement] 1 (1995): 71–74.

Arancibia, Juana Alcira. "Entrevista con Rima de Vallbona." *Alba de América* 8.14–15 (1990): 353–60.

———. "Entrevista con Rima de Vallbona." *Protestas, interrogantes, y agonías en la obra de Rima de Vallbona.* Vol 3: *La mujer en la literatura hispánica.* Eds. Juana Alcira Arancibia and Luis A. Jiménez. San José: Perro Azul, 1997. 401–10.

Arancibia, Juana Alcira, and Luis A. Jiménez, eds. *Protestas, interrogantes, y agonías en la obra de Rima de Vallbona.* Vol 3: *La mujer en la literatura hispánica.* San José: Perro Azul, 1997.

Armas, Wilson. "*Las sombras que perseguimos.*" *Foro Literario* (Montevideo) 14 (1985): 54–55

Baeza Flores, Alberto. "Eunice, la mágica peregrina." *Revista Cultural 2001* (Caracas) April 4, 1982: 14.

Barahona Jiménez, Luis. "La estética en los novelistas del siglo vigésimo (Período 1920–75)—Rima Rothe de Vallbona." *Apuntes para la historia de las ideas estéticas en Costa Rica.* San José: Editorial del Ministerio de Cultura, 1982. 88–90.

Bartolomé Pons, Esther. "Los cuentos de Rima Vallbona: Dignificación de un Género." *Devenir* 7 (1982): 11–12.

Beltrán, Jorge. "El fatídico encuentro con la nada." *La Prensa* (Buenos Aires) May 10, 1988: 3.

Burgos, Fernando. *La novela moderna hispanoamericana* (Un ensayo sobre el concepto literario de modernidad). *Revista Interamericana de Bibliografía/Inter-American Review of Bibliography* 4 (1986): 487–88.

Caamano, Virginia. "¿Seguirá tejiendo Penélope?" *Revista de Filología y Lingüística de la Universidad de Costa Rica* (San José) [supplement] 1 (1995): 59–70.

Cerezo Dardón, Hugo. *A la luz de los libros-Bibliografía Guatemalteca comentada* (1980–1981).
Guatemala City: Universitaria, 1984.

———. "*La obra en prosa de Eunice Odio*" La Prensa Libre December 13, 1981: 12. Rpt. in
Análisis 69–70 (1982): 47–48.

Chase, Alfonso. "Eunice visita por Rima de Vallbona." *La República* (San José) August 15,
1981: 9.

Chase. Cida S. "*Cosecha de pecadores.*" *Alba de América* 14–15 (1990): 353–60.

———. "El mundo femenino en algunos cuentos de Rima de Vallbona." *Revista Iberoamericana* 53.138–39 (1987): 403–18.

———. "*Noche en vela: Discurso y temática.*" Protestas, interrogantes, y agonías en la obra de Rima
de Vallbona. Vol. 3: La mujer en la literatura hispánica. Eds. Juana Alcira Arancibia and Luis A.
Jimenez. Westminster, Calif.: Instituto Literario y Cultural Hispánico, 1997. 83–94.

Chen, Jorge. "Formas de narración íntima y estatuto discursivo en *Las sombras que perseguimos.*" *Revista de Filología y Lingüística de la Universidad de Costa Rica* [supplement] 1
(1995): 75–80.

Chen-Sham, Jorge. "Estrategia epigrafial y doble lectura en Mundo, demonio, y mujer."
Protestas, interrogantes, y agonías en la obra de Rima de Vallbona. Vol. 3: La mujer en la literatura
hispánica. Eds. Juana Alcira Arancibia and Luis A. Jimenez. Westminster, Calif.: Instituto Literario y Cultural Hispánico, 1997. 301–10.

Chinchilla-Sánchez, Kattia. "¿Quién es la tejedora de las palabras? Una medusa, una
sirena, la bruja Circe, una novia o algo más." Protestas, interrogantes, y agonías en la obra de
Rima de Vallbona. Vol. 3: La mujer en la literatura hispánica. Eds. Juana Alcira Arancibia and
Luis A. Jimenez. Westminster, Calif.: Instituto Literario y Cultural Hispánico, 1997.
223–35.

Constanzó, Carlos M. "Sobre Rima de Vallbona." *Análisis* 90 (1984): 8.

Correa, Rafael E. "Rima de Vallbona y el lector: Texto y espacio desiderados." *Alba de
América* 8.14–15 (1990): 85–91.

Cruz, Julia. "La perspectiva mágica de la Circe de Rima de Vallbona." Protestas, interrogantes, y agonías en la obra de Rima de Vallbona. Vol. 3: La mujer en la literatura hispánica. Eds.
Juana Alcira Arancibia and Luis A. Jimenez. Westminster, Calif.: Instituto Literario
y Cultural Hispánico, 1997. 237–46.

———. "Relectura de 'El impostor' de Rima Vallbona." *Revista de Filología y Lingüística de
la Universidad de Costa Rica* (San José) [supplement] 1 (1995): 51–57.

———. "Tema antiguo, trato nuevo en 'El impostor' de Rima de Vallbona." *Confluencia*
10.1 (1994): 98–103.

"El cuidadoso estilo de Rima de Vallbona." *Ancora* (San José) January 20, 1985: 6.

Cuza-Male, Belkis. "Desde Miami de nuevo con Rima de Vallbona." Protestas, interrogantes,
y agonías en la obra de Rima de Vallbona. Vol 3: La mujer en la literatura hispánica. Eds. Juana
Alcira Arancibia and Luis A. Jimenez. Westminster, Calif.: Instituto Literario y Cultural Hispánico, 1997. 385–99.

Daniel, Lee A. "Angustia y evasión en la narrativa de Rima de Vallbona." *Revista de
Filología y Lingüística de la Universidad de Costa Rica* (San José) [supplement] 1 (1995):
25–29.

————. "Ekphrasis en 'El impostor' de Rima de Vallbona." *Protestas, interrogantes, y agonías en la obra de Rima de Vallbona*. Vol. 3: *La mujer en la literatura hispánica*. Eds. Juana Alcira Arancibia and Luis A. Jimenez. Westminster, Calif.: Instituto Literario y Cultural Hispánico, 1997. 183–89.

Decreus, Juliette. "Búsqueda agónica de la fe en los protagonistas de *Noche en vela* y *Las sombras que perseguimos*." *Protestas, interrrogantes, y agonías en la obra de Rima de Vallbona*. Vol. 3: *La mujer en la literatura hispánica*. Eds. Juana Alcira Arancibia and Luis A. Jimenez. Westminster, Calif.: Instituto Literario y Cultural Hispánico, 1997. 123–33.

————. "Rima R. de Vallbona—Romancier du Costa Rica." *Fer de Lance* (France) 83 (1973): 14–19.

Dellepiane, Angela B. "Los personajes protágonicos de las novelas de Rima de Vallbona." *Protestas, interrogantes, y agonías en la obra de Rima de Vallbona*. Vol. 3: *La mujer en la literatura hispánica*. Eds. Juana Alcira Arancibia and Luis A. Jimenez. Westminster, Calif.: Instituto Literario y Cultural Hispánico, 1997. 61–82.

Dowling, Lee. "Perspectivas de la narración y un desafíos ideológicos en algunas de las obras tempranas de Rima de Vallbona." *Protestas, interrogantes, y agonías en la obra de Rima de Vallbona*. Vol. 3: *La mujer en la literatura hispánica*. Eds. Juana Alcira Arancibia and Luis A. Jimenez. Westminster, Calif.: Instituto Literario y Cultural Hispánico, 1997. 19–40.

————. "Point of View in Rima de Vallbona's *Las sombras que perseguimos*." *Revista Chicano-Riqueña* 13.1 (1985): 64–73.

————. "Rima de Vallbona." *Biographical Dictionary of Hispanic Literature in the United States (The Literature of Puerto Ricans, Cuban Americans, and Other Hispanic Writers)*. Ed. Nicholas Kanellos. Westminster, Calif.: Greenwood Press, 1989. 329–36.

————. "Rima de Vallbona: Desafíos ideológicos y perspectivas de la narración en su obra literaria." *Letras* (San José) 11–12 (1986): 193–214.

————. "Rima Gretel Rothe de Vallbona." *Women Writers in Spanish America: An Annotated Bio-Bibliographical Guide*. Ed. Diane E. Marting. Westminster, Calif.: Greenwood Press, 1987. 335–37.

Durán Cubillo, Ofelia. "Rasgos del relato moderno en el orden temporal de *Noche en vela* de Rima Vallbona." *Káñina* (San José) 16.2 (1992): 9–16.

Fajardo, Miguel. "Eunice Odio." *La República* (San José) January 7, 1982; *Análisis* 69–70 (1982): 20–22.

————. "Rima de Vallbona—una narrativa básica." *Análisis* 73 (1982): 41–42.

————. "Yolanda Oreamuno presentada por Rima de Vallbona." *Análisis* 73 (1982): 39–40.

Fernández de Ulibarri, Rocío. "Vallbona en el límite de lo real." *Ancora* (San José) August 21, 1983: 2–3.

Galván, Delia. "Cosecha de pecadores." *Cuadernos de Aldeeu* 1 (1990): 120–23.

————. "Medios de distanciamiento de la realidad en *Cosecha de pecadores* de Rima de Vallbona." *Encuentro de la literatura con al ciencia y el arte*. Ed. Juana Arancibia. Buenos Aires: Ocruxaves, 1990. 451–62.

Gerón, Cándido. "Eunice Odio: poetisa costarricense." *La noticia* (Santo Domingo) March 31, 1982: 8.

Gómez-Parkham, Mary. "Men in the Short Stories of Rima de Vallbona." *Confluencia* 8.1 (1992): 39–49.

Gruber, Vivan M. "*Mujeres y agonías.*" *South Central Bulletin* (Winter 1983): 134

Hansz, Ingrid, and Mary Parham Gómez. "La presencia masculina en los cuentos de Rima de Vallbona." *Revista de Filología y Lingüística de la Universidad de Costa Rica* [supplement] 1 (1995): 25–29.

Izaguirre, Ester de. "Kafka y Vallbona: Exilio del ser o la busca de respuestas al enigma de la existencia." *Protestas, interrogantes, y agonías en la obra de Rima de Vallbona*. Vol. 3: *La mujer en la literatura hispánica*. Eds. Juana Alcira Arancibia and Luis A. Jimenez. Westminster, Calif.: Instituto Literario y Cultural Hispánico, 1997. 173–82.

Jiménez, Esmeralda. "*Las astillas del viento.*" *Letras Femeninas* 3.2 (1977): 54–56.

Jiménez, Luis A. "Bibliografía de y sobre Rima de Vallbona." *Protestas, interrogantes, y agonías en la obra de Rima de Vallbona*. Vol. 3: *La mujer en la literatura hispánica*. Eds. Juana Alcira Arancibia and Luis A. Jimenez. Westminster, Calif.: Instituto Literario y Cultural Hispánico, 1997. 411–32.

———. "Construyendo el sujeto femenino en *Los infiernos de la mujer y algo más*." *Protestas, interrogantes, y agonías en la obra de Rima de Vallbona*. Vol. 3: *La mujer en la literatura hispánica*. Eds. Juana Alcira Arancibia and Luis A. Jimenez. Westminster, Calif.: Instituto Literario y Cultural Hispánico, 1997. 247–56.

Johnson, Roberta. "The Paradigmatic Story Mode of Carmen Naranjo, Eunice Odio, Yolanda Oreamuno, Victoria Urbano, and Rima Vallbona." *Letras Femeninas* 6.1 (1980): 14–24.

Jurado Morales, José. "*Mujeres y agonías* de Rima de Vallbona." *Cuaderno Literario Azor* 36 (1982): 68.

Karsen, Sonja. "*Five Women Writers of Costa Rica.*" *Hispania* 63 (1980): 785.

Kason, Nancy M. "A través del espejo: El proceso de concientización en *Mundo, demonio, y mujer*" *Revista de Filología y Lingüística de la Universidad de Costa Rica* [supplement] 1 (1995): 81–87.

Lasarte Dishman, Amalia C. "Cosecha de pecadores: una carcajada solapada." *Protestas, interrogantes, y agonías en la obra de Rima de Vallbona.*" Vol. 3: *La mujer en la literatura hispánica*. Eds. Juana Alcira Arancibia and Luis A. Jiménez. Westminster, Calif.: Instituto Literario y Cultural Hispánico, 1997. 201–5.

Lázcaris, Constantino. "*Noche en vela.*" *Letras Femeninas* 4.1 (1978): 106–8.

Lindstrom, Naomi. "*Los elementos terrestres.*" *SCOLAS Bulletin* 10.1 (1985): 8.

Lojo, María Rosa. "*Mujeres y agonías.*" *Letras Femeninas* 1–2 (1987): 112–13.

Lojo de Beuter, María Rosa. "*Las sombras que perseguimos.*" *Alba de América* 3.4–5 (1985): 374–76.

López Oroz, María Luisa, and Belén Lagos Oteíza. "Aproximaciones a la temática en *Las sombras que perseguimos*." *Revista Estudios* 7 (1987): 227–34.

Luesma-Castán, Miguel. "Rima de Vallbona: *Baraja de soledades.*" *Heraldo de Aragón* June 26, 1983: 3.

———. "Sombra, dolor y realidad en Rima de Vallbona." *La República* (San José) March 7, 1986: 11.

Matarrita, Estébana. "Macroestructura en el cuentario *Los infiernos de la mujer y algo más*

. . ." *Protestas, interrogantes, y agonías en la obra de Rima de Vallbona*. Vol. 3: *La mujer en la literatura hispánica*. Eds. Juana Alcira Arancibia and Luis A. Jiménez. Westminster, Calif.: Instituto Literario y Cultural Hispánico, 1997. 257–73.

Molina, Nory, and Julia E. Patiño. "La escritura femenina en 'Balada de un sueño' de Rima de Vallbona." *Encuentro de la literatura con la ciencia y el arte*. San José: EDUCA, 1991. 207–20.

Monge, Carlos Francisco. *La imagen separada—modelos ideológicos de la poesía costarricense, 1950–1980*. Rpt. in *Hispania* 69 (1986): 322.

Monté, Nydia. "Mujeres y agonías, un libro que Ud. debe leer." *Información* (Houston) April 1, 1982: 7.

Moreira, Rubenstein. "La obra en prosa de Eunice Odio." *El Diario Español* (Montevideo) July 17, 1982: 12.

Novo Pena, Silva. "Mujeres y agonías." *La Voz* (Houston) July 1, 1982: 10.

Oberhelman, Harley D. "Las sombras que perseguimos." *SCOLAS Bulletin* (1983–84): 5–6.

Páez de Ruiz, María de Jesús. "Mito y realidad en Mujeres y agonías de Rima de Vallbona." *Evaluación de la literatura femenina de Latinoamérica*. San José: EDUCA, 1987. 81–90.

Parham, Mary. "Men in the Short Stories of Rima de Vallbona." *Confluencia* 1 (1992): 39–49.

Parle, Dennis. "Vallbona, Rima. La obra en prosa de Eunice Odio." *SCOLAS Bulletin* 5.3 (1982): 6.

Porras, José A. "La salamandra rosada por Rima Vallbona." *La República* (San José) March 7, 1981: 9.

Portilla-Chaves, Mario. "Encuentro cultural con Rima de Vallbona." *Revista de Filología y Lingüística de la Universidad de Costa Rica* (San José) 1 (1995):

Ramos, Lilia. "Rima Vallbona o Noche en vela." *Fulgores de mi ocaso*. San José: Editorial Costa Rica, 1979.

Ricci, Luis M. "La obra en prosa de Eunice Odio." *Foro Literario* (Montevideo) 11 (1983): 48.

Rivera, Ana de. "Una escritora costarricense en los Estados Unidos." *La República* (San José) April 18, 1982: 16.

Rosas, Yolanda. "Hacia una identidad en Cosecha de pecadores de Rima de Vallbona." *Americas* 19.3–4 (1991): 134–45.

———. "Identidad y voz femenina: Cosecha de pecadores de Rima de Vallbona." *El descubrimiento y los desplazamientos: La literatura hispanoamericana como diálogo entre centros y periferias*. Ed. Juana Alcira Arancibia. Westminster, Calif.: Instituto Literario y Cultural Hispánico, 1990. 107–20.

Salvo, Baccio. "Baraja de soledades." *Análisis* 84 (1983): 23.

Sandoval de Fonseca, Virginia. "Las sombras que perseguimos o una práctica de relectura." *Evaluación de la literatura femenina de Latinoamérica*. San José: EDUCA, 1987. 67–69.

Silvestri, Daniel Alejandro. "Acercamiento psicocrítico a cuentos de Rima de Vallbona." *Protestas, interrogantes, y agonías en la obra de Rima de Vallbona*. Vol. 3: *La mujer en la literatura hispánica*. Eds. Juana Alcira Arancibia and Luis A. Jiménez. Westminster, Calif.: Instituto Literario y Cultural Hispánico, 1997. 143–72.

Tatter, Federico. "Barajas de soledades." *La Ciudad* (Santiago) October 4, 1983. 5.

Umanzor, Marta Aída. "La búsqueda de la salida laberíntica de Renata en la relectura de Mundo, demonio, y mujer." *Protestas, interrogantes, y agonías en la obra de Rima de Vallbona*. Vol. 3:

La mujer en la literatura hispánica. Eds. Juana Alcira Arancibia and Luis A. Jiménez. Westminster, Calif.: Instituto Literario y Cultural Hispánico, 1997. 321–41.

Vargas, Sonia. "Recuperación de valores femeninos." *La Nación Internacional* August 1984: 23.

Velez, Joseph F. "Libro de agonías." *Ovaciones* (México City) July 26, 1984: 8.

———. "Una novela fascinante." *Ovaciones* (Mexico City) April 6, 1984: 8.

Zúñiga-Tristán, Virginia. "Mujeres y agonías." *Káñina* 1–2 (1982): 126.

———. *"Las sombras que perseguimos." Ancora* (San José) August 21, 1983: 2–3.

General Bibliography

Anthologies

Agosín, Marjorie, ed. *House of Memory: Stories by Jewish Women Writers of Latin America*. New York: Feminist Press, 1999.

————. *Passion, Memory, and Identity: Twentieth Century Latin American Jewish Women Writers*. Trans. Ellizabeth Rosa Horan. Albuquerque: University of New Mexico Press, 1999.

————. *Landscapes of a New Land: Short Fiction by Latin American Women*. Fredonia, N.Y.: White Pine Press, 1993.

————. *What Is Secret: Stories by Chilean Women*. Fredonia, N.Y.: White Pine Press, 1995.

Agosín, Marjorie, and Celeste Kostopulos-Cooperman, eds. *Secret Weavers: Stories of the Fantastic by Women of Argentina and Chile*. Fredonia, N.Y.: White Pine Press, 1993.

Ahern, Maureen. *A Rosario Castellanos Reader: An Anthology of Her Poetry, Short Fiction, Essays, and Drama*. Austin: University of Texas Press, 1988

Arkin, Marian, and Barbara Shollar, eds. *Longman Anthology of World Literature by Women, 1875–1975*. New York: Longman, 1989.

Behar, Ruth, ed. *Bridges to Cuba. Puentes a Cuba*. Ann Arbor: University. of Michigan Press, 1995.

Benner, Susan, and Kathy S. Leonard, eds. and trans. *Fire from the Andes: Short Fiction by Women from Bolivia, Ecuador, and Peru*. Albuquerque: University of New Mexico Press, 1997.

Biddle, Arthur, ed. *Global Voices: Contemporary Literature from the Non-Western World*. Englewood Cliffs, N.J.: Prentice Hall, 1995.

Bombal, María Luisa. *New Islands and Other Stories*. Trans. Richard Cunningham and Lucía Cunningham. New York: Farrar, 1982.

Borges, Jorge Luis, Silvina Ocampo, and Adolfo Bioy Casares, eds. *The Book of Fantasy*. New York: Viking, 1988.

Bowen, David, and Juan A. Ascencio, eds. *Pyramids of Glass: Short Fiction from Modern Mexico*. San Antonio, Tex.: Corona, 1994.

Boyce Davies, Carole E., and Molara Ogundipe-Leslie, eds. *Moving Beyond Boundaries. International Dimensions of Black Women's Writing*. Vol 1. New York: New York University Press, 1995.

Breton, Marcela, ed. *Rhythm and Revolt: Tales of the Antilles*. New York: Penguin, 1995.

Busby, Margaret, ed. *Daughters of Africa: An International Anthology of Words and Writings by Women of African Descent: From the Ancient Egyptian to the Present*. New York: Pantheon, 1992.

Cahill, Susan, ed. *Women and Fiction. Short Stories by and About Women*. 2 vols. New York: New American Library, 1975–78.

Caistor, Nick, ed. *Columbus' Egg. New Latin American Stories on the Conquest*. Boston: Faber, 1992.

————, ed. *The Faber Book of Contemporary Latin American Short Stories*. London: Faber, 1989.

Carlson, Lori M., and Cynthia L. Ventura, eds. *Where Angels Glide at Dawn: New Stories from Latin America*. New York: Lippincott, 1990.

Carranza, Sylvia, and María Juana Cazabón, eds. *Cuban Short Stories, 1959–1966*. Havana: Book Institute, 1967.

Cass, Canfield Jr., ed. *Masterworks of Latin American Short Fiction: Eight Novellas*. New York: Icon, 1996.

Castro-Klaren, Sara, Sylvia Molloy, and Beatriz Sarlo, eds. *Women's Writing in Latin America: An Anthology*. Boulder, Colo.: Westview Press, 1991.

Clerk, Jayana, and Ruth Siegel, eds. *Modern Literatures of the Non-Western World. Where the Waters Are Born*. New York: HarperCollins, 1995.

Coelho Pinto, José Saldanha da Gama, ed. *Contistas brasileiros. New Brazilian Short Stories*. Trans. Rod W. Horton. Rio de Janeiro: Revista Branca, 1957.

Cohen, J. M., ed. *Writers in the New Cuba: An Anthology*. New York: Penguin, 1967.

Colchie, Thomas., ed. *A Hammock Beneath the Mangoes: Stories from Latin America*. New York: Penguin, 1991.

Correas de Zapata, Celia. *Short Stories by Latin American Women: The Magic and the Real*. Houston: Arte Público Press, 1990.

Correas de Zapata, Celia, and Lygia Johnson, eds. *Detrás de la reja: Antología critica de Nannadonas latinoamericanas des siglo xx*. Caracas: Monte Avila, 1980.

Coverdale Sumrall, Amber, ed. *Lover: Stories by Women*. Freedom, N.Y.: Crossing Press, 1992.

Cranfill, Thomas Mabry, and George D. Schade, eds. *The Muse in Mexico: A Mid-Century Miscellany*. Austin: University of Texas Press, 1959.

di Giovanni, Norman Thomas, and Susan Ashe, eds. and trans. *Celeste Goes Dancing and Other Stories: An Argentine Collection*. San Francisco: North Point Press, 1990.

Erro-Peralta, Nora, and Caridad Silva-Núñez, eds. *Beyond the Border: A New Age in Latin American Women's Fiction*. Pittsburgh: Cleis Press, 1991.

Esteves, Carmen C., and Lizabeth Paravisini-Gebert, eds. *Green Candy and Juicy Flotsam: Short Stories by Caribbean Women*. New Brunswick, N.J.: Rutgers University Press, 1991.

Fares, Gustavo, and Eliana Cazaubon Hermann. *Contemporary Argentinean Women Writers: A Critical Anthology*. Gainesville: University Press of Florida, 1998.

Fernández Olmos, Margarite, and Lizabeth Paravisini-Gebert, eds. *Pleasure in the Word: Erotic Writing by Latin American Women*. Fredonia, N.Y.: White Pine Press, 1994.

————, eds. *Remaking a Lost Harmony: Stories from the Hispanic Caribbean*. Fredonia, N.Y.: White Pine Press, 1995.

Fishburn, Evelyn. *Short Fiction by Spanish American Women*. Manchester, England: Manchester University Press, 1998.

Flores, Angel. *Spanish Short Stories*. New York: Bantam, 1981.

Fremantle, Anne, ed. *Latin-American Literature Today*. New York: New American Library, 1977.

Geok-Lin, Shirley, and Norman Spencer, eds. *One World of Literature*. Boston: Houghton, 1993.

Gibbons, Reginald, ed. *New Writing from Mexico. A Special Issue of TriQuarterly Magazine*. Evanston, Ill.: TriQuarterly and Northwestern University, 1992.

Gómez, Alma, Cherríe Moraga, and Mariana Romo-Carmona, eds. *Cuentos: Stories by Latinas*. New York: Kitchen Table, Women of Color Press, 1983.

González Echevarría, Roberto, ed. *The Oxford Book of Latin American Short Stories*. Oxford: Oxford University Press, 1997.

Grossman, William L., ed. *Modern Brazilian Short Stories*. Berkeley: University of California Press, 1967.

Halperin, Daniel, ed. *The Art of the Tale: An International Anthology of Short Stories, 1945–1985*. New York: Viking, 1986.

Hanson, Ron, and Jim Shepard, eds. *You've Got to Read This: Contemporary American Writers Introduce Stories that Held Them in Awe*. New York: Harper, 1994.

Howes, Barbara, ed. *The Eye of the Heart: Short Stories from Latin America*. New York: Avon, 1974.

————, ed. *From the Green Antilles: Writings of the Caribbean*. New York: Macmillan, 1966.

Howes, Irving, and Ilana Wiener Howe, eds. *Short Stories. An Anthology of the Shortest Stories*. Boston: Grodine, 1982.

Ibieta, Gabriella, ed. *Latin American Writers: Thirty Stories*. New York: St. Martin's Press, 1993.

Jaramillo, Enrique Levi, ed. *When New Flowers Bloomed: Short Stories by Women Writers from Costa Rica and Panama*. Pittsburgh: Latin American Literary Review Press, 1991.

Jaramillo, Enrique Levi, and Leland Chambers, eds. *Contemporary Short Stories from Central America*. Austin: University of Texas Press, 1994.

Jones Earl, ed. *Selected Latin American Literature for Youth*. College Station: Texas A & M University Press, 1968.

Jones, Willis Knapp, ed. *Spanish American Literature in Translation: A Selection of Prose, Poetry, and Drama Before 1888*. Vol 1. New York: Frederick Ungar, 1966.

————, ed. *Spanish American Literature in Translation: A Selection of Prose, Poetry, and Drama Since 1888*. Vol 2. New York: Frederick Ungar, 1963.

Kalechofsky, Robert, and Roberta Kalechofsky, eds. *Echad: An Anthology of Latin American Jewish Writings*. Marblehead, Mass.: Micah, 1980.

————, eds. *Echad 5: The Global Anthology of Jewish Women Writers*. Marblehead, Mass.: Micah, 1990.

Lawaetz, Gudie, ed. *Spanish Short Stories, Cuentos Hispánicos*. 2 vols. New York: Penguin, 1972.

Leonard, Kathy S., ed. and trans. *Cruel Fictions, Cruel Realities: Short Stories by Latin American Women Writers*. Pittsburgh: Latin American Literary Review Press, 1997.

Lewald, Herald Ernest, ed. and trans. *The Web: Stories of Argentine Women*. Washington, D.C.: Three Continents Press, 1983.

Luby, Barry J., and Wayne H. Finke, eds. *Anthology of Contemporary Latin American Literature, 1960–1984.* London and Toronto: Associated University Press, 1986.

Mancini, Pat McNees, ed. *Contemporary Latin American Short Stories.* Greenwich, Conn.: Fawcet, 1974.

Manguel, Alberto, ed. *Black Water: Anthology of Fantastic Literature.* New York: Potter, 1983.

———, ed. *Black Water 2: More Tales of the Fantastic.* New York: Potter, 1990.

———, ed. *Dark Arrows: Chronicles of Revenge.* New York: Penguin, 1985.

———, ed. *Evening Games: Tales of Parents and Children.* New York: Potter, 1987.

———, ed. *The Gates of Paradise: The Anthology of Erotic Short Fiction.* New York: Potter, 1993.

———, ed. *Other Fires, Short Fiction by Latin American Women.* Toronto: Lester & Orpen Dennys, 1986.

———, ed. *The Second Gates of Paradise: The Anthology of Erotic Short Fiction.* New York: Potter, 1996.

———, ed. *Soho Square.* Vol. 3. London: Bloomsbury, 1990.

Menton, Seymour, ed. *The Spanish American Short Story: A Critical Anthology.* Berkeley: University of California Press, 1980.

———, ed. *Venezuelan Short Stories—Cuentos venezolanos.* Caracas: Monte Avila, 1992.

Meyer, Doris, ed. *Lives on the Line: The Testimony of Contemporary Latin American Authors.* Berkeley: University of California Press, 1980.

Meyer, Doris, and Marguerite Fernández Olmos, eds. *Contemporary Women Authors of Latin America: New Translations.* New York: Brooklyn College Press, 1983.

Milligan, Bryce, Mary Guerrero Milligan, and Angela de Hoyos, eds. *Daughters of the Fifth Sun: A Collection of Latina Fiction and Poetry.* New York: Riverhead Books, 1995.

Moore, Evelyn, ed. *Sancocho: Stories and Sketches of Panama.* Panama: Panama American, 1938.

Mordecai, Pamela, and Betty Wilson, eds. *Her True-True Name: An Anthology of Women's Writing from the Caribbean.* Oxford: Heinemann, 1989.

Morgan, Robin, ed. *Sisterhood Is Global. The International Women's Movement Anthology.* Garden City, N.Y.: Doubleday, 1984.

Muller, Gilberth, and John A. Williams, eds. *Bridges: Literature Across Cultures.* New York: McGraw-Hill, 1994.

O'Reilly Herrera, Andrea, ed. *A Secret Weavers Anthology: Selections from the Secret Weavers Series: Writing by Latin American Women.* Fredonia, N.Y.: White Pine Press, 1998.

Partnoy, Alicia. *The Little School: Tales of Disappearance and Survival in Argentina.* Trans. Alicia Partnoy with Lois Athey and Sandra Braunstein. San Francisco: Cleis Press, 1986.

———, ed. *You Can't Drown the Fire. Latin American Women Writing in Exile.* Pittsburgh: Cleis Press, 1988.

Paschke, Barbara, and Davis Volpondesta, eds. *Clamor of Innocence: Central American Short Stories.* San Francisco: City Lights, 1988.

Penelope, Julia, and Sarah Valentine, eds. *International Feminist Fiction.* Freedom, N.Y.: Crossing Press, 1992.

Picón Garfield, Evelyn, ed. *Women's Fiction from Latin America: Selections from Twelve Contemporary Authors.* Detroit: Wayne State University Press, 1988.

Poey, Delia, ed. *Out of the Mirrored Garden: New Fiction by Latin American Women*. New York: Anchor, 1996.

Ras, Barbara, ed. *Costa Rica: A Traveler's Literary Companion*. San Francisco: Whereabouts Press, 1994.

Reyes, Sandra, ed. and trans. *One More Stripe to the Tiger: A Selection of Contemporary Chilean Poetry and Fiction*. Fayetteville: University of Arkansas Press, 1989.

Rodríguez Monegal, Emir, and Thomas Colchie, eds. *The Borzoi Anthology of Latin American Literature*. 2 vols. New York: Knopf, 1977.

Ross, Kathleen, and Yvette Miller, eds. *Scents of Wood and Silence: Short Stories by Latin American Women Writers*. Pittsburgh: Latin American Literary Review Press, 1991.

Sadlier, Darlene J., ed. and trans. *One Hundred Years After Tomorrow: Brazilian Women's Fiction in the Twentieth Century*. Bloomington: Indiana University Press, 1992.

Salmonson, Jessica Amanda, ed. *What Did Miss Darrington See? An Anthology of Feminist Supernatural Fiction*. New York: Feminist Press, 1989.

Santiago, Roberto, ed. *Boricuas: Influential Puerto Rican Writings—an Anthology*. New York: Ballantine, 1995.

Santos, Rosario, ed. *And We Sold the Rain: Contemporary Fiction from Central America*. New York: Four Walls Eight Windows, 1988.

Sefchovich, Sara, ed. *Mujeres en espejo: Nannadonas latinoamericanos siglo xx*. 2 vols. Mexico City: Folios, 1983, 1985.

Shapard, Robert, and James Thomas, eds. *Sudden Fiction: Sixty Short-Short Stories*. New York: Norton, 1989.

Silva-Velázquez, Caridad L., and Nora Erro-Orthmann, eds. *Puerta abierta: La nueva escritora latinoamericanas*. Mexico City: Joaquín Mortiz, 1986.

Smorkaloff, Pamela María, ed. *If I Could Write This in Fire: An Anthology of Literature from the Caribbean*. New York: New Press, 1994.

Solomon, Barbara, ed. *Other Voices, Other Vistas. Short Stories from Africa, China, India, Japan, and Latin America*. New York: Penguin, 1992.

Stavans, Ilan, ed. *Tropical Synagogues. Short Stories by Jewish Latin American Writers*. New York: Holmes, 1994.

Torres-Ríoscco, Arturo, ed. *Short Stories of Latin America*. New York: Las Americas, 1963.

Troupe, Quincy, and Rainer Schulte, eds. *Giant Talk: An Anthology of Third World Writings*. New York: Random, 1975.

Urbano, Victoria, ed. *Five Women Writers of Costa Rica: Short Stories by Carmen Naranjo, Eunice Odio, Yolanda Oreammuo, Victoria Urbano, and Rima Vallbona*. Beaumont, Tex.; Asociación de Literatura Femenina Hispánica, 1978.

Van Steen, Edla, ed. *Love Stories: A Brazilian Collection*. Trans. Elizabeth Lowe. Rio de Janeiro: Grafica, 1978.

Vélez, Diana, ed. *Reclaiming Medusa: Short Stories by Contemporary Puerto Rican Women*. San Francisco: Spinster/Aunt Lute, 1988.

Yanes, Gabriela, Manuel Sorto, Horacio Castellanos Moya, and Lyn Sorto, eds. *Mirror of War: Literature and Revolution in El Salvador*. Trans. Keith Ellis. New York: Monthly Review Press, 1985.

Young, David, and Keith Hollaman, eds. *Magical Realist Fiction: An Anthology*. New York: Longman, 1984.

Young-Bruehl, Elisabeth, ed. *Global Cultures. A Transnational Short Fiction Reader*. Middletown, Conn.: Wesleyan University Press, 1994.

Criticism on the Short Story, Feminism, and Latin American Women Writers

Acosta-Belén, Edna., ed. *The Puerto Rican Woman: Perspectives on Culture, History, and Society*. New York: Praeger, 1986.

Acosta-Belén, Edna, and Christine E. Bose, eds. *Researching Women in Latin America and the Caribbean*. Boulder, Colo.: Westview Press, 1993.

Agosín, Marjorie, ed. *Ashes of Revolt*. Fredonia, N.Y.: White Pine Press, 1996.

————. *A Dream of Light and Shadow: Portraits of Latin American Women Writers*. Albuquerque: University of New Mexico Press, 1995.

————. "Whispers and Triumphs: Latin American Women Writers Today." *Women's Studies International* 9.4 (1986): 427–33.

Alarcón, Norma, and Sylvia Kossnar. *Bibliography of Hispanic Women Writers*. Chicano-Riqueño Studies Bibliography Series No. 1. Bloomington, Ind.: n.p., 1980.

Aldrich, Earl M., Jr. *The Modern Short Story in Peru*. Madison: University of Wisconsin Press, 1966.

————. "Recent Trends in the Peruvian Short Story." *Studies in Short Fiction* 8.1 (1971): 20–31.

Alvarez Borland, Isabel. *Cuban-American Literature of Exile: From Person to Persona*. Charlottesville: University Press of Virginia, 1998.

Bassnett, Susan, ed. *Knives and Angels: Women Writers in Latin America*. London: Sed Books, 1990.

Berg, Mary. "Rereading Fiction by Nineteenth Century Latin American Women Writers: Interpretation and Translation of the Past into the Present." *Translation Perspectives* 6 (1991): 127–33.

Bergmann, Emilie, et al. *Women, Culture, and Politics in Latin America*. Berkeley: University of California Press, 1990.

Brooksbank Jones, Anny, and Catherine Davies, eds. *Latin American Women's Writing: Feminist Readings in Theory and Crisis*. Oxford: Clarendon Press, 1996.

Brushwood, John. "Mexican Fiction in the Seventies: Author, Intellect and Public." *Ibero-American Letters in a Comparative Perspective*. Eds. Wolodymir T. Zyla and Wendell M. Aycock. Lubbock: Texas Tech Press, 1978. 35–47.

————. *Mexico in Its Novel: A Nation's Search for Identity*. Notre Dame, Ind.: University of Notre Dame Press, 1971.

————. *The Spanish American Novel. Twentieth-Century Survey*. Austin: University of Texas Press, 1975.

Cajiao Salas, Teresa, and Margarita Vargas, eds. *Women Writing Women: An Anthology of Spanish American Theater of the 1980s*. Albany: State University of New York Press, 1997.

Castillo, Ana, ed. *Goddess of the Americas/La diosa de las Americas: Writings on the Virgin of Guadalupe.* New York: Riverhead, 1996.

Castillo, Debra. *Easy Women: Sex and Gender in Modern Mexican Fiction.* Minneapolis: University of Minnesota Press, 1998.

———. *Talking Back: Toward a Latin American Feminist Literary Criticism.* Ithaca, N.Y.: Cornell University Press, 1992.

Castro-Klaren, Sara, Sylvia Molloy, and Beatriz Sarlo, eds. *Women's Writing in Latin America.* Boulder, Colo.: Westview Press, 1991.

Chaney, Elsa. "Old and New Feminists in Latin America: The Case of Peru and Chile." *Journal of Marriage and the Family* 35.2 (1973): 331–43.

Chevigny, Bell Gale, and Gari Laguardia, eds. *Reinventing the Americas: Comparative Studies of Literature of the United States and Spanish America.* New York: Cambridge University Press, 1986.

Colvile, Georgina M. M. *Contemporary Women Writing in Other Americas.* Lewiston, N.Y.: Mullen, 1996.

Conde, L. P., and S. M. Hart., eds. *Feminist Readings on Spanish and Latin American Literature.* Lewiston, N.Y.: Edwin Mellen, 1991.

Correas de Zapata, Celia. "One Hundred Years of Women Writers in Latin America." *Latin American Literary Review* 3.6 (1975): 7–16.

Cortina Rice, Lynn Ellen. *Spanish-American Women Writers: A Bibliographical Research Checklist.* New York: Garland, 1983.

Corvalán, Graciela N. V. *Latin American Women Writers in English Translation: A Bibliography.* Los Angeles: California State University Latin American Studies Center, 1980.

Cypess, Sandra Messinger. *La Malinche in Mexican Literature from History to Myth.* Austin: University of Texas Press, 1991.

Davies, Catherine. *A Place in the Sun? Women Writers in Twentieth Century Cuba.* London: Zed Books, 1997.

———, ed. *Women Writers in Twentieth Century Spain and Spanish America.* Lmpeter, Wales: Edwin Mellen Press, 1993.

De Beer, Gabriela. *Contemporary Mexican Women Writers.* Austin: University of Texas Press, 1996.

D'Lugo, Carol Clark. *The Fragmented Novel in Mexico: The Politics of Form.* Austin: University of Texas Press, 1997.

Dore, Elizabeth, ed. *Gender and Politics in Latin America.* New York: Monthly Review Press, 1997.

Duncan, J. Ann. *Voices, Visions, and a New Reality: Mexican Fiction Since 1970.* Pittsburgh: University of Pittsburgh Press, 1986.

Fernández Olmos, Margarite. "Latin American Testimonial Narrative, or Women and the Art of Listening." *Revista Canadiense de Estudios Hispánicos* (Ottawa) 13.2 (1989): 183–95.

———. "Sex, Color, and Class in Contemporary Puerto Rican Women Authors." *Heresies* 4.3 (1982): 46–47.

Fiori, Mónica Roy. *Streams of Silver: Six Contemporary Women Writers from Argentina.* Lewisburg, Pa.: Bucknell University Press, 1995.

Fisher, Jo. *Mothers of the Disappeared*. Boston: South Bend, 1989.

Fleak, Kenneth. "Latin American Short Fiction." *Studies in Short Fiction* 20.4 (1983): 297–306.

Foster, David William. *Argentine Literary Research Guide*. 2nd ed. rev. New York: Garland, 1982.

————. *Chilean Literature. A Working Bibliography of Secondary Sources*. Boston: G.K. Hall, 1978.

————. *A Dictionary of Contemporary Latin American Authors*. Tempe: Center for Latin American Studies, Arizona State University, 1975.

————. *Mexican Literature: A Bibliography of Secondary Sources*. Metuchen, N.J.: Scarecrow Press, 1981.

————. *Studies in the Contemporary Spanish American Short Story*. Columbia: University of Missouri Press, 1979.

————. *The Twentieth Century Spanish-American Novel: A Bibliographic Guide*. Metuchen, N.J.: Scarecrow Press, 1975.

Foster, David William, and Virginia Ramos Foster. *Modern Latin American Literature*. 2 vols. New York: Frederic Ungar, 1975.

————. *Research Guide to Argentine Literature*. Metuchen, N.J.: Scarecrow Press, 1970.

Fox-Lockert, Lucía. *Women Novelists in Spain and Spanish America*. Metuchen, N.J.: Scarecrow Press, 1979.

Franco, Jean. *An Introduction to Spanish American Literature*. New York: Cambridge University Press, 1969.

————. *The Modern Culture of Latin America: Society and the Artist*. New York: Penguin, 1970.

————. *Plotting Women. Gender and Representation in Mexico*. New York: Columbia University Press, 1989.

————. "Self-Destructing Heroines." *Minnesota Review* 22 (1984): 105–15.

————. *Spanish American Literature Since Independence*. London: Breen, 1973.

Frederick, Bonnie. *Wily Modesty: Argentine Women Writers, 1860–1910*. Tempe: Center for Latin American Studies Press, Arizona State University Press. 1998.

Freudenthal, Juan R., and Patricia M. Freudenthal. *Index to Anthologies of Latin American Literature in English Translation*. Boston: G. K. Hall, 1977.

Galerstein, Carolyn L., ed. *Women Writers of Spain. An Annotated Bio-Bibliographical Guide*. Westport, Conn.: Greenwood Press, 1986.

García, Kay S. *Broken Bars: New Perspectives from Mexican Women Writers*. Albuquerque: University of New Mexico Press, 1994.

García Pinto, Magdalena. *Women Writers of Latin America: Intimate Histories*. Trans. Trudy Balch and Magdalena García Pinto. Austin: University of Texas Press, 1991.

Gazarian Gautier, Marie-Luise. *Interviews with Latin American Writers*. Elmwood Park, Ill.: Dalkey Archive Press, 1989.

Geisdorfer Leal, Rosemary, "Women Writers into the Mainstream: Contemporary Latin American Narrative." *Philosophy and Literature in Latin America: A Critical Assessment of the Current Situation*. Eds. Jorge E. García and Mireya Camurati. New York: State University of New York Press, 1989.

Gimbernat González, Ester. "The Eloquence of Silence: Argentinean Women Writers After the 'Proceso.'" *Fiction International* 19.1 (1990): 72–82.

Guerra Cunningham, Lucía. *Splintering Darkness: Latin American Women Writers in Search of Themselves*. Pittsburgh: Latin American Literary Review Press, 1990.

Gugelberger, Georg M., ed. *The Real Thing: Testimonial Discourse and Latin America*. Durham, N.C.: Duke University Press, 1996.

Hahner, June E. *Women in Latin American History. Their Lives and Views*. Los Angeles: UCLA Latin American Center, 1976.

Harkess, Shirley, and Cornelia B. Flora. "Women in the News: An Analysis of Media Images in Colombia." *Revista Iberoamericana* 4.2 (1974): 220–38.

Harss, Luis, and Barbara Dohmann. *Into the Mainstream*. New York: Harper, 1967.

Hart, Stephen M. *White Ink: Essays on Twentieth Century Feminine Fiction in Spain and Latin America*. London: Tamesis, 1993.

Hill, Marnesba D., and Harold B. Schleifer. *Puerto Rican Authors: A Biographical Handbook. Autores Puertorriqueños: Una guía biobibliográfica*. Metuchen, N.J.: Scarecrow Press, 1974.

Hoberman, Louisa S. "Hispanic American Women as Portrayed in the Historical Literature: Types or Archetypes." *Revista / Review Interamericana* (San German, Puerto Rico) 4.2 (1974): 136–47.

Horno-Delgado, Asunción, et al. *Breaking Boundaries: Latina Writings and Critical Readings*. Amherst: University of Massachusetts Press, 1989.

Hughes, Psiche. "Women and Literature in Latin America." *Unheard Words: Women and Literature in Africa, the Arab World, Asia, the Caribbean, and Latin America*. Eds. Mineke Schipper and Barbara Potter Fasting. London: Allison & Busby, 1985.

Ibsen, Kristine. *The Other Mirror: Women's Narrative in Mexico, 1980–1995*. Westport, Conn.: Greenwood Press, 1997.

Jacquette, Jane. "Literary Archetypes and Female Role Alternatives: The Woman and the Novel in Latin America." *Female and Male in Latin America: Essays*. Ed. A. Pescatello. Pittsburgh: University of Pittsburgh Press, 1973. 3–27.

———, ed. *The Women's Movement in Latin America: Feminism and the Transition to Democracy*. Boston: Unwin Hyman, 1989.

Jehenson, Myriam Yvonne. *Latin American Women Writers: Class, Race, and Gender*. Albany: State University of New York Press, 1995.

Jiménez, Reynaldo L. "Cuban Women Writers and the Revolution: Toward An Assessment of Their Literary Contribution." *Folio* 11 (1978): 75–95.

Johnson, Harvey L., and Philip B. Taylor Jr. *Contemporary Latin American Literature*. Houston: University of Houston Press, 1973.

Kaminsky, Amy. *After Exile: Writing the Latin American Diaspora*. Minneapolis: University of Minnesota Press, 1999.

———. *Reading the Body Politic: Feminist Criticism and Latin American Women Writers*. Minneapolis: University of Minnesota Press, 1993.

———. "The Real Circle of Iron: Mothers and Children in Four Argentine Novels." *Latin American Literary Review* 9 (1976): 77–86.

Kantaris, Elia Geoffrey. *The Subversive Psyche: Contemporary Women's Narrative from Argentina and Uruguay*. Oxford: Clarendon Press, 1995.

Kirkpatrick, Susan. *Las Románticas: Women Writers and Subjectivity in Spain, 1835–50*. Berkeley: University of California Press, 1989.

Kizner, Nora Scott. "Women Professionals in Buenos Aires." *Female and Male in Latin America.* Ed. Ann Pescatello. Pittsburgh: University of Pittsburgh Press, 1973. 159–90.

Knaster, Meri. *Women in Spanish America. An Annotated Bibliography from Pre-Conquest to Contemporary Times.* Boston: G. K. Hall, 1977.

Lagmanovich, David. "Images of Reality: Latin American Short Story of Today." *Dispositio: Revista Hispánica de Semiotica Literaria* 9.24–26 (1984): 53–63.

Larson, Ross. *Fantasy and Imagination in the Mexican Narrative.* Tempe: Center for Latin American Studies, Arizona State University, 1977.

Lavrin, Ascension, and Edith Couturier, eds. *Latin American Women: Historical Perspectives.* Westport, Conn.: Greenwood Press, 1978.

Leal, Luis. "Contemporary Mexican Novel and Short Story." *Contemporary Latin American Literature.* Houston: University of Houston, Office of International Affairs, 1973. 40–47.

———. "Female Archetypes in Mexican Literature." *Women in Hispanic Literature: Icon and Fallen Idols.* Ed. Beth Miller. Berkeley: University of California Press, 1983. 227–42.

———. "Native and Foreign Elements in Contemporary Mexican Fiction: A Search For Identity." *Tradition and Renewal.* Ed. Merlin Forster. Urbana: University of Illinois Press, 1975. 102–28.

Lindstrom, Naomi. "Feminist Criticism of Latin American Literature: Bibliographic Notes." *Latin American Research Review* 15.1 (1980): 151–59.

———. *The Social Consciousness of Latin America.* Austin: University of Texas Press, 1998.

———. *Women's Voice In Latin American Literature.* Boulder, Colo.: Lynne Rienner, 1989.

Lobo, Luiza. "Women Writers in Brazil Today." *World Literature Today* 61.1 (1987): 49–54.

Lozano, Stella. *Selected Bibliography of Contemporary Spanish American Writers.* Los Angeles: California State University Press, 1979.

Luis, William. *Literary Bondage: Slavery in Cuban Literature.* Austin: University of Texas Press, 1990.

Magnarelli, Sharon. *The Lost Rib.* Lewisburg, Pa.: Bucknell University Press, 1985.

Marting, Diane E., ed. *Spanish American Women Writers: A Bio- Biographical Sourcebook.* Westport, Conn.: Greenwood Press, 1990.

———. *Women Writers of Spanish America. An Annotated Bio- Bibliographical Guide.* Westport, Conn.: Greenwood Press, 1987.

Masiello, Francine. *Between Civilization and Barbarism: Women, Nation, and Literature Culture in Modern Argentina.* Lincoln: University of Nebraska Press, 1992.

———. "Subversions of Authority: Feminist Literary Culture in the River Plate Region." *Chasqui* 21.1 (1992): 39–48.

Mathieu, Corina. *Latin American Women Writers, Yesterday and Today.* Pittsburgh: Carnegie Mellon, 1975.

McMurray, George R. "Thematic Incidence of the Revolution in the Mexican Short Story." *Bulletin of the Rocky Mountain Modern Language Association* 18 (1965): 5–8.

Meyer, Doris, ed. *Lives on the Line: The Testimony of Contemporary Latin American Authors.* Berkeley: University of California Press, 1988.

———. *Reinterpreting the Spanish American Essay: Women Writers of the Nineteenth and Twentieth Centuries.* Austin: University of Texas Press, 1995.

————. *Rereading the Spanish American Essay: Translations Nineteenth and Twentieth Centuries Women's Essay*. Austin: University of Texas Press, 1995.

Meyer, Doris, and Margarite Fernández Olmos. *Contemporary Women Authors of Latin America*. Vol 1: Introductory Essays and vol 2: New Translations. New York: Brooklyn College Press, 1983.

Miller, Beth, ed. *Women in Hispanic Literature: Icons and Fallen Idols*. Berkeley: University of California Press, 1983.

Miller, Francisca. *Latin American Women and the Search for Social Justice*. Hanover, N.H.: University Press of New England, 1991.

————. *Women, Culture, and Politics in Latin America*. Berkeley: University of California Press, 1990.

Miller, Yvette E., and Charles M. Tatum. eds. *Latin American Women Writers: Yesterday and Today*. Pittsburgh: Latin American Literary Review Press, 1977.

Minc, Rose. *The Contemporary Latin American Short Story*. New York: Senda Nueva, 1979.

Molloy, Sylvia. *At Face Value: Autobiographical Writing in Spanish America*. New York: Cambridge University Press, 1991.

Mora, Gabriela, and Karen S. Van Hooft, eds. *Theory and Practice of Feminist Literary Criticism*. Ypsilanti, Mich.: Bilingual Press, 1982.

Muñoz, Braulio. *Sons of the Wild: The Search for Identity in Spanish American Indian Literature*. New Brunswick, N.J.: Rutgers University Press, 1982.

Nas, June, and Helen I. Safa, eds. *Sex and Class in Latin America*. New York: Praeger, 1976.

Pazos, Alonso, and Claudia Fernández. *Women, Literature, and Culture in the Portuguese Speaking World*. Lewiston, N.Y.: Edwin Mellen Press, 1991.

Peden, Margaret Sayers. ed. *The Latin American Short Story: A Critical History*. Boston: Twayne, 1983.

Pérez de Mendiola, Marina. *Gender and Identity Formation in Contemporary Mexican Literature*. New York: Garland, 1998.

Pescatello, Ann, ed. *Female and Male in Latin America*. Pittsburgh: University of Pittsburgh Press, 1973.

————. "The Female in Ibero-America." *Latin American Research Review* 7.2 (1972): 125–41.

————. Preface. "The Special Issue in Perspective: The Hispanic Caribbean Woman and the Literary Media." *Revista/Review Interamericana* (San German, Puerto Rico) 4.2 (1974): 131–35.

Picón Garfield, Evelyn. *Women's Fiction from Latin America: Interviews with Six Contemporary Authors*. Detroit: Wayne State University Press, 1985.

Picón Garfield, Evelyn, and Ivan A. Schulman, eds. *Women's Fiction from Latin America: Selections from Twelve Contemporary Authors*. Detroit: Wayne State University Press, 1988.

Rela, Walter. *Spanish American Literature: A Selected Bibliography, 1970–1980*. East Lansing: Michigan State University, 1981.

Resnick, Margery, and Isabel de Cortivron, eds. *Women Writers in Translation: An Annotated Bibliography*. New York: Garland, 1984.

Rodríguez, Ileana. *House/Garden/Nation: Space, Gender, and Ethnicity in Post-Colonial Latin American Literatures by Women*. Durham, N.C.: Duke University Press, 1994.

————. *Women, Guerrillas, and Love: Understanding War in Central America*. Trans. Ileana Rodríguez and Robert Carr. Minneapolis: University of Minnesota Press, 1996.

Rojas, Lourdes, and Nancy Saporta Sternback. "Latin American Women Essayists: Intruders and Usurpers." *The Politics of the Essay: Feminist Perspectives.* Eds. Ruth-Ellen Boetcher Joeres and Elizabeth Mittman. Bloomington: Indiana University Press, 1993. 172–95.

Saénz de Tejada, Cristina. *La (re)construcción de la identidad femenina en la narrativa avidio gráfica latinoamericana, 1975- 1985.* New York: Peter Lang, 1998.

Schaefer, Claudia. *Textured Lives:Women, Art, and Representation in Modern Mexico.* Tucson: University of Arizona Press, 1992.

Shea, Maureen. "A Growing Awareness of Sexual Oppression Among Contemporary Latin American Women Writers." *Confluencia* 4. 1 (1988): 53–59.

Smith, Paul Julian. *The Body Hispanic: Gender and Sexuality in Spanish and Spanish American Literature.* New York: Oxford University Press, 1989.

Smith, Sidonie. *A Poetics of Women's Autobiography: Marginality and the Fictions of Self-Representation.* Bloomington: Indiana University Press, 1987.

Solé, Carlos A., and María Isabel Abreu, eds. *Latin American Writers.* 3 vols. New York: Charles Scribner, 1989.

Sommer, Doris. *Foundational Fictions:The National Romances of Latin America.* Berkeley: University of California Press, 1991.

———. "'Not Just a Personal Story': Testimonios and the Plural Self." *Life/Lines:Theorizing Women's Autobiography.* Eds. Bella Brodzki and Celeste Schenck. Ithaca, N.Y.: Cornell University Press, 1988. 107–30.

Spitta, Silvia. *Between Two Waters: Narratives of Transculturation in Latin America.* Houston: Rice University Press, 1995.

Steele, Cynthia. *Politics and Gender, and the Mexican Novel, 1968–1988: Beyond the Pyramid.* Austin: University of Texas Press, 1992.

———. "Toward a Socialist Feminist Criticism of Latin American Literature." *Ideologies and Literature* 4.16 (1983): 323–29.

Taylor, Diana. *Disappearing Acts: Spectacles of Gender and Nationalism in Argentina's "Dirty War."* Durham, N.C.: Duke University Press, 1997.

Taylor, Diana, and Juan Villegas, eds. *Negotiating Performance: Gender, Sexuality, and Theatricality in Latin(o) America.* Durham, N.C.: Duke University Press, 1994.

Taylor, Kathy. *The New Narrative of Mexico: Sub-versions of History in Mexican Fiction.* Lewisburg, Pa.: Bucknell University Press, 1994.

Tierney Tello, Mary Beth. *Allegories of Transgression and Transformation: Experimental Fiction by Women Writers Under the Dictatorship.* Albany: State University of New York Press, 1996.

Ugalde, Sharon Keefe. "Process, Identity, and Learning to Read: Female Writing and Feminist Criticism in Latin America Today." *Latin American Research Review* 24.1 (1989): 222–32.

Valdés, María Elena de. *The Shattered Mirror: Representations of Women in Mexican Literature.* Austin: University of Texas Press, 1998.

Valenzuela Rodarte, Alberto. *Contemporary Latin American Writers.* New York: Las Americas, 1971.

Valis, Noel, and Carol Maier, eds. *In the Feminine Mode: Essays on Hispanic Women Writers.* Lewisburg, Pa.: Bucknell University Press, 1988.

Vidal, Hernán, ed. *Cultural and Historical Grounding for Hispanic and Luso-Brazilian Feminist Literary Criticism.* Series Literature and Human Rights No. 4. Minneapolis: Institute for the Study of Ideologies and Literature, 1989.

Virgilio, Carmelo, and Naomi Lindstrom. *Women as Myth and Metaphor in Latin American Literature.* Columbia: University of Missouri Press, 1985.

Welles, Marcia L. "The Changing Face of Women in Latin American Fiction." *Women in Hispanic Literature: Icons and Fallen Idols.* Ed. Beth Miller. Berkeley: University of California Press, 1983. 280–88.

Wilson, S. R. "Art by Gender: The Latin American Woman Writer." *Revista Canadiense de Estudios Hispánicos* [Ottawa] 6.1 (1981): 135–37.

Yeager, Gertrude M. *Confronting Change, Challenging Tradition: Women in Latin American History.* Wilmington, Del.: Scholarly Resources, 1994.

Yudice, George, Jean Franco, and Juan Flores, eds. *On Edge: The Crisis of Contemporary Latin American Culture.* Minneapolis: University of Minnesota Press, 1992.

Zimmerman, Marc. *Literature and Resistance in Guatemala: Textual Modes and Cultural Politics from El Señor Presidente to Rigoberta Menchú.* Vol 2: Testimonio and Cultural Politics in the Years of Cerezo and Serrano Elias. Athens: University Center for International Studies, 1995.

Zubatsky, David S. "Annotated Bibliography of Latin American Author Bibliographies: Argentina and Uruguay." *Chasqui* 8.2 (1979): 47–94.

Latin American Women's Works
Not Included in This Volume

Argentina

Borinsky, Alicia. *Dreams of the Abandoned Seducer.* Trans. Cola Frantzen with the author. Lincoln: University of Nebraska Press, 1998.

———. *MeanWoman.* Trans. Cola Frantzen. Lincoln: University of Nebraska Press, 1993.

Bullrich, Silvina. *Tomorrow I'll Say Enough.* Trans. Julia Shirek Smith. Pittsburgh: Latin American Literary Review Press, 1996.

Graziano, Frank, ed. *Alejandra Pizarnik: A Profile.* Durango, Colo.: Logbridge-Rhodes, 1987.

Guido, Beatriz. *The House of the Angel.* New York: McGraw Hill, 1957.

Heker, Liliana. *The Stolen Party and Other Stories.* Trans. Alberto Manguel. Toronto: Coach House Press, 1994.

Kosameh, Alicia. *Steps UnderWater.* Trans. David E. Davis. Berkeley: University of California Press, 1996.

Levinson, Luisa Mercedes. *In the Shadow of the Owl.* Trans. Sylvia Ehrlich Lipp. Barcelona: Salvat, 1989.

———. *The Two Siblings and Other Stories.* Trans. Sylvia Ehrlich Lipp. Pittsburgh: Latin American Literary Review Press, 1996.

Meyer, Doris. *Victoria Ocampo: Against the Wind and the Tide.* Trans. Doris Meyer. New York: Brazilier, 1979.

Molloy, Sylvia. *Certificate of Absence.* Trans. Daniel Balderston with the author. Austin: University of Texas Press, 1989.

Ocampo, Silvina. *Leopoldina's Dream.* Trans. Daniel Balderston. New York: Penguin, 1988.

Partnoy, Alicia. *The Little School: Tales of Disappearance and Survival in Argentina.* Trans. Alicia Partnoy with Lois Athey and Sandra Braunstein. San Francisco: Cleis Press, 1986.

Shua, Ana María. *The Book of Memories.* Trans. Dick Gerdes. Albuquerque: University of New Mexico Press, 1998.

Traba, Marta. *Mothers and Shadows.* Trans. Jo Labanyi. London: Readers International, 1986.

Bolivia

Barrios de Chungara, Domitila. *Let Me Speak! Testimony of Domitila, a Woman of the Bolivian Mines*. Ed. Moema Viezzer. New York: Monthly Review Press, 1978.

O'Hara, Maricarmen. *Cuentos para todos / Tales for Everybody*. Trans. Maricarmen O'Hara. Ventura: Alegría Hispana, 1994.

Brazil

De Jesús, Carolina. *Child of the Dark: The Diary of Carolina María de Jesús*. New York: New American Library, 1962.

Lispector, Clarice. *The Apple in the Dark*. Trans. Gregory Rabassa. New York: Knopf, 1967.

————. *An Apprenticeship, or, The Book of Delights*. Trans. Richard A. Mazzara and Lorri A. Parris. Austin: University of Texas Press, 1986.

————. *Family Ties*. Trans. Giovanni Pontiero. Austin: University of Texas Press, 1972.

————. *The Foreign Legion: Stories and Chronicles*. Trans. Giovanni Pontiero. New York: New Directions, 1991.

————. *The Girl in the Photograph*. Trans. Margaret Neves. New York: Avon, 1982.

————. *The Hour of the Star*. Trans. Giovanni Pontiero. New York: New Directions, 1992.

————. *Near to the Wild Heart*. Trans. Giovanni Portiero. New York: New Directions, 1990.

————. *The Passion According to G. H.* Trans. Ronald W. Sousa. Minneapolis: University of Minnesota Press, 1988.

————. *Selected Cronicas*. Trans. Giovanni Pontiero. New York: New Directions, 1996.

————. *Soulstrom: Stories*. Trans. Alexis Levitin. New York: New Directions, 1989.

————. *The Stream of Life*. Trans. Elizabeth Lowe and Earl Fitz. Minneapolis: University of Minnesota Press, 1989.

Parente Cunha, Helena. *Woman Between Mirrors*. Trans. Fred P. Ellison and Naomi Lindstrom. Austin: University of Texas Press, 1989.

Pereira, Teresinka. *Help, I'm Drowning*. Trans. Angela de Hoyos. Chicago: Palos Heights Press, 1975.

Van Steen, Edla. *A Bag of Stories*. Trans. David George. Pittsburgh: Latin American Literary Review Press, 1991.

Chile

Balcells, Jacqueline. *The Enchanted Raisin*. Trans. Elizabeth Gamble Miller. Pittsburgh: Latin American Literary Review Press, 1988.

Barros, Pía. *Transitory Fears*. Trans. Diane Russell-Pineda and Martha Manier. Santiago: Asterión, 1989.

Bombal, María Luisa. *House of Mist and Shrouded Woman*. Trans. by the author. Austin: University of Texas Press, 1995.

————. *New Islands and Other Stories.* Trans. Richard and Lucía Cunningham. New York: Farrar, 1982.

————. *The Shrouded Woman.* Trans. Richard and Lucía Cunningham. New York: Farrar, 1948.

Eltit, Diamela. *The Fourth World.* Trans. Dick Gerdes. Lincoln: University of Nebraska Press, 1995.

————. *Sacred Cow.* Trans. Amanda Hopkinson. London: Serpent's Tail, 1995.

Mallet, Marilú. *Voyage to the Other Extreme: Five Stories.* Trans. Alan Brown. Montreal: Vehicule, 1985.

Colombia

Chávez-Vásquez, Gloria. *Opus Americanus: Short Stories.* Trans. Gloria Chávez-Vásquez. White Owl Editions, 1993.

Costa Rica

Naranjo, Carmen. *There Was Never a Once Upon a Time.* Trans. Linda Britt. Pittsburgh: Latin American Literary Review Press, 1989.

Oreamuno, Yolanda, ed. *Five Women Writers of Costa Rica.* Beaumont, Tex.: Asociación de Literatura Femenina Hispánica, 1976.

Cuba

Gómez de Avellaneda y Arteaga, Gertrudis. *Sab and Autobiography.* Ed. and trans. Nina M. Scott. Austin: University of Texas Press, 1993.

Montero, Mayra. *In the Palm of Darkness.* Trans. Edith Grossman. New York: Harper, 1997.

Robles, Mireya. *Hagiography of Narcisa the Beautiful.* Trans. Anna Diegel with the author. Columbia, N.Y.: Readers International, 1996.

Valdés, Zoe. *Yocandra in the Paradise of Nada.* Trans. Sabina Cienfuegos. New York: Arcade, 1997.

El Salvador

Alegría, Claribel. *Family Album.* Trans. Amanda Hopkinson. Willimantic, Conn.: Curbstone Press, 1987.

————. *Luisa in Realityland.* Trans. Darwin J. Flakoll. Willimantic, Conn.: Curbstone Press, 1987.

Alegría, Claribel, and Darwin J. Flakoll. *Ashes of Izalco.* Trans. Darwin J. Flakoll. Willimantic, Conn.: Curbstone Press, 1989.

Guatemala

Menchú, Rigoberta. *I Rigoberta Menchú: An Indian Woman in Guatemala*. Ed. Elizabeth Burgos-Debray. Trans. A. Wright. London: Verso, 1984.

Mexico

Ahern, Maureen, ed. *A Rosario Castellanos Reader*. Austin: University of Texas Press, 1988.

Allgood, Myralyn F., ed. and trans. *Another Way to Be: Selected Works of Rosario Castellanos*. Athens: University of Georgia Press, 1990.

Arredondo, Inés. *Underground River and Other Stories* Trans. Cynthia Steele. Lincoln: University of Nebraska Press, 1996.

Berman, Sabina. *Bubbeh*. Trans. Andrea G. Labinger. Pittsburgh: Latin American Literary Review Press, 1998.

Boullosa, Carmen. *The Miracle Worker*. Trans. Amanda Hopkinson. London: Jonathan Cape, 1994.

Campobello, Nellie. *Cartucho and My Mother's Hands*. Trans. Doris Meyer and Irene Mathews. Austin: University of Texas Press, 1988.

Campos, Julieta. *Celina or the Cats*. Trans. Leland Chambers and Kathleen Ross. Pittsburgh: Latin American Literary Review Press, 1995.

———. *Fear of Losing Eurydyce*. Trans. Leland H. Chambers. Normal, Ill.: Dalkey Archive Press, 1993.

———. *She Had Reddish Hair and Her Name Is Sabina*. Trans. Leland H. Chambers. Athens: University of Georgia Press, 1993.

Castellanos, Rosario. *The Book of Lamentations*. Trans. Esther Allen. New York: Marsilio, 1996.

———. *City of Kings*. Trans. Robert S. Rudder and Gloria Chacón de Arjona. Pittsburgh: Latin American Literary Review Press, 1992.

———. *The Nine Guardians*. Trans. Irene Nicholson. London: Canguard, 1958. Rpt. In New York: Guard, 1960; Columbia: Readers International, 1992.

Cruz, Juana Inés de la. *Answer to Sor Filotea de la Cruz. The Answer / La respuesta*. Ed. and trans. Electa Arenal and Amanda Powell. New York: Feminist Press, 1994.

Domeq, Brianda. *Eleven Days*. Trans. Kay S. García. Albuquerque: University of New Mexico Press, 1995.

Esquivel, Laura. *The Law of Love*. Trans. Margaret Sayers Peden. New York: Crown, 1996.

———. *Like Water for Chocolate*. Trans. Carol Christensen and Thomas Christensen. New York: Doubleday, 1992.

Galeana, Benita. *Benita*. Trans. Amy Diane Prince. Pittsburgh: Latin American Literary Review Press, 1994.

Jacobs, Barbara. *The Dead Leaves*. Trans. David Unger. San Francisco: Curbstone Press, 1992.

Mastretta, Angeles. *Lovesick*. Trans. Margaret Sayers Peden. New York: Riverhead, 1997.

————. *Tear This Heart Out*. Trans. Margaret Sayers Peden. New York: Riverhead, 1997.
Muñiz-Huberman, Angelina. *Enclosed Garden*. Trans. Lois Parkinson Zamora. Pittsburgh: Latin American Literary Review Press, 1988.

Nicaragua

Aguilar, Rosario. *The Lost Chronicles of Terra Firma*. Trans. Edward Waters Hood. Fredonia, N.Y.: White Pine Press, 1997.
Belli, Gioconda. *The Inhabited Woman*. Trans. Kathleen March. Willimantic, Conn.: Curbstone Press, 1994.

Peru

Matto de Turner, Clorida. *Birds Without a Nest*. Trans. J. G. H. Emended Naomi Linstrom. Austin: University of Texas Press, 1996.
Riesco, Laura. *Ximena at the Crossroads*. Trans. Mary C. Berg. Fredonia, N.Y.: White Pine Press, 1998.

Puerto Rico

Braschi, Giannina. *Empire of Dreams*. Trans. Tess O'Dwyer. Intro. Alicia Ostriker. New Haven, Conn.: Yale University Press, 1994.
García Ramis, Magali. *Happy Days, Uncle Sergio*. Trans. Carmen C. Esteves. Fredonia, N.Y.: White Pine Press, 199
Vega, Ana Lydia. *True and False Romances: Stories and a Novella*. Trans. Andrés Hurley. London: Serpent's Tail, 1994.

Uruguay

Peri Rossi, Cristina. *Dostoevsky's Last Night*. Trans. Laura Dail. New York: Picador, 1995.
————. *A Forbidden Passion*. Trans. Mary Jane Treacy. Pittsburgh: Cleis Press, 1993.
————. *Ship of Fools*. Trans. Psiche Hughes. London: Readers International, 1989.

Venezuela

Parra, Teresa de la. *Iphigenia: The Diary of a Young Lady Who Wrote Because She Was Bored*. Trans. Bertie Acker. Austin: University of Texas Press, 1994
————. *Mamá Blanca's Souvenirs*. Trans. Harriet de Onis. Washington, D.C.: Pan American Union, General Secretariat, 1959. Revised translation by Frederick H. Fornoff and Doris Sommer, coordinator. Pittsburgh: University of Pittsburgh Press, 1993.

Nora Erro-Peralta is professor of Latin American literature, director of Latin American studies at Florida Atlantic University in Boca Raton, and author or editor of three books and of numerous articles in such journals as *Hispamerica* and *Chasqui*.

Caridad Silva is associate professor and chair of Hispanic studies at Glendon College of York University, Toronto. Together she and Nora Erro-Peralta edited *Puerta abierta: La nueva escritora latinoamericana*, a Latin American literature text.